Rise of the Demon Hunter

A Rael Armstrong Adventure

J. D. DeSain

ISBN: 9798830404112 (paperback)

Rael wakes to find herself at an unexpected crossroads in her young life. She has come on vacation to Europe in hopes of forgetting about the past, including failing at the most critical thing in her life: skiing. Of course, at sixteen nearly everything can feel like the most important thing in your life at any moment. Still, Rael is pretty sure training for six years and losing her big race by a tenth of a second is the lowest possible point her life can reach. Well, she *was* sure of that—until she wakes up in a stone room, alone, bound by rope, and in the care of a vampire. A situation like that is bound to cause a young woman to reevaluate her certainties.

Rael would like to think of herself as the type of person who is far too sophisticated to believe in silly things such as demons. Unfortunately for her, demonic cults are more than willing to believe in her. Well, not in her as a person. It is what is inside of Rael that the demons really want, for Rael apparently has the sort of soul just right for communion with the demonic world. And demonic cults are more than willing to sacrifice her to get what they want: ultimate demonic power. Fortunately for Rael, the world is full of demon hunters too. Hunters turn out to be people willing to stand between her and the demon cults out to get her. Unfortunately, not every hunter is created equal, and it's confusing to her to sort out the good guys from the bad guys in this mixed-up new world. The question for Rael now is whether she can stay one step ahead of all the cults long enough to sort out who she is and what she wants to be. In the end, the best way to defend herself against them all might be to join the club and become a demon hunter herself.

Filled with quirky characters, *Rise of the Demon Hunter: A Rael Armstrong Adventure* is a fast-paced, action-packed occult adventure story.

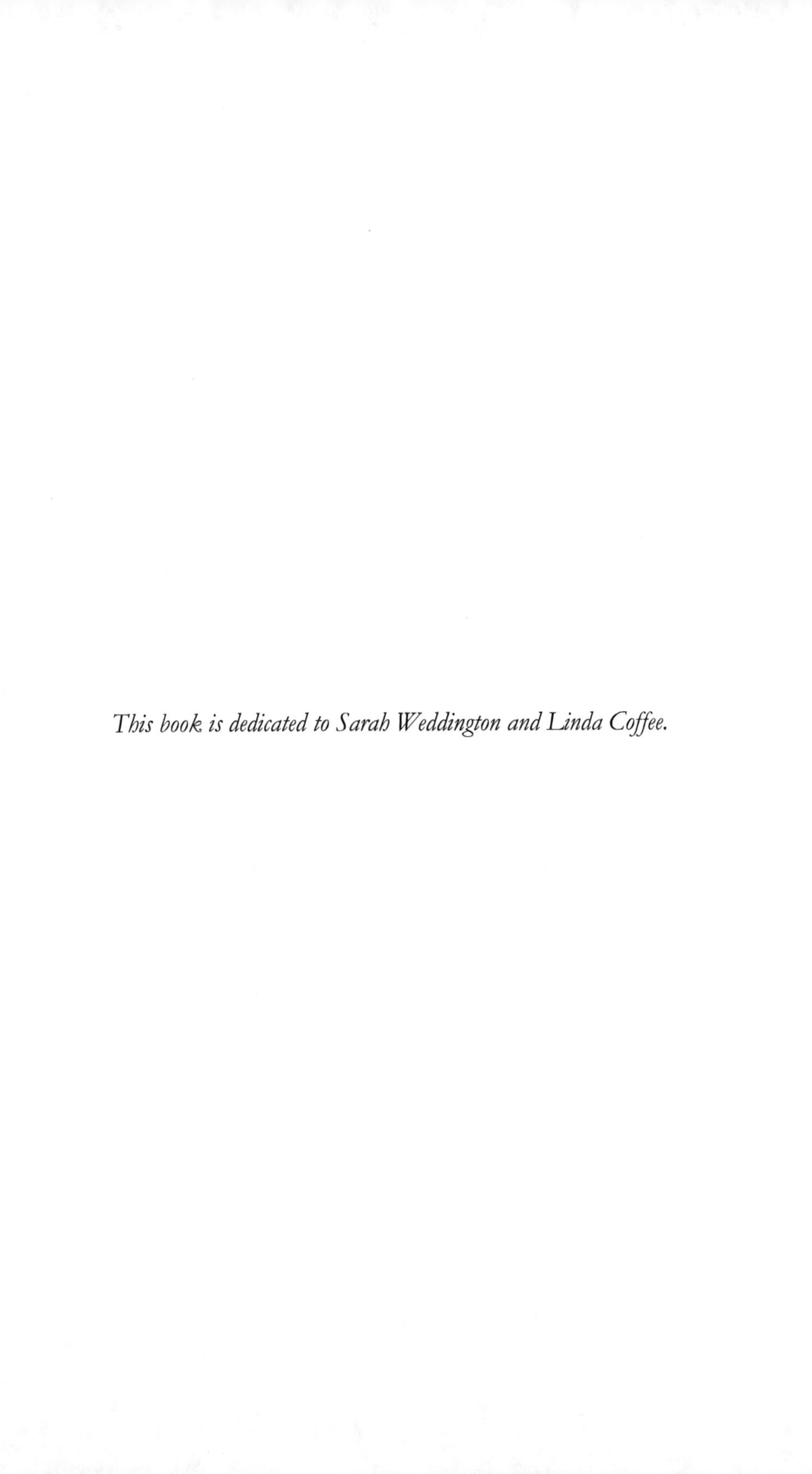

This book is dedicated to Sarah Weddington and Linda Coffee.

Chapter 1

Anticipation is the key to victory. There are no prizes for trying your best. Winning is all that counts in this sport. No one ever remembers the losers. In life, winning is everything. Don't ever be a loser. Focus on your execution; keep your line, hold your form, and today will be your day. You're better than the rest of them, so go out and show it.

The electronic buzzer began its countdown. It beeped in rhythm: one, two, three, go! In a flash, all her father's words passing through her mind melted away. The only thing that remained was the snow under her skis. She needed to conquer it. She pressed her poles into the snow, and she was off. Today's race was a simple one. There was no opponent on the hill with her. It was just her, the snow, velocity, and the flags. The only enemy she was up against was time. Time was an ethereal foe. Yet she knew it was real enough. It was out there counting upward against her. Time haunted her. Time hated her. Time loved the other skiers more. Time never seemed to fall in love with her.

Not today, though. Today was going to be different. Today, time would bow down to her. She crested the last rise, and the finish line was in sight. She tucked and accelerated until she crossed the finish line. At last, she could relax. She loosened her form to slow down. She kicked up loose snow as she turned toward the scoreboard to face the enemy. Her enemy, time, remained frozen on the scoreboard. Her heart sank—her enemy had beaten her yet again. A tenth of a second, that's all it had taken to defeat her. She had been a tenth of a second too late, and time had won again. She was a loser.

She opened her eyes. Stone. That was all she could see. The ceiling and the walls of the room were made of worked stone. She was even lying on a cold slab of stone. She'd never been in this room before. She knew that for a fact. Or did she? *What did she know?* Being in here wasn't right. She knew that much. Something must have gone terribly wrong for her to end up here . . . but what? She couldn't remember. Her memories, where were they? They were lost in a haze. She could seem to recall only shadows of her past. That race, that stupid downhill race. Why did she remember that of all things so clearly? The last thing she remembered was . . . was what? She couldn't even remember her name. Besides that race, all she could remember was a sound. There was a thunderous, deafening roar. It still echoed in her ears, yet this stone room was as silent as a tomb. Her tomb. Was she dead? It was a stupid thought. The dead don't think about being dead.

A voice came to her. She heard the word *go* echo in her ear. But the sound of the word being spoken must have been in her head, for no voice spoke to her now. Why would a voice say that?

Through the haze of memories, she saw white. She feared the white. But that was silly. It was just a color. She focused on the color. The white was moving. It was coming toward her. It was roaring at her. It wanted to consume her. She did not want this white to win, but why? Then another memory returned in a flash.

"Avalanche!" she cried out.

A door opened within the stone room. She could clearly hear the sound of the unoiled hinges. After it opened, she heard faint footsteps. They approached her. She tried to turn to see who had come into her tomb, but her body wouldn't move. It was then that she realized she was strapped down. Her arms and legs were restrained. That wasn't right, not right at all. She briefly struggled against the restraints, but it was no use. The best she could do was angle her head a little as she desperately tried to see who had come in, but try as she might, she couldn't move her head enough to see more of the room. It was then that fear gripped her.

She asked, "Who is in here with me?"

"Ah, you are awake," said a heavily accented man. She did not know the voice. The word *Italy* came to mind. She'd been in Italy on vacation. Yes, she remembered something else now. She'd been skiing there with her family. The fragments of her memories were starting to come together. She had been on an outing set up by her father. It was to help take the sting of losing out on junior nationals. It was a funny gesture on her father's part. Why go skiing to ease the pain caused by skiing? The last six years of her life had been about skiing! Just a tenth of a second faster and her life wouldn't be over now. It was melodramatic to think that way. It had been just a contest, a silly race downhill. There was more to life than that, wasn't there?

She said, "I'm in Italy, and yet you don't sound Italian, so where am I?"

"Ah, that is a good question." A tall man now towered over her face. He looked her in the eyes. His voice exuded power, but his face was gaunt and his hair showed the whiteness of great age. No, his appearance didn't match his voice. He wore a black suit with blood-red accents. His smile showed pearly-white teeth. His enlarged canines could not be missed. They'd make a vampire envious for sure. Maybe she was wrong: Despite being an old man, his appearance did match his voice. He said, "I pay very little attention to national borders these days. They do change so often. But my home, it stays here. You understand, I stay here no matter where the border roams. That is what a home should be. Your home, it is here now too for a little while, so do, please, try to enjoy it."

His reply barely registered with her. Her mind was still trying to remember how to process information. She was just noticing the fact that her ski coat, hat, boots, and goggles were gone. She still had on her sweater and her ski pants, but they felt torn and battered. It occurred to her that she must be at a hospital. She'd had a mishap, and so this must be a hospital. Only that man, he didn't look like a doctor, so who was he?

She explained, "I was skiing with my family. There was an avalanche. I think. No, I know that. The whole slope came down. I guess I outran the worst of it, but it must have wiped me out. How bad am I hurt?"

"Fatally, I'm afraid to inform you."

She laughed. She couldn't help herself. He looked back at her blankly. He was serious! She wasn't in any pain. She replied, "I can't be fatally wounded. I'm not even in any pain."

"You are beyond pain, my child."

"Hello, you do speak English well, right? 'Fatally' means I'm dead—or at least dying. I'm here. I'm alive. Look at me. Alive."

"I have looked at you very closely. That is why I've called for a doctor."

"Ha, you wouldn't call a doctor if I was dying."

"Dead."

"I'm not dead!"

"I am so sorry for your loss," he replied.

"Are all Italian doctors this crazy? I'm here in the hospital talking to you, so I'm alive."

He shook his head. "No, my poor child, you are in no hospital. You are here with me in my castle. I am Count Balog and you are . . . let us say, you are my guest." He checked her restraints and seemed satisfied by them.

"A castle? But why? And why am I tied up?"

"Questions, so many questions, and so few answers I have to give you. I know this much: When the locals found you amidst the wreckage caused by the avalanche, they were most perplexed as to what to do with you. They thought of me and then brought you here. Now it is I who am the perplexed one. You present for me quite a puzzle. It shall take a little time to work it all out."

This is a castle not a hospital? She was so confused. Nothing he'd told her really told her anything at all. Her head felt empty again. She needed to remember more. He was correct: It would take time to figure this all out. Hopefully with time, she'd remember more about herself.

A bell rang. It echoed off the stone walls. "Ah, the doctor is here now. Do try and behave while I am gone. Now, if you will excuse me, my poor dear," the count said.

"Wait, you can't just leave me here strapped down!" But he did. He walked away. The nerve of the man! The door opened and closed. She was alone again. The first thing she did was try to free herself from the restraints. But the ropes were too strong for her.

She'd been knocked out by the snowslide. Someone had found her, brought her here, and then tied her down. She was tied down, helpless, and there seemed to be nothing she could do about the situation. That last part made no sense at all. Unless . . . kidnapped! That's what she was. She was a kidnapping victim. There could be no other explanation. White slavers, they did exist, right? Only the circumstances didn't feel right. Did white slavers often search avalanches for young women to kidnap? No, that sounded crazy. That old man, he didn't seem dangerous either. He looked a touch weird and gave off a menacing vibe, but he had not acted threateningly toward her. Well, besides the restraints. No, there could be no doubt that she was being held here against her will. It was just a fact . . . or was it? Maybe it was all for her own good. She clearly wasn't herself.

The question came to her: who was she? "My name, what is my name?" she said aloud. No one was around to answer her. She tried to remember her face. There was nothing there. She tried to remember something else, no matter how small, but her memories held themselves out of range, taunting her to chase after them.

It wasn't long before the door opened again. The instant it did, she pleaded with the count. "Look, there's been an accident, and I thank you for your help, but I need to find my family. Yes, my family, my mom and dad. They were skiing with me. They'll need help too."

A new face towered over her. The face belonged to a chubby man. He wore a monocle in his left eye and had a walrus mustache. He smelled of tonic. He placed a meaty thumb on her right eye and forced her eyelid up. He spoke at last, but not to her directly. "Her eyes are most unusual."

"They're just blue," she spoke up. Then she realized that she now remembered her own face. Yes, her eyes were blue; her hair was blonde. She was quite proud of her long, straight, golden locks.

"Ah, the patient has a sense of humor," the chubby man said.

"They frightened the villagers, and that is why she is here, Doctor Winkle," said the count.

A doctor! This was the doctor. The count had really brought a doctor to see her. That was good news. Any doctor could tell in an instant that she was alive. The better news was that she hadn't been kidnapped. This was a makeshift hospital after all. She tried to relax. It wasn't easy to do with a meaty thumb in her eye. "Am I hurt badly, doctor?" she asked.

Doctor Winkle asked a question, but not to her. "Her hair, was it once blonde?"

"Judging by that light streak still in her hair, I'd say yes," replied the count.

Frustrated, she said, "Hello, talk to me, not to each other, please. My hair is blonde; my eyes are blue. I'm sixteen years old and I live in Colorado. My name is . . . I can't remember that yet, but I'm remembering more and more things as time passes. My head is clearing."

Doctor Winkle said, "She is very lively for a dead girl."

"Too lively—and I'm an expert on the subject," replied the count.

"No worries, she doesn't appear to be dangerous. I've not seen a case like this before. I doubt anyone alive has. But I believe there is a case in *De praestigiis daemonum*," said Doctor Winkle.

"I'm very much . . ." She didn't get the word out because a thermometer was put in her open mouth.

"She's warm too," said the doctor.

"Devilishly warm?" asked the count.

"No, thirty-seven Celsius exactly," confirmed the doctor, removing the thermometer. Then he jabbed her arm with a needle. She saw her blood being drawn. Fortunately, she had never been one to shy away from the sight of her own blood. "Very red-blooded this American still is," added Doctor Winkle.

"The snowslide should have torn her apart. How can all this be?" said the count.

"Because I am alive, duh," she said.

"I will run a few tests on her blood, just to confirm it," replied Doctor Winkle. He moved out of her view, taking his needle with him. Then she heard footsteps retreating. They were both leaving her.

"Don't leave me again," she begged. They left her alone anyway. *Run some tests to confirm it.* What did that mean? Were they so dense they could not see she was healthy in body and in . . . well, not mind. But in body she felt fine, better than fine. She tested the restraints again. She felt full power in her arms and legs. There was nothing broken. She was alright physically. How were her parents? She wanted to know. There must be a lot of injured skiers. Were they all housed in this makeshift hospital? She had so many questions and so few answers coming her way.

Then there was a noise. It made her forget about everything else. She was alone, so where had the noise come from? It had been a soft noise, barely audible, but it had been real, she was sure of it. Then it came again, confirming that it was real and reproducible. The source was inside the room. It must be a cat creeping across the stone floor. Well, maybe. The stillness of the room masked nothing. She could have heard a pin drop, but this was no pin dropping. She heard it a third time. If it was a stealthy cat, then where was the meow to go along with it? Perhaps it was a mouse instead?

She asked, "Is someone here with me?"

Noises came rapidly now in quick succession. The sound drew nearer until a figure was upon her. The figure wore a black hooded cloak that obscured its face in shadows. She opened her mouth to greet this new visitor, but the ornate dagger in the robed figure's hand made her freeze.

"Be gone, foul abomination of another world," said the cloaked figure. It wasn't the sort of greeting you'd want if you were restrained to a stone slab. The robed figure raised its dagger. Clearly, it meant to strike her. A scream formed in her throat, but her fear was so paralyzing that she couldn't seem to release it. The dagger came down on her throat, but it didn't slice her skin. The figure's hand was stopped by a voice.

"Hunter, you shall not harm her in my domain!" said the count.

The cloaked figure turned away from her and replied, "Count Balog, you rotting old bag of bones. How did you enter this room without me hearing your movement?"

"I have means of entering without being noticed, the same as you," he replied.

The cloaked figure said, "Yes, I was told you're more than just an old bag of bones. You're a vampire from the old school. Sorry, vampire, but my mission here is clear; you will not interfere with it. An abyssal demon was detected in the area. I was sent here to kill it. I fear that the demon I was tracking used this poor girl's empty vessel to gate a horror into our world. You merely have to look at her to know this horror is manifesting itself inside this girl. I was not fast enough, for far too many have died at her hands already. She may look innocent and harmless, but she's a demon through and through. Just look at her with better eyes and you can see she's been taken by the demon."

"I thought the same as you did when I first laid eyes on her," agreed the count.

"And you were wise to restrain her. Now she must be destroyed. You know it, I know it. Let me do my job," said the black cloaked figure.

The count replied, "The restraints are not mine. She was found with them in place. And no, you shall not harm her, and no one defies me in my domain."

"Very well," the cloaked figure said. Those words were just words, however. This figure quickly turned back on her. The dagger plunged into her chest. She had been patiently listening to them argue over killing her as if they were negotiating a trade of collectable Pokémon cards. Now she found her voice. She screamed as the dagger pierced her. Only it didn't pierce her at all.

The cloaked figure stepped back. She removed her hood. Long red hair flowed out. Under the hood of the cloak was the face of a woman. She was beautiful, like the sort of model featured on the greeting cards sold in a hotel lobby. Though this redhead had just stabbed at her, Rael no longer feared the unhooded woman. There was an aura about her that radiated comfort.

The redhead looked at her dagger in disbelief. It was still clean. She shook it as thought it could be malfunctioning. She said, "My viritatus did nothing to her."

The count said, "It is just like a druid of the Order to ignore my sound advice. Your weapon only harms evil, does it not? Had you waited to listen to me, you'd have found out that she is no evil demon. She is an Astralith."

"An Astralith?" repeated the redheaded woman in disbelief.

"Yes, she is the product of an interrupted astral projection. She is now an empty vessel awaiting filling. I think her essence, though once mostly lost, is trickling slowly back inside her from the dark-matter cosmic ether. Her body had been broken, but this otherworldly traveler that so briefly almost claimed her body apparently healed it, with a few added extras from the plane that it came from."

Rael had had enough. She spoke up. "I'm not empty! I'm not any of that. I'm Rael Armstrong." The words came to her. She was Rael Armstrong. She remembered so much more about herself now. She continued, "I'm not a demon. I'm the only daughter of Jill and Ted Armstrong. I was born in California but moved to Colorado six years ago. I . . ."

The redhead put her arm on Rael's forehead and spoke in a comforting manner. "Hush, poor child, for I believe you. We are as confused by your situation as you are."

Rael shouldn't have felt comfort from someone who had just stabbed at her with a dagger, and yet she couldn't help but feel it. This woman's compassion shone like a beacon. It radiated from her emerald eyes. There was a warmth in her that had been lacking in room until now.

The count laughed. "Child, she would not have believed you if the dagger had harmed you. Had she listened to me, the screaming and the stabbing would have been kept to a minimum. You see, hunter, good Doctor Winkle has confirmed that she is no demon by more scientific means."

"A member of the Majestic Seven is here? I should verify this with him," the redhead said.

"He has already left," the count informed her.

Rael asked them, "Demons, stabbing, and false declarations of my death. . . can someone *please* just explain to me what is going on before I go mad?"

The redhead said, "I am called Boudicea Vercingetorix. I am a hunter of the Order. I thought you were my prey. I'm embarrassed and ashamed for my actions against you." That was all she said—as if that was enough explanation. Boudicea used her dagger again. In one stroke, she cut the first of Rael's bindings. Four strokes later, Rael was free. Boudicea turned to the count and ordered, "We shall need a room, a bath, new clothes, food, and a candle."

"It can all be arranged," replied the count.

Boudicea turned her attention once more to Rael. "You have not yet quite reached an equilibrium point. More of your old self may emerge. I've never met a victim like you. Those who plan a communion like the one attempted on you do so to complete the process. Why yours was not finished, I do not know. We are as lost as you as to what to do next. The key thing is what to do with you now. Can you move?"

Rael felt mostly there. There were still some memory gaps, but as to movement, she felt confident that movement could be done. She nodded. Boudicea pulled Rael to her feet. Rael's legs suddenly went weak. Her body shivered. She was not sure she remembered how to walk. She leaned on Boudicea for support.

Boudicea said to the count, "We are ready. Show us the way."

Rael said, "Wait, first tell me what is going on."

"All in good time. You see, we need to learn what is going on ourselves in order to tell you," replied Boudicea.

"You are quite correct, hunter. Time is not in our favor, I fear. The communion was interrupted, but the demon will be back for her soon enough to finish its job. If not the demon, someone else. An Astralith of her magnitude will be a hot property. The doctor had never measured one with her essence in his entire practice. No, I cannot protect her for long in my castle."

The count had looked to Boudicea when saying that. Boudicea replied, "You will not be asked to, I'm sure."

All this talk about vampires and demons, it sounded like a joke, but the count and Boudicea were deadly serious. Boudicea's dagger made it clear she fully believed in this talk. Rael didn't believe in such nonsense. She was a normal modern young woman living in a sensible modern world where demons *simply did not exist*. Still, she relented and started walking with Boudicea's support. Rael wanted to leave the cold room more than anything else. Her past few hours here had seemed like an eternity. She could wait for a little more time to pass to know everything else if waiting meant leaving this cold stone room.

Chapter 2

Count Balog's Castle, the Italian Alps

She sat at the vanity, wrapped in a towel, combing her hair. She had straight blonde hair that had grown out to the middle of her back. One hundred strokes after waking in the morning, one hundred strokes before bedtime was Mother's rule. She'd done the routine morning and night ever since she was a child. She was currently stroking jet-black hair with only one streak left of her natural blonde. She was trying to not let that fact bother her.

Her hair wasn't the only noticeable change in her appearance. She understood their comments about her eyes now. The familiar blue was gone from her eyes. The eyes staring back at her from the silver mirror of the vanity were black as night, with no difference between the pupil and the iris. They looked like a cheap doll's eyes—soulless and empty.

But even that was not the worst of it. The worst of it was the two horns that stuck up from the top of her head. They were only a few inches tall and nearly covered completely by her hair, but they were there all the same. She tried to not let that fact bother her either.

She'd taken a bath to relax, and the fact she wasn't relaxed at all probably had to do with everything that was staring back at her from the mirror. It didn't feel real. None of this did. She kept expecting to wake up and discover it was all a dream. Well, more a nightmare than a dream.

In the upper corner of the mirror, Rael could see Boudicea sitting behind her. Rael remembered she had more than one reason not to feel incredibly relaxed after her hot bath. Boudicea was sitting on the edge of the bed. She had a worried look about her. She kept flipping that dagger of hers in the air. She always caught it by the handle. Whenever Rael asked her anything, Boudicea would stop flipping the dagger, put on a fake air of calm, and pretend things were not such that one needed to be worried about them. It was an odd way for someone who had almost stabbed you to act.

There was no time to think about things deeply. Instead, Rael thought about practical things. Rael asked Boudicea, "Do you think if I permed my hair that it might cover up my horns better?"

As predicted, Boudicea stopped tossing the dagger. In the mirror, Rael could see Boudicea's wide smile forming. She replied, "Yes, that is an excellent idea. I doubt that the count has what we need in the castle to do it, but as soon as we can, we'll try it, if you wish. Until then . . ." Boudicea stood up. She came over and teased Rael's hair. She played with it until it was a tangled, horn-concealing mess upon Rael's head. Well, so much for Rael's brushing regimen. Mother would not have been pleased. Boudicea, though, must have been satisfied because she went back to sitting on the bed.

Rael placed the brush down and sighed. A perm would have looked so much nicer. "I'm sure my family is worried about me and will want to know I'm alive . . . well, alright. Do you think we could ask the villagers for news about my family soon?" asked Rael, suggesting a topic dearer to her heart.

"Yes, I'll ask the count to do that as soon as he returns."

Boudicea seemed eager to agree to any suggestion so long as the return on that agreement would come later, much later. They were to do nothing now but sit in this room within the count's castle and wait. Wait for what, Rael didn't know. It was the one question that Rael didn't dare ask Boudicea because she feared the answer. The dagger started flipping again. She wouldn't push more questions toward Boudicea since her answers were hard to believe anyway.

There was a knock on the door. The count announced, "I have dinner."

Dinner was welcome news. Rael hadn't eaten in . . . she couldn't remember when she had last eaten. Rael replied, "Leave it by the door. I'm practically naked in here." Rael pulled the towel tighter around her.

"Nonsense, when you're as old as I, you've seen it all before," replied the count.

"Yes, no reason to wait any longer. Come in," agreed Boudicea.

Rael was pretty sure the count hadn't seen *her* before, and she didn't feel as accommodating as Boudicea. Even though she did have her towel on and was covered nearly head to toe, it was the idea of it all. This was entirely improper. Mother would not have approved.

The count walked right up to the vanity and set down a silver tray of cooked vegetables. No meat. Rael was partial to meat. Rael considered herself a vegetarian in so far as she liked eating things that liked to eat plants. Yes, plants had never had a bigger friend than her. Rael ate all the plants' enemies.

"No meat?" asked Rael.

"I am a vegetarian," explained the count.

"Oh."

"Don't worry, it is quite tasty. I used a lot of garlic."

"But vampires don't like garlic."

"You know very little of the real world, young lady. I fear that is all about to end for you rather suddenly," replied the count. Then he left the room again.

Drat, she'd forgotten to ask about her parents. How true his words sounded right now, though. Rael thought about all she'd learned from Boudicea while Rael had soaked in the tub. Boudicea had explained as best she could what had happened to Rael. Rael had died in the avalanche. That much was clear. What had happened next was open to conjecture. The avalanche had been some sort of blood sacrifice used to set up a portal to another world. A demon had taken her body just as her last breath was being released and had performed a ritual on her at this portal. It had used her to commune with another plane of reality. Boudicea felt certain about all of that.

The point of the ritual had been to trade away Rael's essence to another plane of reality. Essence was . . . well, Rael didn't know what it was. It didn't matter, probably. The result of the trading of Rael's essence should have been that her empty body was inhabited by a being from another place in another plane. Rael would have been gone.

Whatever all that stuff actually meant, Rael wasn't sure. Sometimes words weren't enough to really explain things. Apparently, those born with the affinity to be Astraliths were prone to such things happening to them. Rael was one of those people born that way. Boudicea seemed sure of the fact, and apparently Doctor Winkle had confirmed it with science, although Rael was pretty sure the main point of science was to confirm that all that stuff wasn't real. Things must really be bad for her if even science was against her.

Rael had learned all this and was just as confused as ever. Again, whatever being an Astralith meant, she wasn't sure of that either. She understood that she was one, though, and it seemed to be rather important. The other important point was that the ritual had been performed so quickly after her death, which meant Rael's death had been planned. Something wanted Rael's body and wanted it badly. Blood sacrifice was often needed to commune, and the ultimate sacrifice, the murder of an Astralith, was apparently a rather potent thing. Rael's essence was to have been moved one way and the creature from another plane's essence moved another way through a gate across the black matter consisting of a sort of ether between the planes. Apparently, that's how astral travel worked. There were no free rides. It was all tit-for-tat.

Fortunately or unfortunately—and that was a matter of perspective—something had gone wrong in the process. That was the last important point, and the reason Rael was still here to know about any of this at all. The ritual had not been finished. Boudicea didn't know why. What she did know was that the interruption left Rael in limbo. Rael's essence—her "soul" to use a more Western notion of things—had returned from her unfinished journey to find the creature from another plane had started to set up shop in her body. The good news was that Rael was somewhat more alive now than she would have been otherwise. The bad news was everything else, though it could have been worse: She might have a red pointy tail as well. The thought made her snicker. She covered her face with her hand.

The dagger stopped flipping. Boudicea asked, "What is so funny?"

"I was thinking how lucky I was not to have a tail."

Boudicea stood up. She came and stood behind Rael. She rested her hands on Rael's shoulders. Rael could feel Boudicea's strength from just her touch. "Yes, that was lucky for us. A hat and glasses hide the rest, but a tail would be much harder to hide."

Rael asked, "This demon will come back for me, that's why you're staying with me, isn't it?"

"Yes, and no."

Count Balog reentered the room. "I come bearing more gifts, and not like a Greek man. For the child, I have these." He placed some clothing on the bed. "I'm afraid it's been some time since I've entertained female guests. I gave up that lifestyle long ago. Still, these are women's clothes, and styles don't change that much with time, I believe. I also have a few Euros in a money pouch and a selection of hats she may want to consider." He paused. "And for the hunter, there is this." He slid a small table into the center of the room. On the table he placed a lone candle. He looked over at the food. He asked Rael, "Something wrong with my cooking?"

"Oh no, it's just that being dead has left me with less of an appetite than I had anticipated," replied Rael, trying not to offend him.

"Yes, it does do that. Now, if you'll excuse me, the sun shall soon rise, and I'd rather not see it. If I do not see you again, my new friend, Rael, I hope you stay safe." He left them again.

Rael said, "There's one thing that I don't understand in all this. Why is it that you kill demons but not vampires?"

"I am sanctioned to hunt only the enemies of this plane. I hunt the supernatural," explained Boudicea.

"I'm pretty sure vampires count as being supernatural."

"Rael, lesson number one about the real world: Let the undead lie where they are. Most are quite satisfied to remain there."

That was about as good an answer as Rael could probably expect. Rael stood up from the vanity and went over to the bed. The clothing on it was definitely from a past era. Perhaps a few hundred years had passed since it had been in its prime. She picked up a light green muslin frock and held it to her body. It unfortunately would fit. She sighed. "The count must be very old to have these clothes."

"Get dressed," ordered Boudicea.

Rael checked the door. She didn't want the count coming back in. He claimed to not want to see the sun, but men did often sacrifice quite a bit to see a pretty woman. The door now secured, she set about dressing. Rael picked up a cream-colored slip. At that moment the room lights flickered. The old castle's wiring could use an upgrade. Then they flickered again. Boudicea took off her cloak. It was an odd item of clothing. Underneath the black cloak, Boudicea was wearing a skintight black Lycra outfit with a blue racing stripe up the side. The suit showed off plenty up top, and Boudicea filled it out quite well. She had curves, height, fitness, that fiery red long hair . . . Was there anything Boudicea was lacking? Her appearance made Rael feel like quite the awkward horn-headed sixteen-year-old girl in comparison. Boudicea tossed her cloak on the bed and went over to the candle.

Rael stopped dressing. Part of the reason was her lack of self-confidence compared with Boudicea. Part of it was the fact Boudicea was clearly up to something. Rael secured her towel tightly and watched. Whatever sign Boudicea had been anxiously waiting for, the room lights trick seemed to be it. Something was about to happen, Rael could feel it.

Boudicea struck a flint against her dagger and the candle flared up. Boudicea clapped and the room lights went out. Well, that certainly made it harder to dress, not that Rael was really trying to at that moment. Boudicea held her hand over the candle flame. Then she lowered it, closer and closer, until her hand came in contact with the flame. The fire licked at her hand like a puppy dog. Rael's interest in dressing was fading faster and faster. She watched as the hunter seared her hand. Only there was no smell of burning flesh. The flame jumped onto Boudicea's hand. It danced there. It bounced from fingertip to fingertip. Boudicea bent low as if she was listening to it. The flame danced for a full minute, and then it extinguished itself. The room plunged into total darkness. The sudden blackness made Rael clutch at the slip in her hand and it tore.

Another clap from Boudicea and the room lights came back on. Rael said, "That was some magic trick."

Boudicea replied, "It was no trick, just a more certain means of long-distance communication than a cell phone. With those things, who knows who is listening in? I've just had a message from the Order. I only wish more complicated messages could be sent the same way. Still, I learned enough. My mission objective has changed. The demon is now second priority to your safety. There is a danger about you the Order doesn't yet understand. You must not be allowed to fall into enemy hands while we learn more about what happened here. You may very well be the most important asset in the world for all we know."

"I can assure you I'm not, as the grand total of Friday night dates I've been asked out on stands at zero," said Rael.

"Dates? Rael, you are an Astralith; that alone has value to those seeking one. Though the demon prepared you to house another, any cult could use you. Some demons trade for a mere drop of blood, some for a life. Few lives are valuable enough to trade for the horror this demon tried to gate in using your essence, but apparently yours might be. The demon will continue to seek you until you're finally consumed. I must prevent that from happening. Creatures from another plane belong where they come from. They're not welcome here."

"I thank you for the offer, but really all I want is to find my family and go back home."

"You will never have a home again—not in the way that you mean. You're an Astralith of some considerable power. Thus, your old life as you remember it is over. Your new life is not yet determined. Until it is, I shall watch over you."

The words stung Rael. They shouldn't have. The idea of returning to normal when you were no longer normal was pure fantasy. In a way, she understood that fact. Still, Rael wished for her old, normal life more than anything. Boudicea took the slip from Rael's hand. She examined the new tear in it by holding it up to the light. Then she grasped Rael's hand tightly. It all was a bit awkward. Nothing was going to be normal again, was it?

Rael asked, "What are you doing?"

Boudicea ignored her words, which was becoming a common theme of the day. She held Rael's hands to the room light. Then she released Rael. "Your hair, eyes, and horns are not all you've inherited from the failed communion. Your fingernails are pure viritatalium now."

"What is that?" asked Rael, now staring at her own hands more closely.

"It is a metal found only in the interspatial zones between planes. A small amount of dark matter may spill over whenever the planes are pierced during astral travel. Viritatalium is the most precious of the black matter for our purposes. The Order prizes it more than anything else."

"Why?"

"It is the only element on Earth that can pierce the hide of a demon and thus kill it. To the good it does no harm; to evil it is deadly in the right hands."

"Then I was being traded dimensionally for a demon armed with claws for killing other demons?" ask Rael.

"Something like that, but so much more. The Order fears you were to be a devourer, a destroyer of worlds. It is what we call a horror."

"I don't understand."

"In this, we are all equal. The Order is still looking into matters, so understanding may come to us with time. Now, come get dressed. Vampires can be friendly and even helpful at times, but their hospitality has its limits. Like most undead, they'd rather be left alone. If you are to have long-term protection, it will come from the Order or an organization of such a kind. For now, it comes from me." Boudicea picked up her cloak and put it back on. "Dress, then eat, for we should leave while it is still daylight. Time is not on our side."

"It never is for me."

"In what way?"

"Oh, it's too hard to explain," said Rael as she finally stopped examining her nails. She looked at her clothing options and frowned. "I'm going to stick out dressed like a Victorian on a ski holiday."

"More like a Georgian judging by these clothes," said Boudicea.

Rael wasn't sure what that meant. She just scooped up her clothing and took it into the bathroom. She placed it on a dressing table and turned to face the bathroom mirror. She saw the table and her pile of clothes reflected in the mirror, but not herself. She waved her hand in front of her face. Nothing. She picked up the clothes. As soon as she touched them, their reflection in the mirror disappeared. She dropped them. They reappeared. She slowly walked out of the bathroom. She said to Boudicea, "I think the mirror in the bathroom is defective."

"Why?"

"It can't seem to see me."

"Interesting. Another shadow trace from the demon that was to gate into your form."

"But the vanity mirror . . ."

"Pure silver. The only mirror that can reflect a vampire's image—and apparently yours."

"Right," replied Rael as if the physics of the situation made perfect sense. She walked back into the bathroom. None of this made any sense. First, there were weapons that only harmed evil, as if the weapon knew who was evil and who was not. Now, there were mirrors that reflected her image and those that would not. If this was all reality, then reality sucked. She looked in the bathroom mirror again. She wasn't there. But she was there. It was her, Rael. Despite the rest of the weirdness, she was still the same person, right?

"I'm still me. I know I am," she said to herself. There was no reflection to talk back to her and reassure her that those words were true. She had gained some things from this attempted demon swap, but had part of her been lost in the exchange? Would she even know what she had lost if it was gone? It was an existential question beyond her ability to answer. It worried her, and yet she didn't want to think about it anymore. She would leave her fate to Boudicea for now. There really was no other option until she found her parents again.

Chapter 3

The Village of Mortem, the Italian Alps

It was about an hour's walk from the mountain peak that held the count's castle down to the valley below. The position of the sun indicated that it was just past noon by the time they reached the village of Mortem. Soon Rael was walking the streets of the mountain village a few paces behind Boudicea. Just a few days ago, it had felt to Rael like a quaint vacation village. Now Mortem had that village-of-the-damned feeling about it. Mostly that was because walking the streets had been a whole lot easier a few days ago. The further into the village they walked, the harder it became to move about. The snow covering the streets was soon knee deep. What Rael wouldn't do for a ski outfit and some skis right about now. Instead of proper gear, she felt dressed more for high tea.

"Should we stop?" asked Rael.

"No, we keep going," replied Boudicea.

Rael trudged along while trying to keep the brim of her silly period-piece hat low and also trying her best not to make eye contact with anyone. The villagers were out in force removing the snow one shovel-full at a time from in front of their houses and storefronts. There weren't many places without piles of snow already, as each nook and cranny seemed covered, so the shoveling progressed slowly. Many seemed to be leaning on their shovels daydreaming about spring. The only good news in all this was that everyone was too busy working or daydreaming to notice Rael, the horn-headed demon child, waltzing by them.

"It's a little hard to walk in knee-deep snow while wearing this outfit. Since the count gave me some Euros, how about we buy something modern for me to wear if we're not going to stop?" asked Rael. Boudicea seemed to be having no problems with the snow. That was likely a benefit of the extra height she had on Rael and the proper gear she was wearing. Rael's words had the desired effect because Boudicea stopped by a storefront. She snatched a newspaper from an outside display. She seemed to be reading it. Rael glanced at the paper, but she couldn't read Italian. "I don't think the newspaper wears any better than the outfit I have on. How about we go inside and see what else they have?"

"It appears one Ronald Bentworth was in town the other day. The wealthy technology billionaire was nearly caught up in the avalanche. Excellent."

"How is that excellent?" asked Rael.

"A person of that means, means a person of your low stature didn't even get a mention in the paper. That is excellent news. The fewer people that know about you, the better off we are. Come, we must go."

"But my clothes!"

"No time. I need to see the communion spot where they found you before nightfall," replied Boudicea.

"Are we going to stop and ask the locals where that was, because I bet a local shopkeeper would know. We could kill two birds with one stone."

"We shall keep all those birds alive, for I don't need outside help. I will determine the correct location using my senses."

Rael had expected that reply. Hoping to elicit Boudicea's sympathy, she added, "Okay, I'm just going to admit that I'm a little cold in this outfit. I really could use some warm, comfortable clothes."

"You've lived a comfortable life up until now. That has changed, and you need to start getting used to it. You have that lovely fox coat to keep you warm, so let's keep moving."

Boudicea's heart strings were apparently not for the plucking right now. Her reply annoyed Rael. How'd Boudicea know what kind of life Rael had led? Sure, thanks to her dad striking it rich six years ago, life had been comfortable for Rael in the sense that she had everything money could buy. But money wasn't everything, and Rael was the victim here. There should be a little sympathy coming her way. Rael grumbled, "It's not a lovely coat, and you know it. It's sort of creeping me out, in fact. I think the fox head is staring at me. Besides I was taught that wearing fur is murder."

"No, Rael, this is murder. This is why we must press on. There are more important things in this world than our comfort."

They'd reached the end of the main village street. Rael knew that ahead of her was supposed to be the snow lodge in an open field that led to the lifts for the ski slopes. She had checked in at the ski lodge with her parents earlier in the week. Only all of that was gone. All Rael could see now was the white of snow. In the stretch of valley between the village street and the slope lay most of the mountain's snow. The scale of the avalanche was beyond anything Rael could have imagined. The snow in the streets of the village was a mild dusting compared with the wasteland before them. Out there had been a ski lodge and slope filled with skiers. How many were lost under all this snow? Boudicea was correct. It had been murder. All these people had been murdered just so a demon could get its hands on her. That was a cold hard fact Rael would never feel comfortable with.

Rael asked, "What force of nature could do a thing like this?"

"Nothing of this Earth. This is the power a horror can unleash. How it was unleashed here, if only briefly, I do not know. It's clear now that the horror didn't permanently stay on this plane, but there are other ways to tap into its power while it rests on another plane."

"That means what exactly?" asked Rael.

"We're dealing not with just a single gated sub-demon but with a cult willing to tap into their own essence to release the power of this horror on our plane, if ever so briefly. The Order knew nothing of this cult before this day. It is lucky the demon was sensed in time, for there is great danger here. A lone demon is not much trouble for me to handle, but a whole cult is different. Come, we must get up to the top of the mountain and seek the source. I can sense the communion site. It's up there." Boudicea pointed up the barren wasteland of the ski slope.

"You can sense it how, exactly?"

"To you it would seem like magic," replied Boudicea, and then she set off across the wasteland.

The world felt anything but magical to Rael right about now. It felt rather tragic. There was great danger here: Boudicea had said there was danger, and then Boudicea had headed right toward it. There were those that saw danger and engaged with it and those that saw danger and did everything to avoid it. Which type of person was Rael? She didn't know herself. There was a danger in downhill skiing, but this wasn't the same thing. She decided quickly. She'd follow Boudicea. She needed to understand what had happened to her.

The ski lift was wrecked, which meant hiking up the mountain was the only option. Well, unless Boudicea's magic included wings, which seemed unlikely. Mountaineering in a Victorian . . . Georgian frock and coat wasn't exactly what Rael wanted to do today. But since Boudicea, in her knee-high black leather boots, was already heading through the wasteland, Rael took a deep breath and followed.

While Boudicea seemed oblivious to the events around her, Rael couldn't help but look. They were passing units of villagers digging deep into the snowfield in search of survivors. *Survivors* being an optimistic term. Rael certainly wanted to be an optimist. Off in the distance, she caught sight of one of the avalanche victims being hoisted out of the snow. She froze in place and stared. She couldn't really understand why. This victim wasn't unlike any of the others. They were, though, in one important way: the coat that they wore. It was torn, but its color flashed in Rael's memory.

She broke from Boudicea's path up the mountain and hurried toward the victim. Rael pushed rescuers to the side. She shouted, "Mother!" It was her mother, but there was no saving her. The body was battered and broken. A shiver ran down Rael's spine. Rael knew that she'd been like that too. Rael had been destroyed by the snow the same way as her mother. Yet here Rael was alive again—or mostly so. She felt a wave of guilt. She went down on her knees hovering over the frozen corpse of her mother.

She remembered her mother's face filled with life. She'd been stern and controlling. It was a form of love. Mother had also been often anxious and sad. She'd tried to hide the sadness from Rael, but a child knows. Rael threw herself on the body and cried. "Oh Mother, what has happened to us?"

A rescuer said to Rael, "*Lei è morta.*" Rael didn't need a translation. The sense was obvious, but the words didn't matter. It was Rael's fault. She had failed in the race. They had come here because of her. This trip had been meant to cheer her up, and as a result Mother was dead. She felt the rescuers trying to pull her off the body, but she didn't want to leave. Then a powerful hand landed on her back. Boudicea lifted Rael up into the air and planted her on her feet.

"It's best not to make a scene," explained Boudicea.

Rael explained, "It's my mother. She's dead because of me. I have to . . ."

"There is nothing more you can do for her. You are here. She is gone. Come, let's go."

"Are you inhuman? My mother is dead," pleaded Rael.

"They're all dead. More will die if we fail to understand what is going on. It is the future we must think about. Never dwell on a past you cannot change." Boudicea turned to head up the mountain.

Rael took one last look at her mother and wiped the tears from her eyes. She'd not remember her like this. She'd not think about today ever again. "I'm all alone now," Rael said to herself. She looked at Boudicea moving through the snow field. Well, almost alone.

Rael looked at the villagers around her. She saw a strange look in their faces. They recognized her now. A group of them had found her somewhere around here. They had deposited her at the count's castle. They had done that out of fear of her. They'd thought they had rid themselves of her, and yet she was back. Rael took a step back from them, away from her mother's body, and then scampered after Boudicea. Whatever her fate was now, it was in Boudicea's hands, because she could never stay here.

As they climbed the mountain, Rael's mind wandered. Boudicea had been correct. Rael had led a rather sheltered life up until now. Her obsession with sports had led to private tutors to keep up with her schooling. She had few friends her own age since she was out of class so often. Really, she'd had no friends at all since leaving California, now that she thought about it. There was no one back home who would miss her. There were the other girls on the ski team, but many of them had taken their first step toward their dreams. Rael had failed at that, and competitive skiing felt like just a dream now anyway. Maybe this was her punishment for failing. She didn't like that idea. Her life had been sheltered, yes, but she was pretty sure it hadn't been so sheltered as to miss the fact the supernatural was real. She pinched her cheek. It did not wake her up. It had felt worth the try anyway.

They had hiked a good deal upward. Rael's feet were starting to hurt. She could take the climbing just fine. Her shoes, on the other hand, were simply not being kind to her. In a way, the fact they bothered her feet at all came as a relief. That her feet could ache just like anyone else's made her feel more normal. She took her mind off the hiking and looked down. She couldn't see anything because the village was now obscured by trees. Funny how only the snow on the ski slope had collapsed. The forest around her seemed completely untouched by the damage. She'd ask Boudicea about it, but figured she'd only reply with more demonic talk.

Boudicea stopped in her tracks. Rael was still busy looking back down the slope, so she ran right into the back of Boudicea. Boudicea turned to face Rael and said, "The place where the villagers found you is, I believe, just over this ridge. Yes, there is a strong negative energy emanating from that direction. There can be no mistake."

Rael suddenly felt it too. She felt a strange pull. There was something out there that was almost calling to her, begging her to return. What was calling her? Rael would know soon enough because Boudicea was headed right for it. Rael followed after her. They crested the ridge and there it was—whatever *it* was. It was a red circular thing on the ground, but it must be more than that. Rael walked around the circle etched in red . . . well, she hoped it was paint. It wouldn't be, though, would it? It wasn't a proper circle either. The circle encompassed a pentagram. At the center of the pentagram was a scrap of clothing. It was part of her torn ski outfit.

"I was here," said Rael with confidence.

"Yes, and so was a demon. No, more than one demon. Yes, two demons have been here very recently. There was a man here as well. More than one man, but only one was a cultist. I don't understand this cult's need for two demons. One would be sufficient power for any cult to have under their control. That means this cult is very powerful. And yet I know nothing about it. Nothing. I don't understand how that is possible."

"Maybe I'm heavier than I look and it took an army to carry me."

Boudicea ignored Rael's words. She was moving away from the summoning circle. She pointed toward the slope. "The evidence suggests that the avalanche started further up. I need to see the source of it to understand what black magic was used."

The comment stirred a memory in Rael. Only, it wouldn't quite come into focus. She replied, "Yes, I remember now. I was at the start of the expert slope when the avalanche began. There was . . ."

"Yes, go on."

"I can't. There isn't more to that memory yet. I remember the wall of white snow chasing me, but not how it started."

"You look tired. Let's take a breather deeper in the forest. Yes, over there by those trees will do nicely," said Boudicea. The fact she'd said that while examining the higher slope instead of turning around to look at Rael or the trees wasn't missed. Rael didn't protest the decision, though. Getting off her feet was a rather welcome idea. Getting away from the summoning circle was even more welcome. The place haunted Rael, but she could remember nothing about the ritual. She'd been dead—well, nearly dead—so in a way she shouldn't be shocked by that.

As soon as they were among the trees Boudicea announced, "There is more than black magic up this mountain. At least one demon lingers close by still. It's higher up on the slope. If there is a second still nearby, I don't sense it. I need you to stay here. I must destroy the one above us alone. I cannot risk you."

"I want to see whatever it was that did this to me too."

"No, I can't allow you near the demon. It's too dangerous."

Rael relented and sat on a fallen log. Rael's curiosity lost out to relieving the discomfort of her shoes. Maybe that was just a convenient excuse. Maybe she was a little afraid to face her demons.

Boudicea went off back onto the slope, climbing ever higher. The midday sun was at least warming the slopes. Rael kicked her shoes off. She rubbed her feet. How did women back in the olden days ever survive without modern footwear? How she longed to have just one pair of decent walking shoes. Back home she'd had the best of everything, including athletic shoes. Her father had never said no to her. She was probably spoiled. When she got home, the family's fortune would be hers. The grim thought soured her mood. Her current outfit was probably the best money could buy a few hundred years ago. Now it was uncomfortable garbage. All she had back home felt very much the same at the moment. Without Mom and Dad, all she had back home felt like garbage. She felt sort of empty. Suddenly she regretted not going along with Boudicea. She needed to do things so her mind was occupied with something other than her current situation.

She tried to brighten her mood. Maybe her father was still alive. She'd not seen his body. The chances of surviving that avalanche were slim. Still, there was always hope. She liked that idea. She was going to try optimism for the rest of the day.

A twig snapped in the distance. It wouldn't have created much of a reaction had the sound of something heavy moving through the dried winter underbrush not followed it. The idea that a demon was after her did cross her mind, but it lost out to the idea of a bear. Bears existed, demons did not, right? Neither a bear nor a demon appeared, however. Instead, walking out of the forest came a thin man smoking a thinner cigarette. He wore a white suit and a red beret. He flashed his tie at her. It was white with a red cross on it. He said to her, *"Tu es la fille dont les villageois parlaient."*

Rael stood up. She replied, "I don't understand. I don't speak Italian."

The man threw his cigarette to the ground in disgust. "Italian indeed! You English are an embarrassment to the world. Ah, but I sense you are not English. American. Even worse. I can't speak American lingo, but I suppose English will do. You are the girl, aren't you? It is a good thing you hail from such a savage country. It makes things easier. I thought that godless heathen in the castle would hoard you like the precious treasure that you are. The dead must not realize or appreciate how precious you really are. Instead, I find you out here among the evergreens. All the better. All the better for me . . . er, the better for our savior Jesus." He made the sign of the cross after saying that.

Her new optimistic attitude was wavering. Something her parents had taught her growing up came to mind: "Do not talk to strangers." And this man felt strange. For a start, what was he doing up in the alpine forest so lightly dressed? However, she was a stranger here herself, and this man clearly knew something about her situation. She was a tad curious. "Who are you?"

He approached her. He took out another cigarette. As he did so, he studied her. She was feeling uncomfortable and thought about calling out for Boudicea. He replied. "My name is Andres de Salete. I am a Templar Knight."

Templar, the word sounded familiar. The Templars were knights, Christian knights at that. She had learned that much from her tutors. Rael relaxed a little. Druids and vampires were one thing, but a Christian knight sounded like just the thing she needed to combat demons. If they really did exist. Then her tutor's full history lesson came to her mind. Something didn't sound quite right about his answer. She said, "I didn't think you people were around anymore."

"Oh, we are and we are not. The king of France tried to eradicate us once, but we had a safe harbor in Portugal. Some of us changed our names, and some retained the ways of the old order: reverence for and fighting in God's good name. Of course, a lot of us are today as we were then—just glorified bankers for the Christian cause. Some things, they say, never change." He took out a silver lighter with an emblem depicting a red cross on a field of white. He lit his cigarette. He blew black smoke out his nose. "None of that ancient history matters now. What matters to me is the future."

"Can you help me? There's supposed to be a demon after me." She felt stupid saying that in public, but there had been no need to feel stupid with him because this man took the news in his stride. Andres almost seemed to expect it. Of course, a Christian knight would know all about fighting demons.

"I know. I've been tracking it for quite some time. Who the leader of the demon cult is has proven to be impenetrable knowledge, but I knew if I followed the demon it would lead me to what is more important. Follow the demon and be rewarded, and so I did. I needed the demon, you see. It was to be very important for the future."

"If the demon has been destroyed by you already, then I'm already safe."

"*Non et non.*"

"I don't understand."

"Hands up or I'll shoot!" he barked. He took out a gun. Rael shot up from her log. He slowly closed the gap between them.

Her new optimistic attitude was dead. It had never really stood a chance against all this craziness. She said, "I thought you said that it was all about my future."

"Not yours, mine. You see, little lady, I've been a good crusader for the cause. I've pillaged the right people and raped the Holy Land better than my ancestors could ever have dreamed of doing. Not physically, but financially. Crusading was in the end mostly just a sanctified business venture for mass murderers. I'd say I got a little revenge on Saladin's heirs in my lifetime, if you will. Now, well, I'm ready to get Christ's rewards in heaven for my good deeds done for the cross. Only there are some that say I don't deserve ultimate rewards. They consider me a sinner. I am upon my death to be damned. That's where you come in. You are a precious diamond and I have you at last."

"Me?"

"You're going to get me into heaven, sweetie. Perhaps I've sinned too much to waltz in through Saint Peter's pearly gates, so I'll gate myself into heaven instead. I don't mind crashing that party. I've been waiting eons for a cosmic mistake like you to appear. Now you've arrived. I tracked that demon for over a year hoping it would reveal the Astralith it had discovered. I thought I'd missed my chance and you were all used up. Instead, here you are, just you and me. A little communion with you later today and I'm in heaven thanks to your essence. Get it?"

"I think I do. You're crazy."

"No, I'm the one holding the gun. Turn around and start marching that way. There is a circle waiting out in the clearing over there that was made just for the two of us. And don't go calling for your druid friend. She won't come as she's otherwise engaged at the moment." He gave a self-satisfied giggle after that remark.

There seemed little Rael could do but follow his orders until a plan came to mind. Nothing immediately did, though. Rael turned and started marching. She could hear his footsteps behind her. Leave it to her to meet up with the least Christian-like crusader left standing. She had a feeling her newfound status as an Astralith was going to give her an opportunity to meet many more colorful people like Andres. Well, if she got rid of Andres first, that is. There was no mistaking the situation—she'd have to make a run for it. Only he'd shoot her pretty easily at this distance. Of course, he'd need her alive—or mostly so—to finish the ritual, right? Okay, she didn't know that for sure. High school taught you the three Rs—reading, writing, and arithmetic—but not the most important R, demonic rituals. It was probably the result of using Common Core. *Think, Rael, you need to create a distraction.*

"You're walking too slowly. I don't have all day to get to heaven."

Andres was a jerk. She could just hit him, figuratively speaking. She looked down at her hands. Hmm . . . maybe more than just figuratively. She could claw him. He was evil, right? She turned around fast and raked her fingernails across his chest. They sliced his cheap suit like butter. He screamed out loud as his gun went off accidentally. He shot it high into the air.

Rael darted off in a flash. He shouted out, *"Je déteste courir les putes."* Rael wasn't about to wait for a translation. This was a race, and in this race, time wasn't her enemy.

He fired off three more rounds. Each struck the ground at her feet. She could hear him huffing and puffing. Smoking had its downside for Andres. She could easily have outrun him, if only she had been prepared for a foot race. Unfortunately, her outfit was not. She ducked behind a tree. This was no good. This stupid dress was slowing her down. She dug her claws in and tore it away below the knees. The dress must have been evil, a fact she didn't doubt for a minute. That was better.

"Come on out, little girl," he ordered.

"Why, so you can shoot me?"

"Yes, of course. I promise to only shoot you in the legs so that you shall run no more, though. Then I will drag your bleeding body back to the site. A good commune needs a little spilled blood anyway. Come, come, it is a good deal that I offer and you know it."

"I'd rather die," she replied.

"Ah, that's the spirit!"

She darted off again, this time making full strides. She wasn't half bad at running. Maybe she should have been a track star. Oh, but Father wouldn't have allowed it. What Father wanted went. He wanted a skier, and so she skied. Had he died happy with her, or had he been disappointed? She'd never know now. Two shots rang out. If she wasn't lucky, she'd soon be able to ask her father that question face to face.

She hit a snag in her plan. It was a thirty-foot freefall cliff-shaped snag. She turned around. Andres was still coming. There was a smirk of sinister satisfaction on his face. He must have known the whole time that she was running into a dead end. Where was Boudicea? Not here, that much was certain.

Andres said, "*Toutes vos bases nous appartiennent.*"

Rael jumped down. Granted it was probably not going to go well, falling thirty feet, but maybe the failed communion had given her super-legs or something. She hit the ground feet first. Her legs went up into her chest. That knocked the wind out of her. She tried to get to her feet fast, but nothing doing. She lay prone on the ground trying to regain her lost strength.

She saw Andres at the edge of the cliff. He said, "I am so relieved to see you alive. Half of those who jump forty-eight feet or more die. It would have been a terrible ending to our meeting for me. Mostly dead and dying is okay; all the way dead is useless. But I see the cliff was not so high, and you are hopefully just horribly injured. Don't worry, I plan to shoot out your kneecaps just to make sure it is so. Then I shall have to lug you back up to the ritual site. I hope you can see that you have been very unfair to me in all this."

He pointed his gun at her. She winced. The shot never fired. Andres went down to the ground like a bag of wet cement. The count appeared at the edge of the cliff. He looked down at her while twirling a silver-handled cane.

She said, "I thought vampires couldn't come out in daylight."

"We prefer not to because it is very bad for the complexion. But I sensed you were in danger. I promised to the best of my power that no harm would come to you in my domain. Your hunter friend is down, but perhaps not out. Do not wait for her." He pointed his cane. "Run in that direction. In the next valley is an old stone church. There is a friend of mine at that church. He can help you further. There you will be out of my domain. This shall be our last meeting, my young friend. I wish you all the best."

He stepped away from the edge. She knew he wouldn't be back. Andres had been thumped on the head. How long would he be out? Hopefully long enough. She got to her feet. She was no worse for wear now that she'd gathered her breath. Boudicea down, what did that mean? Was Rael all alone in this crazy situation? She hoped not. This friend of the count, she had to find them and get help fast. Her breath had returned, so she started running again.

Chapter 4

A Forgotten Church, the Italian Alps

Rael hid in the overgrown shrubbery that surrounded the stone church. The church was small compared with the cathedrals she'd seen in Rome before taking the train to the village. The place looked practically medieval. Of course, it probably was from that period. It was located in the next mountain valley with no village in sight. There must have been one in the old days, though, or else why build it? A better question was why was the church still operational considering the village it served was long gone? Rael didn't know. She was just glad it was here. Night would be falling soon, and she wasn't prepared for a night out in the wilderness alone.

The count had told her to come here for help, but she hadn't exactly found help waiting outside for her. What she had found was a car. It was idling outside the church's front door. The good news was that a car here meant there was a road out of this place. The bad news was that if someone sent you to a church seeking help, the obvious person to offer you help was the priest, and unfortunately he seemed to be busy with another visitor. Only in her nightmare that was the past few days would a vampire send anyone to a priest for help. Nothing made sense anymore, even the nonsense.

Rael snuck through the shrubbery. She would try to spy through a church window to check on the guests that had come with the car. Mostly she wanted to know when they'd be leaving. After one stranger had tried to stab her and another had tried to shoot her, she was pretty much done meeting strangers for a while. The problem with spying inside was the lack of proper windows in this place. The only ones at her level were made of stained glass. They were very decorative but essentially useless for the task of peeking inside. The only way to know anything would be by going inside the church. She crept to the front door. What was the worst that could happen? She'd probably find that out the hard way.

Think positive thoughts, Rael, she told herself. She was having doubts anyway, despite the pep talk. She pulled the oversized oak door and it opened slowly. She wanted no creaks, groans, or squeals from it. She got what she needed. She tiptoed in on her bare and rather chilled feet. After the small entrance room came the nave. This church was old-school, with bleak but sturdy oversized wooden pews set in two rows with a procession aisle between them. The procession aisle led to the altar. Hanging above the altar was a wooden crucifix. Jesus hung there nailed to the cross. Rael could swear Jesus's eyes were looking at her in judgment. It felt a little unfair. It's not like she'd wanted to gate a demon into this world.

Rael always felt like a fish out of water in a church. Rael's parents had never been big on religion. Well, Mom had been at one point, but she had given it up. Dad never had an interest in it. Dad usually had the upper hand in matters like that. The only times Rael had gone to church was for a wedding or a funeral—neither of which had occurred very often. Let's hope today was neither of those. It wouldn't be, though. There was no one in sight. Where was everyone? She figured that she could find a pew and wait it out, only she didn't have time to start acting on that thought. She heard voices. She couldn't tell where their source was because the sound of the voices echoed inside this cozy stone church.

Then a curtain was brushed aside near the front of the church and a man came out. She could see by his collar even at this distance that he was a priest. He appeared to be alone. Maybe it was his car outside. She relaxed. Things were looking up. Then another creature came out. It was a hulking blue beast with an oversized mouth full of jagged reptilian teeth. Its skin was scaly like a serpent's. It must have stood eight feet tall, with ample width. Its appearance caused her to drop to her knees behind the last pew. She'd found Boudicea's demon. Demons were real. Why did they have to be real? Just her luck these days, wasn't it?

She crawled past the marble holy water font and under the last few pews, hoping she was completely out of sight. She had just a sliver of a peeking angle to see what was going on.

The creature spoke in a deep voice. "Father Beno, you joined the Maleficium Society with full knowledge of our plans. Those plans have now failed."

"I had no idea you'd kill so many! You said you were to sacrifice the girl. The girl was nothing to me, but so many people from the village died yesterday—and for nothing. Worse, your lust for death has now brought unwanted attention to us all, and more importantly to me—and with no power from this horror as the reward," replied the priest.

"What am I, chopped liver? Trust me, as long as I am here, there is power," said the demon. Rael was confused. The blue beast sounded like a muppet. So where had that deep voice come from? She wasn't trying too hard to see because the last thing she wanted was to be seen. The source of the deep voice stepped out from behind the curtain. He was wearing a black robe and a hood. It was different from Boudicea's cloak. When the robed man turned his back to her, she could see a blood-red pentagram similar to the one in the summoning area. He must be a Satanist or something. She couldn't see his face. The robed figure said, "Are you having regrets, Father?"

"No, not at all. I still believe in the cause. I've seen the power of Ilitar. If she can move mountains like that from another plane, imagine what she'll do for us when she's here," said Father Beno.

"She'll only be here when we get the girl back. We've been grooming her for far too long to lose her. It is a shame that our demon let her get away with the communion incomplete," said the robed figure in his deep voice.

"I didn't let her get away. I was attacked by an abyssal sentinel. It was that demon that ruined the ceremony. I did my part. It was you that underestimated the power of Ilitar. That was your mistake," said the demon.

Father Beno asked, "But why should another demon interrupt the ceremony?"

"What? You don't believe me?" asked the demon.

The robed figure said, "Enough! What is done is done. Unfortunately, the small release of power from the horror has brought unwanted eyes to this area. The leader is most disappointed. He's moved on. The Society cannot tolerate being discovered. I've been instructed that the whole area is too compromised for us to operate here ever again. This church is no good to the leader anymore."

The father asked, "And what do I do without my church?"

"You die," replied the robed figure.

The demon seized the priest before he had time to react. The beast hoisted the priest into the air. With its two hands it twisted the man of God. Rael heard his back break. Well, she assumed that was the sound of his back breaking. The sound made her sick to her stomach. The idea that she was one discovery away from a broken back herself didn't help. Then again, she apparently was their cat's meow. How had they prepared her for years, though? That part made no sense as of yet. Still, Boudicea had hinted that Rael wasn't a random victim. They had killed all those people just to get ahold of her essence. Her essence must be premium! She'd have felt proud of that fact had it not been bringing her so much trouble.

Bad news: The beast dropped the priest to the floor and started walking in her direction. Rael squeezed herself into a compact ball under a pew. Sometimes not being tall like Boudicea had its advantages. Luckily these old wooden pews were bulky and might just hide a skinny little person like her—at least, that's what she hoped.

"What now?" barked the demon.

"The leader has moved operations down into Rome for now. We must give him a full report on our failures. Let's hope the leader is more forgiving to us than we were to Father Beno. Either way, you, my pet, will soon go hunting again for the girl. You won't lose her a second time."

"You just keep those abyssal demons off me and I'll land the runt."

The church door closed. Rael gave it a good five minutes before she slid out from hiding. She went over to the front door and cracked it open just a peek. The car was already gone. Well, the good thing was that she now knew more people she was up against. The bad thing was, she was all alone in this fight.

She closed the door and tried to size up the situation. The man she was supposed to meet was deader than those designer blue jeans with small pockets that didn't fit your cell phone. That he hadn't been a nice man at all made things feel alright in some ways. Still, the count had sent her to see him. Maybe he was a double agent or something. She would never know now. She moved toward the body. She tried to shield her eyes from looking at his lifeless face. She patted down the corpse. She needed transportation, and she figured God would want her to have this man's car to help in his afterlife redemption. No keys were in his pockets, however.

"Let's hope you have food in the pantry at least," she said to the dead man.

She headed to the curtain. She was a smart enough cookie to know that behind the curtain must be the priest's quarters. She pushed the curtain back. The priest's quarters behind the chapel were small, but clearly most of what you needed to survive a mountain winter was here: a small stove, a bed, food, and a heater. The heater was on, and the room was warm. Rael was thankful for that. Her little toes were still half frozen. As she headed over to the small pantry, her eyes caught sight of a small box labeled "Church donations." Given that she was down to wearing a creepy staring dead fox fur coat and a torn Georgian frock, she was happy to see that box. She pulled out three summer dresses, two pairs of short shorts, and a few sneakers sized for people not called Rael. Who donates summer clothes in the winter? *Well, everyone, Rael,* was clearly the answer. She shimmied up a pair of short shorts. At least they'd keep her bottom warm under the torn frock. She put on the longest pair of socks she could find. Of course, they didn't match. One was red and one was blue. If only she had a pair of shoes, she'd be all set for Fashion Week.

She spied a coat rack by the back entrance to the priest's quarters. She headed over to it. The heavy coat on the rack would make a good tent but a lousy addition to her wardrobe. The boots under it, however, fit. A large man with small feet—there was probably something Freudian in all that.

The outer door rattled next to her. She nearly jumped out of her skin. Someone was trying to open it, but it was locked. She exhaled. Rael moved over to the window to see who it was. *Please be Boudicea,* she thought. She peeked through the curtain. Andres was outside trying to get in. She backed away from the window. She needed a place to hide and fast.

She headed back toward the curtain. No, she couldn't go into the church; that was a dead end too. She'd seen a bell tower. Maybe she could get inside it from here somehow.

"Ah, you must be the girl I was told was coming," said a voice.

Rael turned around in fright. What she saw after she turned around didn't reduce her level of fear. There was a man wrapped in decaying linen holding the curtain open. His face, such as it was, was exposed. His skin was dried and taut. He had black empty space where his eyes and nose ought to be. She blurted out, "You're a mummy!"

"I am Felix Agricola, the former Prefect of Clysma. I am pleased to meet you and at your service, my lady."

Of course, the vampire would never have sent her here to meet a priest. He would have sent her here to meet a mummy—only, why was a mummy here at all? "I'm as pleased to meet you as I am confused as to why you're here at all."

"You know the story: A small-town boy does good. I set off to make my mark in the big world, but I never forgot my hometown. And this is my hometown. Not much to look at these days, but in my time it was wonderful. Come, I'll show you around."

"There's a man outside."

"Do you want me to let him in?"

"No!"

"I see. What do you want?"

"A safe place to hide and something to eat without the man outside ever seeing me."

"I will arrange that. Let's get you safe first. Since there are demons around here as well as men, we must hide you. Come, follow me."

He opened the closet door and went down a secret tunnel hidden in the wall. Rael followed. The mummy walked straight as an arrow. The tunnel opened into a field well beyond the hedges surrounding the church. She looked for signs of Andres. There were none. With any luck he was inside the church.

The mummy was moving beyond the hedges and into a field beside the church. It wasn't long before Rael realized they were walking into an old graveyard. It made sense. These old churches here in Europe often had their graveyards close by. The grave markers that were still standing were all worn. She made no attempt to read them. They were headed for a large slab of marble in the middle of the field. The mummy stopped at it. The letters carved into it were the only ones she could read clearly: *Mors intra cave*. The mummy bent down and lifted up the slab.

"In you go," he said to her.

She looked around one last time. No sign of Andres at the moment. She went in. "It's a touch dark in here," she said.

"Oh, where are my manners? Yes, yes, indeed. I do forget how limited you living people are. Wait here, please." Felix went down into the darkness. He wasn't gone long, and when he returned he was carrying a lantern. "I always keep it filled in case we have visitors. Madam, welcome to the church in the valley after the town of Mortem. We like to call our catacombs Post Mortem." He paused for a laugh Rael didn't give him. "The living are a tough crowd." He waved her down deeper.

"My name is Rael Armstrong."

"A pleasure to meet you, Rael."

She went further down into the tomb. The mummy followed her, carrying the light source. She could hear the scraping of the marble stone closing back up. Normally she'd worry about who had just closed that, but these weren't normal times.

The mummy said, "Wait here. There's no need to go down deeper into the main catacombs. I wouldn't like you to get lost back there. Anyway, I dug up a nice little casket here for you to sleep in. It has a silky-smooth satin lining with a small, plush pillow. This century. Quality stuff. I traded the owner a few baubles to let you have it for the night."

Rael looked at the open casket. It looked about as comfortable as she could expect to be when sleeping inside a tomb. "Thanks," she replied. Her stomach rumbled.

"Oh, there go my manners again. I promised you a meal." He put the lantern down on the ground. "I'll be right back in a few." He went off into the darkness of the catacombs, leaving her alone. Well, not alone per se. Opposite her lovely casket was a closed wooden coffin. The walls of the catacomb had been hollowed out to form multiple shelves. On each shelf was a pile of bones. Perhaps there had once been markings to tell a visitor whose bones they were, but Rael couldn't see any now. It was surprisingly warm inside the tomb, at least.

The marble slab moved up top. Maybe that was dinner coming. She got excited. Then again, maybe it was Andres. She looked for something to use as a weapon. She didn't find anything to hand. Rael stopped the search when she saw a cloaked figure walking into the crypt. Rael wasn't alarmed, because the tangle of red hair sticking out of the hood gave its identity away. Boudicea removed her hood completely and tossed her dagger into the nearest coffin. The blade sunk down to the hilt. Her blade couldn't cut Rael but was hell on old wood. This new-world physics was going to take a little getting used to. The marble slab closed again. Boudicea said, "This is a good place to hide. Smart thinking."

"What, no hello?" replied Rael.

"I see you've upgraded your wardrobe. Good thing you kept the coat." Boudicea tossed something to Rael with her right arm. Rael caught it. She examined it in the light of the lantern. Boudicea explained, "Tracking acorn. Its partner is planted in your fox coat. That's why I wasn't keen to go shopping in town." Boudicea shrugged off her cloak and winced in pain. The source of the pain was obvious. There was a huge bite mark on her left shoulder. Blood was flowing freely from many puncture wounds made by teeth.

Rael gasped. "You're hurt!"

"It's nothing."

The limpness of Boudicea's left arm seemed to say otherwise. Rael remembered both Andres and the count hinting that Boudicea hadn't been alright. They'd been correct. Rael suggested, "I can sew a little. Maybe I could stitch you up before you bleed out . . . if we had a needle and thread. When the mummy gets back, I can ask . . ."

"It's nothing to worry about. A red abyssal sentinel demon got the jump on me is all. Amateur mistake on my part. I'm more disgusted in myself than hurt at the moment. It could have told me a lot more about what happened here, I'm sure of it. If only I had captured it. My mind was on other matters when it should have been focused only on demons, and it nearly cost me my life."

"Other matters?"

"You."

"Oh."

"Luckily for me the red demon just tossed me off a ledge rather than kill me outright."

"Red demon? Wait, I just saw a blue one."

"A blue chaos demon? Where?"

"It was in the church when I arrived, but it's gone now."

"There's too many demons here for my liking. You're a hotter property even than I feared you were."

"I think all this has something to do with some society. I overheard the demon's conversation with the priest before it . . . sort of double-crossed him and killed him. Oh, and there was another man, a demonic priest or something like that, with the demon. The demon seemed to take orders from him. Oh, and then there was another man . . ."

"You've certainly been busy." Boudicea sat down on the coffin next to her blade. "And you've done better than me at sorting things out. Congratulations. Divicia would be proud of you."

Rael asked, "Divicia? Who is that?"

"A great man. I was his apprentice. My parents gave me to him when I was three months old. He was to mold me into the Order's greatest champion. At times I feel I've not lived up to his expectations of me."

"Oh, I sort of know how that . . ."

"Who wants McDonalds? I know a ghoul that lives in the sewer under the McDonalds in the town in the next valley, and boy does he deliver fast," said Felix as he returned from the darkness of the catacombs. He stopped in his tracks upon seeing Boudicea. "Oh, a huntress. Had I known you were expecting company I would have ordered two bags."

Boudicea replied, "I am just a hunter and I require nothing."

"Hunter, huntress? I'll never get a handle on this English language. I do wish people still used proper Latin. Now, there is a noble language, and it is far more civilized for use when looting and pillaging. Who would ever have thought the backward Picts' bastardized lingo would catch on . . . no offense to you, Brigante." He looked at Boudicea's wounds and added, "I've got plenty of bandages if you need them."

"I need nothing," replied Boudicea.

Rael took the bag from Felix. "Thank you, Felix. I think she wants to be left alone."

"You know, the druids said the same thing to Caesar, and . . ." He covered his mouth. "I probably shouldn't talk about that. There's still a little bad blood over it all. No thanks are due for my help. I am only trying to be a good host."

Rael said, "You are most kind."

"I do my best. Now, you eat up and have no worries, because you are safe here. This catacomb has a thousand eyes and ears on alert for your enemies. Five hundred noses too, but well, you could probably work out the math yourself."

He drifted back into the inky darkness of the inner catacombs and was gone. Rael climbed into her casket and opened her bag. The smell of hot fast food hit her nostrils. She had a keen fetish for it. Her father had never allowed her to eat it, though. Fast food was not for young women who were training their bodies, he had lectured her time and time again. He was gone now.

Boudicea's words about her mentor reminded Rael of her own worries. Had her father died disappointed in her? She suddenly realized how hungry she was. Now was not the time for mourning her parents; now was the time for eating. She started stuffing fries into her mouth. Stuffing fries was more fun than dwelling on the unchangeable past. She looked up and saw Boudicea just sitting there staring into darkness. Rael said with her mouth full, "Are you sure you won't have some?"

Boudicea got to her feet. She picked up her cloak and draped it around herself. "My cloak provides me all I need." She pulled out an apple from the sleeve. "It can feed me, heal me, protect me, guide me. To you it would seem like magic."

"Everything seems like magic to me these days," Rael replied.

Chapter 5

A Forgotten Church, the Italian Alps

Rael opened her bleary eyes. She stretched her arms, and they immediately clunked against the side of the casket. Her nails made a scratching sound against its stained wood frame. She hoped the dead man that Felix had traded for her to use it wouldn't mind the damage. All this was a not-so-subtle reminder of where she had just spent the night. It felt too early in the morning for those types of reminders. Not that she was sure it was morning, given that it was never not nighttime down here in the dark.

Rael sat up and cracked her neck. Caskets were surprisingly uncomfortable to sleep in. She hadn't gotten nearly as much sleep as her body wanted. Still, she hadn't had any nightmares last night. These catacombs were tailormade to induce nightmares. How did the dead manage to sleep so soundly year after year stuck in a place like this?

The lantern burned brighter as Rael turned up the fuel. "Good, you're finally awake. We can get started," Boudicea greeted her.

Rael looked over at Boudicea. She appeared to be on the mend already. Indeed, she was practically good as new and already doing yoga stretches in her completely repaired black Lycra outfit. There was nothing worse than a morning person-type roommate when you weren't one yourself. What Rael needed was breakfast and not yoga.

Right on time she heard a friendly voice calling to her out of the dark. "I've got some Egg McMuffins, hash browns, and coffee!" Felix had arrived with breakfast! Rael snatched the coffee from his decaying hands.

"Cream and sugar, madam?" asked Felix.

Rael popped the plastic top off and started drinking. She liked her coffee hot, black, and super-sized. Mostly she liked the caffeine; the rest of the coffee was superfluous.

Boudicea said to Felix, "I need to be alone with Rael. It's time for us to discuss our next move."

"Of course, your hunterness, so sorry to have taken up your valuable time. Only . . . yes, I do think you might be interested in . . . well, no, it can wait for a less busy time."

Boudicea grabbed a loose linen wrapping on the mummy and drew him closer to her before he could scamper away into the darkness. "Tell me what you think can wait for me to hear."

"Ah, then you do want to know right away about my news?"

"'I'm dying to hear it," added Boudicea.

"I'll ignore that pun at my expense. I'm happy to inform both of you of my news. There is a demon, a rather large red one at that, with big scary teeth and all. It is inside the church as we speak. I didn't catch its name. Should I go ask?" Felix explained.

"What's the demon doing inside the church?" asked Rael.

"Talking to the priest from what I saw," replied Felix.

"But the priest is dead," said Rael. She looked over at the mummy and added, "No offense."

"None taken. You wouldn't be the first to assume the dead can't speak. Let me tell you . . ."

"It's getting them to shut up that's the hard part," interrupted Boudicea. Boudicea put her cloak on. Her dagger slid out from her sleeve. That meant only one thing. They were about to go hunting, and here Rael hadn't even had one refill of coffee yet. The marble slab above them started to move, which confirmed it.

"I know you might not want to hear more from me, but I know a secret way into the church. Much better for a stealthy approach," said Felix.

"He did know a secret way out of the church that prevented Andres from seeing me," added Rael.

The marble stopped moving. "Who is Andres?" asked Boudicea.

"I sort of told you about him yesterday. He tried to kill me while you were off fighting demons and before I stumbled on the priest-killing demon and his cultist friend."

Boudicea didn't reply to her. She turned to Felix and said, "Show me the secret way inside."

"Can I just finish eating breakfast?" asked Rael.

Boudicea wasn't agreeable to the suggestion. "Grab it to go. I've got a night of shoulder pain to return as a favor to this fiend."

Felix grabbed the lantern and was off into the catacombs. Boudicea followed. Sitting there in the dark eating didn't seem like a good option, so Rael grabbed her bag of breakfast and headed after them.

The catacombs had a lovely mildew smell to go with the occasional creepy-crawly that scampered under Rael's foot. The centuries of dust did little to hide the general disrepair of the place. Felix didn't seem to mind. He moved through it like he'd had an eternity to memorize every centimeter of the establishment.

He stopped and pushed through a spiderweb. Then he climbed through a cubby hole and crawled through a long tunnel on his hands and knees. They followed him, with Boudicea in front of Rael. The tunnel came to an end in what appeared to be a small room made of worked stone. This room was, to all appearances, a dead end.

"What next?" asked Boudicea.

"You go up," replied Felix. He reached up and tugged on a rusted iron ring embedded in the ceiling. The ceiling came down. Not like it had collapsed, but more like a trapdoor that had swung open. Felix said, "Ladies, I give you the secret entrance to the bell tower."

"Great, now how do we get up?" asked Rael. Boudicea sprang up and caught the ledge with her bare hands. She then effortlessly hoisted herself up. Rael said, "Great, now how do those of us who can't fly get up?"

"Perhaps I can be of assistance, madam," said Felix. He leaned over. Rael climbed on his back then moved up on his shoulders. Felix hoisted her up. "Sorry if it's a bumpy ride, but my back is a little stiff this morning. Indeed, I'm a bit stiff all over this morning." There was silence. He added, "Tough crowd. What, does no one get jokes anymore?"

The ride up on his shoulders was fine. He was rather strong for someone who looked as if he was one swift breeze from unraveling into dust. Rael stepped off Felix's shoulders. She looked down through the trapdoor and said, "Thank you again, Felix."

"Don't mention it. I died to serve, as they say."

"That one was funnier," said Rael. The mummy seemed pleased. Then he went off.

Rael was up and down at the same time. She was up out of the catacombs and down on the bottom floor of the bell tower. The important thing was that she was there alone at the bottom of the bell tower. Where had Boudicea gone off to? She opened the door, but that just led outside. Thoughts of Andres still roaming out there somewhere came to mind. He'd be a fool to stay the night, but he *was* a fool, so it seemed possible.

One thing was certain: There wasn't a good way to get inside the church through the bell tower since it didn't connect to the rest of the church, at least on the ground level. She closed the door and looked up the spiral staircase that wound round and round as it went up to the bell on top of the tower. There was naturally only one direction Boudicea could have traveled. At least Rael wasn't afraid of heights. She put her foot on the first step. It felt as sturdy as a wooden step built in medieval times might feel. Well, it had held Boudicea's weight already, so it would hold hers too, she hoped.

The bell tower stairs didn't only go all the way to the top of the tower. Rael soon discovered that there was a landing at the roof level and the stairs kept going up beyond that point. There was no door on this landing, but there was an open archway that served as an exit. Rael could spy Boudicea out on the church's roof. She was lying face down on the slate that formed the covering of the roof. Rael set out to catch up with her.

Rael knelt down beside Boudicea and asked, "What's going on?"

"Shhhh, I'm listening?"

"To what?"

"The demon is still talking to the dead priest."

"What are they saying?"

"I'd know if there was more quiet up here and less talking."

Rael could take a hint and clammed up. She pressed her own ear against the slate. There wasn't anything to hear. Maybe her cloak gave Boudicea special hearing powers. Only she didn't even have the hood on over her head, so how that worked was beyond Rael. Rael started to hear her tummy churning; it would probably be happier if it was churning on that McMuffin.

Boudicea raised her head. "I heard something . . . one word. I heard the word *society*. You mentioned the same word to me last night. It's important that we learn as much about this society as possible."

Rael replied, "Yeah, the Maleficium Society . . ." she paused. "I remembered the whole name this time. Funny how things pop back into your head, isn't it?"

Boudicea stood up. "I might have to start eating brain food like you do. What more do you know about it?"

"Nothing . . . I think, and yet there's something else trapped in the back of my brain."

"Don't try to force it; it will return to you in time."

Rael opened her bag and pulled out the hash browns. "What's our next move?" She bit into one.

"You are staying put." A rope shot out of Boudicea's sleeve. The metal grappling hook on that rope dug into the masonry of the church. "I'm going inside to question a demon, and kill it if needed. This time I'm not playing nice." She tossed her dagger to Rael. Rael dropped her hash brown and also missed catching the dagger, which fell harmlessly onto the slate. Boudicea pulled a long sword out from her other sleeve. To Rael it looked a lot like more magic stuff going on. As Rael bent to retrieve the dagger, Boudicea launched herself off the roof. She swung down and went directly through a stained glass window. Rael heard the sound of what was very likely priceless antique stained glass shattering. Not long after that a demon howled out in what was hopefully pain.

Rael grabbed the dagger and headed for the tower stairs. She was taking the long way into the church, via the front door. If Andres was still around, she no longer cared. After what the demons had nearly done to her and her family, she was partial to seeing one finally get some payback.

She sprinted down the stairs and darted out the tower's door. She was running a lap around the hedge toward the front door. She yanked it open with one hand, armed with the dagger in the other. She was in the midst of a pure adrenaline rush. It was just like downhill racing, only the enemy was real. She entered the nave to find the action already dying down.

The demon had its back to her. It looked totally different from the blue one she'd seen previously. It looked sort of like an oversized, balding ape. It was seven feet tall and sported impressive claws at the end of its arm. Notice the word *arm*, because it only had one. The demon was without one of its arm, and orange goo was streaming out from the shoulder wound where the other had once been attached.

Boudicea was standing on the altar with her sword at the ready should the demon make a move toward her. Boudicea said, "Tell me about your Maleficium Society?"

The demon spit at Boudicea. Its aim wasn't too impressive. The spit missed and burned on the crucifix behind Boudicea, just like acid might have. It replied, "It's not my society, you stupid, weak huntress."

"I'm a hunter, same as any other."

"The only good hunter is a dead one."

"Brave words for a demon about to be sent back to its plane in pieces."

The demon swung its good arm at Boudicea. Boudicea leaped into the air. She did a flip, avoiding the demon's grasp and delivering another blow. And just like that the demon had run out of arms.

The red demon didn't acknowledge any pain from the blow. It snarled at Boudicea instead. "My existence here in your world is not for you to give, hunter. Ilitar has learned what she needed to know from my time here. Thus, my work here is already done. I can leave this plane at any time now. Ilitar has other agents to finish the job that needs to be done."

"What job is that?" asked Boudicea.

The demon didn't respond verbally. It rushed at Boudicea instead. She easily dodged the bull rush and sliced a gaping wound into the demon's side. That didn't stop the demon one bit. It kept steamrollering down the procession aisle. It occurred to Rael that the demon was headed straight at her. She had just been standing like an idiot watching the events unfold.

Rael held her dagger out in anticipation of receiving a blow, but the demon stopped short of her. Its orange goo loss apparently was getting to it. It seemed light-headed and started to topple over. With its last grasp, the demon seized the marble font next to Rael. Holding itself up by the rim, it drank from the basin. The beast laughed fiendishly. The sizzling began at once, and within seconds it burst into orange flames. It had an odd grin of satisfaction as it turned into a pile of charred red ash before Rael's eyes. Well, that had put her off eating her McMuffin for now.

Rael stopped flinching. She shrugged. "Who knew that holy water stuff actually works?"

"The demon knew. Now we'll get no more information from it," replied Boudicea.

"Chalk one demon up for our team." Rael flipped the dagger in the air and tried to catch the handle as she'd seen Boudicea do countless times before. She missed and it clanked upon the floor.

Boudicea said, "Don't get too cocky. This one got what it needed from the priest. It was just a sentinel demon. It was a dime-a-dozen warrior. Sacrificing a drop of blood from a chicken will net you one of those. Now it's back in the abyss ready to reform and tell all that it knows to its master, Ilitar."

Boudicea used her boot to scoop the dagger from the floor onto her toes. Then she flexed her foot and the dagger flew back up into her hand. The dagger and the sword were then both stored into their proper sleeve. It was a neat trick. Rael figured she'd master flipping one first before she attempted it.

Boudicea turned and went back down the aisle. "We must locate more information on this society. I've never heard of it before, and yet they were organized enough to be working with a chaos demon and using you to bring Ilitar here. They clearly know more about you. Yes, I need to know all about you from them." Rael scampered after her. Boudicea pushed back the curtain. "Ah, the priest's quarters."

"I searched it yesterday. There is nothing much in there," explained Rael.

"A lot can change overnight."

Boudicea went through the curtain. Not much looked different to Rael since she'd last been inside.

Boudicea seemed excited all the same. She said, "Three chairs moved at this table, three cups in the sink, and the bedsheets folded down three inches. Freemasons have been here and have searched the place."

"Freemasons?" replied Rael.

"That's not all." She pulled a pan from the top of the stove. She turned the pan over on the table. Black soot and char spilled out. "Faustian minions have been here as well."

"How do you know that?"

"The soot is the remains of the priest's Bible. Devil worshipers are big on the written word. They'd not be able to see a Bible and not destroy it. Funny, given our priest was not a practice-what-you-preach type of man."

"What did he preach?" asked Rael.

"A good question." Boudicea opened a cupboard. She pulled out religious garments. "Catholic, Catholic . . . ah, abyssal in worship." It was a black robe like the one Rael had seen the other man wearing.

"It's like the one the other man wore," said Rael.

"Pretty common demon-worshiping cult gear. It doesn't tell us much about the Society. I fear we might need to resort to more messy means to learn more."

"Meaning?"

"We must get information out of the dead priest."

"How?"

"He won't be willing, but I will force it out of him."

"That didn't really answer my question."

Boudicea was already moving back through the curtain. Near the altar were the remains of the priest. Boudicea picked the dead body up and propped it on a pew. Then she started undressing it.

Rael had followed her. She asked, "Do we have to strip him?"

"There's no rule against it."

"But it's not decent!"

"We can't desecrate a fallen priest."

"Not exactly what I meant. You see, I've never seen a grown man naked, particularly a dead one. I'm good with not starting now."

Boudicea tore his shirt off. The sight of his bloated stomach made Rael a touch queasy. Rael turned away and faced the altar. She saw the pants fly over her head and land on the altar. The underwear soon followed. *This is so not right*, she thought.

Boudicea said, "As I expected. He has a tattoo of a double circle with an I in the middle. We know the brand of Ilitar. He's pledged himself to the cult of Ilitar."

"Great, who is this Ilitar?"

"Ilitar the Destroyer. She's a demon horror from the seventh circle. Born of the afterglow of the coalescence of the abyssal plane. She is a queen there, thought to rule over a realm that encompasses the better part of the seventh circle. She is powerful and ruthless. Those who want the same often worship her. Few, though, dare to summon her from her throne. Besides, the power needed to do that is beyond any chicken; even most born an Astralith don't have the essence to spare for the task. The best someone normally does with a horror such as her is tap into her power—but bringing her here in the flesh, I've never heard of such a thing. Still, they must have tried with you. A foolish thing . . ." She looked Rael over closely in silence. "At least, I hope it is foolish."

"Thanks, I think."

"Come, let's speak to him now."

"Ah, he's still dead."

"Watch and learn."

"Could we throw a blanket on him or something before I have to see him?"

"Already done."

Rael turned around. There was a gray blanket covering the body. Where Boudicea had got the blanket probably wasn't worth asking, so she didn't ask. Only his head stuck out exposed to her now. His lifeless eyes were staring at Rael. The look of shock he'd worn when the demon had killed him was still frozen on his face. Boudicea pulled a silver acorn out of her sleeve. She forced open the dead man's mouth. She shoved the acorn in and closed his mouth. Then she began to speak. As she spoke, she poured a green substance over the face of the dead man. She said, "*Bruidhinn rium an duine marbh.*" The green liquid turned to vapor. It rose up from the dead man's face. The green vapors made an exact copy of his face in the air before them, only it looked more alive than the man did now. Boudicea said, "*Tha thu ag innse dhomh caite a bheil e.*"

The green face of mist replied, "*Non loqui.*"

"*Tha thu ag innse dhomh.*"

There was a pause. The body started giving off a faint odor. Then it burst into green flames. The face of smoke pursed its lips. It tried not to speak. It was no use. It gave in. "*Abierunt Romam.*"

Then the face of smoke blew away. The body crumbled into green dust. "He tried to fight me, but his will was weaker," boasted Boudicea.

"All we got was two words, though." exclaimed Rael.

"Those two words were all we needed. He thought he was clever to speak in Latin, but we got what we needed from him. It's time for us to leave."

"To where?"

"The forest. If we're to follow this priest's lead, then we will need help. I'm starting to believe that you're no ordinary Astralith. If that's true, we will need a lot more help. In the forest there is always help."

Chapter 6

In the Forest, the Italian Alps

Rael found herself in her usual position of late: trailing behind Boudicea, wondering where exactly they were going. Snow had started falling, and they hadn't stopped for lunch. Not that she had much with her to eat except that McMuffin. Well, Rael didn't have any other food on her other than that McMuffin, and she was pretty sure it was past its prime delicious state. Boudicea probably had a cornucopia up her sleeve, but she wasn't offering. Instead, Boudicea kept marching on and on.

There was only so much trekking Rael wanted to do in a dead man's boots that almost fit her. Her usual preference was none. The dead man had said two words and that had been enough to get Boudicea moving. Only, Rael was pretty sure what he'd said didn't translate to "wander around an alpine forest during the winter looking for help among the squirrels." Rael wondered what it would take to get Boudicea to stop walking and start explaining to her what the plan was.

The high alpine forest evergreens did shield Rael from the falling snow. That was a relief. It wasn't a blizzard outside today. No, it was more of a slight snowdrift. There were exactly zero signs of civilization out here, which came as less of a relief. Fancy Rael being in the only part of Europe without a soul around.

"Pretty quiet out here, huh?" said Rael.

"It *was*," replied Boudicea.

Okay, conversation wasn't Boudicea's specialty. Rael knew that already. Slicing and dicing seemed to be all she cared about. It had been sort of exciting to watch the demon fight. Not that Rael had done more than watch. Still, she'd been there for the kill. It had killed itself, though. That felt sort of un-demon-like, if that was a word. It should have fought till the end. The death had avenged Rael's parents' death, but it hadn't really helped stem the feeling of loss.

"I was just thinking as I was walking. About things, you know?"

"What things?" asked Boudicea.

"About my parents mostly, I guess. I wonder what they'd have said about all this. I mean, I've never really been away from them. They were sort of strict. My mother was more the smothering, nurturing type, and my father was sort of demanding . . ."

"It's best not to think about them at all anymore."

"But they're my parents."

"Were."

"Now you're just being grim. What is appropriate to talk about if not my parents?"

"What is to come."

"You mean fighting more demons, right? It was kind of weird, that demon killing itself like that, huh?" asked Rael.

"It must have known too much and was afraid I'd make it talk. I would have too."

With brief answers like that it was pretty much a given that Rael was never going to know too much about anything. She was feeling less knowledgeable than ever these days. Everything she'd learned from her tutors was wrong anyway. The past few days had shown her the world was a crazy place. Why was this fact never told to people anywhere but late at night on the History Channel?

She pulled her near-frozen McMuffin from her shorts pocket. She desperately wished her short shorts were more modest and her high socks were higher. There was a distinctive thigh gap in her thermal protection. Thermal underwear would come in handy right about now.

She opened the brown paper bag and unwrapped the McMuffin. Now, normally she was more a fries and burger type of person, even for breakfast—not that her parents ever allowed it—but a beggar couldn't be a chooser out here. She bit into it with delight. It was a small amount of normal in a day's worth of the paranormal. With her tummy at least partially satisfied, she shoved the wrapper into the bag and tossed it onto the ground. Boudicea suddenly stopped. Finally, something was going on. She turned to face Rael. She pointed at the bag and said, "Don't trash Mother Nature's gift."

That was not exactly what Rael had been expecting. "The bag is biodegradable, you know."

"Then we are in agreement: We do not wish to degrade the biosphere."

"I don't think that's what the word biodegradable means."

Boudicea pointed to a tree. "You must be careful, Rael. The ravens are watching you. Wherever you go from now on, expect eyes upon you. If you're as powerful as I fear you might be, then you're never going to be lonely again. Your actions have meaning to all with eyes, remember that. If we're to gain help, then you must act like someone worth helping. An action can turn an ally like a raven into a foe so easily."

Rael studied the black birds sitting high on the branches around her. One was looking right at her. Then it hissed at her and flew off. Rael asked, "The raven, who does it work for?"

"One never knows." Boudicea started walking again.

It was starting to feel like Rael was trapped in a demonic dystopia with her stepmother. Rael snatched the paper bag and hurried to catch up. She was facing death—or another death—on multiple fronts, and all her self-sworn protector cared about was littering! She thought, *Look at this place. Who would even see the trash but a bird?* There was no one else. No one. Just trees, rocks, and endless snow . . . only, where was the snow? Rael suddenly realized there was nothing but dead brown grass beneath her feet.

Rael looked around her. They'd entered a clearing that was an open circle with no snow. At the borders of the clearing stood five pure-white megaliths. On the faces of the stones were jagged scars. Boudicea was up against the tallest of the stones. She was running her hands over it. Then

Boudicea turned around to face Rael. Rael knew that look of concern all too well by now. Rael could swear that there was almost a tear in Boudicea's eye this time. Rael asked, "What is it? What is wrong?"

"I came to this place seeking guidance and help, for this is a druid's grove. These groves are sacred places to us." She turned to face the stone again. Her voice became bitter. "It's been desecrated."

"By the demons?"

Boudicea smelled the air. "No demons this time. This was done by a devil."

Rael took a sniff. There was the distinct, if faint, odor of sulfur. She asked, "Aren't they the same thing?"

"No, devils are much more logistical. Whereas a demon wouldn't care that this was a grove, seeing the presence of the Order written on these stones would drive a devil crazy. A devil wants to claim territory and erase others' claims to it. We will need to reclaim this place for Arianrhod before it will be of use to us."

"Who?"

"The goddess of the weaving of cosmic time and fate."

"Never heard of her."

"What you have never heard of could fill a book, perhaps a library. They've tried to erase her from history, but she survives in our hearts." Boudicea knelt by a flat stump at the base of the tallest megalith. She showed Rael what had been placed on the stump. "Acorns, painted black. This is a sarcastic message from our devil friends." Boudicea brushed them off the stump. She pulled two silver acorns from her sleeve. Apparently she had a near-endless supply of them. She set them down where the black acorns had been.

"Rael, join me. We must renew this place."

"I'm not really religious or anything," said Rael.

"This isn't religion, this is . . . well, to you it would seem like magic."

Rael knew the meaning of those words by now. Boudicea was going to do something that felt exactly like magic. She knelt beside Boudicea in anticipation of what was to come. Boudicea said, *"Máthair ag éisteacht linn."* She turned to Rael and said, "Repeat it with me."

"Could we do it in a language that I know?"

"The tongue doesn't matter, only what is in your heart," replied Boudicea.

"I don't think that's going to help. I told you that I don't believe in religious stuff."

"Your heart doesn't care what you believe in; it cares about what you care for. Repeat after me, then search your heart for that you hold dear and confess your inner heart to Arianrhod."

"Okay, I guess I can do that."

Boudicea said,

Mother, listen to me.
Raise the sacred oak tree.
Use the acorn to heal the land.
I will obey your wise command.
I seek within my heart
Calm, peace, love, a new start.
Use your power, for time can cleanse
This place where we gather with friends.

Well, that was corny. It must have sounded better in Boudicea's native gibberish. Rael looked to Boudicea to see if they were done. Boudicea seemed to be in a trance. She was probably searching her heart. It wasn't exactly clear what that meant. What did Rael hold most dear? Skiing obviously. It was her life. It's what she lived for. It was her dream. Only, was it? No, she hated it. She really did. It had been so much trouble. It had been her whole life up to now. Had she died on the mountain, she'd have missed out on so much because of it. She had no close friends, she'd been on zero dates, and she'd sacrificed her social life for what—a few trophies and medals? Those things had meant so much to her father, though. Each one had been his little prize, and they'd brought a small amount of praise and approval from him. But beyond that, they'd really never meant anything to Rael. They had just been a means to an end. What she'd really wanted was her father's love. Now that he was dead, she'd never have it again. She had lost when it mattered most to her father anyway. She'd lost by a tenth of a second in her biggest race and let him down. She would always be a failure to him now. No, she hated skiing. She hated it forever.

Boudicea said to her, "Clear your mind. Listen to your heart. What does it say?"

Rael's heart was dead silent. She stalled for time. "You first."

"Divicia, it never says anything else. And you?"

"My heart . . . ah, it cries for my mother." Rael clamped her mouth. She was shocked the words had come out. She didn't know where those words had come from, but they rang true. She'd been thinking of her father, but her heart belonged to her mother. The words were true. She'd not seen her dead father's body, but she'd seen her mother battered and destroyed. Her mother, her poor mother, was gone. Those words brought tears to her eyes. Her tears fell onto the silver acorns she was kneeling in front of. As the first drop struck them, the grass of the clearing turned green beneath Rael. Rael felt warmth, a tremendous warmth, within the grove all around her.

Boudicea stood up. She showed off the grove. The megaliths had changed. There was one word now carved on each one. *Grá, saol, am, talamh, màthair.*

Rael asked, "What do those words mean?"

Boudicea replied, "Love, life, time, land, and mother."

Rael replied, "Mother, really! I was just thinking about my . . ."

A howl echoed through the forest. It broke the mood. In an instant Boudicea had her dagger in her hand. "The devils are not amused by our magic."

"They're still here?"

"Yes, and they are coming to take back what we've reclaimed. It's their mistake."

As she said that, a black dog came into the clearing. It was as large as a wolf, but it didn't have a wolf's head. It didn't have a dog's head either. It looked like the head of a sabretooth tiger. It snarled at Boudicea and then howled. Boudicea took out her sword.

"What the heck is that?" asked Rael.

"Exactly, it's a Heckhound straight from the bowels of Heck itself."

"Wait, where?"

The hound jumped at Rael, but Boudicea got between the animal and its target. It snapped at Boudicea and received a dagger in the skull for its efforts. The beast tried to shake loose, but Boudicea twisted the blade and the hound expired and fell to the ground.

"That was easy," said Rael. Her words were poorly chosen, for another howl echoed in the surrounding woods, and then another. Soon there was a choir of hounds out there.

"They're circling us, waiting to come in for the kill. We need to hold our ground and fight," said Boudicea.

"That's great. What am I using to fight with?" asked Rael.

"Everything you've got," replied Boudicea as a hound dashed into the grove. It homed straight in on Rael. Boudicea intercepted it again. It got skewered by her long sword.

"They keep coming for me," said Rael.

"They're predators; they always cull the weak one in the herd first," explained Boudicea.

Rael felt less than flattered. Weak one out of only two in Rael's herd! The first two hounds must have been feeling the situation out because the pack now broke from the forest. They were all charging toward the clearing at once. It wasn't exactly a good time to be the weak one in the herd.

Boudicea said, "We'll be okay so long as none of them can breathe fire."

Rael turned to Boudicea and replied, "What?"

The hounds were leaping through the gaps between the megaliths. Boudicea dashed at one and caught it mid-leap. Down went another of the bad guys' team. Unfortunately, this left Rael exposed. Another hound leaped on top of her. She caught it and in the process dug her nails into its hide. The hound bellowed in pain. She'd managed to disembowel it. She'd have felt pretty proud about that had she meant to do it. That and the fact the dog's blood had splattered over her dampened her giddiness. The only thing worse than being dressed tackily is being dressed tackily while covered in blood straight from a hound of Heck. She rolled the dog off her and stood back up.

No more dogs were charging in. They weren't leaving either. Instead, they stood in the gaps between the megaliths barring the way. Boudicea said, "We better get up the tree fast. Their leader is arriving, and she will try to roast the area."

"What tree?" asked Rael. No sooner had she said that than the stump was gone, replaced by a mighty oak tree. Rael would have asked Boudicea how that had happened, but she was pretty sure the answer would be "Blah, blah, blah, like magic."

Boudicea jumped up and grabbed the nearest branch. Rael had never been much of a tree climber as a kid. Mostly because her house in California didn't have trees. It didn't even have a yard. They hadn't been able to afford better until six years ago, when her dad had struck it rich and moved them to Colorado. It couldn't be that hard to learn how to climb. Not when you came equipped with claws. Rael dug into the bark with her fingers and climbed. As her feet left the ground, the leader of the hounds opened up her arsenal. Red flames spewed from her gaping mouth. The dead priest's boots nearly got roasted.

Higher and higher into the tree they climbed. The beast drew in close to the mighty oak. The closer she came, the higher she could send the flames up. The oak tree, though, refused to burn. The hounds, getting furious at this, started leaping at the branches. Finally, a few of them started gnawing at the base like beavers. That their teeth were being dulled to nubs in the process didn't seem to bother them.

"I think we might be in trouble," said Rael.

"No, for there is hidden strength in the forest on our side. We've delayed the hounds long enough. Now we can signal to our allies because they are near. Give me a pine of cone," replied Boudicea.

"You mean a pinecone?"

"No, I mean a pine of cone. Give one to me."

"I would but we're up a magic oak tree. It doesn't have a single cone." No sooner did those words leave her mouth than the tree sprouted a pinecone within Rael's reach. She almost suspected the tree could hear her and had produced the pinecone in a show of sarcasm. Rael picked the cone and tossed it to Boudicea. "Okay, what are you going to do with that?"

"This," replied Boudicea. She tossed the pine of cone in the air. It burst into white-hot flames that streaked through the sky like a firework. That was all it did. The hounds were halfway through the base of the tree. If their teeth held out, Rael's goose would be cooked.

Rael said, "I don't understand what giving the hounds dinner and a show did for our benefit, given we're the dinner part of the equation."

"Wait and see," replied Boudicea.

An arrow shot out of the forest. It struck one of the hounds between the eyes. Two more arrows followed suit, and down went two more hounds. The hounds' focus quickly went off the tree. They looked at the forest suspiciously. They weren't the only ones. Rael too wanted to know who had shot those arrows.

Boudicea acted now. With the hounds distracted, it was easy for her to pounce on one. Rael shrugged and dropped from the tree as well. She caught the pack leader by the tail. She tore into her with her claws. The hound barked flames out her mouth, probably out of surprise at being clawed. The flames roasted the dog next to her. Never let it be said that Heckhounds are resistant to their own flames.

More arrows shot out of the forest. The hounds were losing badly now. The largest of the pack howled then darted into the forest. The rest of the pack broke off the attack and followed the injured leader. They'd won. All thanks to this mysterious archer. The mystery was short-lived, for another cloaked figure soon walked into the grove.

The figure said, "*Geia.*"

Despite his being their rescuer, Boudicea didn't seem happy to see this other figure. Boudicea exclaimed, "Only one of you? Where is Archon?"

"The Order requested his presence in person. They request yours too. I bear that message to you. There is to be a gathering. My orders are to take over watching the prisoner and send you off to the gathering."

"I am not a pri . . ." Rael stopped talking as the figure removed his hood. He was a young man around her age. He was tall and blond, with eyes as blue as the Pacific Ocean. His hair was tied in a knot on top of his head. He had one of those "I could have shaved but I didn't" stubble beards that only teenagers can keep. She continued, "I mean, I am Rael Armstrong. I mean, I was before I died. I guess I still am, but it's complicated. I don't normally dress like this, nor am I normally covered in hound blood or do I have horns . . ." She was saved from making a bigger fool of herself as she felt Boudicea's hand cover her mouth. She was rather grateful for the gesture.

Boudicea said, "We did not come to this grove just for me to leave her here with an apprentice to guard her. I came here because she's such a hot commodity that even I need help to protect her. You could never do it alone."

"There is no choice in this. The Order cannot communicate with you any other way but in person. The oracles are listening everywhere. Who works for whom, no druid knows. But don't worry. Look, I'm good. You saw how I dispatched those hounds with my bow. Archon trained me well."

"Like Divicia trained me?"

The young man turned red and moved away from Boudicea. Whatever Boudicea had meant by her remark, it had apparently struck her intended target as well as the target could strike a hound with his bow and arrows.

Rael was rather annoyed at Boudicea. She seemed ungrateful for the rescue. Rael struggled out from Boudicea's grip. She walked up to the young man. She held out her hand to him and asked, "Your name is?" He looked at her hand quizzically. She took his hand and shook it. "It's how we say hello," she said. He smiled at her. His teeth were white like snow, which normally would be rather attractive to her if they didn't remind her of the avalanche, but she bet she'd forgive him for that.

"I'm Dynami from Atlantis."

"Oh, like the underwater city in the comic books? So, you can breathe underwater and talk to fish?" asked Rael.

That left Dynami with a queer look on his face. After a pause, he looked over to Boudicea. "Is something wrong with her?"

"She did die just the other day," replied Boudicea.

"Oh, right. I guess that would leave anyone a bit confused. We'll need to stay here through the night. Then, Boudicea, you must leave for the

Order. I'll set acorn landmines around the perimeter and then collect my arrows. Each arrowhead is a precious gift. I mustn't leave them lying about," said Dynami.

"Good, you do that. Rael and I will set up camp for the night within the grove," replied Boudicea.

Dynami set off into the forest. Boudicea didn't spring into action to set up the camp. Instead, she frowned and kicked the green grass beneath her feet. "Arianrhod, I cannot just leave her with him. I tell you she is more than an ordinary Astralith. I can feel it." She winced and fell to her knees. The oak tree grew bitter black fruit upon it. She relented. "Your will is my will, as always, Arianrhod." The black fruit ripened on the limbs.

"Are you okay?" asked Rael.

"No, I am an obedient servant. I always have been. What do you think about Dynami?"

"Oh him, he's . . ."

"Cute."

Rael shook her head. "No, he's not my type at all."

"Good, because I must leave you alone with him in the morning. Two young fools out in the forest by themselves is just asking for trouble, so you'll not stay in the forest. Instead, walk east toward the sunrise at first light. There's a border town in that direction. Get there and catch the first train back to civilization." A golden acorn slid out from her sleeve. She tugged and a chain extended from it. She placed it around Rael's neck. "I came to this grove seeking help, and now I can't even help you. This is the best I can offer you for protection. I want you to wear it always. It was once Divicia's gift to me. Now it is my gift to you. It will get warm when danger is near. Let it be your guide."

"What will I do without you?" asked Rael.

"Go to Rome. As the dead priest told me, so it should be done. I will have Dynami take you to Rome."

Chapter 7

Austria–Italy Border

Rael pulled a T-shirt off of the rack. The front read *At least I'm not Hungry*. She figured it was meant as a joke, only she didn't get it. She held it up against her body. She wasn't sure about the color. She turned to face Dynami and modeled it for him. "Do you like the red one or the white one on me?"

"I don't like either of them on anyone," he replied.

He *had* responded to her question. That was something. Indeed, that was the most he'd said to her since Boudicea had set off. You had to give him credit. He was a very honest person. Honesty was not needed at the moment. Sure, both shirts were hideous; on the other hand, a new shirt was badly needed. Hideous was a step up from what she was currently wearing. Anything was better than the "I survived the zombie apocalypse" ensemble she was currently in.

Rael was hardly spoiled for choice at this small gift shop at the Austrian border town's train station. It had taken twelve hours to walk here. Nothing had attacked, stalked, or killed them during the journey. Dynami had said next to nothing the whole walk here. Every time she'd tried to strike up a conversation, he had noted that the birds were listening. She had almost been tempted to talk to the birds just to be able to say something. She held the souvenir T-shirt up once more. Ugh, nearly everything was better than what she was wearing, but why did everything in this store have to be low-stitch-count Slovenian polyester? She went with the red one and put the white one back on the rack. If she gutted another Heckhound while wearing it, at least the blood wouldn't show.

She went through her mental list of other needs: shoes, socks, hat, gloves, and winter coat. It was impossible to obtain any of them here. She took a pair of Latvian skinny jeans off a shelf. They were two for one, but she didn't even want the one. She'd have to go by her estimated size because there was no dressing room. That was living dangerously, but that was her new normal. Skinny jeans . . . didn't Europeans know that mom jeans were back in style? There was no place to put her cell phone in these jeans. Not that she'd seen her cell phone since the avalanche. A few days ago she couldn't go half an hour without checking that thing. Now she didn't even know where it was.

She looked over at Dynami. He was tapping his foot and looking ten shades of impatient. He'd just have to wait. He had his magic cloak, and Rael had nothing suitable to wear. She wasn't sure how she felt about being traded off to another protector by the people who ran this Order thing. They sounded like very bossy people, but they weren't the boss of her. She could go where she pleased. Well, in spirit, that is. In reality she would stick it out with these druids because being with them beat being with demons any day. She had just been getting used to Boudicea, though. She looked over at her new protector. Dynami sure was tall. It wasn't all bad being stuck with him instead of Boudicea.

She should get a magazine. Dynami might be nice to look at and all, but he held a conversation worse than a funeral parlor held birthday parties. She could pass the time on the train catching up on the world. Not the real world, but the one shown in most magazines. She spotted a problem: Most of the magazines on the rack were in languages Rael couldn't read. She already had something nice to look at on the train; she wanted reading material. The only English magazine was one of those wealthy lifestyle ones where you learn how nice it is to live rich. It had been nice when Dad made his money. Having money had made many things easier for the family. And yet, it hadn't really made things better for Rael. There was something about money that had ruined the family. It was a terrible thought she'd just had. She shook her head. *Stop thinking about your family in negative ways, Rael,* she told herself. She scanned the magazine's front page to take her mind off things. Apparently someone named Ronald Bentworth had just built England's tallest building. Rael had had enough heights for now. She'd pass on that story.

"Time is ticking," said Dynami.

Rael gave him a look but conceded he was probably correct. It was time to head to the train. She lugged her load up to the cashier. She asked, "You don't have any underwear by chance?"

"*Nem értek angolul,*" replied the cashier.

"I'll take that as a no." Rael pulled out the bag the count had given her. Rael dumped some Euros on the counter. Carrying around those puppies had been one big pain in the butt—oh well, she would have pockets now to keep the change.

"Are you almost done?" asked Dynami. "I think I hear the train whistle."

"Almost," she replied. She was actually done, but a good girl keeps her man waiting. Not that Dynami was her man. He was currently fidgeting with his foot. Guys! They were always impatient to get what they wanted. That was the thing about being with Boudicea. Sure, she might stab you from time to time, but the relationship with her was easier. With Dynami there was added . . . well, there was nothing added. *It's all in your head, Rael. You walked twelve hours with him today and he barely said a word to you. He clearly isn't interested in you. And you're certainly not interested in him. Not at all.* She sighed. She wished she was a better liar.

The clothes got tucked into a plastic bag, and the change went into the small pouch she had tied around her waist. Once they got on the train, the torn frock and blood-stained short shorts would be history. It was a small victory toward the goal of returning to some kind of normal existence.

"Come on, the train will be leaving soon. If I miss getting you on that train, Archon will have my behind." Dynami tugged at her arm and she let him move her out of the store. There were some words you didn't want your Greek-speaking young man to say to you, and those were most of them all in one sentence.

Dynami reached into his sleeve and pulled out two passports and two tickets. He handed one of the passports to Rael. "If anyone asks, we're a brother and sister from New Zealand on holiday."

Rael opened up the passport he'd just given her. It had her picture inside and it was issued by New Zealand, not America. She replied, "Dynami, you can't use fake passports."

"Why?"

"It's illegal."

"Don't worry, then. These are very real and official . . . mostly." He slid two more out. "Would you rather be from Australia instead?"

"Where did all these come from?"

"To you it would seem like magic," he replied.

Oh no, not him too.

They moved to the start of the railway platform. There was a man in a booth checking IDs. He said, *"Reisepass."* It was time to see how good Dynami's sleeve's magic really was. Dynami handed his passport over to the man. The man opened it. He examined it with a UV light. He flipped through it looking at the stamps. He must have been satisfied because he handed it back to Dynami. He added, *"Und die Frau?"*

Rael handed over her . . . well, *the* passport. Her real one would be buried deep under snow somewhere now. The man opened it, looked at the picture, and handed it back. *"Gute Reise,"* he said and waved them through the turnstile. They pushed through and were on their way.

Rael said, "That was easy."

"Maybe too easy. Quick, act like you're kissing me."

"What?"

Dynami flipped his hood up; then he twirled her until she faced him. He swept her off her feet and raised her to his eye level. He had rather strong hands, and they were around her waist. Then he leaned over until his cloak obscured her face from view. It was all a bit sudden. That was love, though; it hit young men suddenly—at least it did in the movies. The only thing wrong with his current action was that he wasn't kissing her!

After thirty seconds of *almost* being kissed by the young man from Atlantis with the ocean-blue eyes that she was staring straight into, he put her down rather than taking her out for a sail.

"That was a near thing," he said.

"Yeah, it was nearly something, that's for sure," replied Rael.

"See that black man getting on the train right over there. He was right behind us. I had to do something to hide your face from his view. He is very suspicious," he said.

"You're not a closet racist, are you?"

"Nothing like that. That man goes by the handle Wat Tyler, but he's no tiler. He's a Freemason hunter. I've studied all the cults—it's part of my training. A Freemason on the train with us . . . I wonder what he is really doing here?"

Dynami said that like it was a question, but she knew he knew exactly why the man would be here. The answer could only be her. In some ways it was nice to be wanted by a man—only it always seemed to be the case that you're wanted by the man that's not the man standing right next to you. Actually, having had zero dates in her life, Rael couldn't say for sure that was always the case.

"He's on car eight, and we're on car ten. Let's hope he didn't make us. Freemasons can be helpful at times, but they can also be trouble. Either way, my mission with you is to steer clear of people like that."

"Then steer away," she replied.

They walked down the train platform. The conductor was waiting by the entrance to the car. He looked at them with a twinkle in his eye. He said, "*Jungvermählten?*"

Rael whispered, "What's that mean?"

Dynami didn't get a chance to answer before the conductor extended his hand. Dynami placed the tickets in it. The conductor punched them and handed them back. He elbowed Dynami as he did. The conductor said to him, "*Wundervolle frau! Schlafwagen, kein gepäck, und kein ring.*" That twinkle in his eye got a little more sparkly and a wide grin was added. He waved them onto the train.

Dynami said to her, "I think he has the wrong idea about us. He must have seen our fake kiss."

Rael replied quickly, "That's to our advantage. A boyfriend and girl-friend stepping out is a better cover story. We should keep up the act."

"Oh, yeah. I hadn't thought of it that way," he replied in a tone of voice that made it clear that he was anything but game. Indeed, he looked a bit queer about the idea. *Calm down, Rael,* she told herself. *Your teenage hormones going into overdrive is the last thing you need. Well, maybe.* Oh man, she'd really wanted him to kiss her. That was crazy thinking; they'd just met. You shouldn't kiss a man you'd just met, particularly if you just met them during a mass slaughtering of Heckhounds. That was probably in the *Young Woman's Guide to Proper Dating Etiquette.* She sighed and hoped her attraction to him didn't show. She'd been so good at focusing on skiing all this time that she'd barely even tried with the boys. Now that her skiing days were over for good, perhaps she should start trying. *No,* she scolded herself. *Focus on surviving.* The thing was, what was the point of surviving if it was just for the sake of surviving?

Dynami opened the door to their compartment. Rael followed him inside. It wasn't a luxury hotel room, for sure. It was just a small sitting room with a bench seat built into one wall. On the other wall was a pull-down bed. Finding personal space here was going to be hard. Dynami sat down next to the window on the bench. Rael went about setting the place up to be their home for the duration of the trip. She was pretty sure that if she'd told her mom she planned to ride the train to Rome sharing the same train car with a cute young guy from Atlantis, she'd not have been allowed to go on the trip. Well, Dynami wasn't that cute. She gave him a quick glance. *Nah, not that cute at all.* She really needed to get better at lying to herself because Rael hadn't believed that line for even a second. She pulled a latch built into the wall and one tiny bed came down.

She said, "Look, there's only one fold-down bed. Maybe we should get separate rooms."

"I can't let you out of my sight, so the bed is all yours. I've been trained to go days without sleep. I will just sit here and watch."

"Oh, you're the kinky type who likes to watch a lady," she replied.

"What do you mean by that?"

"It's a joke. You know, just a little teasing between friends."

"Oh jokes, I've heard of those. The Order has no time for those."

Okay then, Dynami was the super-serious type. Atlantis must be a fun place to be from with that sense of humor. *Okay, Rael, you're going to spend the night with a guy in your room. Just calm down. He doesn't seem super-interested in you.* Rael laid her bag on the bed. She took out her jeans and T-shirt. Normally she liked to wash her new clothes before wearing them. No time for that now, though. What's the worst that could happen wearing them unwashed? The answer was, nothing worse than dying, and she'd done that once this week already.

She couldn't just change in front of Dynami, no matter how uninterested he seemed to be in her. That was mostly because if she did, he might just sit there like a bump on a log, and that would do wonders toward sinking her already fragile ego. She was, if nothing else, modest like her mother had taught her to be, so she opened the door to the bathroom. It was more a closet with a toilet and sink inside, but it was the best available around these parts. She'd love to have a hot bath right about now, but a little toweling off was all she was going to get in here.

She noticed the toothbrushes and exclaimed, "Oh, complimentary toothbrushes, so needed." She cracked the plastic on them and put on some toothpaste. She stood just outside the door to the bathroom, brushing while looking in the mirror. She caught sight of Dynami in the mirror. That was easy to do since she had no reflection. His hood was down at his shoulders and his eyes were staring right at her posterior. No, that couldn't be right. He was a trained hunter with one thing on his mind: killing demons. She wiggled her bottom a little. His eyes followed every sway. That fink! He was totally checking her out. He was interested after all. Oh no, he was totally checking her out. *What do I do?* she thought. Flirting was all fun and games until it worked.

While she brushed, she asked him, "Being a druid must be tough, what with that vow of celibacy and everything."

"What vow? There is no vow," he replied.

"Oh, you're not one of those," she paused and made a scissor motion with her fingers, "eunuchs then, are you?"

He stood up and protested, "Of course not! Where do you get your knowledge of druids? While it is true an apprentice is forbidden to even kiss, a full druid has a proper place for everything. We do not go about kissing willy-nilly. I'll have you know that when the moon is out and full, it is said that the druids gather in their sacred grove around Arianrhod's mighty oak to perform the ancient ritual of renewal to rebirth the fertile earth. They say that there is singing, dancing, and lovemaking all night long. Druids are incredibly passionate about that type of stuff."

"What type of stuff?"

"You know . . . ah, kissing and all that other stuff."

"You mean the birds and the bees."

"I don't think animals are involved."

"You sound like you're very experienced in the art of making love."

He turned away from her. He looked a little embarrassed talking about it. Rael felt like she'd been a little mean to him. After all, who was she to boast about knowing that much about the art of love.

He said, "I don't know all that much myself, I admit. I can't go to the sacred gathering until I'm twenty-one and elevated to hunter class. Just ten more years as an apprentice and I'm going to be elevated. I can feel it. I need to stay focused on my training. Everything else can wait. I can't fail this mission. It's the biggest thing I've ever been asked to do."

"Wait, go back. You said ten more years until you're twenty-one?"

"Yeah, it's a fifty-year internship program."

"Fifty!" Suddenly the idea that she was alone in a sleeper car with a dirty old man came to her, and nothing seemed fun about that. She asked, "How old are you now?"

"Almost seventeen."

Rael stopped brushing. Either Rael's math was bad or something wasn't adding up. She'd always got good grades in math which meant the word *magic* would be the answer to any question she could ask as a follow-up. If he was like forty or so going on seventeen, how old was Boudicea? The whole idea made her head hurt. Rael probably should have guessed that when you pal around with a cosmic time goddess's druids, time would become a fluid thing to the members of her Order.

She decided not to torture Dynami anymore with this conversation. "Be right back." She grabbed the clothes bag and tucked into the bathroom. She placed the bag on the toilet. She looked into the mirror and said, "Everything is so crazy right now." She couldn't see herself. It was so frustrating; she realized that she couldn't have a proper conversation with herself in a mirror ever again! *I have just got to get one of those silver mirrors to carry around because I'll go nuts if I can't talk to myself.*

She pulled the frock off and then the shorts. She tossed them in the wastebasket under the sink. Then she washed up as best she could using the tiny paper towels provided. They gave you complimentary toothbrushes, so you'd think they'd at least have proper hand towels too.

She put the souvenir T-shirt on and then shimmied up the pants. They must come extra skinny in Latvia. She sucked her tummy in, which wasn't hard given how little she'd eaten lately, and secured the button. If only she had underwear. When they reached Rome, she was wiring the US embassy. She'd get an advance on her inheritance. Then she was going to go shopping with reckless abandon. Real clothes would help her feel normal. She felt something loose about her neck. She reached down and felt the necklace Boudicea had given her. It was loose and above her shirt. She played with it in her fingers. It was warm to the touch. For the first time in days she actually felt safe, but its temperature was supposed to signal trouble. Love, it was trouble in a way.

"Sorry, necklace, I don't think he knows the first thing about love. No trouble here." She tucked it under her shirt and teased her hair. It was impossible to know what it looked like. She just hoped she had teased it enough to cover the horns. "I really am a hot mess right about now," she said to the blank mirror.

The train lurched forward. Rael tumbled against the bathroom door. She'd not latched it, so it gave way. This sent her headed for the floor, only she never hit it. Dynami caught her before she hit the floor. He hoisted her up and said, "Careful, the train is starting up. It can get a touch bumpy." He then gently placed her on top of the bed.

"My, you have really strong hands," she replied. Ugh, she had not just said that to him! She made a mental note not to let her mouth say things that were not officially sanctioned by her brain from now on.

"My people get that from all the swimming we do in Atlantis."

"Then it is underwater."

"No, it's a joke. I'm teasing you." He cracked a smile at her and then went back to sitting by the window. That necklace lying over her heart had just got a tad warmer.

Chapter 8

Train to Rome

Rael could see her mother's face. She could easily read that face. Mother wasn't happy. There was an anxious look in her eyes like she was waiting for a bus. She had worn that look on her face all the time instead of a smile. Why did Rael remember her that way? Rael wanted to remember her mother as being happy, but the truth was she'd not been happy often these last six years. Rael had never understood why. How could becoming rich have made Mother so unhappy? Rael didn't know, and she'd never asked. Mostly she hadn't asked because Rael feared the blame for her mother's unhappiness must lie with Rael. Rael's skiing was all the family had cared about—or at least, Mother had tried to care. But had she cared? Had she known Rael didn't care that much about it either. She had, though, back then. It wasn't that long ago that losing that race had felt like the world had ended. Now Rael's world had really ended, and that race didn't matter at all. She had skied all that time to please her father. He'd seemed pleased by it. Whether it had pleased Mother . . . well, that was hard to tell. It hadn't appeared to.

Despite the loss, Father had still been excited to take Rael to Italy to ski. Mother had come along too, but she had been unhappy during the whole trip. And by that, Rael meant that Mother had appeared to be more unhappy than usual. Maybe that was just Rael reading something into that anxious look that wasn't really there, though. Rael had never asked, so how could she know how Mother really felt?

Rael called out to the image of her mother before her. "I was so self-centered, Mom, sorry. I should have asked how you felt." The face couldn't hear her. Why hadn't she asked about her mother's unhappiness? Had Rael not been all Mother hoped she would be, or was it something else that had bothered her? Had her mother known about Rael all along? Had she known Rael was special? How could Mother have known? It seemed impossible that she could have. And yet, a mother always knows—or at least, that's what they say. The face of her mother seemed so real just now. Rael tried to touch it. She wanted to comfort her mother and say she was sorry, for if Rael hadn't been this Astralith thing, Mother would still be alive. Rael had killed her mother. There was no other way to look at it. Had Rael not been who she was, Mother would still be alive. It was Rael's fault, hers alone.

Rael heard a knock. The sound stirred her from the thoughts of Mother, and so she opened her eyes. The sound had startled her. She'd been drowsy, perhaps even asleep. Yes, she had been asleep, if only in a light daydream. The noise had awakened her to full consciousness now. Her mother's image was gone from her mind. Rael knew she shouldn't worry about her family anymore. Instead, she now wondered about the source of that knocking. She rose up in bed and looked over at Dynami. He was still sitting on the same spot on the bench. His attention was focused on the door. The knock came again. This time, the source of the sound was obvious. It was someone at their compartment door.

"Are you going to answer it?" asked Rael. Dynami shook his head.

"*Abendessen!*" called out a voice from the other side.

Rael asked Dynami, "What is it?"

"Just the conductor asking us for our dinner orders. We don't need to order. Just lie back and return to sleep," he replied.

Rael tossed the blanket off her and swung her legs off the bed. "Don't believe what you read on my shirt. I'm more hungry than sleepy, so ask him in at once."

Dynami looked reluctant to do it. "I was ordered to keep you safe. The fewer people we talk to on this trip, the better off we will be."

"It's only dinner," replied Rael.

Dynami frowned, but he eventually stood up and went over to turn the lights on. "If you wish to eat, I cannot stop you. Remember, say nothing to anyone. I will talk for you. We're just tourists from New Zealand. Nothing strange going on here." Then he unlocked the bolt on the door and said, "*Die tür ist offen.*"

The conductor entered. He gave Rael a once-over, and that twinkle she'd seen before returned to the conductor's eyes. It made her feel a little uncomfortable. He handed menus out to both of them. Dynami didn't look at his menu. Rael scanned hers hoping for anything extra-filling. They weren't very long menus. There was just one full meal and an alternative option of a snack available. Rael didn't need to decide. She said, "Order the full meal. In fact, get two."

"I'm not hungry," replied Dynami.

"Trust me, I'm hungry enough to eat a horse, two horses even!"

"I think it's a pasta main dish."

"It's just an expression."

"Oh."

Dynami said to the conductor, "*Das abendessen.*"

"*Und die frau?*" asked the conductor.

"*Gleich,*" answered Dynami.

"*Ausgezeichnet!*" exclaimed the conductor and then he left.

Dynami bolted the door again. He asked, "Lights on or off?"

"On. I couldn't fall back asleep knowing food will soon be coming." She started to rub her bare feet as she thought again about her mother. Why hadn't she been happy even in Rael's dreams? Rael hoped she was happy now, at peace. The idea that Mother wasn't happy worried Rael greatly.

"Are they bothering you?"

"Who?" asked Rael.

"Your feet."

"Oh, my feet . . . yeah. You should try hiking in boots made to fit someone else."

"I could use my strong hands to rub them."

"Oh, I wouldn't want to . . ." He seized her right foot and started to massage it. She lay back down. He really did have strong hands, and he seemed to know how to use them . . . on feet. She closed her eyes and thought of something to get her mind off her parents. She thought of chocolate ice cream, with chocolate syrup, with chocolate sprinkles on top. It felt like it needed more chocolate, but it would do. She'd take that over a pasta main dish any day. Her father had never let her have snacks like that. Not while she was training. Once in a while she'd sneak a McDonalds visit or ice cream in, but she always felt guilty about it. She felt like she was letting him down. Even when she wasn't training. He wanted her to be at her best, always. She was to be the best ever. Ha! She'd been a tenth of a second too slow to be even good enough. Well, not thinking about her parents hadn't ended as planned.

A pain struck her chest at that moment. There was an intense burning sensation on her skin. She shot up straight and fished down into her shirt. She pulled out the necklace. It was no longer warm; it was legitimately hot.

Dynami stopped the massage. He asked, "Was I running my thumbs into your sole too hard?"

"What? Oh, the foot massage—no, it was wonderful. It's just that this necklace Boudicea gave me is getting hotter by the minute."

"How hot?"

"Too hot to handle."

Dynami started to pace the compartment. "That's a clear sign of trouble. Divicia's necklace is never wrong. But we're alone in here. Still, we must prepare for danger at once." He pulled his bow from his sleeve.

"Is Divicia that good a hunter that he is really never wrong?"

"He was the best. The very best."

"Was? What happened to him if he was the best?"

"I thought everyone knew."

"No."

"Boudicea killed Divicia."

Rael waited a few seconds. The words needed to sink in. Even after they did, she still couldn't believe what he had just said to her. "But he was her mentor!"

"Yes. I don't know the details, as it was before my time. But it happened. All druids know that it happened."

"Why?"

"I couldn't tell you. You would have to ask her about it." He went back to sitting down in his spot on the bench. The massage seemed to be over. That was too bad, as she had a second foot that would have loved one too. Dynami looked rather sullen. The topic had clearly disturbed him. Rael mentally kicked herself. She always brought up the wrong subject. But how was she supposed to know things had ended badly between Boudicea and her mentor? Boudicea's weapons only harmed evil, and so it stood to reason that if she'd killed her mentor, then her mentor had gone evil. Thus, a druid of the Order could be evil. It was a terrible time for an idea like that to strike her. The idea worried her no end as she was completely dependent on Dynami at the moment. She wanted to trust someone, but based on this information, there was no one she could fully trust. She looked at Dynami. She'd have to trust him. She couldn't face this crazy lifestyle alone.

A knock came at the door. "*Dein essen.*"

Dynami didn't look pleased. "That didn't take very long."

"Don't be so suspicious. They probably have it all pre-made," explained Rael.

Dynami went over to the door and unbolted it. The conductor rolled a cart into the compartment. There were two serving trays with stainless steel covers on the cart. He asked them, "*Willst du wein?*"

Dynami said to her, "He wants to know if we want wine."

"My parents would kill me if they found out I drank alcohol. I guess they can't find out now. Still, I think I'd rather have a Coke."

Dynami said to the conductor, "*Einer Coca-Cola.*"

The conductor went out into the hallway. He returned momentarily with a can of Coke. He popped the soda can open. He turned over a wine glass and poured in the soda.

He turned to Rael and asked, *"Frau will einen trinkhalm?"* He held up a straw. Coke always tasted better sucked through a straw. Whatever the physics involved that improved the taste, Rael didn't understand it. She just knew it to be true, so Rael nodded her head.

The conductor didn't place the straw in the glass. Nor did he hand it over to Rael. Instead, he put it to his lips. If pre-using a person's straw was a European thing, then this was one old-country tradition Rael could easily pass on. A dart blew out of the straw. It hit her in the neck. Within seconds she started to feel loopy.

The conductor pulled a gun. Dynami began to ready his bow, but the conductor had the drop on him. He said to Dynami, "Enough games, boy child, load the girl onto the cart or else you get it." His English had improved as fast as Rael's health was going downhill.

"Who do you work for?" asked Dynami.

The conductor swept his free arm across the cart top, knocking the trays and covers to the floor. He said, "No questions. I can shoot you and then do it myself, so, please, follow orders and load the girl onto the cart like a good, obedient child."

Dynami gave in and came over to Rael. She was seeing everything through a haze. She blinked but nothing seemed to come into focus. She could hear everything just fine. The rat fink had hit her with a poison dart. Didn't he know better than to mess with a hungry lady's dinner? She'd scratch his eyes out. Well, not now . . . later, after a nap. *No, don't nap, Rael. You have to fight this.* The worst part of all this was that Dynami had been correct to be suspicious. They should never have opened the door until they hit Rome, even for dinner.

Dynami picked her up. "That's a good boy. Now put the girl on the cart," instructed the conductor. After he said that, another knock came at the door. The conductor didn't let it cause him to lose his concentration. He kept his back to the door and his gun on Dynami. The conductor said, "We are busy here, so go away!"

Another knock didn't come at the door. Instead, three prongs of a trident came right through the door. They went right through the conductor too. Had Rael not been so loopy due to the poison dart, the sight of that happening would probably have made her sick. The trident prongs were retracted back out the body and the door. The conductor flopped to the floor like a dead fish.

The door jerked open and Wat Tyler came in carrying his trident. He took one look at Rael and reached over to pull out the poison dart. He sniffed the end. "He drugged her—sleeping dart. They don't want her dead; they want her very much alive."

"Who wants her?" asked Dynami.

"The whole train is run by Faustians. You two bought a one-way ticket into a trap."

If Rael could have seen his face right now, she was sure Dynami would be pouting. Dynami said to Wat, "I'm Dynami of the Order. This is . . ."

Wat grinned at Rael. "She is the Astralith everyone is talking about."

"I need to get her out of here. Can you help?"

"I wouldn't have interfered now if I hadn't been sent here to help. Follow me."

Wat went into the corridor. Dynami followed him, carrying Rael over his shoulder. She wanted to say hello to the man who'd just saved her, but her mouth wobbled and dribbled instead of making sensible sounds.

Two train staff stood in the corridor holding butcher knives. Wat said to Dynami, "I can carry her and still fight, whereas you need both hands to shoot your bow. Let's trade." The two staff charged toward the three of them. Dynami didn't hesitate. He tossed Rael onto Wat's left shoulder. In a flash, his bow was in his hands, and arrows were then soon in those men's skulls.

"Come, we can make for the last car and detach it from the line," suggested Wat.

He started moving. Dynami didn't object; he followed. Rael felt like she might puke. It was probably impolite to puke all over the back of the man who had just skewered the bad guy and saved you, so she did her best to hold it in.

They pushed through the outside door. Two Faustian railwaymen were outside the door to the next car. They were armed with machine guns.

One of them shouted, "It ends here! Put the girl down!"

Wat shouted back, "You're at a disadvantage. You want her alive, whereas we don't care if you're dead."

Dynami shot an arrow over Wat's shoulder. It struck one of the Faustian cultists before he knew what had happened. He toppled from the train. The other cultist got angry and discharged his weapon at Wat. Wat ducked back inside the door as bullets ricocheted off it.

"I do believe I touched a nerve," Wat boasted.

"Unfortunately, he's blocking our path," replied Dynami.

"Nonsense." Wat thrust his trident through the metal door. It cut that door like butter. It also bridged the gap between the cars and skewered the machine-gunner like butter. The hail of bullets stopped. Wat smiled. "It's good to have ten feet of reach." He yanked the trident back in.

He opened the door again and jumped the gap between cars. They hurried through to the next car. Rael was still draped over a shoulder, and thus was mostly seeing what was behind them. What was behind them was a gathering mass of cultists. They were armed with whatever weapons they could find. They weren't dressed like railwaymen. They must be passengers. Where were they? On the express train to hell? Of course they were—that would just be her luck.

A compartment opened up as Wat passed by. Without looking, he spun the trident through the open door frame. He caught a cultist before they could react. Meanwhile, the mass of cultists were jumping onto their car. Dynami fired an arrow into the mass. It was impossible not to hit one, but also impossible to hit them all. He'd need a machine gun to do that.

"I do believe there are too many of them," said Rael. She could talk! She was so excited to be able to use her mouth again.

"I think she's recovering," said Dynami.

"Good, because we're almost at the last car," said Wat. He popped the outside door open. This time no one was outside to greet them. "It looks empty, but you should check it out to be sure."

Dynami jumped the gap onto the last railcar. Wat's trident came down hard on the coupling. The last car detached. There was one problem with the situation. Rael was still on Wat's shoulder, and Wat was not yet standing on the last train car.

Wat said to Dynami, "Sorry kid, finders keepers, losers weepers."

A few arrows came sailing Wat's way. Dynami had clearly shot in frustration, not with the aim of hitting him. He'd never have risked Rael, or so she hoped. It seemed like a waste of priceless arrowheads. He must like her that much. Unfortunately, the rest of the train was rapidly leaving him behind. Rael suddenly wished she had puked on Wat.

Rael used whatever strength she had to start pummeling Wat's back. His leather jacket must have been thick because her claws didn't do much damage. Then again she was far from full strength. She wasn't far from that mass of cultists, though. Wat was about to be swarmed by them.

Wat said to her, "Don't worry, my lady, we're leaving too."

That was good news because at the front of the pack were now four or five men armed with machine guns, and they were fast approaching them. Only, jumping off a train was not Rael's preferred escape plan. Wat hurled his trident into the thick of the men. One dropped dead. Then Wat jumped with her still on his shoulder. The men's machine guns erupted. A hail of bullets surrounded her as they leaped from the train. Rael felt like she should be falling, but she wasn't. The ground kept getting farther and farther away instead. The bullets passed under her. They were flying, but how?

She looked up. There was a helicopter above her, a rope ladder extending from its belly. Wat started to climb. How he could manage to climb a ladder while still securely holding her worried her. Rael hoped his grip was that secure. Clearly he was strong. Strong enough to send that trident through metal doors. She hugged him just in case he wasn't strong enough for this climb.

They reached the top and Wat unceremoniously dumped her inside the helicopter. He laughed, grinned, and boasted, "Another successful mission." He looked her in the eyes. "Don't look so afraid. I'm one of the good guys."

"So was Dynami," she replied bitterly.

"He's only a rookie. I wasn't about to leave as hot a commodity as you in the hands of an amateur like that. Do you understand how valuable you are?"

She wanted to strike him again just to wipe the silly grin off his face. That would require standing, and she wasn't quite up to that task yet. Poor Dynami was all she could think about. When Archon found out Dynami had lost her, he'd be in deep trouble with the Order.

The helicopter banked and they were off. Wat turned his attention from her to the pilot. He knocked on the Plexiglas separating the pilot from the back of the helicopter. It opened. Wat said, "Roger, take us to England." There was a pause. "Hey, you're not Roger. Where's Roger?"

The pilot replied, "*Tot.*"

"Uh oh," said Wat.

Uh oh what? wondered Rael. Wat didn't need to explain because it didn't take long for the situation to reach the uh-oh level of problem. She should have been used to it by now because facing uh-oh problems seemed to be her new way of life. The pilot slammed the Plexiglas window shut. Then a green cloud of gas billowed inside the back of the helicopter.

Wat screamed, "Poison gas!" He fell to the floor, struggling to breathe, and ended up lying next to her unconscious. His hands were still around his throat. At least the silly grin was off his face.

Poisoned twice within fifteen minutes. These people really knew how to treat a woman badly. This time the poison must have had a little more kick to it, because Rael completely blacked out.

Chapter 9

Parts Unknown

There was searing pain. It came from no place in particular. It was more of an all-over body pain. This intense pain was so overwhelming that she'd quickly gone numb. Then there came the blackness. It hadn't just surrounded her. It had actually penetrated Rael. It was strangling her. She was fighting against the black nothingness, and she was losing. She knew she was losing badly. There was no hope. The weight of the snow above her pressed down and crushed her as its movement tore her apart. She couldn't get air anymore. Her lungs were broken beyond repair anyway, even if there had been air to breathe under the snow. Her body wouldn't work correctly ever again. It was over. She was gone. Death would all too soon overcome her.

Into the blackness came the color blue. It was cold and uncaring, but it gleefully seized her from the hands of death. The silence of death was over, for she could hear voices again. The blackness was fading, and the blue hue was growing more intense. It was singing to her, almost chanting. Yes, something was chanting in a language she didn't know. It was then that her essence began to drift out of her body. It was floating as if on top of water. She left the blue behind, and now there was the eerie silence of deep space. She was sailing on the solar winds far away from Earth. There were stars, whole galaxies, all around her. And then them, too, she left behind. There was just a big empty, a nothingness that went on for seemingly forever. Under the nothingness something stirred. She was not alone. She could feel her, though she could not see her. She called out to Rael. The calls were not to bring them closer together. They were to ward her away, for she hated Rael. She hated her passionately, though they had never met. Why did she hate her so much? And then suddenly there was an intense red flame. Rael was standing on the surface of another world. It was hot, burning, and lifeless. But no, it was not so lifeless as it had first appeared. It was only devoid of life as Rael knew it. Her essence was nearly consumed. Her being was phasing in and out. Then Rael saw her in the distance through the blazing inferno around her. She was a horror. That was the only way Rael could describe her. She howled with bitter anger at Rael, but Rael could not fight back. Her strength was growing as Rael's was failing. Rael was dying a second death. Not just death, though, but the loss of all that was her as Rael's body and soul were both to be consumed. Who was she dying for? Who was out there that hated her so much? The horror howled and she saw the face of the red-skinned demon now. It had Rael's face!

Rael woke up. That had been one hell of a dream. Only it hadn't been a dream. It had happened—it had really happened to her. It was a lost memory returning to her. Only, what was it that she had finally remembered? Ilitar. Rael had almost been exchanged body and soul for her. Only, the communion hadn't been finished. The dream offered no insight as to why.

Rael went to rub her forehead and discovered her arms didn't move. She looked up to see a chain dangling down from the living violet velvet-skinned ceiling fifty feet above her. That chain dangled all the way down, ending at cuffs that restrained her arms above her head. Her toes barely touched the floor. Not that the floor could be called a floor. The floor felt solid enough beneath her, but its appearance was anything but solid. It was a violet mist that trickled up to lap against her ankles. She'd been in this position before. She was helplessly trapped at the hands of someone or something. But always before she'd been in some place . . . well, if not normal, then *almost* normal. This place was different. It was otherworldly.

"What the heck?" she said.

The mist spoke to her. "Please, don't flatter me with prayer, for your prayers cannot influence me. I'm already under contract, and once I have a signed contract I always follow it through." Out of the violet mist rose a demon. He was tall and thin in a purple business suit with black trim. He was bald and wore a black skull cap. His ears were pointed, and so were his leathery black bat wings.

Okay, while this was about the same level of weird as the rest of her new normal, it wasn't a pleasant weird either. Being trapped and chained by a demon was not the best way to wake up after being poisoned. Rael needed to size up the situation fast. She asked, "What do you want with me, demon?" She hoped her voice sounded deep and authoritative. She wasn't feeling particularly authoritative, but it couldn't hurt to bluff it.

He put his hand on his breast. "*Moi*, a demon? Don't insult me, for I'm a devil through and through."

"Then I'm in hell!" she exclaimed.

The devil howled with delight. Then he shook his head at her. "Now you do try to flatter me. If only Lucifer could hear your boasts, he'd roast us both alive. I am merely Siberion, a humble servant of the type-one sub-devil class from the outer forty-first plane of Heck."

"Then I guess I need to ask what the heck do you want with me?" asked Rael.

"Me? I want nothing. I'm merely fulfilling a contract. You see, I am what you call a middle-devil. When young ladies are abandoned, the treasures within them are put up for auction. I'm just the auctioneer."

"I wasn't abandoned. Your people kidnapped me!"

"My people did no such thing. I received you from a group of Yugoloth mercenaries. Luckily for you, they are indifferent to your astral treasures, but they were quite enchanted with the Earthly treasures you would bring them at auction. That's where I come in. I'm a devil that knows how to get maximum value for a client."

A female voice spoke out of the mist. "Siberion, paging Siberion, there is a call for you on line three."

He rolled his eyes and looked at her. "You will have to excuse me, because I am a busy type-one sub-devil."

Rael tried to shrug, but it was a pointless action while she was bound. "Answer your call, see if I care. I'm not going anywhere."

"Not for a few hours anyway, you're not," he agreed. He pulled a small bat with an oversized head from out of the mist. He put it up to his ear like it was a phone. "Yes, Siberion speaking."

The bat said in a female voice, "The Freemasons have paid the ransom. It appears that it will be a two-for-one kind of day, your excellency."

Siberion grinned from pointed ear to pointed ear. "Already paid in full, you say? Perfect! I like a motivated client." He tossed the bat into the air and it flew away. Siberion called out to the mist, "Bring up the Freemason from the prison!"

Rael heard the sound of gears grinding away. Out of the mist slowly rose Wat inside a steel cage. There was only enough room in the cage for Wat to be on all fours. It seemed to be a fitting cage for a dirty dog that had double-crossed Rael. Wat looked over at her and said, "Sorry about all this, kid."

Wasn't that just like a person to do that? As soon as Rael had worked up a good dislike for them, they played on her sympathy. She would have liked to tell Wat to go to hell with his apology, but it seemed pointless given the circumstances. Neither one of them was likely to get any closer to hell today than they already were. Siberion said to Wat, "Your soul has been paid for in full, so you're free to go."

"What about her?" Wat asked.

"She's to be auctioned off to the highest bidder," explained Siberion.

"The Freemasons will pay any price for her. Name the price and I will pay it," replied Wat.

"Does someone need an explanation on how an auction works? The Freemasons will get their chance to bid at the appropriate time, and not until then. Now, remove him from my sight!"

Two imps rose up from the mist. Together they flapped their little imp wings and started to fly Wat's cage away. Wat pleaded to Siberion, "Please listen to me. You don't understand how dangerous she will be if she gets into the wrong hands. She's not just another run-of-the-mill Astralith. Let me take her with me. Sell her to me before it is too late for all of us."

"Sorry, I'm not under contract to care," explained Siberion while holding up a contract signed in blood. The ceiling opened up, and the imps whisked Wat away. Siberion clapped his hands together. "It is going to be a two-for-Tuesday type of day. One soul sold and another about to be put up for auction. Good, my clients are going to be so pleased. Money does make this world of you foolish humans go round." He then turned toward Rael. "And now for you, my little scarecrow."

If it was money he wanted, then Rael had a chance. Rael said, "I'm pretty rich . . . I mean, my parents were. I guess I inherited the wealth, so I am now rolling in it. I could . . ."

Siberion yanked on the chain and lifted her up off the ground. He placed his face inches from hers. "The one who's being auctioned is not allowed to bid on herself. It's in the fine print of the contract." He held up the contract. It was an eight-by-eleven sheet of white paper. The sub-devil snapped his wrists and the sheet of paper unrolled until the bottom of the sheet disappeared below the mist. "It's all here, here, and here. A standard contract written in certified goat's blood. No loopholes." He snapped his wrists again and the contract rolled up. "In two hours' time, I'm expecting the bidding to be hot and heavy for you. Why, I've already heard inquiries from the Faustists, Freemasons, Gnostics, Orphics, Hermetic Order of the Golden Dawn, Templars, Mysteries of Set, Saturni, Illuminati, Cult of Isis, Greys, Mesmerists, and Harper Valley PTA. Who knows who else will join in the bidding by auction time?"

"And the druids?" asked Rael.

"Don't be a silly girl—the druids never bid at auction. Nor do they wear buttons for some odd reason. Cults . . . who can understand their odd rules?" He was so close she could taste his sulfuric breath. He ran his hands through her hair. He said, "Horns, black eyes, drab hair, and the worst wardrobe I've ever witnessed on a young woman. You're not helping matters at all. I want maximum profit, and this 'little miss scarecrow' look of yours isn't going to bring it in. We need to up-market you, sweetie."

"I'm not a product," she barked back.

He ignored her and shouted, "Karen, work to do!" Then he turned away from Rael and clapped his hands. Out of the mist rose someone new. She was voluptuous, if you were into that sort of thing. Her curves were too curvy to be real. All the wrong parts of her were barely tucked out of sight by black leather straps. Her skin was pale blue. She must be another devil, for she had a pair of black bat wings, black horns, and a pointy blue leathery tail.

"Your excellency, how may I be of service?" Karen asked with a curtsy toward Siberion.

Siberion pointed at Rael. "Her! Do something with her for me!"

Karen looked Rael over and sighed. "Another her. I was hoping for a him this time around. What's the point of being so ravishing if there's no one ever to ravage with it?" She started filing her claws.

"Karen, I have no souls to be ravaged today by you."

Karen tossed the nail file into the mist. "Very well, a succubus's job is never done. Then it is just to be a simple painful disembowelment for this bound girl?"

Siberion replied, "Nothing so tragic. Just a makeover. The word of the day is *up-market*. The bidding begins soon, and I need a product worth bidding on." After delivering his orders, he sank down into the mist.

That left Rael alone with Karen. Karen moved over to her. She gave Rael the once-over. "Has anyone ever told you that you look tacky and cheap, like a used Yugoslavian furniture store?"

"All the time," replied Rael.

"A bit of lip on you, huh? You're not one of those woke types, are you? Men hate the woke types. If you want to wake a man up, sink your claws into him, honey, and rip his heart out. Whatever you do, don't give me any of that b-attitude, though. We're both women; we can treat each other respectfully."

She pawed at Rael, tugging at her clothes. She then ran her claws through Rael's hair. "You've got stuff to work with, honey. Don't worry about a thing because I'm just going to hurt you." She ripped through Rael's train station–bought clothing with glee. Then she pulled a leather corset with studded metal straps from out of the mist.

"I thought he wanted to up-market me, not have you torture me," said Rael.

"It's not torture, honey; it's called fashion."

"Please, just stay away from me," Rael begged.

"Why? I'm trying to help you."

"Your type of help is nothing that I want."

"Isn't it though, isn't it though? Look at my sex appeal. You wish you had it. I could teach you how to have it. There's a man in your life isn't there?" Rael shook her head. "Liar! You want a man. At your age, girls always have a man they want, so sure you do, but you won't get him looking like you do. I can show you the tricks of the trade. Give you some pointers on how to seduce the right one or, better still, the wrong one." She winked at Rael. Karen sang as she dressed Rael,

Do you hate me for my red eyes?
The little way that I tell lies?
I'll tell you girl, to make their world,
You need to be much more feminine wise.
You need to have it, to know how to flaunt,
Because it's what men want.
Their heart is the least direct route.
Better to have tight hard round glutes.
Climb up the stairs, jumping on squares,
Will make them want to play you like a flute.
Tone until you're a derriere savant,
Because it's what men want.
Steer clear of eating greasy fat.
Sweets, savory, we can't have that.
You play it thin, for you to win.
A good girl has abs oh so flat.
Starve yourself until your middle is gaunt,
Because it's what men want.
If you want their cute eyes to home,
Plump up your top with silicone.

Nothing absorbs like firm round orbs.
Trust me, double Ds are never alone.
Plump up your breasts like two fluffy croissants,
Because it's what men want.
Oh, that natural complexion
Doesn't bring you much affection.
Fair, huh, love ain't, wear the war paint.
Hunt them down with artful crass seduction.
Pull your face until your wrinkles are taut,
Because it's what men want.
Just a few minutes of your time.
A quick washing off of your grime.
With my advice, a touch of vice,
And you'll never be lonely again at bedtime.
I'll pass you off as a glamorous debutant,
Because it's what men want.

Rael shouted back, "My man wouldn't care if I took any of your foul advice because he loves me for being me."

Karen howled in laughter. "That man doesn't exist outside of your imagination, honey. They all want it. They all need it. Give it to them, and they'll give you anything you want in return, even their soul. I always get what I want from a man, one way," she bared her fangs and bit the air in front of Rael's face, "or another." Karen took a few steps back. "Sometimes, as an artist, I amaze even myself. Done!"

Done? She hadn't even started, or had she? Rael had been so seduced by Karen's singing voice she hadn't noticed she'd been made over from head to toe. She looked down. Her outfit was changed. How'd that devil manage to put a shirt and pants on Rael while Rael was still bound by that chain? The answer was probably magic, but it seemed such a waste of good magic. She wished she had a mirror just to see herself. Then again, that wouldn't help much, given her condition. Siberion rose up from the mist. Well, she'd know in a minute if the succubus had transformed her into class or trash. Siberion took one look at Rael and licked his lips. If a sub-devil did that toward you, was it because you looked like class or trash? Rael wished someone else non-devilish were there to offer their opinion.

"I love what you've done with the place," Siberion said to Karen.

Karen showed Rael off. "As you can see, I went with a perm, light dusting on the cheeks, a hard black pencil outlining the eyes to bring out the natural goth freak in her, and then heavy on the brow pencil. Ruby-red kiss-me-now lips, overdone to make them look fuller without injections. It's so in right now. Blue pantyhose under Seven jeans, with a peek of the matching blue thong straps at the hips. Old-school trashy, but still chic. Dolce and Gabbana sneakers on the feet. Up top we've done a heavy renovation with a pushup bra to lift and press and a stretch T-shirt from Fendi, this season, with a nice high cut-off to give plenty of window view at the belly button below and a nice low plunging neckline to give a peek at what we lifted and pressed. For jewelry, all she's got is that tacky acorn around the neck. It's gold, though, not cheap, so it stayed. I could pierce her belly button and ears, among other places, but that would cost you extra. Do you want extra?"

Siberion waved her off. "I'm not auctioning her off to potential husbands. I just need her to be presentable for an auction. After all, whoever buys her is just going to spend all her essence to transfer an astral figure here from the outer planes."

"That sounds rather kinky, but not my kind of kink. Am I done here or what?" asked Karen.

"Done."

"I'll be sure to send you my bill." Karen gave Rael one last wink and sank into the mist.

No sooner was the succubus gone than a hail of gunshots erupted above the chamber ceiling. A cacophony of footsteps followed. Then the bullets came again. Perhaps it was a rescue attempt. Rael looked over to see how Siberion was handling the situation. He was cool. He simply pulled an hourglass from his pocket and checked the sand falling. The ceiling tore open and a rope fell down until it reached the mist floor. A masked man wearing a white mask with a red cross across the face started climbing down from the ceiling. It was a long climb, and he didn't seem to be the most agile of climbers.

Siberion looked annoyed to have to wait on the man. He muttered, "What bother is this now?"

Rael replied, "Don't ask me, I'm just a prisoner here."

"Don't be a clever clogs."

The man made it down to the mist. He was sporting a submachine gun and had it trained on Siberion. Siberion didn't seem to care. He looked at the visitor and said, "You're early. Bidding begins in one hour. Can't you Templars wait?"

As those words were being said, imps rose from the mist carrying guns. They were so small that the recoil from the guns they held would probably send them reeling if the trigger was pulled. Well, if physics still worked, but from Rael's recent experiences physics didn't seem to matter anymore.

The man pulled his hood off. It was Andres. Rael would never forget him. He was the last man she wanted to see come to her aid. That meant this wasn't going to be a rescue attempt so much as a transfer of ownership. Maybe the imps would kill him. Her imprisonment would at least have an upside then. Andres said, "I've come to make a bid."

The imps stopped training their guns on Andres and looked toward Siberion. Siberion replied, "Andres, I should have known it was you. Always the impatient one, aren't you? Did you have to shoot some of my best imps just to make a bid in person inside my pocket plane when it's all done online these days?"

"Yes, because I'm bidding for myself and not the Templars as a whole," replied Andres.

"I don't care so long as you bid at the appropriate time—in one hour."

"I'm bidding now, or the bullets start to fly!" Andres informed him.

Siberion still appeared bored by the situation. "Fine. If you must kill, then you must. They are only imps, so you may shoot them at will. I suggest staying for the bidding, dead or alive. It is your choice." He showed Andres the hourglass. "As I said, it starts in an hour. No exceptions!"

Andres pulled a white bag from his pocket. "I repeat, the bidding starts now because there are always exceptions."

Siberion shook his head. "Need I remind you that I'm under contract?"

"Your contract states there is to be an auction. The time and date are set by the auctioneer. The winner is the party that offers the highest bid."

"Yes, I do know the language of the contract, thank you very much."

"I repeat, you set the time and date. It doesn't say you can't reset it, if needed."

"Why would I need to do that?"

"I have an offer you can't refuse. In this bag is one of the Templar's greatest relics from the Holy Land. The original thirty pieces of silver given to Judas for betraying Jesus. The ultimate payment for fulfilling a contract. What honest devil could resist owning them?"

Siberion mopped his suddenly sweaty brow. "The highest bid is not based on what's valuable to me, but my . . . they do come with papers of authenticity, right?"

"I got them in my pocket."

This sounded bad for Rael. She said to the devil, "One hour. . . remember the terms of the contract. Who knows what else someone might bid?"

Andres tossed the bag he was holding at Siberion's feet. The bag disappeared under the mist. Then the sound of coins spilling out and rolling across the floor could be heard. Siberion dropped to his knees to gather them.

"I think we have a winner. Box her up, imps," boasted Andres.

Rael screamed at Siberion, "Look how up-market I am now! Don't settle for thirty coins, because I'm worth so much more than that!" It was no use. The sub-devil had made a deal. His focus was on the dirty silver coins. A wooden crate rose up from the mist until it engulfed Rael. The chain broke from the ceiling and fell down around her. Indeed, the chains coiled around her, filling up the box, and squeezing her in tight. Then the imps clamped the lid down.

"Don't forget to poke some holes in it. I need her alive for a little while longer," ordered Andres.

Chapter 10

Santa Maria del Priorato, Rome

Being boxed up is not a lot of fun. That little factoid was one of those things that Rael had never planned on learning in life. She ended up learning it quickly, though—the hard way. Being boxed up like Christmas ornaments on January second was just not something she had planned on ever happening to her.

It was sort of ridiculous that it was happening to her of all people. She'd never been that special. She wasn't the best at anything. She was a tenth of a second from even being in the running for adequate. Now, all of a sudden, she was worth boxing up like the fine china. It was an absurdity that could only have happened this past week. Good thing for her she wasn't particularly claustrophobic, so the confined space didn't bother her much. What bothered her was that those imps had forgotten to put a "This end up" sticker on the box. No one wanted to be in a box, but even less did they want to be upside down inside a box for as long as she had been. The blood had long ago rushed to her head. She felt a little past loopy.

She could hear the sound of the truck stopping. She didn't get her hopes up. It could just be another red light. But then she heard the sound of the back door opening. She was sure of that sound because Andres couldn't afford grease for the hinges. She peered out of the little holes made for air but saw nothing. She was still inside a truck upside down, so the holes were useless.

The box tipped and came down hard on its side. This was something of a relief for her head. How some women managed to do all that upside-down yoga, Rael didn't understand at all. It had always given her such a head rush—in a bad way. She was dizzy for hours after just fifteen minutes of yoga. Rael peeked out the holes again. There was daylight at last. There was more than that. She could see she was next to a building of some sort. She didn't recognize the place, but it did look old.

"*Avec grand soin, idiot!*" exclaimed Andres, a man whose voice she would not soon forget.

"*Mordimi,*" said a voice back.

A quarrel soon followed. It was one of words, not fists, most likely, but Rael wouldn't mind if Andres took a few lumps on the chin.

"Stop this fighting at once!" said a third man.

"Of course, Father Giovanni," replied Andres.

The box lifted and Rael was on the move. She could hear the squeak of the wheels of the cart they'd loaded her onto. Through the holes in the box, she saw what seemed to be a golden dome in the distance. It shone like a beacon of heaven. Andres couldn't drive to heaven, could he? The box lurched as a loud squeak announced that one of the cart's wheels had caught on something. Only Andres would have a defective cart.

"Careful, that door is famous because the keyhole looks out on Saint Peter himself," said Father Giovanni.

"Who cares? Where's the entrance that matters in this place?" asked Andres.

"It is at the altar," replied Father Giovanni.

Rael was trying hard to keep track of the names that went with the voices. She'd get one chance at pleading for mercy when the box opened. Well, she hoped. The Templars were a noble name. Not everyone in the Templar order could be as corrupt as Andres.

Now the box went up and down again. There was a long pause. Then she heard crowbars at work. The top of the box came off and light flooded in. The box tipped, and she slowly slid out of the box and onto the stucco altar of a church. It was a Christian church—well, no surprise there. A large statue of Piranesi towered over her. She shifted her eyes away from the statue and onto Andres. She saw him eyeing her eagerly. Next to her were two men in dresses or robes or vestments or whatever it was that priests wore. They looked a little silly to her.

Andres said, "Father Giovanni of the Templar Knights and Father Rezzonico of the Knights of Malta, I give you an Astralith beyond your wildest dreams, as I promised." Then he placed his hand on Rael's head. He said directly to her, "So nice to have you in my possession again."

"Our possession," corrected Father Rezzonico. "Andres, she better be real. You've cost us one of our greatest relics. Santa Maria del Priorato will never be the same without it."

Andres snickered. "About that." He pulled a white bag from his coat pocket. "Thirty pieces of silver." He tossed them at Father Rezzonico. The father looked quite baffled to see the coins again.

"But how?" asked Father Rezzonico.

"Every good banker knows that greed blinds all," replied Andres.

"You mean you cheated Siberion with worthless coins and kept the real ones," interjected Rael.

"I just finessed the situation like a good banker does. One silver coin is very much like another. He is just a devil, so he wouldn't know the difference. I offered thirty pieces of silver, and that's what he got," corrected Andres.

"Enough! Devils were made to be cheated; I wasn't. Promise me she is the real deal," said Father Giovanni.

"She's everything you ever dreamed about and more. I've seen her once in action," replied Andres.

"Then how can she still be here?" asked Father Rezzonico.

"A red demon from the abyss stopped the ceremony as I was watching it happen. Strangest thing I've ever seen. It saved her, much to the annoyance of the cult members that were sacrificing her. But oh, what a benefit to me . . . us . . . God," explained Andres.

Father Giovanni replied, "Then you have redeemed yourself for your past sins."

It felt like now or never for Rael to plead to these men, two men of the Church. The odds that at least one of them would find mercy in his heart if he heard her story weren't bad, according to her. She pleaded, "Please help me. Andres is not what he seems. He wants to . . ."

"Bring back our beloved Jesus using you, my child," interrupted Father Rezzonico.

"What?" asked Rael.

Father Rezzonico explained, "We Templar Knights and Knights of Malta have kept the faith all these years. The Holy Father just over the hill, he promises us for centuries that our Jesus will return at the end of days. But of that day and hour no one knows, not even the angels in heaven, nor the Son, but only the Father. I have, frankly, become tired of the waiting. And then Andres here, he comes to us with an answer to our prayers. A millennial Astralith has been created by the grace of God and has now set foot in our world. You can open portals to the outerworlds. It is a miracle! You are that miracle. For you can be sent up to heaven in exchange for our dear Jesus coming back down to us."

"By force if necessary," added Father Giovanni.

"You're both mad," said Rael.

Father Giovanni grabbed the chain that bound Rael's hands. He pulled himself closer to her. He said to her, "No, not mad. I just love my Jesus too much to not want him to return. I know the hour of his return, and the hour begins now!"

Father Rezzonico added, "Agreed, let us begin. The summoning circle is in the Templar base below us." The two priests climbed onto the stucco altar next to her. Andres pulled a hidden lever on the altar statue. The altar started to sink down into the ground. Andres hustled over to get on board.

As they rode the elevator altar down, Father Rezzonico spoke. "We've arranged it all, Andres. In the hidden chamber below there is the summoning circle."

"And all our friendly noble knights?" asked Andres.

Father Rezzonico explained, "All sent away. The church is officially closed for the day. No one is here to interfere with us. Not even a mouse."

"Good," said Andres.

The altar sank one hundred feet into the ground. The altar stopped in place and formed another altar inside another, much more ancient church below the Aventine Hill church. The vast chamber was lit by electric lights, for the place had been modernized and yet was old at the same time. The walls were decorated with mosaics of knights in battle with infidels, depicting real events and possibly depicting some that were imagined. Red crosses adorned one wall and black crosses adorned another. The sarcophagi of dead knights lined the walls around the chamber. The lifelike lids depicted the dead soldiers dressed in their armor, as they had been in battle—or how the sculptor imagined they had been.

The nave had been cleared of pews. Located there instead was a pentagram painted with pure gold. It must have been fifty feet across. Incense burned in a circle around the pentagram.

The priests stepped off the altar. "See, it is all as it should be," said Father Giovanni to Andres.

Andres grabbed Rael by the chain. He forced her to follow him. Rael resisted momentarily. She was never going to let him get her to that circle. "Gentlemen, a little assistance," said Andres.

The two priests seized her. Together the three men carried her into the pentagram. She could have kicked and screamed, but it wouldn't have done any good. No, she bided her time. She would save her energy in hopes of a moment when using it would matter. The heavy chain made running away impossible anyway. The extra weight was too much for her to bear for long. Besides, there didn't appear to be anywhere to run away to down here.

They dumped her in the center of the pentagram. They used the chains to strap her down to iron rings embedded in the floor. Then they took new chains and strapped down her legs.

Rael said to the men, "It's not too late to repent, for what will Jesus say when he finds out what you've done to me?"

"Poor child, he knows more than any other the importance of self-sacrifice. What you do for the world today is the noblest of such saintly services. Your name shall be remembered forever—whatever it is. Should we record her name?" asked Father Giovanni.

"Why bother? It will hardly be worth knowing in the future kingdom," replied Father Rezzonico.

Andres said to the priests, "Now, out of the circle, so I may finish the ritual."

"Shouldn't you leave too?" asked Father Rezzonico.

"Yeah, about that." Andres pulled a gun from his pocket. He fired twice. Once for each priest's heart. The men of God crumpled to the floor.

"You killed them!" exclaimed Rael.

"Of course. They wanted to bring Jesus here, but I want to go to him instead. My will was stronger. Besides, you need fresh blood to start the communion, and I wasn't about to use my own. You're going to heaven, and I'm riding there in your wake. Soon you will cease to exist, whereas I shall break into paradise and receive my Earthly rewards on my own terms. But do not think my act is entirely evil, for as you depart, so shall an angel be gated back here to take your place inside your empty vessel."

"You're tearing an angel away from heaven and you don't think that's an entirely evil act?" She asked.

"I guess now that I think of it, I really just don't care." He dipped his fingers in the dead priests' free-flowing blood and used it to trace a pentagram on her forehead. Andres spoke,

Dies irae, dies illa,
Solvet saeclum in favilla,
Teste David cum Sibylla.
Quantus tremor est futurus,
Quando iudex est venturus,
Cuncta stricte discussurus.
Tuba mirum spargens sonum
Per sepulcra regionum,
Coget omnes ante thronum.
Mors stupebit et natura,
Cum resurget creatura,
Iudicanti responsura.
Liber scriptus proferetur,

In quo totum continetur,
Unde mundus iudicetur.
Ludex ergo cum sedebit,
Quidquid latet apparebit:
Nil inultum remanebit.
Quid sum miser tunc dicturus?
Quem patronum rogaturus?
Cum vix iustus sit securus.
Rex tremendae maiestatis,
Qui salvandos salvas gratis,
Salva me, fons pietatis.

The gold circle around her began to glow. Andres kept chanting in verse, but his words faded out. Then the whole room began to fade to black. The chains around her came off and she was free. She was drifting through space and time. She'd been here before. She was in the big empty between worlds. She wasn't on the same path as before, though. There was a light ahead. It glowed with a golden hue. She felt at peace because there was no hate here. She approached the glow and all she could feel was love. She could see a faint image of an angel, and the angel saw her. There was pity in the angel's eyes. She knew Rael was doing this without a choice. Rael began to fade into blackness too. Her mind was going, along with her body. The angel was becoming more defined. They were merging. Rael would lose her body to the angel as Rael's soul was expended.

Andres's voice bellowed, "It's working, it's working."

The angel spoke to Rael. "For this, I forgive you."

And then in a flash of blue light the angel was gone. Rael was back body and possibly soul. She was being dragged across the stone floor. The chains rattled as she slid. She was on her back, and all she could see were the frescoes of the hidden chamber below Santa Maria del Priorato above her. She knew she'd been returned to Earth. The question now was who her savior was.

Andres shouted, "No, I was so close!"

"The girl is ours," snarled a voice. Her chains broke free from her hands. Her feet had already been freed. A blue hand hoisted the chains up and tossed them at Andres. They hit him square in the chest. Andres was taking longer to recover from the astral trip than Rael. She had experience in astral travel, after all, and he didn't. She tried to get to her feet, but the demon nabbed her and placed her onto its scaly blue back. What was it with everyone carrying her about! Even King Kong gave Fay Wray a break once in a while. She shook the remaining cobwebs from her mind. It wasn't like before. Her memories weren't so clouded this time. Andres must not have gotten as far as the last failed communion. She knew exactly what had happened. The blue demon had interrupted the summoning circle and saved her. Not for any more noble reason than to save her for himself, but she was alive and free, albeit a prisoner at the same time.

Andres had roused himself enough to unload his gun into the demon. The blue demon was anything but happy about this. The bullets, though, could not penetrate its hide. The demon turned and charged Andres. Andres was rapidly reloading. He was too late. With one swing of its arm, the demon knocked Andres high into the air. The fallen Templar landed with a thud on one of the knightly stone sarcophagi in the room. Andres wasn't getting up for a long time after that.

The demon started to gather a long rope. "The thread of Ilitar, perfect for binding you so you won't be any more trouble," he explained.

Rael had saved her energy hoping for a chance and it paid off. Now was her chance, and she acted in haste. She raked her claws across the demon's back. It screamed in pain. Unlike Andres's bullets, Rael's nails were made of the stuff that penetrated the hides of demons. As the demon lurched to end the agony, she fell from its back. She didn't take time to decide what to do; she just ran. Only, she quickly discovered that there was still no place to go.

"You're more trouble than you're worth . . . nah, you're worth it," said the demon.

Rael was pressed up against a wall with no more room to run. She could run around in circles inside here forever, but she couldn't escape the demon that way. Something told her demons had pretty good stamina anyway. She eyed the stucco altar. What goes down must go up. The beast charged at her. The demon was aiming to put her in the least friendly bear hug ever. As it reached to hug her with its rope, she went low. Indeed, she went right between its legs. Hah! Being short had its advantages. She sprinted toward the altar. She could feel the demon nipping at her heel. She was faster. She leaped onto the altar. *Hah, I finally won a race!* Now, what did she win? She said, "Up." She kicked the altar. "Go up." She jumped up and down on it. "Why won't you go up?"

The demon hurled itself at her, but there was nothing for it to grab. It landed on the empty altar. She was going up. Only there was nothing under her feet. She laughed. She couldn't help herself. She was flying. Sprouting from her back were two pairs of white dove wings. They glowed with angelic light, illuminating the hidden chamber like never before. They were gently stroking, lifting her ever higher. She looked at Andres crumpled in agony on the sarcophagus. She had to thank him in a way. At least he'd finally done something to help her. The second failed communion had altered Rael yet again. This time in a more angelic way.

Rael soared one hundred feet up, out of the sub-chamber of the church and right into the church itself. Like so many other escapes of hers, this one simply led to more danger. The nave was filled with twenty black-cloaked figures. They were members of the Maleficium Society, she had no doubt about that. Most were carrying weapons, and she was trapped in here like a bird in a cage.

"Look, the church is defended by an angel," shouted one figure. All of them got down on their knees. It was nice to be respected for once.

All but one cultist had gotten down, that is. The remaining cultist stood in the middle of the nave and scolded the others. "Don't be fools. That is the girl we came to seize. She's lost more essence. Pray she still has enough for us." She'd heard his voice before. It was the same man who had been inside the church where she'd first seen the blue demon. They were members of the Ilitar cult alright. They were the ones who had changed her into this thing. The only good news was that they had already failed once. She couldn't wait to make them fail again.

"Come, catch me," she said to them. Too bad this church didn't have a very high-domed ceiling. She could only get so far out of their reach. If they shot at her, she was a sitting duck. But no, they didn't want her damaged this time around. No bullets came her way, so she perched on top of the statue on the altar. There was a round stained-glass window above the main door across the nave from her. If she worked up a good enough head of steam . . . she might break her neck trying to fly through it. *You're not Boudicea who can go through glass without being harmed. You need a non-stupid plan. Think, Rael, think.*

The black-cloaked figure approached her, walking straight down the nave. Other members of the cult were either activating the lever to bring the altar back up or surrounding her. When that blue demon arrived, she'd have real trouble again.

"This does not have to end unpleasantly. I could shoot you. I almost want to for the fun of it. But we've wasted far too much of your essence. No, it's safer to preserve as much of you as possible. Please, instead, fly down and join us," said the main cultist. Then he removed his hood.

Shocked, Rael flew up higher into the air. She exclaimed, "Father!" It was him. His voice was different, but his face, she would have known it anywhere. He wasn't dead. Only she wished now that he was. She didn't want to cry, but it was impossible not to. Her own father had tried to kill her. Her own father had killed her mother. Her own father was the cause of this whole mess.

"My daughter, my one and only daughter, you will come down and join with me now." His voice sounded normal now. The same voice that he'd used to push her to ski all those years.

She wiped the tears away. "You killed Mother. You nearly killed me. You've become a monster!" she said in anger at him.

"No, I merely tried to make you stronger. You're a rare gift. Because of you, a wealthy man gave me money. All we have as a family is due to your gifts. I've grown quite powerful and rich because of you. It was determined you would peak in power just after your sixteenth birthday. It was time to bring you to your true form. You see, you have essence worth the ransom of a demon queen. We have the means to control her here on

Earth. Dwelling inside your empty body, Ilitar could make us powerful beyond imagination. You'd want that for your father, wouldn't you? Ultimate power . . . what daughter could give her father more?"

"Go to hell!" she barked back.

"That's the spirit," replied her father.

Rael was going to need to work on her trash talking. All those old, standard catchphrases no longer worked when the world was actually crazy. The front door of the church exploded into splinters, which saved her from thinking up new material on the spot. Sometimes you go to hell, and sometimes hell came to you. A red demon charged in on all fours. It was different from the last red demon Rael had seen. This one was more beast than man. It was here for one purpose, and that was to fight. It had two tusks on its snout, and it used them to gore the nearest cult member.

"Why can't these foul red demons stop spoiling our fun?" lamented her father.

The cultists unloaded their weapons into the red beast. It snarled and then bull-rushed another member of the cult. As it trampled the body, it looked up at Rael. Of course it looked at her. Everyone wanted her. She knew what Andres wanted from her, she knew what the two dead priests had wanted from her, and now she knew what her father wanted from her, but what did this red demon want? Not the same thing as the blue one, that much was certain. Red and blue demons didn't mix. She understood that much now. The front door was open thanks to the red demon bursting onto the scene. Indeed, it was in splinters. The bird was caged no more, so she beat her wings toward the opening.

"Come back, Rael. I command it!" shouted her father.

She would never come back to him. In her heart, he was dead to her. She soared outside and was finally free from them all. There was nothing but blue skies ahead of her. She could go wherever she wanted—only she had no safe place to go to. She had no home anymore. She couldn't fly forever, though. She needed some place to land. Then she saw it: the golden sphere of Saint Peter up ahead. If they couldn't help her, no one around here could.

Chapter 11

Vatican City

The one thing Rael had to hand to the Italians was that they knew how to make a good cup of coffee. The coffee at the gas stations here probably tasted better than the coffee at an American five-star restaurant. The cup Rael was holding didn't even come from an Italian gas station. It had been sourced for consumption by a much higher class of clientele. She finished the last drop and looked at the cup. It had a picture of the pope on it. She wondered if she would get to keep the cup as a souvenir. She glanced over at her guards. They looked like they meant business. They'd probably not let her keep the cup.

There was a knock on the door that the guards were guarding so carefully. The priest who had been standing watch over the service cart left her side to go answer it. The two guards of the Italian Guardia Svizzera parted, and the priest opened the door. A man dressed in red vestments entered the room. "*Devi andartene,*" he said to the priest. He didn't need to ask the priest twice. The priest left immediately and closed the door behind him. The guards then resumed their position in front of the door, halberds at the ready.

Rael couldn't decide if the guards were stationed at the door for her protection or to make sure she, as their prisoner, stayed where they wanted her. She'd not heard much one way or the other on that matter from those she had spoken with up to this point. This new man looked important enough that she might finally learn her fate from him. Yeah, he definitely had a serious look about him, and that meant official business was going to be discussed. Rael hoped he wasn't afraid of her, but given that the guard had had to pry her off the roof of their fancy church, on which she'd landed about two hours ago, she figured he probably was.

The man of God walked up and inspected Rael. She wondered what he expected to see. A young girl with devil horns and angel wings, no doubt. He said to her, "Could you please keep the coffee cup off of the armrest? It's priceless. Clement II used to sit on that chair, after all."

"Oh, sorry," she replied, lifting the cup.

"No need to be too sorry, because it is just a small detail. Small details, though, can be important ones. You are very small, yet to me you look very important, so you understand now how it is." He retrieved the empty cup from her hand and placed it back on the service cart. "Would you care for some more biscuits or cakes?" he asked.

"No thanks, I ate about twenty already."

"Flying like an angel must have made you very hungry."

"About that . . ."

He held his finger up. "Hush. I need no explanations. There are no wings on you now, I see."

"I don't know where they went either. They seem to come and go as they please. You see, they're sort of new," she replied.

"Half the tourists in Vatican City saw you flying about with those angelic wings. We were torn between claiming you were just a weather balloon, a reflection in the atmosphere off of low-flying clouds, or a fool with a wingsuit. We went with the weather balloon story. It usually works. Whatever the story, most of our believers will see you as a miracle. Miracles are good for our business, so no harm has been done to us. You, though, I fear have seen great harm in the past few days." He poured a cup of coffee for himself. Then he sat next to her. "I envy you. You've been to a place where men like me dream to go."

"I haven't felt very lucky lately," replied Rael.

"Nonsense, young lady. You're very lucky to still be alive, for you are temptation itself, Rael Armstrong. Even a man of my stature is tempted by what you could bring me. Even my boss is not immune to your temptations. Do you understand how important you are?"

"I'm beginning to."

He explained, "Good. I am Cardinal Santiago. My boss sent for me as soon as you landed on Saint Peter's sphere. I am the Church's resident occult expert. And you are made of the stuff that the occult is made of."

"You mean to say that I'm an Astralith."

The word didn't shock him in the least. He already knew the truth. Everyone seemed to know about it. She wished she had known sooner. He continued, "You're much more than that. You are much more powerful than a common Astralith. One like you is born every millennium or so. Now blood, a chicken, or a lesser Astralith, if you're lucky enough to acquire one, is not an abnormal sacrifice to commune between planes of reality. That might net you a sub-demon minion or a minor devil if you're a not-so-honest man. A man such as myself could hope for a conversation with the planar creature of my choosing. But it takes someone like you to really move between worlds. You understand, it requires such a very rich essence to do the near impossible. By using you, someone could travel to a place only dreamed about in legends, or by using you, a much more powerful being could be brought into this world. You're a one-use ticket, however, and the next one may not get printed for a thousand years or so. A thousand years is a long time to wait, and most men are not so patient."

Rael replied, "I know all this already. In fact, I've lived it."

"Now I will tell you something you don't know. If a cult were to locate the phylactery of a demon and then gate this demon into our world using your soul, well, they'd control the demon so long as they controlled the phylactery. Imagine tearing a queen demon from her plane and enslaving her here inside your body. Something so powerful as a queen horror could do immeasurable damage to our world. We would be at the mercy of whoever controls her. We have reason to believe the Maleficium Society has such a device to enslave Ilitar. They damaged Santa Maria del Priorato this afternoon trying to retrieve you. Without you, you understand, their phylactery is essentially useless. With you, they could rule this world. They must be stopped at all costs.”

That didn’t sound good. It sounded horrible. It wasn’t that unusual for a parent to try to have their child fulfill their failed dreams for them. Usually such father–daughter relationships only manifested as your father dictating to you whom you were to marry, where you were to go to school, or your choice of profession. Rael had always seen her dreams of being a famous skier as more her father’s dream. Now she knew it was all just a distraction from his real goal for her. She’d been groomed by her father all this time to be used to gate in a horror. She wasn’t meant to ski. She wasn’t meant to fall in love. She was never meant to have a life of her own. She was meant only to fulfill his dreams of madness. That was not the sort of thing you get over quickly. And he’d killed Mother in the process. There was hate in her heart now, and she couldn’t help it if that hate was lodged permanently inside there. It was his fault.

“I think my father is in this cult,” she said.

The cardinal placed a handkerchief to her face and dried it. “And that is why I see stale tears clinging to your cheeks. Then I am very sorry for you, but being sorry for you won’t help matters. We must retrieve this item from the cult to neutralize them.”

“And then I’ll be safe?” she asked.

“No, now that it is known that the power inside you is so great, you will never truly be safe again.”

“People keep saying that to me. I guess I should start to believe them.”

There was a knock on the door. The cardinal motioned the guards. They parted. The door opened and Boudicea came in. Rael wanted to leap from the chair and tell her all that had happened to her. But she didn’t move, because Boudicea didn’t look very happy to see Rael. Indeed, she appeared extremely unhappy.

The cardinal went over to Boudicea and said, “This is the young woman that we inquired to the Order about. I am told you’ve met her already.”

“Yes, though she couldn’t fly the last time I saw her,” replied Boudicea.

"Yes, the more angelic parts of her appear to have been the work of a fallen Templar named Andres de Salete. He is now in our custody. I will retrieve him. We have many questions for him."

"Do go get him, while I fulfill my part of our deal. Am I now allowed to be alone with her?" asked Boudicea.

"No, druid, you are not to be alone with her. The guards will remain here. But I shall give you temporary leave of my presence. I believe that is all that is called for. The guards do not speak English. They will not understand anything said between you two. And there are things to be arranged by you. Let us pray that they go our way." The cardinal then left the room.

They were alone, sort of, for the first time in a while. Things felt as awkward between them as ever. Mostly because Boudicea towered over Rael. Rael thought of standing up but decided against it. Boudicea said, "You look rather turned out."

"I sort of had a devilish makeover," Rael explained.

"Rael, you can't just go flying about in public glamoured up from some Rome fashion boutique. You have just alerted every cultist on the planet to your presence here! Worse yet, the Society has now fled Rome. We've lost our only hope of finding their leader."

Now Rael stood up. She replied, "Look, I'll have you know that I almost died, and died, and then maybe died again. There were Satanists, Freemasons, Templars, Knights of Malta, a blue and a red demon, and a couple weird things straight out of Heck all trying to get me."

Boudicea sighed, "What am I going to do with you?"

"Hopefully not lecture me anymore. You're not my mother." It felt good to say that at last. She expected a sharp tongue in return for a statement like that. It's how her own mother would have responded. Boudicea pulled a cloak out from her sleeve. She held it up in front of Rael. It was Rael's size. Rael had not expected that.

Boudicea explained, "It has been decided. You've shown some ability to stay alive despite all that has happened to you. The only way to keep you safe from being turned into some horror is to hone that natural survival skill inside you. Thus, you are to become my apprentice—if you wish. The

Order doesn't usually ask a person at all. The decision is made for hunters long before they know themselves. It is made while they are still babies. This is a one-time proposition, a special offer. Take it or leave it."

Rael stood up. She reached for the cloak and stopped. Rael said, "Tell me what happened between you and Divicia."

"He was my mentor."

"Dynami told me that you killed him."

Boudicea dropped the cloak to the floor. She turned her back to Rael. "He should not have told you that. He will be punished for it. That is the Order's business and nobody else's. Dynami is already being punished for losing you. I don't think he will make it to hunter grade at this rate. Archon had such hopes, but he's a failure."

Punished! Rael was livid. "He shouldn't have been punished for losing me. It wasn't his fault. There was a Freemason. He was helping us, and then he sort of wasn't. What I mean is, he was only helping us because I got us into trouble. Dynami was against opening our door to begin with. It was my . . ." She paused. Her words wouldn't matter to Boudicea. She wasn't listening to them. She was bound up in the rules of the Order. As Siberion had suggested, cults had rules that were not easily understood by outsiders. There was only one way to understand them, and that was to join. Rael didn't really have any friends, and now she certainly didn't have any family. She didn't belong anywhere. Rael picked the cloak up from the floor and put it on. Instantly her outfit changed. She was wearing a black Lycra suit with a yellow racing stripe up the side to match the golden streak in her hair. "I wasn't exactly expecting that!" she exclaimed.

Boudicea turned around. She looked worried. It was that worried, unhappy look Rael's mother had always had. Now Rael knew the source of her own mother's unhappiness. She must have suspected Rael's father was up to no good. She probably couldn't imagine the truth, though. Who could ever imagine that? Boudicea faked a smile. Rael already knew her fake smile by heart. Boudicea took out an all-black ballcap from her sleeve. She placed it on Rael's head to cover the horns. "Good, now it is done."

Rael spun the cap around and pulled a tuft of hair through the loop in the front. She said, "There, now it's done. Now that I'm in the Order, Dynami's failure on the train is my failure. Agreed?"

"We will discuss it later," replied Boudicea.

Rael wanted to protest more, but she was stopped by a knock on the door. The guards parted again, and the door opened. The cardinal had returned. He was not alone. There was a short, white-haired woman with him. She was round like a beach ball and wore a black nun's habit. She carried a green set of rosary beads in a clenched fist. She had a deep scar down the right side of her face that would make her stand out in any rogues' gallery. The nun grimaced at Rael and then cracked her knuckles.

The cardinal asked Boudicea, "How did we fair?"

"She accepted the cloak. It is done," replied Boudicea.

"That is all that is required?" asked Cardinal Santiago.

"There are no formal requirements for an apprentice starting at Rael's late age. We're winging it," explained Boudicea.

The cardinal took a deep breath and exhaled. "Good. I had brought Sister Isabella with me just in case the alternative was needed. I am so happy to hear that it is not."

"What alternative?" asked Rael.

Boudicea replied, "There were only two ways to ensure you didn't become a horror. One was to train you to defend yourself better. And the other was to destroy you before you were used for harm."

"Wait, you were all planning to kill me?" exclaimed Rael.

The cardinal waved that off. "The needs of the many, child, outweigh the needs of any one of us, so there is no call for anger. Besides, I have faith. I knew you would choose wisely. For not one moment did I believe the alternative would be needed."

"Still, you brought Isabella with you," interjected Boudicea.

"Yes, but only because I have other uses for her abilities. We need to get all we can from Andres," replied Cardinal Santiago.

The door had never shut. Two Swiss guards entered, dragging a chair that Andres was tied to. Rael couldn't help but smirk. It was about time he got the other end of this prisoner stuff.

Cardinal Santiago ripped the duct tape off Andres's mouth. The man immediately started complaining, "What right does the Church have to do this?"

"The same right you took upon yourself to kill two men of the cloth," said the cardinal. The cardinal removed Andres's blindfold next, and his eyes found Rael quick enough. Once you'd seen paradise, it was hard not to keep looking at its source. She could see in his eyes the desire to kill her for another chance at paradise. She stepped back from him. "Now, Andres, you must answer for your crimes."

"This doesn't look like a courtroom," said Andres.

"That is not the kind of answer that we need. Let me introduce you to Sister Isabella. Her ancestors were very big in the Spanish Inquisition. Some things you just can't get out of a bloodline," said Cardinal Santiago.

"Am I supposed to be scared?" asked Andres.

"No, you're supposed to be in pain," said the sister. She then implanted her balled-up fist holding the rosary into Andres's forehead. Andres and the chair he was sitting on went over backwards. She made the sign of the cross after decking Andres. "Father, forgive me for what I do."

Rael said to Boudicea, "You can't just hit a tied-up man like that."

"I didn't. She did," replied Boudicea.

Rael said, "We should . . ."

Boudicea interrupted Rael, "We should stay back and watch. This is between the sister and Andres. She's good—she could take you in a fight—so don't interfere in other people's business. That is your first lesson."

It didn't sound like a very moral lesson. Sister Isabella tilted Andres back upright. The imprint of the crucifix was stamped into his forehead. He was trying to shake the cobwebs out of his brain. Sister Isabella asked him, "How did you come to learn of the existence of Rael?"

Andres looked back at her with anger in his eyes. He was a schemer at heart. Rael knew that much. He was weighing his chances against the sister. There were two paths he could take: silence or talk. Apparently it was a quick calculation. He began speaking. "I was in Lebanon on business. A missile sale to the Syrian government needed financing. They were in a civil war. There's always good money to be made from a war. That's right up the Templars alley. While I was there, I crossed paths with a man recruiting disillusioned jihadists. They make good minions, so I've heard."

"And?" asked the sister.

"And I joined this cult—not really, but I faked it. I was curious. I got as far as learning about the Society's secret demon business. I learned all about their devotion to a demon queen. Nasty stuff, but right up my alley, because worship means money. After I saw what was going down and who was the best person to track in secret, I split. It took me a full year of tailing cultist after cultist until I found the right one. That led to me finding out about an ordinary, if wealthy, American family with an extraordinary daughter. That information came to me from a fallen priest who lived in a church in the Italian Alps. It was there that the girl was to be sacrificed for the greater good of the cult. All it took was a million dollars of Templar funding to net me that information from the priest at the church. It looks like he didn't cover his tracks too well because now he's dead at the hands of his own men. Sucks for him."

"It was you who saved Rael that first time they tried to use her then," said Boudicea.

"Please, let the sister do her job," said Cardinal Santiago.

Andres said, "I don't mind answering. No, it wasn't me. A red demon beat me to the punch. It royally messed up her daddy's plans. It played right into mine, though. I'd have scooped the girl up and been in heaven by now if the avalanche rescue team had not beaten me to the summoning circle. Tough luck, because they hid her in that damn count's castle."

"Who controls this red demon?" asked the sister.

"I don't know," Andres answered. She balled up her fist again. He flinched. "I don't know, you crazy nun, and I mean it!"

"Ask the big one so we can be done with him," said Cardinal Santiago.

"Who owns the phylactery?" asked the sister.

"What phylactery?" he replied. She kicked him in his shin. He gritted his teeth. "Look, I wasn't lying, you b—"

"Enough," said Boudicea.

"I think he's lying," said the sister.

"No, he doesn't know," said Boudicea.

"A night in an iron maiden might settle the issue once and for all," suggested Sister Isabella.

Cardinal Santiago said, "No, no, we've got enough from him. I worried he would be mostly useless for learning what we really need to know. The existence of a phylactery would be a closely guarded secret. A man that was merely in and out of the cult as he claims would never have been near it. Possibly only one cult member even knows of its existence: the cult leader."

"Is my father the cult leader?" asked Rael.

Cardinal Santiago replied, "No, he works for another. Someone beyond our means to locate so far." The cardinal turned to his men. "Guards, to prison with Andres. He is the Vatican court's problem now. Double homicide—it should be an easy case to make against him."

Andres said, "Hey, wait just one minute. I could help you guys. I know people within the Society. If there's this phylactery thing somewhere in there, I could help you find it."

The cardinal put up his hand. The guards paused. The cardinal looked toward Boudicea. She shook her head back at the cardinal. Rael was relieved. Andres was just about the last person she wanted to team up with.

Cardinal Santiago said, "Have it your way, hunter. Sorry, Andres, no deal."

"You'll regret this," said Andres. The guards removed Andres. He spent his exit trying to bargain with the room, but he'd run out of chips. The door closed, and the two Swiss guards resumed their position at the door.

"What do we do if we don't use Andres to work our way to the leader of the cult?" asked Cardinal Santiago.

"An oracle will be able to locate the phylactery's whereabouts for us. We merely need to ask the correct one," said Boudicea.

The cardinal didn't take the suggestion too well. He looked toward Sister Isabella. She said, "They are not the most trustworthy of sources. If you tell one oracle what you are searching for, the whole world will soon know about it."

"The sister does have a point," agreed Cardinal Santiago.

"I know one oracle I can trust with my life," said Boudicea.

"Such an oracle does not exist," replied the sister.

"Divicia trusted her with his life," added Boudicea.

The cardinal said, "That name is not unknown to me. If a hunter of that stature trusted her . . ."

"He did," insisted Boudicea.

"Very well, where is she located?" asked the cardinal.

Boudicea explained, "Rael and I must go to Crete at once."

Cardinal Santiago agreed to the request. "Very well. I offer Sister Isabella here to assist you on your journey. I can have a plane fueled and ready to leave in fifteen minutes. It's yours if you want it."

Rael had a feeling it was an offer of help that they wouldn't refuse.

Chapter 12

Flying over the Sea of Crete

Rael pulled her goggles down and stared out at the slope. As far as the eye could see below her, the day-trippers and tourists were skiing. It was nice-and-easy stuff down there. Up where Rael was, the slopes became a challenge. Indeed, she was about as high up as the resort's liability insurance allowed a skier to go. They called this the pro slope. It did nothing to take her mind off her problems. She'd lost a race. It hadn't been just any race. It had been . . . well, it didn't matter now. This vacation in Italy was going to erase all those bad memories. Her dad had promised her that much.

The family vacation to date hadn't done much to break her out of the funk she'd been in since her racing loss, though. Daddy could buy just about anything these days, but funk-free wasn't a product on a shelf. It was a state of mind. Rael had moped about for days now, not really enjoying Europe at all. She thought to herself, *You're in Italy. This vacation should be fun.* But skiing was never just fun for her these days. To her father, this was business, and so it meant business to her too. Tourists had fun; today, she had demons to conquer out here on this slope. They were personal demons, the hardest kind to defeat. Still, she should be having fun while doing it. There were no competitors here, no clock to race against; it was just her and the fresh powdered snow. The tourists did the lower runs because they couldn't handle the course up here. She could. She was something special, maybe not Olympic grade, but still a cut above the madding crowd. She should appreciate that fact. She should be proud of herself.

She took a deep breath of cold mountain air. "Be proud, Rael, be proud." She didn't feel super-proud, though. That was Little Miss Self-doubt talking. She didn't want to hear from her anymore. She dug her poles in. She would have a nice fun run and then hot cocoa in the ski lodge. She'd have fun on this vacation even if it killed her. Fun—she was allowed to have it now and then, wasn't she?

"Rael, can I have a word with you before you start down?" asked her father.

Fun—no, it wasn't allowed. Not by Father anyway. This was supposed to be a vacation, but to him everything was a means to an end. She turned to her father. She replied sheepishly, "Now?"

"Yes, exactly now."

"Yes, Daddy." She slid over to him. He immediately seized her arm. He squeezed a little too hard and she winced.

"Must we talk about it? We've been waiting forever . . . let's just do it and be done with it," her mother said.

"We will when I say we will," Father replied.

"Wait—that's all I ever do. Then I will see you at the bottom of the hill. And, Ted, don't traumatize Rael too much." Her mother started down. Rael felt that Mother was so lucky to get away. That was the freedom that came with being an adult.

"Traumatize?" her father repeated in disgust. He let go of Rael's arm. He took his glove off and dropped it into the snow. "I've never traumatized you, Rael. I've always done what is best for you. I've waited years for this day to really bring out the best in you."

"Oh, I didn't know this vacation meant that much to you."

"You're sixteen now. Last night was the first blood moon since your birthday. That means today is a very special day. Today is the day I start a whole new way of life. You too, in a way."

Rael had no idea what he was talking about. Business, probably. He had been obsessed with it these past six years. He'd been sort of a normal bossy coaching father living his life through her until he'd started to make real money. Now his mind was always on money . . . well, the power that went with it. Only it didn't sound quite like business that he was talking about right then. It sounded sort of loony what he was saying. She really didn't care one way or the other. She wanted a little fun for once. She wanted to be free to just ski with no worries attached. "When can I start skiing?" asked Rael.

"Soon. We're about to have a race."

"Oh." Then it was to be a competition day after all. It was *so* like Father. He liked winning at business and at life . . . well, at Rael's life. He was too old to compete, so she competed for him. Even a holiday couldn't be pure fun. No wonder she couldn't break this funk she was in.

Then he cut his wrist with a razor blade. Blood was flowing freely onto the white snow beneath his feet. Only, no, she looked down, and at her father's feet was a golden chalice. It had ruby red gems around it. Rael just stood there looking rather stupid for a second. She wasn't stupid, though. It was what was going on that was stupid. She couldn't believe that had just happened. Her father must have lost it. He'd cut himself. Mother was always warning him this business of his would drive him over the edge. It must have really done so. Finally, Rael shook the disbelief away long enough to speak. "What did you do that for?"

"The future, Rael, the future. I only need a little blood to finish this, and look at everyone out on the slope, plenty to choose from. Let's have them all, my dear little girl. Let's have them all. A blood sacrifice is needed, and I'll use them all. Including your mother," replied her father. Then her father added,

Come to me now, Queen Ilitar,
Make them all a competitor.
Make the mountain of ice and snow
Start to crumble down and free flow.
Watch them as they race for their lives,

Dying a death before our eyes.
We need their fresh blood, death, and gore
To unlock your abyssal door.

Rael was always suspicious of adults when they slipped into verse. She hadn't experienced anyone doing it since nursery school, though. Her father had an insane look in his eyes. He had always been a little high-strung. Well, not always. He'd changed in the last six years, after he had gotten the new job, though she had been too young at first to notice it. They'd become wealthy, but he'd lost his warmth.

Rael's eyes moved toward her mother. She was skiing downhill below. She was too far away to hear Rael's scream. Father had finally gone mad, and Rael was alone up here with him and didn't know what to do.

The snow on the mountain started to move. It was shaking up and down. It could be an earthquake. Italy did have them, right? It was rumbling like one. Only, it seemed to be just the snow around her. The snow around her moved. It was alive. A beast, a great blue thing, rose out of the snow. She was frozen in place, too afraid to move.

The blue beast said to her father, "We need the blood sacrifice to start the ceremony, so begin."

Her father said to the beast, "It has already started. Can you imagine the power I'm about to have?"

"I don't need to imagine it, I've lived it," replied the beast. "Just don't kill the girl too much. She needs to be fresh meat for it to work." He pointed at Rael while saying that.

"She will not be permanently damaged. As her last breath leaves her body, you, my friend, will summon Ilitar with her soul," her father commanded the beast.

Then her father walked away. Rael was too confused for words. Only, words were greatly needed. She called out, "Father!"

He turned to her with flaming red eyes and said, "Go!"

The mountain gave way. The snow was sliding down the slope at her. It was an avalanche. She dug her poles in and set off down. She had to get away from the snow. But more importantly, she had to get away from him.

For this was madness. The last thing she heard over the rumbling snow was the blue beast complaining, "Must we do it this way? I'm going to just hate digging through all that snow to retrieve her body."

Rael opened her eyes. She heard the hum of the plane's jet engines. She was lying down on a long bench in the back of the plane. She looked over to see Boudicea sitting opposite her. Her eyes were open, watching her. How lucky she was to be able to go without sleep for days. She probably never had demon-filled nightmares like Rael had just had. Rael sat up. Had it been a nightmare, or had it all happened just like that that day on the mountain?

"You are shivering. Pull your cloak tighter around you and you shall not know cold," said Boudicea.

Rael sat up. "I'm not shivering because I'm cold. I think I just had a lost memory come back to me in a dream. No, not a dream. It was a nightmare. It was one memory I wish I had never remembered. It can stay lost forever as far as I'm concerned. You see, it was about my father."

"Yes."

"He caused the avalanche. He killed all those people."

"Yes."

"He killed my mother."

"Yes."

"He killed me . . . well, mostly."

"Yes."

"What do you mean, yes?"

"I mean, yes. It is the truth. It happened. You cannot change it, so do not punish yourself for it. Focus on the future. It is there; we can still make a difference," replied Boudicea. That sounded really profound and empty at the same time. Boudicea reached over and pulled Rael's cloak tighter around her. Rael did instantly feel warmer. The cloak had magic within it. It was her magic now.

Rael said, "I wish I knew how this magic cloak of mine worked."

"Since we have the time, I will give you a lesson," said Boudicea. She took a silver acorn from her sleeve. She placed it in the palm of her hand. "Now it's in my right hand, and now it is not." She raised her arm and the acorn rolled down it and into the sleeve of her cloak. "And now it is back again." She lowered her other arm and the acorn rolled from the sleeve until it stopped in the palm of her left hand. She tossed the silver acorn to Rael. "And now you will try it."

"Okay, that looked easy enough. The old magic sleeve trick." Rael held out her right hand. She put the acorn in it with her left. "Now it is in my hand. And now . . ." She raised her arm. The acorn rolled down her arm, missed her sleeve, and rattled as it rolled across the floor of the airplane.

"And now I see that it is on the floor," said Boudicea.

"Tada!" replied Rael, feeling every bit the failure.

Just then her chest felt warm. She took her focus off the acorn on the floor and pulled the acorn necklace out from her suit. It was getting hot. She said, "I think there's trouble." The back of the plane suddenly went black. An alarm went off, followed by a blinking red light. Rael forgot all about the acorn on the floor. Magic could wait. "What's going on?"

Sister Isabella shouted from the cockpit, "We have two bogeys coming in hot!"

Boudicea scrambled to the front of the plane and sat next to the nun. She asked, "Whose?"

"Don't know yet. They look like ordinary prop planes from afar, but they're moving too fast. They've been upgraded. I think they mean business," said Sister Isabella.

One broke formation and moved on them. It came on them fast. Gunfire erupted. The bullets pelted the side of the plane. The plane roared its engines and flew past them still in one piece. Sister Isabella replied, "Two P-35 Tomahawks equipped for action. Don't worry, this is a papal personal jet, so it is bulletproof."

"Small planes like that shouldn't be able to keep up with this jet; we should be fine," said Boudicea.

One of the planes buzzed them high and tight as it passed by. "Like I said, they've been heavily modified," said Sister Isabella. The plane circled around again and was coming straight at them. As it did, it fired a small missile.

Rael asked, "Are we also missile-proof?"

"There's no such thing," Sister Isabella informed her. She turned hard, and the jet did a half-roll. The missile skimmed the jet's bottom but didn't detonate until they were safely past it. Rael found herself sitting on the ceiling. She wasn't there long because the jet quickly rolled back upright. She landed with a thud between benches.

Boudicea turned around to look at her. She shook her head. "Oh, Rael, do behave back there."

Rael rubbed her sore bottom and got back on her bench seat. She tried to protest that she hadn't been playing at all when the plane went into a hard dive. Sister Isabella said, "There's two more at two o'clock. Judging by their markings, they're American."

"I don't see any markings," said Boudicea.

The sister explained, "That's because there are none. Only American Psychic Ops would use unmarked modified prop planes for combat. Everyone else would just use an ordinary fighter jet, because no one else would have the budget for such useless items."

Rael heard the word American and her ears perked up. Americans! They were her people. She was saved at last. Only, they were attacking her. She asked, "Why are the Americans attacking us? I'm an American! They should be helping me."

Sister Isabella explained, "The whole of US Psychic Ops, as well as over a third of the American government, have been supplanted by lizard people from the Psilon Moon of Raptor. Their main goal is to fatten up citizens and then eat them—sort of like sheep. Besides helping themselves to you, they got little use for you."

"They probably want to deny humanity your power. That would be just like the lizard people," added Boudicea.

"What?" exclaimed Rael. When she thought about it for a minute, it did sort of explain the American government's actions ever since she'd been born. "Are you telling me my own government is infested with reptilian aliens?"

"Don't be silly, Rael, they're interdimensional beings. We're living in a modern, civilized age. No one believes in space aliens anymore," corrected Boudicea.

"And they're going to kill us!" shouted Sister Isabella, steering the plane through another hail of bullets.

"Why again?" asked Rael.

"They must see you as a threat to their ideals of a new world order. It's an order with them on top and everyone else as hors d'oeuvres," explained Boudicea. She got out of her seat and went to a cabinet in the back of the plane. She opened it up and took out a backpack. She asked Sister Isabella, "How close are we to the drop zone?"

"Close enough," she replied.

"Open the hatch," ordered Boudicea.

"Hatch? What hatch?" asked Rael.

A ramp at the back of the plane began to drop. The cold wind rushed into the plane's fuselage. Boudicea started strapping the backpack onto Rael. Only, it wasn't a backpack, was it? It was a parachute!

"We're not jumping, are we?" asked Rael.

"We are. Remember, free-fall as far as possible before opening the chute or they'll strafe you as you slowly float down," replied Boudicea. Then she grabbed a pack for herself and proceeded to jump out the back of the airplane. She hadn't even put it on first. She'd probably be doing that midflight. Show-off! Sister Isabella left the cockpit and headed to the cabinet.

"Who's flying the plane?" asked Rael.

"No one."

"I have a small problem, Sister Isabella. I'm not sure I can just jump out of the back of a perfectly good airplane," explained Rael.

As if on cue, the starboard engine chose that moment to explode, right after taking a direct hit from a missile. "Don't worry, you're not," replied Sister Isabella. She made the sign of the cross, and then she jumped.

Rael inched toward the ramp. As she did, she stepped on the silver acorn. She picked it up. She could use some magic right about now. She looked into it. She could see her own reflection. It was heavily distorted, but it was there. She said out loud, "Okay, Rael, you can do this." Her reflection didn't look all that confident. "No, seriously, you can do it. We're not any higher up than we would be if we were skiing on a mountain, so it's just like skiing—only without the mountain being there." She looked at her reflection. It was giving her a "What the heck does that mean?" stare. She didn't really blame it.

The port engine went out. They were dead in the air. Correction: She was dead in the air. Everyone else had already left. She closed her eyes, kissed the silver acorn, and jumped. She opened her eyes again just in time to see one of the four lizard planes shoot a missile into the open hatch. The pope's plane exploded above her. Rael hoped the plane hadn't been expensive.

Okay, next step: Find the cord thingy. Rip cord? Right, that's what they called it. Only she didn't want hers to rip. Okay, find the totally-not-going-to-rip cord. It was such a better name. Only, where was it? She patted her front. It had to be here. Don't panic, it's here. A plane circled in the air in front of her. The other three were nowhere to be seen. She didn't care where they had gone. She only cared about the one that was left. It hit its booster jets and roared right at her. Okay, panic. It unloaded its machine guns at her. She flinched and tumbled in the air. The bullets struck the back of her cloak. The impact hit her like a ton of bricks. The bullets might have bruised her, but they didn't penetrate her at all. They bounced off. Ha, the cloak was bulletproof. Then she heard her parachute pack tear apart. It proceeded to disassemble itself in short order. The cloak was bulletproof, sure, but the parachute pack was not. Trouble. *What am I going to do now? I'm dead meat unless I can fly . . . wait, I can fly! I totally forgot.* She shouted into the empty sky, "I can fly!" Her wings appeared and unfolded themselves. She immediately stopped falling. She saw Sister Isabella's chute open below her. Boudicea was already drifting in for a landing. It must be nice not to be everyone's target.

She stroked her wings and darted toward the plane. *Let's see how they deal with a moving target.* The guns opened up, but the plane was lagging behind her. *Hah, I'm faster than they think.* It roared past her, having missed its target.

As it flew by her, Rael hurled the acorn into the jet intake. The engine exploded and bellowed black smoke. "How do you like them apples . . . er . . . acorns?" The plane exploded midair a second later. Rael hadn't even known her acorn was loaded. *And to think, I was going to roll that up my sleeve.*

She made for the ground now, beating her wings as fast as they could go. The other planes were nowhere to be seen. Perhaps they thought they had finished their job? She didn't care where they went. She was just happy they had left. She landed next to Boudicea, who was already disconnecting her parachute.

"I see that you didn't listen to me, so now every reptilian on Earth will know about your added features," Boudicea greeted her.

"Yes, I'm fine. Thanks for asking," replied Rael.

"I'm not," came Sister Isabella's voice. They darted into a thicket of dense underbrush. All Rael could see was the fabric of the nun's chute, but no nun to go with it. Boudicea yanked the fabric back to reveal the sister still under her chute. She was barely moving. Rael worked to get the chute off Sister Isabella's back. Once it was off, Boudicea bent down to examine the nun.

"Broken ankle," said Boudicea.

"That's what I was afraid of. I'm no good to you both in this condition, so leave me behind," said the sister.

"Are you sure? The lizard people might be back," said Rael.

"They will be. Those other three planes will be back on the hunt soon enough. That is all the more reason for you two to start moving. I'm not afraid of those soulless vermin," replied Sister Isabella.

"May good luck guide you," said Boudicea to her.

"And God bless you," replied the sister.

Boudicea walked off. Rael trailed after her. "You can't just leave her."

"I can, and I am," replied Boudicea.

"After all that she just did for us!"

"Because of all that she just did. She will catch up with us when she's on the mend. That old lady is tougher than she looks. It is up to us now to finish this leg of our journey. Now we must find the oracle that we seek. We're on a hunt, and nothing can delay us."

The land around them was mostly bare rock or sand, with only small thickets of shrubs here and there. What Rael didn't see was anything, within walking distance, that felt like a destination. "This oracle is where exactly?"

"This way."

"Are you sure?"

"I am more than sure. I know this place like the back of my hand. I practically grew up here. We go this way." Boudicea took a few steps to the east. Stopped. Turned back on herself. "I meant this way, toward the shore."

Chapter 13

King Minos's Maze, Crete

Rael dipped her toes in the warm waters of the Mediterranean Sea. Life could be a lot worse right now than spending time lounging on the sandy shore watching the waves roll in. It would be even better if she wasn't dressed in a black Lycra suit, which tended not to be the best choice of beachwear when the sun was high in the sky. She looked at her cloak lying on the sand next to her and wondered if the thing came with a built-in AC unit.

"I found it," announced Boudicea.

Rael turned her attention from the endless roll of the waves to the white rocks behind her. Boudicea had been searching through them for hours. Rael was starting to suspect something was wrong with the back of Boudicea's hand. Knowing things like the back of one's hand was, frankly, a silly expression. After all, it was one of the parts of their body people knew the least about. The back of her own hand could have been stepping out on her and seeing other people when she wasn't paying attention for years. She'd hardly have noticed. She looked at the back of her own hand. How well did she really know it? Her eyes, nose, hair, nails, and even her gams got far more of her attention. Her hand's back barely got an honorable mention most days.

Perhaps all these thoughts were silly. They were the kind of silly things you think about while sitting on the hot sand and dipping your toes in the warm water. Maybe they were not productive thoughts, but they felt somehow cosmically relevant anyway.

Rael stood up to see what Boudicea had finally found. The sun cast her shadow on the untouched sand around her. She frowned. She turned to look at her posterior. She asked, "Do you think this uniform makes my butt look big?"

"Men like big butts," replied Boudicea.

That was distinctly not a no. It was simple courtesy to answer no to such a question. Treating it as rhetorical would have been far better than giving that particular answer. The thing was, Rael cared little what men liked. Men liked movies about chunky men driving around in cars while shooting at—but, oddly, never hitting—each other. They were hardly to be counted on as authorities on anything related to aesthetics, and she considered her butt a work of fine art, or at least a work in progress. She cared most of all about what she liked. She would like it very much if her official demon-slaying uniform didn't make her butt look big. *My butt isn't too big*, she assured herself. *It must just be a trick of the light on the sand.* She scooped her cloak up and moved through the rocks.

"Okay, where is this secret entrance?" asked Rael.

Boudicea didn't reply. She had vanished somewhere among the white boulders. Well, that was certainly annoying. It was then that Rael saw exactly why Boudicea had gone into hiding. There was a man walking along the beach toward them. He was wearing a black suit with black sunglasses and carrying a black semiautomatic machine gun. He looked, in a word, suspicious. Rael didn't want to wait to say hello so she could get to know how friendly this man was. She hadn't met many friendly people lately. Besides, the warm necklace around her neck told her all she needed to know. She crouched down behind a large boulder. She crumpled into a ball and hoped her big butt didn't stick out and give her away.

She could hear the man's footsteps now. He wasn't stealthy at all. He was moving through the boulders, judging by the direction of the noise he was making. This was not a good development. He could stumble upon her at any moment. Temptation got the better of her, and she peeked out to see where he was. He was standing about twenty-five feet from her looking out across the boulder field. He didn't seem to be focused on her. What was he looking at? He opened his mouth and a long red tongue shot out. It latched onto what appeared to be a wharf rat. The man's jaws widened like a snake's, and he slowly slithered the still-alive rat into his mouth whole, without chewing once. He sucked in the rat's tail almost like a strand of spaghetti. Finished, the man wiped his chin with his sleeve. Okay, that was officially gross. One thing was for sure: These American lizard people had not given up the search even after Rael had managed to destroy one of their planes. Rael hoped Boudicea had finally found that entrance, because they were going to need a secret place to hide, and she didn't want that place to be this guy's gizzard.

The man's forked tongue snaked out again. He was tasting the air. Then he was on the move and headed straight toward Rael. She slunk back down behind her boulder. Very soon it would be time to spring into action. Now would probably be a good time to have a dagger or sword or gun. But her lessons hadn't gotten that far yet. All she had was her claw-nails. They were probably good enough to slice and dice him, as she was assuming this man was evil. He did work for the government after all.

Rael noticed loose sand falling between the boulders into her hiding place. He must be real close now. She sprang into action. "Have at you!" she shouted. It was a terrible catchphrase. She'd need to work on a better one later. She went to claw him but discovered the man was further away than she had thought. Sand must roll a long way between these boulders.

"You are doomed, human," he said. Rael suddenly felt better about her own catchphrase. He darted his tongue at her. It wrapped around her wrist. Then he lurched forward and fell off the boulder he was standing on. His sticky tongue dragged Rael down with him. Rael ended up face down in the sand beneath a boulder with the still-twitching reptilian corpse lying next to her. There was a twelve-inch viritatalium dagger with squirrel-themed ornamentation sunk into the back of his skull.

"You know, your butt doesn't look so big from this angle," said Boudicea.

Rael rolled over in the sand to see Boudicea standing on top of the boulder looking down at her. "Really?" She composed herself. "I mean, I wasn't really concerned about such trivial . . ."

"Good, never get distracted by the trivial." Boudicea dropped down next to the man. She reached into the man's pocket and pulled out a box. "A tracking device. So long as the man is still moving, they won't get suspicious about where he is." Boudicea pulled a wharf rat from her sleeve. She used a rubber band to strap the tracking device onto its back and then let it go. "We should be safe for now. Grab my dagger and your cloak, and then follow me. Ariadne awaits us."

"Who is Ariadne?"

"The oracle. She lives alone in the dark inside a secret cave here."

"That sounds pleasant." Rael stood up and dusted herself off. Well, she tried to dust herself off, but the sticky tongue refused to let go of her wrist. She used the thumb and forefinger of her left hand to peel the offensive object away. She then grabbed the dagger with her left hand and pulled. Then she grabbed it with both hands and pulled. Then she squatted, grabbed it with both hands, and pulled. The dagger finally released itself and Rael was planted on her bottom again. She stood up, dusted herself off, retrieved her cloak, and scampered off after Boudicea.

"I got your dagger. When do you think I'll get my own weapons?"

"When I think you won't cut off the end of your nose with one," replied Boudicea, retrieving the dagger from her. She stored it up her sleeve.

Rael put her cloak on. She said, "Okay, cloak, don't listen to her. How about some weapons?" Twenty ordinary acorns rolled down her sleeves. "Hey, the cloak did something magical for me for once! I mean, not what I wanted, but it's a start."

"Yes, it is a start, and this is a start as well." Boudicea rolled a large boulder a few feet, revealing a cave behind it. Boudicea explained, "These boulders around you do not look like much now, but they are all that remains of King Minos's grand port that welcomed ancient Athenians into his kingdom. Back then, this place was more than pleasant. It was the height of luxury. You do know who King Minos was?"

"He's the muffler guy with the Midas touch that turns everything into a car discount coupon, right?" Rael replied.

"Almost. He's the man who conquered the Mycenaeans long before what we think of as ancient Greece existed. He demanded fourteen slaves, seven male and seven female, from them as tribute. Two batches were sent to their doom inside this cave, until Theseus put a stop to it. But I'm sure you know that the history told to you, like most history, is a myth."

"Of course. Theseus was the guy with the flying horse, right?"

"That's Bellerophon."

"He found the golden fleas?"

"Fleece. And that's Jason."

"He tricked the Cyclops?"

"That's Odysseus."

"Okay, I don't know that myth."

"What do they teach kids in school these days?"

"I'm not really sure myself. I spent a lot of time with private tutors, which isn't so different from what I'm doing right now, I suppose."

"Then follow me, listen, and learn," said Boudicea. She went into the cave and Rael followed. There was a small entrance chamber with rows of torches on the wall. Boudicea picked one up. It lit as soon as it left its holder. "If my memory serves me, it is this way through the maze."

"Maze?"

Boudicea started walking the corridors of the worked-stone cavern. As she guided Rael through the maze, she talked. "Yes, King Minos had Daedalus design this labyrinth to hold his son, the minotaur. You know what a minotaur is, right?"

"Not really."

"A beast, a man, born from the union of the queen and a bull."

Rael interrupted, "Why would one . . ."

"It's best not to ask questions such as that. What is important to know is that this half-man, half-bull ate the flesh of those Greek slaves delivered to King Minos. Theseus put an end to that with the help of the original Ariadne, the king's own daughter. She fell in love with Theseus and helped him kill the minotaur."

"And they fell in love and lived happily ever after, and this oracle Ariadne is descended from Theseus and Ariadne."

"No, she is descended from Ariadne and Dionysus."

"But you said Ariadne fell in love with Theseus and helped him kill the minotaur, so what happened?"

"Perhaps her butt was too big for him."

"Haha, very funny."

"Rael, a woman doesn't always marry the first man she falls in love with."

"Is that another lesson?"

"It is just a fact. Theseus abandoned Ariadne on the Island of Naxos soon after she helped him."

"That fink! Uhm, then shouldn't Ariadne be on this Naxos and not Crete?"

"All that was long ago. People do move about, Rael, even people of legendary origin."

"I'm not sure what that is supposed to mean."

A howling sound swirled up through the white stone cavern. The dust on the floor picked up and danced around them. The howling winds picked up their pace until the torch finally blew out. Then in an instant the winds were gone. The torch lit up again.

"That means we can go see her now."

Rael asked, "Is there still a minotaur down there?"

"I told you, Theseus killed it."

"Lately I am finding that it's not like things to stay dead."

"His spirit still roams the lower levels of the maze. Only a fool travels down there. It will not harm you so long as you stay away from there. Follow me. You will be quite safe."

"Boudicea, I have one more question."

"Go on then."

"How is it that you practically grew up here?"

Boudicea pulled two silver acorns from her sleeve and held them out in her open hands. "It is a short story. Divicia was in love with Ariadne. When we were not out hunting, he'd come back here to her with open arms." Boudicea clapped the two acorns together and the cavern exploded in a blaze of white light.

In an instant the winding maze passages were gone. They were now standing in a room of polished white marble. On the walls were frescoes of celebration. The predominant motifs were wine, armored men, and women jumping over bulls. Giant gold braziers burned at the four corners of the room, and in the center of the room was a white-haired woman in a snow-white tunic with purple trim. She wore all manner of golden bracelets and trinkets. The old woman said to them, "Ariadne was in love with Divicia. Divicia had a young child that followed him like a puppy dog wherever he went. Even here. You have some nerve to come back here, my grown-up dog."

Boudicea ran up to the woman. She tried to embrace her, but the old woman did not open herself up to being embraced. She just stood before Boudicea with a defiant look in her eye. Boudicea settled for getting down on her knees before the woman and looked at the floor. Boudicea said, "Ariadne, I should not have stayed away from here so long."

"Why, because I've grown old and ugly in your absence? It is age, Boudicea. It is what happens to you in the course of time."

Boudicea clutched at the hem of Ariadne's tunic. "No, it's not that at all."

Ariadne stepped away from Boudicea and circled her. "Why are you here then, if not to flaunt your youth and beauty at me?"

"I need your help. There is a phylactery that can house a powerful demon queen. I must locate it before it can be used for great harm."

"You would rather use me, then. My gifts, that is all I ever was to you—just a means to an end."

"You know that is not true."

"Perhaps once, but now I am not sure. And the child with you?"

"She's my apprentice, Rael."

"You are the teacher instead of the student this time around. Hah, pray that you fare better than my beloved Divicia in that game."

She walked up to Rael. She removed a bracelet and peered through it at Rael. She moved it around her face. Through the bracelet Rael could see

Ariadne as she had been, and not as she was. She had been young once and beautiful. It was no wonder warriors had fallen in love with her. It then occurred to Rael the bracelet must work both ways. She wondered how Ariadne saw her. Ariadne turned to Boudicea and said to her, "Please, do not dirty my floor. Stand up like a woman, my child. For the sake of old memories, I will help you now. Come with me and receive a reading, and then leave me alone. For my poor heart cannot bear the sight of you a second longer than I have to. The memories you bring to me aren't all pleasant ones."

A stairway leading down appeared in the middle of the marble floor. The old woman walked down the stairs. The four braziers burning in the grand marble room went out. All Rael could see was a faint glow coming up from below. Rael said, "She seems nice."

Boudicea stood up. She wiped her eyes. "I often dream that time can heal old wounds, but time just wounds us more and more as we age." She didn't say that to Rael. She said it more to herself. Boudicea headed for the stairs, and Rael followed her. Rael was confused by it all—as usual.

Down below they found Ariadne sitting behind a marble table that stood on a mosaic floor. The part of the mosaic Rael could see showed a woman lying on a stone bench with vapors around her head. A man stood next to her with parchment and stylus in hand. It must have taken a long time to put all the little stones that made up that mosaic into place. Ariadne fanned out a deck of cards. She said, "Pick a card, any card." Boudicea reached for one, but the old woman pulled the deck back into her hand. "Not you. Rael must choose your fate, for she is to be the cause of it."

Boudicea stood back. She looked at Rael and said, "Go ahead."

"Is it to be a magic trick?" asked Rael.

"Yes," replied Ariadne. Ariadne fanned the deck out in her hand and offered the cards again. Rael was quick to pick one. On the back they were all very much the same, so one card seemed to be as good as any other. Although that's not how these tarot cards worked now, was it? She didn't really know. In a sane world they didn't really work at all, but the world was hardly sane. She knew that now.

"Let me see it, Rael," said the old woman. Rael handed it to Ariadne. "Ah, the lovers card. Is that what you want? Attraction, beauty, love? Those qualities are so tempting. What young woman could resist having them?"

Rael's eyes grew big. Was she really to fall in love? That sounded nice. It sounded a bit scary as well. She wanted to know more. She wanted to hear all about it. Although that would ruin the surprise of it all. Wasn't love supposed to be a surprise? It was a thing that happened to you before you realized it had already happened to you. Yes, it was supposed to be a surprise.

Boudicea added, "It could also mean a trial that has been overcome. And that is what she wants. It's what we all want for her. Help me end this poor girl's suffering."

The old woman gathered the deck up and put it away. She scolded Boudicea, "Let Rael speak for herself!" Boudicea shrank back from Ariadne like a wounded child.

Rael said, "I would love not to be almost killed all the time, so I guess Boudicea is correct."

"That is far better than the alternative: to be killed!" Ariadne reminded her. "You would have been better off falling in love. As painful as death is, as lovely as life can be, that is what love is, but it is not in the cards for you right now." The lights went out. It stayed dark only briefly before a crystal ball at the center of the table illuminated the room. Ariadne's eyes rolled back in her head. She placed her left hand on the crystal ball. She said,

Follow the path winding north, nature sourced, south of where the
  Nile does flow.
Lair of hate, care do take, demon cry, grown men die, dares no
  man to go.
Animals, gear laden, walk you to oasis, their white palm haven.
Out in the dry desert dwells a step pyramid. Under sand it recedes.
Deep in there lurk cultists, Ilitar-loving men, planning their foul
  deeds.

The room went dark again. Again, they were only briefly in darkness before a light illuminated their surroundings. The source of the light was a burning torch that was now back in Boudicea's hand. Rael saw that the room she had just been in had completely vanished. She was now back in the cavern maze. All traces of Ariadne were gone from view. The howl of the minotaur's spirit echoed again. It sent a chill down Rael's spine. It was hard to think Boudicea could have seen this as her home once.

Boudicea said, "And that was Ariadne."

Rael replied, "Okay, that was weird, but what did any of what she just said mean?"

"It means that we are headed south across the sea to Egypt. The rest we will figure out along the way."

"And how do we get there?" asked Rael.

"This way. I have a plan on how we get there."

Boudicea led her out of the maze. Rael was rather glad to leave. The place might have been a little too weird even for the new normal. As they traced their steps, she thought of Ariadne's words, but they didn't stir up a meaning for her. They felt like the kind of words whose meaning only made sense after the words happened to you. The pyramids were in Egypt, as was the Nile, so Boudicea's plan seemed an appropriate one.

They emerged from the maze. As soon as they left it, the stone rolled back into place. Boudicea climbed the nearest rock. She said, "Our dead lizard friend came from this direction. Hopefully he came alone." Then she dropped down from the rock and set off along the sandy beach.

More tongue-shooting, rat-eating government workers Rael didn't really care to meet. Boudicea clearly didn't want to meet one either. Rael had a suspicion that Boudicea only wanted his plane. They soon found it parked on the shore just over the horizon. If Boudicea knew how to fly it, they were in luck—and Rael took it for granted Boudicea would know how to fly it because she knew just about everything else.

There was one problem with the current plan. Another lizard man stood guard over the plane. Boudicea said to Rael, "Wait here." Rael planted herself in the sand. Boudicea drew her dagger. The lizard man looked to be armed with a submachine gun. It didn't feel like a fair fight at all. He should have come much better prepared to go up against a hunter like Boudicea.

Chapter 14

A Paddle Ship Sailing on the Nile, Egypt

he little ceiling fan circled slowly round and round. It was doing nothing at all but making Rael dizzy from staring at it while she wondered what its actual function was. Rael suspected it had been placed there just to mock her. If a breeze blew from it, it was a very subtle one. Rael's new uniform was just about the least comfortable thing to wear in the sweltering heat of the cabin. Apparently, druids don't pick their demon-hunting uniforms based on comfort in high heat. The only good news to be had was that today marked the third day since someone had last tried to kill her. It was a new record, and one that she sure hoped would be continuously broken. She was lying on top of the sheets of her bed inside a stateroom of a paddle ship slowly sailing south up the Nile, wondering why she was there at all.

Boudicea came out of the powder room wrapped in her cloak yet looking cool as a cucumber. Rael sighed. "How can you stand this heat?"

"It is a bit warm in here," agreed Boudicea as if the subject was open to debate. She ran her left hand up the opposite arm's sleeve. Out came a peach-colored cotton summer dress. She tossed it at Rael. "If you need to dress better for the heat, you can put this on."

Rael shot up out of bed. She replied, "You mean the whole time I was freezing my butt off up in the Alps, you could have puffed out a warm set of clothes for me from your magic cloak?"

"Don't be silly, Rael." Boudicea slid another dress out. "I bought these dresses after we landed in Cairo and while you were distracted looking at the pyramids."

"I wasn't distracted by them. I had thought we were going inside them. Ariadne mentioned them in her little poem."

"No, she did not mean those pyramids."

"How can you be sure?"

"Confidence makes me so sure. We seek a step pyramid, lost in the sand, closer to the source of the Nile, yet out by an oasis. I've never heard of this place. The best we can do for now is get as far as the Aswan Dam on this ship. I strongly suspect by then I will have learned much more about what we seek. Hopefully I shall learn it much sooner than that, as I am expecting news."

"From whom?"

She shrugged. "If one is silent and listens, one never knows who may tell you what you need to know. Come now, get dressed. If we stay in this cabin for the whole journey despite this heat, people will think we're acting suspiciously."

"You mean we're going out in public without our cloaks and unarmed?"

"The wits in our head are lethal enough for most occasions."

Rael had never seen Boudicea kill a demon using just her wits yet, but she hardly doubted the statement. Rael was actually more grateful than alarmed to be leaving her current outfit behind. If Boudicea felt they were safe, they must be.

Rael got up and peeled her outfit off. That's what her own deadly wits were telling her to do, and she wasn't not going to listen to them. She dropped the Lycra on the floor. It immediately folded itself up. She picked it up and placed it on the bed. It was the oddest garment she'd ever had. It never ripped or stayed dirty for long. It was rather convenient. She looked over and saw Boudicea was already slipping into her own sundress. It was emerald-green to match her eyes. Rael asked, "Don't druids wear under-wear ever?"

"Why do you ask?"

"It's just that if you go out like that and the sun hits your light-colored dress, the men around here are going to get sore eyes from staring."

"They are men. They will stare no matter what you wear. They are such simple creatures. If you require to wear more, I do believe I bought all that you'll need, and it is kept in our closet."

Rather than listen to more advice on men, Rael opened the closet. Boudicea might lack basic modesty, but Rael saw no reason to abandon it. Indeed, the idea of chafing under her dress in the hot sun sounded nothing like comfort. She found that the closet was filled with everything she would require. The thought that occurred to her was that she had spent the previous night sweltering in a Lycra bodysuit when she could have been much more comfortable much sooner. She said, "You couldn't have bought all this while I was looking at the pyramids. I only looked at them for a few minutes. Besides you don't even have any money."

"It is a mystery now, isn't it?"

Rael strongly suspected magic was at work. More than that, she knew now for sure that she'd frozen her assets off in the Alps for nothing. Only, it was probably not for nothing. Everything, every day was a lesson. Even back then did Boudicea know they'd end up working together? She must have. What the ultimate point of most of these lessons would be, Rael had no idea. She did know that Dynami had spent forty years learning them, and he was still an amateur—albeit a cute one. Forty years. Rael had quite a hill to climb and a long time to climb it. When she reached the top maybe she'd understand the point of all these lessons. Until then, she was wearing underwear at the very least.

She pulled the sundress over her head and rechecked her hair. It needed to be properly fluffy to hide the horns. It would have helped if she could see herself in the closet door's mirror, but all she saw was Boudicea standing behind her watching as she patiently waited for her.

"Do you like the dress?" asked Boudicea.

"It's a bit, you know, short. My mother would never . . ." She stopped. The thought of her mother, even in disapproval of such a dress, pained her.

"Yes, your mother would *what?*"

"It doesn't matter."

"Mothers matter, Rael, they matter greatly."

"I'm not sure how you know, seeing as you never had one."

"Ariadne was like a mother to me. She still is."

Rael probably should keep her big mouth shut at times. There was no reason to have brought up mothers at all. Still, Boudicea didn't seem to mind the topic any. Rael gave up trying to fix her hair without being able to use a mirror and placed a wide-brimmed sun hat on instead. She asked, "Aren't you going to put on a sun hat? You're so fair-skinned you'll burn to a crisp without one."

"Devils burn, not druids," replied Boudicea. She snapped open a pair of sunglasses with a flick of her wrist and put them on. Then she opened the door. "Good. Now remember we're daughter and stepmother out on holiday from Canada."

"Last time I was out on holiday, I ended up on the train trip to hell. Are you sure it's safe on this boat?"

"Check your necklace if you doubt me." Rael pressed the necklace to her chest. It was cold. She relaxed. It was sort of fun to be on holiday. She snapped her own sunglasses with her wrist. They snapped out of her hand and fell to the floor. She picked them up and put them on gently.

"We're ready. Let's go break some hearts," announced Boudicea.

They walked the outer deck of the ship and went up some stairs to the top deck patio. It was labeled "sundeck," and the label wasn't a lie. The sun beat down on it. An Egyptian waiter looking uncomfortably warm in his white suit met them at the top of the stairs. Rael could see him look them over with disapproval. But he said nothing. Boudicea said, "Is there a place for two available?"

"Sun or no sun?" he asked.

Boudicea replied, "As you can see by our milky white skin, we're Canadian. We Canadians don't care for the sun, eh."

He led them past several other passengers. There seemed to be people of all nationalities. An obvious pair of Americans stood out: He wore an American flag speedos, while she wore a string bikini, and both displayed more confidence in their appearance than reality warranted. He watched

Boudicea pass by; she didn't. Rael had known they'd attract attention with Boudicea looking like that. Still, everyone else here was dressed for the sun, even the old ladies sitting around a table. It made Rael feel less exposed.

The waiter dumped them off at two lounge chairs placed under sun umbrellas. "Ladies, would you care for a drink?" he asked.

"I'll have a mojito, and my daughter will have a strawberry Italian pop," announced Boudicea.

"With lots of ice," added Rael.

Boudicea lay down and pulled out a book on Egyptian history. Rael wondered where she'd got it, but she knew it wasn't worth asking. She just wished she had a book of her own. All she had was a glass of soda, which arrived a few minutes later. She sat back and people-watched through the safety of her sunglasses. She needed to hone her people-reading skills. She'd been surprised far too many times by people lately, and this seemed like a good time to work on her hunter skills. A good hunter could read a room and pick out the prey.

There was that American couple, but they seemed harmless. Beside that couple, there was an Arab. He was dressed in a white thobe with black headgear. He seemed interested in watching the Nile scenery pass by. He didn't appear suspicious. There was also an Asian couple that appeared wealthy, judging by the labels on their clothing and accessories. He was studying a tour book, and his wife was fast asleep. There was a smattering of retired folks talking around a lounge chair circle in European languages that Rael couldn't distinguish. All in all, they must be harmless, as the golden acorn on her necklace was the same temperature as the ice in her glass. She remembered her drink and began to sip it. The ice had already melted.

It was then that he walked up the steps and onto the sundeck. He was tall and well-built and gave off a hint of having seen a little action, just like a solid classic American muscle car. He was the type of man a woman would notice if she were into that type of thing. He was clearly Egyptian, but he dressed in Western casual. He had a gold chain with an Egyptian fertility symbol inside his mostly unbuttoned Hawaiian shirt. It kept his mat of chest hair company. The waiter approached him, but the man brushed him off quickly. His eyes fell straight on Boudicea. Well, of course they did. Rael looked over at Boudicea. She was nose-deep in her book. He started to approach them. Rael tried to look busy, but all she managed to do was bite on the end of the straw and stare at him.

He stopped just short of them, making sure to cast his shadow over their bodies. He said, "My friends call me Amen, and I can feel almost instinctively that we are going to be good friends." Rael opened her mouth to answer but stopped. He wasn't looking at her at all. That comment was meant only for Boudicea.

Boudicea pushed her glasses up with her book. She replied, "A man? I don't remember ordering a man."

"No Amen, not a man. Amen Johonson to be precise. I'm a paleontologist from a prestigious university in England."

"Probably Leeds from the looks of it. Amen, I've always thought that a paleontologist should stick to studying interesting lifeforms from the past, so that rules me out," replied Boudicea.

"I like to make exceptions for interesting lifeforms from the present. I do it all the time. For instance, have you ever seen an Egyptian crocodile? They're very big and extremely dangerous but well worth seeing. Seeing one would be bound to give a woman like you quite a thrill. You can get a spectacular view of one near my cabin on the lower sundeck."

"We're not here to interact with wild animals," Boudicea replied.

"We?" he asked quizzically, finally looking in Rael's direction.

Boudicea gestured over to Rael. "My daughter, Rael." Rael gave him a sheepish wave. He'd already lost interest in Rael and moved back to focusing on Boudicea. It was rather annoying to wear a mother-disapproved short sundress and have all eyes fall on the friend you're with.

He said, "She looks too old to be your daughter."

"Step-daughter, but I feel as if she's my own. And as I said, neither of us are in need of interaction with wild animals."

"A shame, because the wild ones, so I'm told, are the best to interact with," he replied.

Boudicea swung her legs off the chair and stood up. Rael figured this rudely forward man was in for it. Boudicea's book got tossed onto the lounge chair. "I suppose I shall have to see it for myself then. Rael, wait here. I do know how the sight of reptiles has upset you lately."

Rael said, "But I could . . ."

"Just wait here," interrupted Boudicea.

Rael slunk back down into her lounge chair. Boudicea walked off toward the stairs, twirling her sunglasses by the earpiece. Rael was pretty sure her hips didn't have to sway as much as they did right now to walk over there. Amen didn't rush to catch up. He got a good look first, and then he followed. They disappeared below the deck as they walked down the stairs together.

"Did that just happen?" Rael exclaimed to no one. She looked around. No one else seemed to even care. *Okay, Rael, that did just happen.* Now she just had to know what that was all about. She downed her drink and scampered over to the rail. It would be snooping to just peek at them. Then again, maybe she'd see the crocodile too. She'd never seen one before. *Oh, forget the pretext, just look.* She casually glanced down. They were gone from view. Now, where had they gone? Maybe they were under the upper-deck awning in the shade. Rael placed her hands on the rail and leaned over as far as she could. They still weren't within view.

A pair of rough hands pressed down on hers. She looked up. She was staring into the eyes of another man wearing black headgear. The Arab was standing over her. He was well over six feet tall. He said to her, "You are Rael Armstrong." It wasn't posed as a question. He knew her name, which wasn't a good sign. Rael tried to get away, but his strength pinned her hands to the rail. He wouldn't do anything here, not with so many people watching, she hoped.

"What do you want?" she asked, stalling for time.

"The same thing as you. Ilitar realizes that now. We both want the same thing. That is a good thing, no? If Ilitar had realized that we could be working together sooner, much time could have been saved."

Oh great, a talking Ilitar cultist, and Boudicea nowhere in sight. That acorn around her neck must be faulty; it was hardly doing a thing. "Sorry, but I'm not into ruling the world right now." She wiggled in her place, trying to free herself from him, but she was pinned. She was still able to fly. Maybe she'd take him for a ride and see how he liked it.

"You'd be unwise to spread your wings and alert everyone to your extraordinary powers. We abyssal demons are not your enemy. You must understand that our queen already rules a world vastly greater than this dump you call home, so why would she want to come here to be a slave to a mere man in this one?"

That actually made sense. She remembered now that the other red demon had attacked the Maleficium Society to save her. The cult's demons were blue. She stopped struggling. She said, "Very well then, what would you suggest?"

"Turn back. You're going the wrong way. We both want to stop them, so turn back. Listen to me: Join me, and together we can end this." He released her and backed away. Rael spun around ready for a fight, only he wasn't anywhere to be seen. She glanced at the remaining guests. The retired people were still gabbing away. The Asian couple were now both napping. The Americans appeared to be eating chips. No one cared about what had just happened with Rael.

She went over to the waiter. "Did you see a tall Arab man leave the sundeck just now?"

"No." That was all he said in reply. He didn't appear interested in offering more. Okay, what was that about? Ilitar and Rael wanted the same thing? He couldn't have given her more information on that? It felt like an important point to expand upon. The difference between the blue and red demons now interested Rael a great deal. This was all so confusing, and only a mentor could tell her what it meant. Now, where was she?

Rael hustled down the stairs. Boudicea wasn't on the lower deck looking at crocodiles. Rael walked the deck until she caught sight of Boudicea. She was standing on the bow of the ship. Amen was next to her. They were holding hands and talking. Then they were doing more than talking. He kissed her! It wasn't a short kiss either. Rael forgot all about the cultist. Clearly some druids could kiss anywhere when they wanted to. She ducked behind a collection of wicker baskets near the bow. She couldn't just interrupt them. She shouldn't watch them either, yet she did. She thought of Dynami and his boasts of how druids made love at the full moon like they were filled with madness. Judging by this kiss, Dynami was right. Druids knew more about love than Rael had realized. They certainly weren't celibate.

They parted at last. Amen said, "Boudi, we've just come together again. Must you leave me so soon?"

"I must act on Ariadne's information."

"I know other, more trustworthy oracles we could consult."

"There is none I trust more than Ariadne."

"At one time maybe, but now the old witch has it in for you."

"Nonsense, she is more my mother than any other woman ever has been."

"Parents are not always to be trusted."

"If the pyramid I seek is the one you spoke of just now, then Ariadne's words will have come true. Therefore, I must go there and end this. After that, I will be back to see you again soon enough. You understand, Rael will not be safe until this is over. It's my duty to defend her to the last. I must act quickly."

"You care that much for this young woman with you?"

"I'm her mentor now. I shall care for her as Divicia did for me."

"I see, but with a girl like her, will it ever be over for you? Can we ever be together?"

Boudicea replied, "I don't know."

"Boudi, don't let the Order get you killed. I need you alive."

"I don't die so easily." She kissed him again. They lingered. His hands explored her.

Rael was starting to feel quite the third wheel right about now. Then they parted. Boudicea was walking in Rael's direction. Rael might die of embarrassment if Boudicea discovered she'd been spying on her. Rael climbed into the nearest wicker basket and pulled the lid over her head. Only, the hat prevented that from working at all. She tossed the hat and settled in. A few moments later, she popped the lid again. Boudicea was gone. That had been a near thing.

She took one last look at Amen. Who was he? Whoever he was, he was staring off at the Nile, lost in thought. He loved Boudicea. That much was clear as day. It was Rael's fault they weren't together. Rael would apologize to him for being such a bother if they ever met again.

Rael headed back to the sundeck. Boudicea was already lounging with her book. Rael headed back to her own chair. She needed to act casual. *Don't make her suspect a thing.* She sat back on her chair and picked up her glass. She sucked on the straw, which made a noise, reminding her she'd already emptied it.

The noise made Boudicea lower her book. She looked toward Rael. Even with the glasses on, Rael felt she had a pair of accusing eyes dead set on Rael. "When I returned, I found that you were gone. Did you have fun wherever you went off to?" asked Boudicea.

"I just went to the bathroom," Rael replied.

"That does sound like fun."

"Did you get to see the crocodile?"

"There wasn't time."

"Oh, such a shame."

"I am still hoping that there will be time later for another chance." She tossed Rael's sun hat onto her lap. The book went back up over her face.

Okay, that confirmed that Boudicea knew Rael had spied on her. Of course she knew. . . she knew everything, and she didn't seem upset about Rael's spying. Rael wanted to ask who Amen really was, but she couldn't. Boudicea clearly wasn't interested in explaining who he was to her. Instead, Boudicea had played a ruse. Rael was certain of it. Boudicea had come here to meet him, and he had told her something important. Oh, Rael remembered: She knew something important too. Rael lowered her voice, "Boudicea, I learned something important while you were gone."

"About men?"

"No, not about that stuff. There is a cultist here on the boat. He told me that we're going in the wrong direction. He wants us to team up with him and turn back."

"What would you expect from a cultist but a lie?"

"But he claims to be an Ilitar cultist, and I do recall the red demon attacking my father's men. It helped me escape. I think he's here because he wants to help us somehow."

"Demons only have their own side. Your father thinks he can control them, but the demon always wins if it can. Beware of them always."

"Oh, right. But then, why didn't this cultist just try to kidnap me again?"

"A good question. If we see him again we'll be sure to extract that answer from him at dagger point. I did not expect to make it through to their pyramid undetected, though I hadn't wished to be detected so soon. We will need to cut the boat part of the trip short now."

The idea of using violence against the man made Rael uneasy. He'd been forceful but not violent with her. Still, he was in a demon cult. That meant he was a liar, right? What about Boudicea's man? Was he a liar too? No, Boudicea wouldn't kiss a liar. And what a kiss it had been. It was all enough to make Rael feel . . . sort of jealous. No, that wasn't it at all. She felt disappointed. Yeah, that's how she really felt. Clearly Dynami could have kissed her had he wanted to. After all, Boudicea had just kissed someone.

Rael said, "Dynami said druids can only kiss each other within a druid grove at full moon."

Boudicea lowered her book. "Am I supposed to respond to that statement?"

"I want clarification. It's important. Well, not *important* important, but all the same, I'd like to know the rules."

"Because you wish to kiss Dynami?"

"No! It's just that . . . well, no one gave me the official rundown, you see? I wouldn't want to turn into a pillar of salt or anything because I broke a sacred druid rule."

Boudicea replied, "Yes, I understand now. You want a lesson on the druid rules of love."

"Yes," replied Rael sheepishly.

"Remember that a dedicated hunter never allows a distraction such as love to interfere with a mission."

"But you just kissed . . ."

"What you're allowed to do by the rules and what you are capable of doing are two different things."

"But what if the Order found out?"

"Arianrhod can see what's in your heart. There is no fooling her. That is the only truth that matters. Everything else is just a formality of mannerisms."

"I don't understand."

"Yes, that sounds very much like love to me." Boudicea put the book over her face again. Rael very much doubted she was reading it. Boudicea didn't play by all the rules. That was living dangerously—or was it? Rael felt warm again. She'd need another glass of ice-cold soda.

Chapter 15

Valley of the Kings, Egypt

"I feel like a Bedouin dressed like this," complained Rael, walking down the ramp and exiting onto the shore.

"If we're lucky, people will mistake us for two of them," replied Boudicea.

"Then we're no longer posing as Canadian tourists?"

"Not for much longer."

It was official, then: They were leaving the boat, and the vacation part of the trip was over. It seemed rather pointless to book a boat trip up the Nile and depart before it reached the end of the trip. Then again, most of the passengers were departing today anyway for a day trip. This was a major tourist spot, and the shoreline was bustling with activity. The thing was, while everyone else was departing to see the sights, Boudicea had a more permanent exit in mind. Which was odd, particularly if the source of the Nile was what they were seeking—and Rael had assumed it was, given Ariadne's message. This boat was sailing further up the Nile, so why get off before the end?

Rael heard the stubborn grunt of a camel. Soon after, the captain of the boat arrived with two camels in tow. He said to Boudicea, "I have had my people pack up your things onto these two camels, as you requested.

I do warn you, it would be better if you stayed with the tour. The open desert can be a dangerous place for women."

"We will be okay," replied Boudicea.

"You crazy Americans take too many chances," he said.

"We're Canadian," corrected Boudicea.

He threw his hands up in the air and replied, "If you will not listen to reason, then Allah please look after you with fortune, because I will not be responsible for you." He returned to his boat ramp to escort other guests.

Boudicea handed the reins of a camel to Rael. She said, "You do know how to ride a camel, right?"

"Sure, we did it all the time back home in Colorado."

Boudicea mounted, and her camel stood up. Rael climbed aboard hers. It just sat there. Rael pulled on the reins. "Up!" she commanded. It lay down. She could feel Boudicea watching her, judging. Camel riding seemed like a dirty test to throw at an American teenager. Rael complained, "I think mine is defective."

Boudicea lectured, "It is easy. Just remember, the camel dislikes you, and it will bite you and spit at you when needed. It is up to you to show it who is boss. Only then will it respect you."

"That sounds just lovely." Rael's camel was already eyeing her with suspicion. She'd almost suspect it of being a demon if not for the smell. No, it couldn't be a demon, because no demon smelled as bad as this camel. She gently pulled the reins again. "Giddyap, up, up, up." The camel wasn't buying what she was selling and appeared to fall asleep.

Rael looked to Boudicea for help. Boudicea looked distracted. She was watching a party from the boat heading off into the distance. They were all setting off to sightsee. If Rael were acting like a normal tourist, then she'd be doing the same thing. Rael suspected the cultist showing up had forced them to scrap those plans. The thing was, he hadn't showed up a second time. Where had he gone? He wasn't coming off the boat. Rael was pretty sure that she'd have recognized him if he had come off. Rael caught sight of Amen as he came down the ramp and claimed a donkey to ride. Rael swore she heard Boudicea sigh as Amen ignored them both. Perhaps they were leaving for more than one reason. Amen rode off into the distance, and Boudicea turned to Rael. "Let's go. There is nothing left for us here."

Rael said, "I thought we were heading to the source of the Nile."

"This is it. Over that way is the Valley of the Kings. The pharaohs were the source of the Nile's power for generations." She pointed into the desert. "Out beyond that is the open desert. It is a desolate place. In most places around the world, white is the color of light. It is the symbol of life, rebirth, and renewal. The opposite is true of black. It is the color of the night. It is the symbol of death and decay. That is not so in Egypt. In Egypt, the black of the fertile Nile soil gives life, and the white of the endless desert brings death. I've been told there is a place called the Oasis of the White Palms out in the shifting sands. Near it there is said to be a lost pyramid. Inside that pyramid, we will find our cult."

"You were told all this by whom?"

Boudicea replied, "The prophecy of Ariadne and no other." Boudicea kicked her camel and it moved off into the desert. Rael figured someone other than Ariadne had had a hand in this information, but for whatever reason Boudicea wanted to keep her obvious source a secret. It didn't matter to Rael, so she kicked her own camel. Her camel opened a lazy eye and then spit at her. It landed a direct hit to Rael's left eye. The camel almost laughed. Then it reluctantly got to its feet and followed after Boudicea.

The traffic leaving the valley was light. Once they'd made it past the tourist zone and crossed the last road, things grew pretty grim. After another two hours, they found themselves alone. Alone, yes, but with plenty of sores in all the wrong places. Camels were as pleasant on Rael's posterior to ride as she'd figured they would be. She could use a break. More like, she could use an ice bath. Chances were slim of a single cube of ice around here, though.

"Do you think we could rest?" asked Rael.

"You can't be tired. All you're doing is sitting; the camel is doing all the real work," replied Boudicea.

"My bottom feels otherwise."

"Then we should stop." The response took Rael by surprise. She'd already opened her mouth to argue further and hadn't expected to win so easily. She never won these types of conversations with Boudicea. Boudicea dismounted. Rael's camel was less obliging. Now that it had gotten into the rhythm of moving, it didn't seem to want to stop. Boudicea grabbed the reins. She said, "Sit tight."

"Me or the camel?" asked Rael.

"You." Rael had been afraid of that. The whole point of stopping was to get her butt off this beast. Well, for her, that was the whole point. There must be something up. They wouldn't just stop to rest. She felt for her necklace to feel its temperature.

"You there, put your hands up!" shouted a voice. The need to know the temperature quickly faded. Two men came riding up on camels. They were dressed as nomads. They had AK-47s with them. How had two men managed to sneak up on them on camelback? Rael turned to ask Boudicea that very question, but she was gone. Of course, they hadn't snuck up on them at all. Boudicea had seen them coming. The men rode up to Rael. They noticed Boudicea missing. "Your friend, where is she?" one asked.

"She's indisposed," replied Rael.

"Indisposed?" questioned the nomad.

"You know . . . potty break," explained Rael.

He responded by swinging the butt of his gun at her. It caught her on her head. She proceeded to fall off the camel. The desert sand was supposed to be soft, but naturally Rael fell on what appeared to be a defective patch.

The two men were off their camels now. They clearly weren't nomads, but bandits. The captain had tried to warn them it wouldn't be safe out here. Rael had to agree he'd been correct about that. One bandit said, "Quick, tie up the camels. We will take them back loaded."

"And this girl?"

"We can leave them both out here to die. It's better than shooting them. If their bodies are found, no one will be any the wiser this way."

"But her money and jewelry?"

"We've made enough already. Just leave her to the elements. Let's go."

Rael didn't like the sound of that conversation. She started to get up, but one of the bandits trained his gun on her. He warned, "Not so fast. At least against the sun you have a chance. Against my gun, not so much." He followed that with a laugh. Rael frowned and gave in. He did have a point, even if it wasn't as funny a point as he thought.

It was then that the camels on which these two men had arrived started to run off. The man with his gun trained on Rael swore and shouted for his friend to stop them. His friend didn't answer. The man ran over to where his friend had been gathering up Rael's and Boudicea's camels. From a distance, Rael saw that his bandit friend was face down on the ground. The man kicked at his friend to turn him over. Rael had seen enough death for a lifetime lately, so in an instant she knew this man was dead.

Rael said to the remaining bandit, "I'd give up if I were you."

He wasn't her. He was pissed off that his friend was dead. She had a feeling he was thinking about taking it out on her. He moved on her in anger. Boudicea moved on him quicker. Rael didn't see where she came from, because Boudicea moved like the wind. He was paying attention to Rael and not her. It was a fatal mistake. Boudicea pierced his gun hand with her blade. He bellowed in pain as he dropped the weapon.

Boudicea yelled at the bandit, "Run!" He hesitated. Boudicea added, "Against the sun you stand a chance." She paused to kick his weapon up into her hands. She pointed it at him. She continued, "Against me you will have no chance."

His eyes darted to Rael. Having been knocked on the head by him, Rael was feeling less than sympathetic to his cause. She scooped up his friend's gun and pointed it at him. He cursed, "May Allah take from you all that you have!" Then he ran off into the sand.

Boudicea watched him disappear over the horizon and then took the weapon from Rael's hand. Boudicea reassured her, "Don't worry, Allah doesn't like bandits any more than we do." She pointed over to the dead man. "Strip him."

"We're not going to talk to the dead again, are we?"

"Just do it."

Rael was less than enthusiastic about the assignment. She approached the fallen man. Rael could see his throat had been slit. She tugged off his outer clothes and stopped. There was no need to go further. He had a white uniform under his garments. Just like the ones the crew on the boat wore. She examined his face again. He was the waiter from the sundeck on the boat. She remembered his face. Rael said, "So, there were more cult members onboard than just the man who talked to me."

Boudicea kicked the sand. "No, it would appear that these men are just ordinary thieves. Sent out by their captain to rob us and leave us out here to die, no doubt."

"But when we left, the captain seemed concerned for our safety."

"Yes, he did seem concerned."

The prospect of being hunted by cultists was starting to feel normal to Rael. The idea that she had almost been killed by ordinary highway bandits felt almost prosaic by comparison. She looked at his lifeless face and turned away. She asked, "Must we kill everyone we meet?"

"He wasn't worried about doing the same to us. Still, I do worry about it. I had stopped here with the thought that we had attracted some cultists. It would have confirmed Ariadne's prophecy, but it was not to be, so we will press on until we find them."

"What about our rest?" asked Rael.

"Rest is for the dead. Just ask him how it feels now that he has it." Boudicea mounted her camel. Rael looked at the dead waiter in the sand. There was nothing more she could do for him. What would become of him out here she did not know. Rael had a new worry now. She worried she might become like Boudicea. She worried she might become too used to death and killing. She mounted her camel and rode off after Boudicea.

It didn't take long for Rael to become disappointed in the high desert. That moment of action involving the boat crew was the end of the exciting part of the desert. The endless shifting sand failed to materialize for the most part. The land they moved through was relatively flat. It was barren of anything that was not rubble or a boulder. Once in a while they got lucky and spotted a shrub. Why the shrub bothered to hang out in such a drab place was its own business, and certainly they never stopped to ask one why it chose to be out here.

The traffic out here in the sand was minimal. She heard an airplane off in the distance from time to time, but they saw no one. They settled into a routine of moving between dusk and dawn, when the sun made it more tolerable to move. During the day they sat in a tent made of camel hide, which Rael strongly suspected just caused more bitter feelings on the part of her mount. Fortunately, they never ran out of water, as Boudicea seemed to always have a full canteen to share. What they didn't have was an oasis or a white palm after three days of being out here.

It was noon on the fourth day, and all they were doing at lunchtime was sitting out of the sun waiting to move again. Their tent was tucked behind a large mass of boulders. It gave them a little shade—not that it helped much. Rael sat on a mat suspiciously eyeing the cold porridge in her bowl. How could this wet glop stay so cool when everything else out here was piping hot? It was so hot today that she couldn't manage to have an appetite. The bland meal didn't help matters.

Boudicea lifted the tent flap and entered. "Care for some figs to liven up the meal?"

"Thanks, but I don't think I care one fig for this meal at all."

"Patience. Eat now, for you may need your strength later."

"Is that a lesson?"

"No, it is basic biology. We all need to eat. Food, drink, and love: They're the basic requirements of all humanity to stay alive."

"I don't think love and eating are on the same level of importance."

"When you're starved for both, you may think differently."

Boudicea lifted the flap and left. "Okay, what did that mean?" asked Rael of her porridge. It had no answers about either eating or loving. It was just bland porridge. She set it down. Rael put on her sun hat and went outside. Boudicea was sitting on a boulder flipping her dagger in anticipation. Rael instinctively felt her necklace, but it was not warm to the touch. It hadn't warned her of the bandits in time either. There seemed to be limits to its powers. She had no idea what those limits were, though, because none of this made a lick of sense.

Rael found a boulder to sit down next to her mentor. She said, "You're waiting for something to happen today, I can tell."

"In a way. The truth is that nothing has happened to us recently, and that worries me. A cultist spoke to you on the boat, and yet four days later, here we sit as perfect targets and nothing comes for us. Yes, the lack of something happening worries me a great deal. These cultists should be chomping at the bit to reacquire you, and they're clearly not. They seem content to wait in their lair for us. It doesn't feel right."

It made sense to be worried about that, and yet Rael didn't believe her. Boudicea was worried about more than that. The odds of her telling Rael what was really on her mind, though, seemed low. Rael had a suspicion who she thought might come after them, and it wasn't just cultists. Rael said, "Boy, speaking of needing love, how about that Amen fellow from the boat? I'd love to meet a guy like that. I mean, a guy like him but more my age and not all old and stuff."

"We were not just speaking about love."

"You were talking about how much every cult member would love to catch me, and so, naturally, I assumed the topic of love was in the air. And since it was, I thought about you and your love, Amen. He is your secret love, isn't he, and we're waiting for him, right?"

"He's just a man."

"Just a man! He's so . . . well, *so*. He's the type of guy that makes everything sound like innuendo. He could be, like, 'I need to pick up some milk on my way home from work,' and you'd be, like, 'I know what that means. It means . . .' You know. Secret, non-sanctioned kissing and stuff."

"No."

"Oh, I'm pretty sure that it does."

"No, *he* is just a man." Boudicea pointed her dagger out into the desert and jumped down off the rocks. Rael saw a lone man walking toward them. Boudicea had done it again. She'd spotted trouble coming while Rael was blind to it. Rael was also wrong again. They clearly weren't waiting for Amen to arrive. They were waiting for this new man, whoever he was. Rael jumped down from her boulder.

"Who is he, another bandit?" asked Rael.

"I do not know. Go in the tent and stay out of sight," ordered Boudicea. Rael didn't like the idea of that. She wanted to see who he was. She was the apprentice, though. She'd agreed to the role, so she had little choice but to obey. She went inside. Then she lifted the flap a hair to peek out. Boudicea hadn't said not to, so it wasn't like Rael was disobeying orders.

The man was within speaking distance now. He called out, "*Χαιρε.*" Rael tried to clean the wax from her ear, because she was sure he'd just spoken gibberish.

Boudicea replied, "*Ογωμ, Cω?*"

Was there a language that Boudicea didn't know? Rael felt quite the poorly educated fool. Here Boudicea spoke just about a million languages, including Canadian, and Rael knew only English—and not real English, where they spelled color, colour, but the American barbarized version of the language.

The man waved Boudicea off. Boudicea asked, "Do you know English?" Oh good, finally Rael would understand what was being said. No luck there, though.

"*Xéro ellinikí glóssa,*" he replied.

"*Kalós,*" Boudicea replied. She laid out a mat in the shade. The man came to their camp and sat down. He was old. His face showed the weathering of the sun. No wonder, given he wandered around out here. He didn't seem like a bandit since he was armed with just a book in his hand. He opened the book and placed it in front of Boudicea. She flipped through a few pages. Then she said, "*Psáchno gia mia ekklisía.*"

"*Giatí?*"

"*Gia na to katharísete,*" Boudicea replied. The man smiled a near toothless smile at her. Then he flipped through the pages of the book. He took out a pen and wrote something in the margin of the book. Rael had no idea what he could have written, but she wanted to know very badly. Their voices lowered. They were mere whispers now, but the words came quickly on both sides. Rael could see only so much of what was going on, and now she could hear very little of it as well. She was in the dark again as to what was going on in her own life.

At last Boudicea glanced at the book and said, "*Sas efcharistó.*" Then she turned toward the tent. "Rael, come out." Something she understood at last. Rael sprang into action. She appeared on cue, but she couldn't think of any more to do than just stand there looking awkwardly at the man. Boudicea suggested, "Pay him."

"With what?"

Boudicea replied, "Show him your wings." Rael hesitated. Showing off to strangers felt exactly like the wrong thing to do. Was this a test? Boudicea prompted, "Go ahead." Okay, apparently it was not a test.

"Fly!" commanded Rael. Her wings spread and she lifted herself into the air. She didn't go up very high. She didn't need to.

"*Angeloi*," he said. Then the man made the sign of the cross and got on his knees. All of that simply made Rael feel more awkward, so she landed. The man got up. He was practically beaming with excitement. He reached out and touched Rael's face. There was a happiness in his face that made Rael quite jealous. Then he turned from Rael and wandered back off into the desert.

"Where's he going?" asked Rael.

"Away," replied Boudicea.

"But he forgot his book."

"It's our book now," explained Boudicea. Boudicea opened the book and showed it to Rael. There was a map of sorts written in the man's hand in the margin, along with a lot of writing Rael couldn't read. She continued, "He's a Coptic Christian Monk. He is wandering around selling wisdom to make ends meet. This is his Bible. He's given it to us. I don't speak enough Coptic even to get by, but lucky for us he also knew Greek."

"Why Greek of all things?" asked Rael.

"Eons ago they formed a monastery out here to avoid Byzantine influence on their religion. The old ways die hard for the monks that still run it. Their wisdom has survived in their hands for a long time. That is, until very recently. His monastery was taken over by bad men about a year ago. They tossed the old monks out in the cold, so to speak. The old monks are currently holed up in a Roman fort near an oasis that is just south of us."

"Did he say who the bad men were?"

"No. All he knew was that they were not locals. They were strangers and treated his church members badly."

"Why'd you want him to think that I'm an angel?"

"It was the only thing we could give him worth the information he gave us. He gave us his most prized possession because he thinks we've come to return his monastery to him and his fellow monks. And perhaps we will. The cultists seem uninterested in coming to us, but we're still gunning for them. We know where we have to go now, thanks to this monk. His monastery is our pyramid, I'm sure of it. These bad men can only be the Society. Ariadne's words have come true. Our search is drawing to a close. Get ready, we're moving on the cultists' position after sundown."

Chapter 16

The Lost Pyramid, Egypt

"We're here," announced Boudicea. It was hard to confirm that by the map in the old man's Bible because it was far too dark to read the notes scrawled there. How Boudicea managed to steer through the darkness, Rael didn't know. It was hard enough for Rael just to keep track of Boudicea, given they were both dressed in black. The darkness of the desert was unlike any darkness Rael could remember. What she noticed most about the darkness out here was that the cloudless skies displayed the stars like no other place she'd ever been. There were so many of those stars up there. She'd not appreciated how impressive the night sky really was. The modern lighting and pollution of so much of the civilized world hid the stars. As she stared up at the night sky she counted the stars, but it was a hopeless task. There were thousands of them, thousands of thousands of them.

She understood now that so much of the world had been hidden away from her. She was only just beginning to see the world as it really was. The real world was a spectacular place at times, and this was one of those times. Some of it, like the night sky, was worth finding out about. Sadly, too much of the real world was disappointing because it felt so pointlessly violent. She wanted more still nights filled with wonder and less violence.

Boudicea pulled on one of her horns, and she knew she'd not get what she wanted for the rest of this night.

Boudicea said, "Are you daydreaming, or do you plan to go with me into the pyramid?"

Whatever Rael wanted, she wasn't going to get it tonight. Violence seemed to be the only way of life for the hunter. Rael replied, "It's nighttime, so how could I have been daydreaming?"

"There is always daylight somewhere." That sounded pointlessly profound, but not as pointless as Boudicea's digging. She was digging with her hands into the chalky white sand around them.

"We're not digging up the whole pyramid, are we?" asked Rael.

"Rael, don't be silly and help me dig."

Rael must not have gotten her point across. She had thought Boudicea's digging was the silly part of it! Rael shrugged and scooped up a handful of dirt. She then scooped up more and more. She soon felt the edges of a block. The block was about a meter square. Within minutes they'd cleared the top of it. One block down and about a thousand more blocks to go to see the whole pyramid. She didn't think she was up to the task of unburying a whole pyramid tonight.

"Help me lift it," said Boudicea.

"What, the whole pyramid?"

"Don't be silly. We need only lift this block."

Rael got on one end and Boudicea the other. Rael was ready for a strain on her back, but the block lifted easily. This block was quite thin. Apparently it was just a capstone. It uncapped a passageway that led into darkness. Rael said, "This place reminds me more of a tomb than a pyramid."

Boudicea explained, "In Egypt all the pyramids are tombs. That means that this is both a pyramid and a tomb, and then again it is neither. This part we've revealed is just an old air vent made for the original diggers. The actual pyramid would have stood above us. Its red clay bricks eroded away eons ago. The burial chambers and passageways were dug into the solid rock beneath the pyramid. They were used by our friend the monk as a church. The monastery used this air vent as a secret passageway in and out. It was mostly reserved for use as their means of escape in case of attack."

"It was lucky we bumped into that old man."

"There is no luck in this life, Rael. The fates move him in his direction, as they move us in ours." Boudicea rolled a silver acorn from her sleeve. She squeezed it, and it started to glow. She tossed it into the passageway.

Rael asked, "Do I get a light too?"

"That's up to you. You get what you bring inside." Boudicea moved into the passageway. Rael searched her sleeve, but it was empty. She could spread her wings and let them glow again, but there wasn't going to be much need for flying underground. She moved into the passageway toward the light.

The passageway had held up to the test of time quite well. The walls were heavily decorated. The ceiling was painted dark blue with yellow dots. It took her a few seconds to realize what the dots were supposed to represent. She'd just come from outdoors and saw the same stars depicted here by some long-ago artist. Rael said, "This air vent is quite beautiful."

Boudicea replied, "All around us is the story of the afterlife. The hieroglyphs here are written spells from the Book of the Dead. With them and the aid of an Astralith like you, one could travel through Duat to reach the afterlife. The owner of this small pyramid was a vizier called Djau, and the spells were placed here for him and his family. Whether they worked or not for him, I cannot tell you. His resting place here on Earth has long ago been retrofitted, so I doubt we shall meet him or travel through Duat tonight."

"Good, because I've done enough of that type of traveling for a lifetime."

"Agreed."

The passageway ended in a rather disappointing way. They were in a small chamber. The room had been obviously converted into a dusty old library. In her mind, Rael lingered on the *dust* bit. It was everywhere, choking the air. The walls were lined with decaying wooden shelves that held decaying works of literature. They were very likely the prime source of the dust. On the shelves were papyri and books from long ago, hidden here by the monks. There appeared to be no other exit from the room. The passageway made for a less than convenient escape path if this room was the only place it escaped from.

"It appears to be a dead end," said Rael.

Boudicea didn't reply. She was searching the shelves. She pulled a crumbling scroll off a shelf and showed it to Rael. It had writing on it, but not in a script Rael knew. It was half gone due to great age. Boudicea explained, "These are too old to be what we're looking for. They hail from the time of the great liturgical rift between Alexandria and Constantinople, I'd say. They must be sacred to the monks, but they are not very useful to us."

"Oh," replied Rael, trying to search her memory for lessons on ancient history involving any of that. She didn't think she had ever received one.

"This is more promising, though," announced Boudicea. She had moved on to another shelf with bound books. She ran her fingers across the dust-encrusted tomes. She stopped where a gap appeared on the shelf. Into the gap she placed the old monk's book. The bookcase clicked and then swung open. "We are no longer at a dead end," announced Boudicea. Without hesitation, she moved into the hallway the bookcase had just revealed. Rael wasn't going to linger around catching up on her reading, so she followed.

The stonework was similar to the passageway they had just been in, but the walls were painted differently. The hieroglyphs were gone. In their place were paintings in a more Christian theme. Most of them appeared to have been hastily repainted over the original art. This must be the proper monastery, but there was one thing missing: the evil cultists who were supposed to have taken over. Rael couldn't hear even a hint of anyone being down here with them, and the passageway seemed ideal for bringing an echo to them from any place inside the pyramid.

They stopped at a fork in the passageway. They had three options to choose from. They all looked equally vacant and dark to Rael. "Maybe these bad men left already," suggested Rael.

Boudicea replied, "That would explain the lack of cult activity on our journey to date. It would be good news for the monks too, but bad news for us because it would be impossible for us to complete our mission." Boudicea paused to smell the air down each path. "This way leads to the surface, this way leads to old storage rooms for the monks, and this way leads further down. Djau's burial chamber would have made the best place for the monastery chapel. It would be the biggest chamber down here. If there is even one cultist remaining in here, they will have left evidence of their presence there."

"We've come a long way to find just one cultist, if that's all there is here."

"All we need is one if it's the correct one."

They moved down deeper into the pyramid's chambers. The next half hour consisted of searching the passageway's many side chambers. Apparently Djau had intended to bury his whole family with him and had done an amazing job at preparing for that. And he'd had a big family, judging by the number of chambers they ended up searching through. None of his family were still to be found among the chambers. They were lost to the ages. The chambers appeared to have been converted into quarters for the monks, kitchens, and dining areas. They were not the most glamorous of accommodations. It must have been grim living down here in the dark. But then, no one was living here now. The age of the current room's setup was hard to guess. Perhaps the monks only came down here in times of need or on certain religious high holy days. The cultists might be the same way: living up on the surface and rarely venturing down into the dark abyss of the pyramid's hidden chambers.

At last, they found the burial chamber of the man of honor. It was much larger than the remaining chambers. Rael's stars were back, painted so high up on the ceiling that no one had been able to reach up there to repaint them. The room had been converted to the Christianity of the monks. A granite sarcophagus that was far too heavy to move had been converted into an altar instead. There were no pews, just simple prayer rugs on the floor. The walls were painted with murals. Stained glass was, of course, impractical for underground churches. On the wall behind the altar was a painting of a man. Rael was used to seeing Jesus, but typically she saw the passion of Jesus. Here he was depicted as a teacher instead. He was holding a book and appeared to be lecturing. An odd sort of teacher, though.

"Jesus. It checks out as Christian," said Rael, pointing to the painting behind the altar.

Boudicea corrected her, "That is a portrait of Mark. He brought the good news to the land of Egypt and is a central figure in the monks' beliefs."

"Why does he have a cow's head?" asked Rael.

Boudicea frowned. "It's clearly a bastardization of the monks' original painting. I suspect we have our first trace of cult activity."

"Is Ilitar a cow demon?"

"No. Yet this clearly does show a half-man, half-bull. It draws my interest."

"It reminds me of the minotaur in Ariadne's maze," said Rael.

"You have learned something from me! I was beginning to think all my training was going up in smoke. The Minoan culture spread far and wide during its heyday, until its bronze age collapse. It remains within society, even if society doesn't know it. To this day, when people pay to see bull fights or rides, they're seeing a glimpse of the past. Let's see if the cult that chased out the monks left any more traces of their form of worship so we can guess which exact cult they belong to."

"I thought they were part of this Maleficium Society."

"Every society has different factions within—perhaps with different beliefs."

Rael took her word for it, as the occult was still new to her. Boudicea grabbed the light source off the wall and moved to the altar. There was something chiseled into the black granite. It read,

The Eternal Olam has made a covenant oath with us,
Asherah has made a pact with us.
And all the sons of El.
And the great council of all the Holy Ones.
With oaths of Heaven and Ancient Earth.

Boudicea said, "It would appear that they're devoted to Baal. Odd, I would have thought Apis more appropriate for Egypt."

"Who is Baal?"

"The Lord of dew and the rain."

"Isn't a desert a weird place for a Baal cult to hang out"

"No place needs his power more than the desert," said Boudicea.

"Okay, you got me there, but aren't they the wrong cult for us?"

"Yes, I've never known Baal worshipers to be interested in a demon queen like Ilitar. Mot worshipers, maybe, but never Baal worshippers," replied Boudicea.

"Then the cultist on the boat was right. This is the wrong way for us to have gone."

"Maybe, but Ariadne sent me here. I trust her. And yet, her ways are never direct. They have meaning, though. There must have been a reason to send us here. There's something down here we need to find."

"Beats me what it could be," admitted Rael. They had started this journey south with clear goals. Now they seemed muddled. Rael was ready to leave. As fun as poking around in the dark had been, there was no one down here. She was already wondering what they'd do next. They couldn't go back to the boat and sail back to Cairo, for obvious reasons. If not back to the river, where? This society her father had joined could be located anywhere. The one thing Rael knew was that they'd be after her eventually. Nothing she'd accomplished in Egypt to date would stop that.

Boudicea didn't look eager to give up on this place yet. She stood there, seemingly lost in thought. Perhaps they'd head to the surface and see if cultists were really up top. No such luck, though. Boudicea suddenly had that look like she knew something extraordinary. She pressed against the mural of Mark. She moved her hands across the painting, searching for something. She didn't seem to find whatever it was she wanted to find.

"Are we finished?" asked Rael.

"Not yet." Boudicea reached up high on the wall. Mark had a book in his hand. The book was closed. Boudicea pulled at it. The stone the book was painted on gave way and opened. There was a lever behind it.

Boudicea pulled it. The mural opened to reveal a passageway behind it. Boudicea said, "We had yet to find Djau's treasure chamber. Now I think we have."

"Will we get to see Egyptian treasures beyond our wildest dreams inside it?"

"I imagine they're all well plundered by now."

That was disappointing. Rael would have liked to have found treasure. The adrenaline rush of the sudden find eased. It was replaced with that empty feeling that goes with staring down a pitch-black passageway. Only a mole would be living in there. That wouldn't stop Boudicea from searching it, though.

Boudicea lit an acorn and rolled it down the passageway. Nothing stirred. Boudicea started walking down just the same. Rael followed. The walls here were bare. No hint of gold or precious gems. Just bare worked stone extending down at a slope, gradually leading them deeper underground. Boudicea was a determined searcher. She was going as deep as she could. Rael had no choice but to follow.

The passageway went a full two hundred feet down, but Rael had no way to judge the distance. She only knew she'd gone a long way down. She could see the end now, far off in the distance. It appeared to be a small chamber with little antechambers around it. They were dark, so at this distance there was no knowing how big the whole complex might be. What she could see was barren and empty.

Then a light went on in one of the small antechambers. It took Rael by surprise. Only it wasn't just a light. There was something moving around in the light. She could see it making shadows.

Rael said, "We're finally not alone, and I'm not sure if that's a good thing or a bad thing."

"We can only find out by investigating." Boudicea moved closer to the light. Rael followed with a sense of caution. She was about as cautious as she could be, given they were in a barren passageway with no place to really hide. The figure in the light didn't seem to care that Boudicea was coming for it. Well, that *they* were coming for it, because Rael was following closely behind.

Rael heard a voice. It called, but not to her. It spoke again, and it clearly said, "Boudicea."

Rael said, "It appears to know you." Boudicea didn't respond. She continued to move closer, at a more rapid pace.

The voice called again. "Come to me."

Boudicea now ran. Rael had no choice but to follow at their new pace. Boudicea was faster than Rael by a lot. She had already entered the small chamber at the end of the passageway. Rael saw now that the light she was seeing had no clear source. It must be magical in nature. There was a man moving around within the light. He was white as snow, dressed in a white robe. He had a long, snow-white beard.

Boudicea exclaimed, "It can't be you!"

"Who, who can't this be?" asked Rael.

The man paid no attention to Rael. He gestured toward Boudicea. "It is me. I've waited ages to see you again."

"By Ariadne's blessing, Divicia, it is you." Boudicea moved into the light with him.

Divicia? Rael had been told he was dead. More to the point, Boudicea had apparently killed him. How could it be that he was here? More importantly, why would he chase some old monks away just to sit here in the deep alone? There were too many questions and no answers. Only there was his necklace around Rael's neck, and it suddenly felt warm to the touch.

Rael called out to Boudicea, "I think we're in danger!" Boudicea ignored her. She was lost in memories. This was not good. There was something very wrong with all this. Boudicea stood right next to him now. Rael was dreading going into the light after her.

Boudicea said, "I've dreamed of this day."

"I know," replied Divicia. "Come and let me hold you in my arms again." He held out his hand.

Rael's necklace was so hot it could have seared her. It was Divicia's necklace, so there was no reason it shouldn't like him, yet it didn't. "No, don't do it. Something isn't right about all this!" cried out Rael. It was sort of wishful thinking on her part. There was no talking sense to Boudicea. Not about Divicia.

Boudicea reached out to touch his hand. The second she did so, a flash of energy was exchanged between them. Then another, followed quickly by a third.

"Why?" was all Boudicea could say before she fell to the floor. Divicia faded away, soon gone. The light remained, though. One by one the antechambers became ablaze with fresh light, until all of the space around Rael glowed bright. And then men stepped out of the chambers. They wore horns on their heads and red robes.

One of them stepped closer than the rest and spoke. He must have been the leader. He said to Rael, "He was just a hologram. Crude, but it worked for our purposes. The witch told us you'd eventually come. She is the keeper of the minotaur's spirit, a servant of Baal. She told us that if we took care of her treacherous daughter for her, she'd show us how to use you to defeat Mot. Now the daughter is nearly dead, and our reward stands with us." He commanded his men. "Strip the cloak from the hunter and burn it so she cannot heal herself. Then we will leave her here to be buried in this tomb. As for the little one, tie her up. She's worth everything and more."

They approached Boudicea's fallen body. "Not so great a hunter after all," shouted one. They all laughed. The men grabbed at the helpless Boudicea and tore her cloak. With torches they set it ablaze. It burned with a sweet green flame.

Rael was stunned. Ariadne had betrayed Boudicea to these men, but why? Rael realized it didn't matter why. What mattered was what she did next. Boudicea was out, and Rael needed to act, or all would be lost. Rael tried to back away, but she was surrounded. The underground space gave her no chance to fly. She'd need to fight it out. Two men approached her with rope in hand. She lashed out at them. She managed to scrape one up real good. But the other seized her hard.

"I'm going to make her pay for scratching me!" shouted the one she'd injured.

"Don't damage her, fool!" the cult leader warned the man holding Rael. Rael assumed the word *yet* was left unspoken at the end of that statement.

The other cultists were busy finishing off Boudicea. They were poking her fallen body with cattle prods. They kept torturing her in delight. They would not stop until they'd had their fill of fun, Rael knew that much.

Rael shouted, "Leave her alone!"

The cult leader explained, "We must kill her. Mot must be defeated, and then Baal can have his final victory. It shall come to pass, and it will all be thanks to your sacrifice. We will always remember your spirit. That you can count on."

Rael didn't care about their mythos. She cared about her friend. Only, there didn't seem to be much she could do to help her. Worse, she had a feeling she was going to be their Astralith and be sent on a final journey. Well, she wasn't just an Astralith; she was also a hunter now. They were evil cultists. She'd have to act. She bluffed, "Stop now and I'll let you all live." They stopped torturing Boudicea long enough to have a laugh. Not what Rael had been going for. She'd need to back up those words. She stomped on the foot of the cultist holding her. He let go. She raked his face. That stopped his laughter.

She darted for the passageway leading up. Three men barred her way. She shouted, "I'm warning you!"

"Or what?" asked one of the men.

This was answered in the most unexpected way. Even Rael was quite surprised by it. A burning red beast charged down the passageway and burst through the three men. It was a demon with tusks like an elephant, moving on all fours. It tossed the nearest cultist with its tusks.

The cult leader screamed, "What manner of the devil's witchcraft is this?"

"Demon!" shouted another.

"A hunter came down here with a demon protector? Impossible!" said the leader.

The demon stomped a few cultists, which sort of negated the cult leader's doubt. The red demon turned its fury on the leader. The leader by now had realized it was in fact possible and turned to flee for his life. Rael was having mixed emotions at this point. The enemy of your enemy theory only went so far. The demon could never be a hunter's friend, could it?

The leader went after it with a cattle prod. His weapon did nothing against the red demon. The red demon impaled him with its tusks and tossed him aside. The rest of the men scattered. They ran for their lives up the passageway. The demon chased after them. They'd never see daylight again, Rael knew that much.

Rael didn't follow. She ran to Boudicea's side. She rolled her fallen body over. Boudicea was cold to the touch.

Rael said, "Don't die on me."

Boudicea opened her eyes. She said, "She was like a mother to me, but I killed her beloved Divicia. For some acts, there is no forgiveness. Rael, I am sorry for being a fool." She then passed out again. Rael tried to pick her up, but she was too heavy to carry all the way to the surface. Rael's cloak could heal her, maybe. How did it work? Rael didn't know. She needed help. She heard the grunts of the demon. It was back. It snarled at Rael. Rael readied her hands; she could pierce the beast with her claws. But she didn't need to, because it changed form. Gone was the beast. The tall Arab Rael had met on the boat was in its place. Rael exclaimed, "You're a shapeshifter!"

He said, "I tried to warn you, but humans always take the longest path on any journey. It is their nature, I suppose."

Rael replied, "We must get my friend out of here."

"I could have let the servants of Baal destroy your essence, but Ilitar demands greater security than merely your destruction. Ilitar sent me here to help you defeat the Maleficium Society and secure that which could control her. Her, the hunter, I have no care for."

"She is a part of me. Helping her helps you, for no one I know is better at this type of fight."

"And yet she lost today."

"I will not leave without her."

The demon didn't appear happy to hear that. He gave in, though. He replied, "Very well. There is no need to fight about it when it is so easy for me to carry her to another place to die." He came and picked Boudicea up with ease. The oasis was the natural place to retreat to. All Rael needed to do was navigate her way there. There would be monks there that could help Boudicea. It couldn't be too hard to find an oasis at night in a barren desert, right?

"We need to get to the Oasis of the White Palms," said Rael.

"We?"

"I assumed, now that you've revealed yourself, that I'd have a lot of trouble losing you ever again."

"That was a good assumption. We will go there if it means finally getting on the correct path."

"I think that it will."

Chapter 17

The Oasis of the White Palms, Egypt

Rael paced the floor. Well, Rael paced on the white sand, which in this place was all that was left of the floor. She was just outside the oasis proper, inside the remains of an old stonework Roman fort that sat decaying in the sun. She was alone and feeling quite annoyed about everything in general. Mostly she was annoyed with herself, but it never felt quite right to feel annoyed with oneself, so she took her annoyance out on the rest of the world.

She paused pacing and said, "Rest, Rael." This never worked. It just focused her mind on the fact she wasn't restful at all, even if she should be. She needed to take a break, because that was why she was here in this room, but she hadn't rested for a minute since coming in here because she was restless, and hence the endless cycle of sleeplessness rotated ever onward. She closed her eyes and tried to empty her mind. In an instant, Boudicea was there to haunt her thoughts. She opened her eyes again. There was no doubt: She couldn't relax her mind. It was annoying.

After climbing out of the pyramid's sub-basement, the demon had carried Boudicea to the doorstep of the monks. When not trying to kill her, these demons were quite useful—or at least this one had been. He'd seen through the darkness as if it was day and brought Rael straight here to the fort at the edge of the oasis. He was still here somewhere, lurking outside and watching her. He had refused to enter this makeshift church, but Rael knew that he would not leave her alone again for long. Not until this Maleficium Society business was taken care of *or* the demon double-crossed her. Maybe both—the two ideas were not mutually exclusive.

After they'd arrived the previous night, the old monk had seemed pleased to see them again, even though Boudicea was hardly in victorious condition. The monks had taken Boudicea from Rael as soon as they'd seen her condition. They seemed confident they could help her, or at least that was Rael's impression of her conversation with them. Not being able to speak to any of them made things difficult to interpret. Mostly she got smiles and hand gestures. It all felt very reassuring, but a smile was a dangerous thing to interpret those days because it could turn into a frown so quickly.

After taking Boudicea in, the old monk had brought Rael here to this room. She must have looked tired and ragged. He had thought she wanted to rest, and she probably did. . . no, it was more than probably, she did want to rest. She wanted to sleep and wake up and have this whole thing be just a dream. She couldn't rest because it was not a dream. As tired as she was, she couldn't shut herself down to rest. She was too worked up and annoyed by her situation.

Annoyed was not the correct word, though. She was sort of frustrated. Yes, that was much more accurate. She had let the monk take over the situation. She'd acted like a child, glad to have someone else assume responsibility for Boudicea's well-being. Now she felt guilty for fleeing here with thoughts of putting her problems to rest. The monk's kindness was frustrating because it had allowed the worst in her to win easily. She was a hunter now, or at least a hunter in training. She needed to take charge of a situation. She wanted to know how Boudicea was doing. Nothing else mattered. If she knew for a fact that Boudicea would survive, she might feel her duty satisfied and begin to rest. But how could anyone guarantee that? The oasis had limited medical facilities from the looks of it. Granted, she'd only seen it from afar and at night. Perhaps she should seek more help. No, she should help Boudicea directly. "Think, Rael. How can you help Boudicea more?" said Rael. She sighed. Asking herself a question she didn't know the answer to was no help at all.

The old monk they'd met in the desert came in with a smile. He seemed to instinctively know the cultists inside the pyramid were all dead and their old church was safe to return to. Come to think of it, maybe he also thought she was his avenging angel. She wasn't, though. It was just another thing to feel guilty about. Still, their church was restored to him and his fellow monks, so perhaps her guilt was misplaced. Rael said to him, "How is she . . ." She stopped herself. He spoke two languages—possibly more, she didn't know. He knelt before her and then left some water and a little food for her as if she were a dog. Then again, maybe they were an offering to a god.

"I'm not an angel, you know," she said to him. He just smiled pleasantly at her and then left. The food he had left for her was dates and bread. She didn't want any food; she didn't have an appetite at all. Well, until the smell of the bread hit her nostrils. The bread was hot, fresh out of the oven. It was just like the bread her mother never made, because they bought it prepackaged at a store. Rael was used to lifeless American bread wrapped in plastic and cut into slices. That bread was starved of taste by preservatives; it sat on shelves cold and lifeless for months. This bread, though, seemed alive. She popped the fresh bread in her mouth. It was the best bread she'd ever had. Maybe that was the desert desolation talking, but this real stuff tasted so much better than what she was used to. She sat down on the floor and ate it all.

As she ate, she thought harder about her situation. These monks could help Rael get out of her current situation, yes, but she needed more help than just them. She needed to get word to Dynami or Archon—or anyone else in the Order for that matter. Rael would need the Order's help to get out of this place and more than that to save Boudicea. If Boudicea didn't make it, the need for more help would be tenfold. She felt guilty to think that Boudicea lived just to save Rael from situation after situation. Amen's words on the boat haunted Rael. He'd known Rael was a burden, maybe even a curse, upon Boudicea. But it hadn't been Rael that caused Boudicea to fall in the pyramid; it was Boudicea's own past used against her. It had all been a trap, obviously, and had done nothing to further their quest.

This hunter business was too much. She looked at her cloak. Boudicea's was gone, but Rael's remained. Magic cloaks felt sort of comical. This way of life was sort of stupid. No, it wasn't stupid; she was. She was in the Order now but knew next to nothing about its magical ways. Rael wasn't even good at fighting. She didn't feel particularly good at anything. Dynami had forty years of training on her and he still made mistakes; she had about a week in the Order and knew next to nothing.

The annoyance creeped back in. She felt useless and blamed herself for being that way. She should be better than she was. Boudicea's cloak could heal Boudicea; Rael had seen it in action before. If only Rael knew how to activate the powers of her own cloak, she could use it on Boudicea while she was unconscious. She finished her dates and picked up her own cloak. She had to learn to make it work. She said, "Come on, show me the way." She reached up the sleeve. Nothing. Not ever a lousy acorn. What was the use of this thing to her?

A small Egyptian boy of about five came into the room. He asked her, "You are dumby, yes?"

Oh good, someone she could actually talk to. He spoke English . . . well, sort of. She replied, "I am called Rael."

"Yes, good, the priests, they come to White Palms seeking someone that can talk to the dumby that they can't speak with. My father says I can speak to dumbies, and so here I am."

The one thing Rael couldn't knock this boy for was a lack of honesty. Still, there were key parts of his story she wished had been left out. Rael asked, "My friend, is she okay?"

"I have just met you, so how should I know your friends? The priests, they say nothing to me about dumby's friends. They just want me to tell the dumby that they're very happy you saved their church. They wanted you to have this." The young boy dropped a wooden cross into Rael's lap. It was different from the Christian crosses she was used to. The four points were equal in size and had elaborate loops.

The boy must have felt done with her because he started to leave.

"Wait, I still need you to translate a message to the monks for me," Rael called out after him, but the boy kept going. He was a fast little bugger. She stood up, placed the cross necklace around her neck, and raced after him. She reached the door to find that he had already happily skipped around the corner. Well, that happened. Rael toyed with the Coptic cross around her neck. It was rather nice, given the monks had so little to offer. Still, their helping Boudicea was thanks enough.

She was outside, and thoughts of resting now seemed so silly that she abandoned them completely. She looked out across the oasis to the small city beyond. She had imagined groves of palm trees and a flowing fountain of water. It wasn't like that at all. There was just a small town of about thirty thousand or so huddled around a depression below sea level in the surrounding higher desert. Being below the water table allowed water to gather in the depression. It brought life to the desert. Mostly it brought scrub trees, which gave the area a little greenery, and a few goats to eat that greenery. It wasn't much to look at, but it beat the high desert wasteland they had walked through.

That made her think about the camels. They'd left them out there by the pyramid that wasn't a pyramid. It would be cruel to just leave them there. She should find the old monk to send him after them. She walked around the stone fort searching for the boy to talk to the monk for her. Hopefully, he hadn't gone all the way home.

She rounded the corner and instantly forgot about the boy because she saw a white SUV parked by the fort. This vehicle was built for traveling through sand. One thing was certain: There was no way this vehicle belonged to the poor monks. Maybe they had sent for a doctor and he'd arrived. She walked over to it. The vehicle was empty. No one seemed to be about.

"Doctor, a very smart man, he is inside," said the boy.

Rael turned around and saw the child peeking at her around the vehicle. She walked toward the boy. She asked, "The doctor is inside with my friend? I am relieved."

The boy didn't seem to notice she'd spoken to him. He played with a tire. He was scooping up white sand and letting it sift down to the ground along the treads. She thought of repeating herself, but she had doubts it would do any good. He was too young to really care about her situation. She'd find the doctor on her own.

She called out, "Is there a doctor about?"

A flap over an opening in the fort lifted. Her heart raced a little in excitement, but it was short-lived. The old monk came out. He beamed a smile at her again. She displayed his gift to her to show she was grateful. He seemed unmoved by it and wandered off. She looked at the boy to explain to him that he needed to tell the monk about the camels, but the boy was gone. She walked around the car. He was nowhere to be seen. She looked under the vehicle. He wasn't there either. It was like he'd just upped and vanished. Yes, the little bugger could move pretty fast. He was too fast and too young to be of real help. The camels were doomed, and it was just one more fact to annoy her. She had failed again.

"Can I help you?" asked someone.

Rael noticed a pair of feet standing next to her wearing sensible shoes. The doctor was here, and he spoke English! Rael was excited and embarrassed at the same time. It must be a little awkward to find someone on all fours looking under your vehicle. She planned to explain to him that she wasn't a thief or anything. She got to her feet and dusted off her knees. She looked into his face and was immediately disappointed and interested at the same time. He was a doctor, but not the medical type. It was Amen Johonson, the paleontologist from the boat. "You're here."

"I am," he replied.

"But how did you know we'd be here?"

"What makes you think I knew?" he replied.

"I know you know Boudicea better than you suggested on the boat."

"You know that, huh? Yes, I did send Boudicea in this direction, but don't think I followed her out here. I wouldn't have come, but a strange fellow turned up on the boat looking for you two. A Freemason who went by the name of Wat Tyler. It got me spooked, so I came, but apparently I came too late."

"This wasn't done by Wat. I've not seen him around here. It was agents of Baal that did this to Boudicea."

"That's good news in a way. I didn't think the Freemasons would normally bother Boudicea, but I thought they might bother you. You're an unknown quantity to me. I haven't really sorted you out at all."

"Join the club. I'm a mystery even to myself. All I know is that the Freemason was probably just trying to help me, sort of. It doesn't matter. What matters now is Boudicea."

"Agreed. I've just come from seeing Boudicea. She's in terrible shape. My worst fears about her mission have been confirmed." He sounded angry. Maybe at Rael. She remembered his words on the boat again. He'd not thought Boudicea should risk so much just for just her, and maybe he'd been correct on that matter.

Rael replied, "I wish I could help her more, but I don't know how to."

"No one expects a child to be a doctor. I will have to try to drive her to one. If she survives the trip, she will be very lucky. It would be better to help her here and now, but that is not possible."

Rael sighed, "I should be able to do it. It's just that I'm a beginner. I don't have any magic with which to help her. Her cloak can't heal her now because it was destroyed, and mine is useless. If only I knew how it worked."

Amen seemed to brighten up. "You've got an idea forming. I like the sound of it. You've still got a magic cloak of your own and everything, so there's hope. Now we must tap into that hope."

"But I don't know how to use it."

Amen rolled his eyes at her. "Great, just great. An attitude like that, we don't need right now. I told Boudi not to trust Ariadne's words, but she's never been one to listen to me. You will be different. To tap into your cloak's power, let's start by you explaining to me how this happened to Boudi in a touch more detail? Then we'll work from there."

Rael explained, "The cultists used Divicia's image to lure Boudicea into a trap. They made her think he was still alive. I guess she felt guilty about killing him, so she was easy to fool. Once she had been lured toward the image of Divicia, they struck her down before she knew what was happening to her."

"What is this now about Boudi killing Divicia? I know that's how she sees it, but it's not true in the strictest sense of the meaning. Ariadne obviously sees past events as Boudicea killing him, and I think she's convinced Boudi to believe it too out of guilt. But Divicia did it to himself to save her, I tell you."

"What do you mean?" asked Rael.

Amen explained, "That damn cave of Ariadne's has a dark spirit in it. It frightened Boudi terribly as a child. Whenever they were not on a hunt, Divicia would go there to Ariadne and take her along. They were very much in love, Divicia and Ariadne. I am told it was a happy time and Ariadne treated Boudi as if she were her own. Of course, Boudi is Boudi. Which means, when Boudi was just about your age, she got it into her head that to become a hunter on her own she needed to face her darkest fears. She went down deep into the maze to see the minotaur spirit for herself one day. Well, she ended up doing more than confronting her fears; she ended up fighting it. She should have let the dead lie undisturbed, because this was a fight she could not win. It had nearly killed her by the time Divicia came to her rescue. He was no match for it either. A life for a life, he fought off the minotaur spirit long enough for Boudi to run away, but there was no escape for him. Ariadne has never forgiven Boudi for Divicia's death. Boudi has never come to grips with the idea that Ariadne's love has now turned sour on her. It is nothing now that she feels for Boudi but pure hate."

"That's terrible, but it explains so much. Ariadne sent us to our doom. How could Boudicea have behaved so recklessly not to see through it, though? How could she have gone to face the minotaur spirit? It doesn't sound like her."

"It doesn't. She didn't behave recklessly any way you size it up. It is my firm belief that Divicia would never have let her even get to the lower maze alone unless he wanted her to go there. It was a test. The day he died, she graduated and became a hunter."

"But she lost."

"Life is not a game to be won or lost."

"That sounds very un-profound."

"I'm sorry to disappoint you. I am, in the end, just a university professor. The ways of the Order seem pointless to me. Unfortunately for my dear heart, Boudi values the Order above all else. In a way, I feel for Ariadne, for I know what it is like to be always waiting for my love to return to me from a battle." Amen placed his hands on Rael's cloak. "If we can teach you how to use this, Boudi, my love, may still be saved."

"Can you contact the Order and get me a lesson?"

"No, but all this talk has given me an idea. We need to get help, and I know someone local that may help both of us."

"But you said that no one local could help Boudicea."

"It is not Boudicea I am thinking needs the most help; that person is you. I know someone that might help you tap into your inner magic. Boudicea would never let me try to contact him, but she cannot stop me . . . *us* now. One oracle betrayed you, but there are others in this world. We will try to find a local one. He is supposed to be near here."

"Who exactly?"

"Names are not important. He is another oracle, but one I trust more than the fallen Ariadne."

"When I heard a doctor had arrived, I thought you were the help I needed," Rael said.

"I may still be, indirectly." Amen opened the door to the SUV. Rael climbed in. Amen set a course for the oasis proper. It was a short drive.

Amen parked the vehicle and climbed out. The people of the oasis appeared to be living a lavish life compared with the monks, but the area around the oasis was not a rich one by Rael's standards. Rael looked for even one white palm, but there was none. A name is sometimes just a name. The town was different from other places in Egypt she'd been to so far. Most of the people here weren't Arab or Egyptian, but Berbers. Amen went to the open-air marketplace. He went market stall to market stall asking questions in Siwi, which he seemed to be quite fluent in. Rael was, as usual, in the dark as to what was being asked.

They left the last stall empty-handed. Amen was looking a little frustrated. He said, "Someone here must know. We must find that someone. Maybe at the mosque we will get lucky."

"Or maybe that someone will find you," said the demon. Rael turned and saw the red demon. The demon was in its human form and standing just a few feet from them. A merchant moved toward him and offered him some goods, but the demon ignored him.

Amen whispered to Rael, "I do not know this man."

Rael whispered back, "This is no man, but a shapeshifting demon in human form."

"Are you going to kill it? If so, please not here," whispered Amen.

"No, I'm not going to kill it," replied Rael.

The demon said, "I know you wish to find the oracle that dwells near here. I know where he is."

Amen said, "I don't think it is wise to trust the word of a demon. Boudi would be dead against it."

"We have no choice but to accept the demon's offer of help," replied Rael.

"The little one learns quickly. I don't wish to help the hunter, but the sooner this is over, the sooner Ilitar can be safe. Thus, let us get this over quickly," said the demon.

It walked down the street. Rael followed. Amen looked concerned, but he went along. The demon headed for the source of the water. The small oasis lake was at the edge of the town. The demon stopped at the water's edge to shoo a few goats away from the shore. Once the shore was clear, he pointed into the water. "The Oracle of Ammon is down there."

"Who is this oracle?" asked Rael.

Amen explained, "Amun-Ra was an important deity to the ancient Egyptians. Though most of his people have long forgotten him, his power remains on the outer planes. His oracle can still channel it."

Rael didn't doubt it. Not after everything she'd seen. Still, being underwater meant this oracle was not the most helpful of people. "Okay, how do I see him if he's under the oasis?"

"Do humans know nothing of their own world? Ilitar forgive me for praising one from another plane," said the demon in disgust. He then tossed a handful of sand onto the water right where the orb of the sun reflected off its surface. He said, "The illuminated ones turn toward him. Adorning the two lands by his coming forth. Hail to thee, Amun-Ra, lord of the throne of the two lands! His city loveth his rising." The water's surface broke and receded slowly, forming steps down. "The oracle is down there waiting for you," said the demon. Rael didn't hesitate. She started down the stairs because she needed to know what was down this magical path. Amen tried to follow, but the demon grabbed his arm. "The child must do this on her own."

"I don't like that idea," said Amen.

Rael turned to Amen and said, "I will be okay."

"Boudi's overconfidence has rubbed off on you," he replied.

That might have been true. If so, it was in a good way. Divicia's necklace signaled no danger at the moment. If there was someone here that could teach her how to tap into her own magic and revive Boudicea, she'd go to them. She had to do it, because she had to help her friend. Rael descended into the oasis. As her head sank below the waves, the water around her turned from blue to golden yellow. Suddenly Rael was not underwater at all, but in the presence of a bright light. The glowing yellow stairs beneath her feet continued down. Soon the light became too bright for her to see, and she closed her eyes to avoid being blinded. She moved by touch alone. Down into the heart of Ra she traveled, one step at a time.

She stumbled and found there were no more steps left. She'd reached the landing to which the stairs led, for what it was worth. Not being able to see meant she had no idea of the value of her journey. She dared not leave the steps, for if she wandered blindly into the light then she might never find the stairs again. There must be someone down here. She called out, "I am in need of help."

A man's voice responded to her call. "An Astralith of some means here visiting me? Yes, I do believe you are in need of help. As Ra travels on the Mandjet, thus also does Ra travel on the Mesektet. Open your eyes and now be able to see."

Rael opened her eyes. The light was gone. She was in blackness. Then, stars began to appear all around her. One by one, they lit up the world around her. They were embedded into the firmament that composed this place. They were like a living form of the pyramid paintings. Inside the living ceiling she saw a tiny boat sailing across the stars.

"Impressive is not the Duat, the ether between worlds, between planes of reality?"

"I've been to this place before," said Rael.

"I can see that."

Rael's eyes adjusted to the room she was in. She saw before her now a man. He was bare-chested, with an ornate white wrapping around his waist. He wore a strange headdress shaped like the head of a bird. He reached over and patted her hair to touch the horns on her head. "Not many can say they've had such a journey through the Duat and lived to tell the tale. Tell me, what help do you need from the living Amun?"

"It's rather complicated. I need a lesson in magic, but I guess I don't know how to ask correctly about it because I know so little about magic."

"Tell me your story, and I will know the correct words that form the proper question."

"My story? Okay. We sought information from Ariadne about a thing called the Maleficium Society. We think they have a device that when combined with my Astralith powers can trap a powerful demon. Ariadne gave us a reading, but she did not help us. Instead, she led my friend, a druid hunter, astray. Now I need to know how to use the magic in my cloak to save my friend's life."

"Ah, so we got to the need in the end. That's a lot to ask of Ra. But I will see if his will matches yours. You may be in luck. You have a good heart, Rael. When weighed against a feather from Maat, it won't betray you."

He held out his hand and pricked a finger with a pin. A drop of blood dripped into a cup made of lapis lazuli that appeared in his hand as the blood dropped down. The cup started to glow with white light. A ray of light shot from the cup and shone directly on the boat sailing through the living painting. Then the cup went dark again. The man clapped his hands and the cup was gone. The cup of the oracle might have vanished, but it blazed an image in her head. Only, the cup in her head had red stones and was held in her father's hand. She'd seen that cup in a dream—except the dream was a memory of an event that had really happened. She needed to know about that cup.

"I know all you need to know," said the oracle.

Rael said, "I don't think so, because I need to know more now."

"How like a child it is to be always in need of knowledge. How like a parent it is to be in need of teaching it. Tell me what you need to know."

"I want to know about your cup. It reminded me of something from a dream. I've seen a cup like that before. It was in my father's hands when he commanded an avalanche to kill many people, including my mother."

"How evil a deed. My cup that you saw is my summoning cup. For a drop of blood, it allows me to commune with the living Amun-Ra. It cost me but a little of my Earthly essence. I fear communing with his cup for such an evil deed cost your father much more."

"Then, using magic is like my gating to other worlds?"

"Yes, eventually the channeler will run out of essence and there will be no more magic. All oracles are slowly killing themselves. A hunter's life such as yours will not be infinite. There is a price for everything in this world. If you use your magic cloak, you will be slowly killing yourself."

"Then I have cost you just now by asking you questions. I am sorry to have done so."

"No need to be. As the hunter does what they do to satisfy a need inside them, so an oracle does. Amun-Ra chose me, and I accepted his price to speak with him. Here is what I know from asking him for you. I know now that Ariadne's prophecy was not false. She told you how to find an object of great danger held by the Maleficium Society, and thanks to your journey you've now acquired the meaning to get it."

"The shapeshifting demon," said Rael.

"Yes, the demon that saved you is the key, and not anything else you found inside the pyramid. Ariadne set a trap for you, yes. But in doing so, she revealed the answer to your need. I sense you understood that much already. It is the way of those Greek oracle types: Always at the end does your understanding of the words get twisted; always at the end a little tragedy. We Egyptians do it differently. And that leads us to your real answer. The one that will save your friend. The magic you seek is the magic you already possess. It is within you. You only have to believe in yourself to tap into the power you possess that many wish to take from you. Only when you believe in yourself will the magic flow. It is better for you to use it than have others waste it. You were wise to choose the life of a hunter."

The stars went out. The white light flashed into Rael's eyes. She closed them before the brilliance blinded her. It seeped through even her closed eyelids and hurt. And then the intense light dissipated. She opened her eyes and she was standing in a mudbrick shack located within the shallow waters of the oasis. On the muddy floor sat an old man dressed in tattered clothes. She could hear the flies buzzing happily around him. He reached out his hand and opened it. It was empty.

Amen came to her side. He asked her, "Did you learn something?"

"Yes, I hope so."

Amen dropped some coins into the old man's hands, and the old man closed his hands around them. Amen said, "I will not ask you more about how this shack came to be here. I will simply take you back to Boudi and hope your newfound knowledge proves useful."

Chapter 18

The Oasis of the White Palms, Egypt

Rael pushed back the curtain and entered the room. The old monk was standing watch over Boudicea. Rael knew he was trying to help her, but she also knew that his vigil was doing nothing for her. It was all up to Rael now. Rael moved over to Boudicea's side, with Amen close behind her.

Rael had forgotten how bad Boudicea had looked after the fight in the pyramid. Then again, maybe she hadn't wanted to remember. That's because she also didn't want to remember something else: Her mother's body had been battered even worse. Battered by the avalanche that her own father had sent against her. Her father had murdered her mother. The painful memory flooded back. She couldn't save her mother that day because she was naive about how the world really was. She hadn't known how badly her father sought demonic power. She hadn't known that she was the key to him obtaining that power. Had she known that, she would have saved her mother. Things were different now. She knew she had power within her. She'd not lose Boudicea the same way she'd lost her mother. All it took to save her was self-confidence, according to the oracle.

Amen bent down to check Boudicea's pulse. The monks had bound her wounds, but they couldn't revive her. Even Amen's gentle touch couldn't stir a reaction from Boudicea. Amen said to Rael, "She has grown weaker since I last saw her. She'd have never survived the trip to the big city. We were right to trust in finding the oracle, to trust in you. She won't have long if you don't act soon."

Rael understood. It was up to her. It was up to her magic to save Boudicea. She replied to Amen, "I think it's best that I be alone with her."

"I can arrange that," said Amen.

Amen exchanged a few words with the monk. The monk looked to Rael and said, "*Malak*." Amen nodded his head and they left together.

Rael was now alone with Boudicea. Rael wasn't sure she was glad about that fact. It was up to her to save her mentor, and truth be told it didn't feel right. She was only sixteen. It shouldn't be up to her to do anything. Yet this was a task only she could do.

Rael said, "Okay, Rael, do it! Visualize success." She kneeled beside Boudicea. The key thing was to believe. She worried about that. In some ways it was easier to believe in demons and cultists than it was to believe in herself. She was still the same young woman who had failed at skiing by a tenth of a second. She wasn't a hunter yet. She wasn't even close to being one. She said, "Oh, Boudicea, I don't know if I do believe in me. I believe I need you, though. And now you need me. I guess we both have family issues. We're a lot alike. We've become a team. Is that enough belief to save you?"

Boudicea didn't reply, for obvious reasons. That was always the way. You could always tell people how you really felt about them when they couldn't hear you. Rael took a deep breath and wrapped her own cloak around Boudicea. She said, "Arianrhod, master of time, giver of acorns, and a bunch of stuff like that, you must aid me now in my task." Nothing happened. Okay, maybe she needed to work on her chanting a touch. Then again, maybe her cloak was a dud. They had to have lemon magic cloaks just like they had lemon cars, right? It would be just her luck to end up with a defective magic cloak. Maybe she needed to jiggle the handle—only, it didn't have a handle. "Come on, magic cloak, get with the program!"

Okay, shouting at your magic cloak wasn't going to help matters. Still, she felt a little better because of it. She pulled her cloak off Boudicea. She stood up and tried to compose herself. She paced around. She had to believe. She needed things to believe in. What did she believe in? She believed in demons now because they were real. She had seen them. She believed in other worlds now because she'd been to them. She believed in lizard people, devils, and even sexy devils with odd fashion advice that sang weird, poorly advised songs. She believed she was valuable and people like Andres and her father wanted her gift for selfish reasons. She believed in good people too because she'd met some along the way on her journey to date: druids, vampires, and even a mummy who liked to order fast food. She believed in all that, but did she believe in herself? Why shouldn't she?

"Forget about your failures at skiing. You can fly anywhere you want now!" she said to herself. She thought about how she had blown up the lizard people's plane, which was totally awesome. She was a hunter in training. Not just anyone could say that. "You have a lot to believe in, Rael, even magic." She reached into her sleeve. She closed her eyes. "Believe, Rael, believe!"

She pulled out a silver acorn. She then immediately dropped it, of course, because she had been as surprised by its sudden appearance as that acorn probably was. She laughed a little. She could do magic too. "I believed and it happened," she said. She took her cloak off and wrapped it around Boudicea again. She repeated, "I do believe. I do believe."

"What do you believe?" asked Boudicea.

"You're awake!" exclaimed Rael.

Boudicea sat up. She noticed Rael's cloak around her and handed it back. She said, "You announce it like you doubted I would ever awaken again, yet you say you believe. How strange."

"I . . ."

"Need not say more," interrupted Boudicea. Amen burst in, which was just the distraction Rael needed, as she didn't want to explain to Boudicea that she'd ever doubted herself. He said, "I believe that I heard my Boudi's voice." He saw Boudicea awake and bounded toward her side. He embraced her. Boudicea didn't appear overjoyed by the attention. At least while Rael could see that she was getting it. Amen didn't seem to care.

Amen said to Boudicea, "Rael's magic is real, and my little desert flower is awake!"

Boudicea broke free of Amen. "Amen, please don't talk like an idiot. And more importantly, what are you doing here?"

"A Freemason arrived at the boat looking for you two. I came to tell you this fact—and a good thing too, because you needed my help," he explained.

Boudicea replied, "The Freemason is not a concern. The cultists in the pyramid are my . . ."

"They are all very dead," said Amen.

"How?" asked Boudicea. Her eyes fell on Rael, but Rael didn't get a word in edgewise. Not because she couldn't have, but because she could see Amen was more than eager to take up the task.

"It is a long story. It is wise to just move on from what happened in the pyramid and remember that I am here now helping," Amen replied.

"This mission is too dangerous for you to help with it. I thought I made that clear to you on the boat. There are demons about, and they mean business. You're a professor, not a hunter," scolded Boudicea.

"Yes, all that you say is true. Indeed, there is one demon just outside the door to confirm it," agreed Amen.

Boudicea reached to pull a blade from her sleeve, but there was no cloak. She looked completely displeased. She balled a fist and asked, "Where is this demon, for we still need to find the phylactery?"

Rael grabbed her arm. "No, it's not like that. The demon outside is here to help us. He seeks what we seek."

"Rael, have you learned nothing from me so far? There is no such demon as a helpful one," said Boudicea, pulling away from Rael.

"But he saved your life and mine inside the pyramid. He killed those cultists, not me. He saved both of us. He has already helped us so much. Please, talk to him and see that he seeks what we seek," explained Rael.

Boudicea cast a concerned eye toward Rael. Then she turned to Amen. She asked, "And you were a party to this befriending of a demon?"

Amen replied, "The demon has been of some help to us, yes. He helped find the Oracle of Ammon for us so that Rael could unlock the secrets of her cloak and save you with it. I should think you'd thank all of us for your rapid recovery."

Boudicea ignored Amen's suggestion. She said, "You spoke to another oracle? That was unwise. There are many ears listening to the vibrations of the ether. I fear that this whole area will soon become too hot for us to handle. We must get away from here at once."

Rael was a little annoyed. After all they had done to save her, Boudicea seemed rather ungrateful about it. Boudicea went to stand up but nearly fell to the floor trying to take a step. Amen caught her in time.

"You're still too weak to move, my love," said Amen.

"I am nobody's love. And we have no choice but to move," said Boudicea.

Amen shrugged and said to Rael, "You can see how it is with us." Rael tried to suppress a laugh. It was too bad, as she needed one. "Very well. Rael, get under one arm. I will support her on the other side. We shall get her to my SUV. I can drive you anywhere you need to go," said Amen.

Rael helped prop up Boudicea, and they moved her outside and headed for his vehicle. They placed Boudicea in the passenger seat. She grimaced from the jostling. Amen said, "Sorry, my love."

"Less apologizing and more movement. I can feel trouble approaching," said Boudicea. She then grabbed Amen and pulled him toward her. She kissed him. Then she slapped him across the face. "Next time, listen to me. I don't want to lose you too." Amen rubbed his face and winked at Rael. Boudicea must be one tough girlfriend for a guy to have.

Amen got in the driver's seat and started the engine, while Boudicea cupped her left ear. Rael listened but heard nothing. Rael opened the door to the back seat and climbed in. She saw the old monk peering out of the fort. Then the other monks emerged. They had their possessions on their backs. With Boudicea healthy again, they were ready to return to their pyramid that really wasn't much of a pyramid. Rael felt satisfied. At least some good had come of their desert trip. They had restored the pyramid . . . well, to the monks. The rightful owner was likely still lost to history for good. There was only so much a hunter could do.

"Drive!" ordered Boudicea.

"What about the demon? We can't leave it behind," said Rael.

"Drive!" Boudicea ordered a second time.

Amen sped off into the desert. They had just cleared the town when Rael heard the sound of helicopters. She looked out the back window. The swirling blades of black helicopters cast shadows on the sand. Three of them suddenly flew over their heads and swarmed the oasis. Amen floored the accelerator and they darted away, leaving the black helicopters in the distance.

Rael asked, "Who are they?"

"Agents of Ghanal, but you know them by another name: the Maleficium Society," said the red demon. Rael pressed against the door because the demon was now sitting beside her. Where'd it come from? She didn't know, but it didn't matter. "There is no reason to worry about those helicopters for now. An agent of theirs left a tracking device on this SUV, but I found it and tied it to a local goat. They'll be very confused when they find that goat, but because of it they won't know where we are for some time. Hopefully long enough to get out of the desert."

Rael asked, "Who is Ghanal?"

Boudicea said, "It's a demonic agent of chaos. I do not understand, nor does the Order, how blue chaos demons can be working in an abyssal cult like the Maleficium Society, but it does appear to be true."

The demon replied, "Listen to me, for I teach great lore."

Rael said, "I'm all ears."

The shapeshifting demon explained, "Neither Ghanal nor any of its kind are a match for my queen, Ilitar. In my world, Ilitar rules the blue chaos demons, and they are her obedient slaves. They deserve no other existence. They are pathetic and weak. Long ago, they were foot soldiers of Neubewar. In the great war when the worlds were new, they were not good enough when the time came and failed him. Ilitar makes them pay for their failures! However, they have long dreamed of their own kingdom, and this Ghanal fancies itself their would-be liberator. It escaped to this world and has clearly formed a plan to banish Ilitar here. The abyssal plane without my queen might indeed fall to the chaos demons, and my way of life would be over."

Rael said, "Ghanal is the blue demon I've seen with my father then."

The demon explained, "Yes. It might have been stopped by now, had a hunter not killed one of our best soldiers in an old church in the Alps."

"I killed it because it was an agent of Ilitar and the Maleficium Society is an agent of Ilitar. You are lying to us. It tried to destroy Rael to gate Ilitar here," replied Boudicea.

The demon said, "You are wrong. It was Ilitar's demon that stopped the commune and saved Ilitar from a foul fate. During the resulting battle between the demons, Rael was found and moved by the villagers to the count's castle. It was most unfortunate for Ilitar."

Rael admitted, "I don't understand this chaos versus abyssal stuff."

The demon continued, "The cult of the chaos demons, this Maleficium Society, will use Ilitar's power to control this world, while Ghanal will return to rule the abyssal plane in Ilitar's absence. I am just a drone in Ilitar's currently unbeatable forces. All that matters to me is Ilitar, my queen. She has ruled her realm in the abyssal for nearly five billion years, since the fall of the old kingdom of Neubewar. It was a simpler time when Neubewar ruled the negative planes. The gap between worlds was not so vast when the worlds were new. Anyone could find an Astralith capable of traversing it. The great king was able to bridge the gap between the positive and the negative planes with a soul bridge, and then the king started an invasion of the positive planes. It was a bold move, too bold even for those simple times. The great Neubewar faced magic he'd never seen before and was destroyed by the combined forces of the positive worlds. His realm fell into the hands of his minions, Ilitar being one of them. Neubewar himself was scattered into the ether, never to reform again. However, the war left lasting damage that not even Neubewar could foresee. The positive plane-dwellers created powerful artifacts to control Neubewar's generals during the battle. When the war was over, their need diminished one thousand-fold. These phylacteries have now been forgotten to the ages."

"Until Ghanal found one and seduced the members of the Maleficium Society with the idea of using it to control Ilitar," said Boudicea.

"Yes, that is what happened," agreed the demon.

Boudicea asked, "What does the phylactery look like?"

"To you, it would look like a golden calf. Of course, that was five million years ago, when it was last seen by an abyssal demon. Its exact shape now is not known to me," replied the demon.

"Where is this object now?" asked Boudicea.

"Ilitar believes it is in London, but my queen does not have forces here on Earth strong enough to breach their lair and take it by force. It is preferable to eliminate the phylactery altogether and free Ilitar from future worry. The Astralith would be of no importance to her if that were to happen."

"I sense a great need for the two of us to work together then. I can supply the manpower; you find me the exact location of the phylactery," said Boudicea.

"Then you are willing to make a deal with a demon?" asked the demon.

Boudicea said, "I do have that will. Amen, take us to Alexandria. We must secure safe passage to London at once."

"We will drive day and night until we are there," replied Amen.

Rael settled back into her seat. She didn't understand half of what the demon had explained. She had a feeling that with more training she might someday understand it all. What she did know was that there was nothing left to discover in the desert. The Oracle of Ammon had been correct: Ariadne had steered Boudicea toward the information she had sought in the long run. They just hadn't got it the way they assumed they would.

Chapter 19

Alexandria, Egypt

It was just an ordinary day in middle school. Nothing special at all. Rael hit the sidewalk with her backpack strapped to her back. She was walking home with thoughts of the weekend on her mind. It was only Wednesday, but she was already thinking about asking her father if they could head out to the mountains to go skiing all weekend. He'd likely say no. They couldn't afford to go skiing all the time. Winter never came to this part of California outside of the mountains, and so one had to spend money to go skiing. The past week's rain in the valley would have made for ideal skiing conditions in the mountains. She liked skiing, but her father *loved* it. It was always a fun time together when they went. Maybe today he'd say yes. Fun did sometimes overcome thoughts of fiscal responsibility.

She rounded the corner and saw a moving truck parked on the road, blocking traffic. That was a normal part of California life in an area heavily populated by condos. Someone was always moving in or out of a place, so Rael never took much notice. Since people came and went like the clouds, she never really bothered to get to know them well. As she neared home, she noticed that today was different. This truck was parked in front of Rael's unit. She distinctly saw her kitchen table being carried into the truck.

Though her mother had agonized over that table every night, Rael had never thought much about it until now.

Her father was on the sidewalk waiting for Rael. "There she is at last. Rael, how would you like to go skiing this weekend?" he asked her.

She was confused. You didn't need a moving truck to go skiing. She replied, "I'd love to, but why do we have a moving truck here?"

"I've got a new job. It means the best of everything from now on. This place isn't the best of anything. That means we're leaving it. We're leaving here for Colorado. We can ski more often there. Why, we could even make a run at your dream."

"My dream?" Rael distinctly remembered dreaming about a chocolate chip cookie last night. She didn't have to make a run at it. It simply sat in a jar until she opened it. She figured he meant *dream* in the bigger sense of the word. The sense that included ambition. Only, Rael was ten and didn't have much ambition, did she?

"We won't settle for anything less than you in the Olympics."

"Oh right, my dream of the Olympics. I . . . don't know, Dad. What about school?"

"I'll get private tutors."

"My friends here?"

"You won't need them. They're losers anyway. I want you to get to know more winners."

"Winners?"

"Don't worry about anything. I've taken care of it all. From now on, I'll take special care of you. You're special, I know that now." She looked into her father's eyes. They were eager eyes. This moving states business had come out of nowhere. She still didn't understand it. To move at a moment's notice like this, it wasn't like her father at all. In an instant he had changed. Something had happened to him, but she was too young to really care what. She had gone along without questioning it at the time.

Rael opened her eyes. Her dreams at times were so real. In this case it was because it had really happened. The question was, what *had* happened to her father? She didn't know. Somehow her dad had joined a cult all those years ago. She'd dreamed about the very day, she now knew, that he'd joined. Only, that knowledge was gained in retrospect. Retrospect wasn't good for much. It only made Rael feel stupid for not having seen events more clearly all those years ago. She had been ten with a normal family life back then. After that day, they were wealthy and working toward her dream. Only it was his dream they were working toward, and skiing was a distraction from that real dream.

She had never lived a normal life again after that day. She never saw friends, never stayed in school long, and was always preparing. All of that was a distraction until the day her father tried to sacrifice her. He hadn't gotten a new job. He'd joined a cult that had plans of murdering her for their gain. That very day he'd known that one day he'd kill her. Most of her life had been lived as a lie. Had her mother known? She must not have, because he'd killed her. They were a cruel cult, though. They even killed their own. Rael had seen that fact first-hand. Rael couldn't face it if Mother had known too. She'd not believe it without proof. The weight of the idea sent a shiver down her spine.

Rael stretched as she sat in the backseat of the SUV waiting for Amen to return. She must have dozed off due to boredom. She wanted to think of something else, anything else but her father, so she turned her thoughts toward Amen. He was out on the docks trying to secure a boat ride for them. It wasn't clear to Rael who was still working after dark out on these docks. She imagined all types of nefarious people out there. That might just be her not-unreasonable paranoia speaking. From time to time she saw dockworkers pass by the parked vehicle. They looked more tired and busy than nefarious, though. This city was famous for an ancient lighthouse that was considered one of the great wonders of the ancient world. Today the docks at Alexandria glowed a pale yellow from the modern electric lighting. The docks appeared, though, as busy as they ever had been.

Boudicea said, "Hand me your cloak."

Rael looked toward the front seat. Boudicea was staring at her. It took a few seconds to register that she'd asked for her cloak. Why would she need it? Then it occurred to her why. "Do you think Amen is in danger?" asked Rael.

"I didn't ask you for a question. I asked for your cloak," said Boudicea.

Rael relented. The boredom of waiting appeared to be over. She was too interested in what Boudicea was up to not to give in. Rael handed the cloak over to her. Boudicea stepped out of the SUV and put Rael's cloak on. It wasn't a good fit, which accentuated the differences between them. Boudicea didn't seem to care how silly she looked in Rael's cloak.

Rael opened her door. She said, "If there is to be a fight, then I'm coming too."

"Be still. There is no fight—at least, not yet. There's only a wardrobe change." Boudicea reached up the sleeve. She pulled out another cloak. She snapped it and dust flaked off. She smiled, "Good as new." She took Rael's off and handed it back to her. She put her new cloak on. "I'm starting to get back to full strength. Which is good, for the dangers ahead will be formidable. Rael, the two of us are not so different. We both have our issues with family. The thing to remember about family is that we're your family now. The Order. When we face your father again, you must not think of him as your father. You must accept what might need to be done to stop him. He is the enemy; that is all."

It seemed like a strange topic for Boudicea to be lecturing Rael on after the whole Ariadne thing. Rael very much wanted to never think about her father again. Wanting and being able to were two different things. Rael opened her mouth to explain, but the demon interjected. "She means we will kill him when we find him." The sound of its voice made Rael jump. It was always appearing out of nowhere.

Boudicea scowled at the demon. She said to it, "If that is what is needed, then, yes, that is what will be done to him."

"Don't patronize the child. Tell her the truth: We will gladly kill her father. He is nothing to us," said the red demon.

Boudicea replied, "Demon, be silent, but if you must speak then tell me your name, for I do not care to keep calling you demon."

"My name is nothing to you, because it could not be pronounced with a human tongue," he replied.

"So be it. You are a shapeshifter, and for lack of a better name, that will be yours from now on," said Boudicea.

A ship's horn sounded in the distance, and the group fell silent. Rael remembered the hate she felt for her father. There was enough of it inside her to have killed him the last time they had met. But was there the will inside her to do it? After that day with the moving van, her father had never been the same man. Still, there was the time before the cult. There were many good times with him to remember. She'd kill those memories too if she murdered him. Rael didn't think of herself as a killer at heart. She was a lover at heart. But hunters were killers by trade, were they not? She'd do what she had to do when the time came. She thought that with less confidence than she probably needed. She looked toward Boudicea. The demon was correct: She'd kill Rael's father in a heartbeat. She might object to the raw honesty of the demon, but Boudicea would kill him if needed. That's why she had asked Rael to accept that fate. Rael never doubted the fact for a minute. She hoped the decision was Boudicea's to make. Rael did not wish it to be hers.

"I will do what a hunter must when the time comes," said Rael.

"Mere words," scolded the demon. The demon saw through her words, and Rael didn't defend herself.

"Her father is not here to turn Rael's words into action, so what do you expect but mere words?" interjected Boudicea. Rael was glad for Boudicea's stern defense of her, even if the demon probably wasn't wrong. The response shut the demon up—although the approaching footsteps on the dock may have also made it keep quiet.

They belonged to Amen. He immediately asked, "Why did you all get out of the SUV?"

"That doesn't matter. Did you find a ship willing to take us?" asked Boudicea.

"I did, but you might not like it," replied Amen.

"Why?" asked Boudicea.

"I found a formidable craft willing to take you onboard. It is captained by a Knight of Malta. He is waiting for you in berth thirteen. His name is Gerard," said Amen.

Rael objected, "The last meeting I had with the Knights of Malta makes me wish it would remain my last meeting."

Boudicea was not so quick to reject the news. She asked, "Do you trust him, Amen?"

"I cannot say my trust in him is boundless. I did know his father, who was always an honorable man. The adage 'like father like son' is not always true, though. What is true is that he is willing to sail with you onboard, and that is more than I can say for any of the other captains I spoke with. The Knights of Malta are at least a known known," said Amen.

"Agreed. So, we go with this captain," decided Boudicea.

"What about me? Why don't I have a say in our means of travel?" balked the demon.

"Because you don't," said Boudicea. The demon relented again. Rael would not object a second time. She knew her place by now in her relationship with Boudicea, and the demon was learning its place.

Boudicea started down the dock and the demon followed. Amen didn't follow. He called out to her, "I will say goodbye, because I have work to do in Egypt and I've been distracted from it for too long." He paused, but Boudicea did not turn around. He looked over to Rael. He added, "Not that I wasn't willingly distracted." He said the words with bravery, but Rael didn't believe them. He wanted to leave with them. She could feel it.

It was the demon who stopped. It turned and said, "Very touching." Then it sneered and continued down the dock in search of the boat.

"She didn't even say goodbye to you," said Rael.

"It would hurt her too much to say such things. Nothing can stop a hunter from their mission, not even romantic feelings. What were you discussing while I was gone?" asked Amen.

"Oh, nothing big—just family," replied Rael.

Amen smirked. "The topic of family is nothing big? Boudicea is your private Hathor. You're lucky to have her, and she, you." Amen waved Rael away. He said, "Go now, Rael, and feel no sorrow for me. Think only of my joy when I get to see you both again in the future in better circumstances."

"I will, and I thank you for your help," replied Rael. She left him alone at the start of the dock.

The dock housed many cargo ships. However, the boat in berth thirteen turned out to be not so much to look at. The cargo vessels all around them dwarfed this small craft. The good news was that it wasn't a slow tugboat. The bad news was everything else about it. It was only twenty-five feet in length, and rust was its primary décor. The boat was christened the *Puta Mahmuga*. It flew a half-white, half-red flag with a small cross in the upper left.

One by one, they hopped onto the boat. Rael hit the deck and said, "I was expecting a bigger boat to sail the open seas."

A younger man, maybe as old as twenty, came on deck from down below. He had olive skin and dark hair. He wore a white T-shirt, cargo shorts, and sunglasses even at night. He said to Rael, "She is not much to look at, but she floats. That is what matters most in a boat, right?" Rael felt a little ashamed to have been overheard by the captain. Luckily, she wasn't the only one with doubts. Boudicea immediately added to Rael's doubts.

"You are Gerard?" asked Boudicea.

"I am," he replied, bowing to Boudicea.

"How old are you?" asked Boudicea.

"I am nearly eighteen."

"Isn't that a little young to be a knight?" asked Boudicea.

"I inherited my title and position after my father died in battle," replied Gerard, lowering his head.

"Oh, in what battle did he die?" asked Rael.

"The one with alcohol, my dear young damsel in distress," replied Gerard.

"I am not in distress at the moment," said Rael.

"Around me, all young ladies' hearts are in distress. I have that effect on them," boasted Gerard.

"Rael, please don't get distracted. How big is your crew?" Boudicea asked.

"I'm about this tall," Gerard replied, measuring himself with a free hand.

"A crew of one, then. That will be simple enough to keep track of. We push off immediately, for time is not on our side," ordered Boudicea.

"There is the little matter of my payment before this boat leaves the dock," said Gerard.

"The Order will pay in full when we arrive safely, you know that," replied Boudicea.

"Money—is that all you humans care about. Power matters; money does not. These matters do not concern me, so I'll be in the cabin below," said the demon. The boat wasn't even sailing yet and it already appeared to be getting a little pale green in the face. Rael wondered if the retreat below had more to do with *that* fact.

Gerard smirked and elbowed Rael, "An abyssal demon, even disguised as a human, can never fool a knight of God's order. It is sick because there are no oceans in its godless abyss."

"We do have them. They are just oceans of flames," replied the demon and then went below.

Gerard said to Rael, "Come with me to the pilot house, pretty Astralith, as we set off to the sea."

He climbed up to the top deck, which sat above the cabin. Rael looked toward Boudicea to see if she was comfortable with her being with Gerard. Boudicea wasn't paying attention at all. She was looking back toward the docks, lost in thought. She had put up a good front, but affairs of the heart were hard. Clearly Boudicea wasn't ready to leave Amen. She probably wanted to be alone, so Rael climbed up top with Gerard.

Gerard said to Rael, "The knights of old had horsepower, and so do I." He started the boat's motor. The boat lurched forward, blew a cloud of black smoke up a stack, and stopped. He then shouted down toward Boudicea. "A little help, please."

Boudicea shook herself out of her funk to toss the mooring lines off the boat. The boat slowly idled from the dock. As horsepower went, Rael had seen more impressive displays. Indeed, she'd seen ducks at the park swim faster than they were moving. Gerard talked as he steered. "Rael Armstrong, the famous Astralith on the loose. As Astraliths go, you don't look like much to me."

"Oh, what do they normally look like?" asked Rael.

"I don't know. You're the first one of any significance I've met. Still, for all the fireworks you've caused in Rome, I expected more."

"Sorry to disappoint you."

"I am not disappointed yet. It takes a lot to disappoint a man like me." He elbowed her again. He added, "The ladies, though, are never disappointed when I'm around. As I've said, horsepower matters in a man." He stretched and attempted to put his arm around Rael.

Eww, thought Rael, as she dodged him. Rael moved slightly away from Gerard. "I am not really interested in your horsepower. You see, I am a sixteen-year-old druid of the Order, with a vow of celibacy and all that goes with it."

"I thought you druids made mad love by the moonlight, and unless my eyes are mistaken the moon is full tonight."

Rael looked to the moon and said, "Waxing gibbous, I believe."

"That's full enough for me." He paused as he passed by an oil tanker. "I am just making conversation, you understand. I mean nothing by it. Sexy talk, it is the way of the romantic knight."

"As long as that's all you're making, then we're fine."

"You are a hard one."

"Count on it. I'm as tough as they come."

"Your reputation is known to me. You did quite well in our church in Rome. My elders were impressed. They were also very sad to learn that one of our own tried to harm you. Now that I see how pretty you are, I too am very sad about the matter. Gerard, like the knights of old, has a heart that clings to a higher sense of honor when it comes to women, the old code. You know how the old code of the knights works?"

"You mean *you* practice chivalry?"

"But of course. You sound surprised by the fact. But I am the very model of a chivalric knight. Have I made a pass at you, a damsel in distress, while on my boat?"

"Er . . . yes!" replied Rael.

"That was a rhetorical question. Anyway, you do not know what you speak of. Let me explain the moral code of the modern romantic knight:

> Chivalry is a very noble thing, from that moral fountain my values spring.
> I place the female on a pedestal, then I look up, if not preventable.
> I, for one, never kiss on a first date, to go further is open to debate.
> In all dealings I am to be polite, especially if your buttocks are tight.
> I shall not reveal in my love affairs, I shall hate it if you show me your wares.
> Until marriage I do keep myself chaste, still leaving the door open just in case.
> Before asking, first remove the ring, a married hand is not my kind of thing.
> In danger, I would gladly give my life to save any girl that is not my wife.
> In love I practice modesty. I spread gossip on Facebook, never audibly.
> At service to the needs of my lady, will I call her tomorrow? Well, maybe.

"And to think I'd heard chivalry was dead," replied Rael.

"It is a common misconception."

They cleared the port entrance and were in open waters. Gerard set the controls to full throttle, which apparently changed their speed, though Rael didn't notice much difference. Gerard put the boat on autopilot, which unfortunately gave him a second free hand that she'd have to dodge. Fortunately, his free hands fumbled around in the compartments of his boat and appeared indifferent to her. Gerard popped open a compartment next to him. He pulled out two small white boxes. "Ah, we are free to roam where we need to roam in these waters. We need a toast to our success." He offered a box to Rael. "Rael, would you do me the fine honor of toasting the sea with me? I have some of Detroit's finest boxed wine."

Before them was the infinite sea, the blackness of the dark waters extending into the blackness of the night sky. The waves of the Mediterranean at night reminded her of the living stars of the Oracle of Ammon's chamber. It was rather romantic, in a way. Well, if Rael had been sailing out in it with any young man but Gerard. Rael replied, "I don't drink."

Gerard pulled the plastic straw from its wrapping and poked it into his boxed wine. He took a sip and asked her, "Then how do you maintain the proper levels of your bodily fluids?" Rael didn't reply. Her heart was on fire, and the flames weren't being lit by Gerard. She pulled her necklace up and held it in her hands. There was danger coming their way. "Hello, are you okay?" asked Gerard, waving his hand at her.

That was a good question. Rael looked down at Boudicea, but there was no need to warn her. She already knew what the necklace was telling Rael. Boudicea looked up at Rael. Boudicea said, "Our friends from the desert finally caught up with our trail. Four black helicopters are coming our way."

Gerard asked, "These helicopters are friends of yours?" Rael shook her head as she looked toward the black night sky. She saw nothing. Then four bright floodlights turned on. They illuminated the boat. There were two helicopters in front of them and two behind. They were trapped between the four helicopters.

Boudicea shouted, "Gerard, if you want to live, you'd better give it all you've got."

Gerard understood the seriousness of the situation. He dropped his boxed wine and scrambled to the wheel. He pulled up a secret panel and jammed a red button on it. The boat accelerated, now splitting the front two floodlights. The boat went up on hydrofoils and took off at speed. The helicopters didn't anticipate Gerard's craft having that kind of speed. They opened fire but the bullets trailed behind the boat. Gerard looked over at Rael. He said, "You see, I have a lot of secrets inside my trunk. As I have said, it all comes down to horsepower with us knights."

The demon came out from down below. It didn't look happy. It snarled, "What's going on here?"

"The Maleficium Society's black helicopters have found us," replied Boudicea.

"Out here? I don't believe it!" snarled the demon. A helicopter opened up another round of gunfire.

"Believe it. They're not trying to kill us so much as disable the boat and board us. They want Rael alive." As fast as Gerard's hydrofoil could go, helicopters could go faster. Boudicea asked Gerard, "Do you have any more tricks on this boat?"

"Do I?" Gerard nudged the console next to him. Another secret panel dropped down. He hit a button and a machine-gun turret rose up on the bow of the boat. "I got a cabin full of hand-held automatics below. Feel free to use them."

The demon helped itself to a machine gun. It fired it in the direction of the gunning helicopter. All it did was take out its light. Without its light, the helicopter got bolder and moved in closer, and the demon took out the whole helicopter in an explosion. One down, three to go.

The other helicopters responded to the fire-fight by shooting a lot more at them as well. Except for one, which flew too high above them for the demon to hit it. The helicopter swooped and circled around to face them. Something dropped into the water from the underbelly of the copter.

Boudicea shouted, "Torpedo!"

"I don't have anything to counter that," said Gerard.

"Steer into it at full speed," ordered Boudicea.

"Wait, what?" replied Gerard.

Boudicea climbed up to the pilot house and removed him from the steering wheel. Boudicea went full throttle and turned into the on-rushing torpedo. The torpedo hit their hydrofoil and bounced off.

"A dud. We got lucky," said Gerard.

"No luck. The torpedo hadn't been armed yet," explained Boudicea.

"They won't make the same mistake with the next torpedo," snarled the demon.

"You just keep shooting at them then," ordered Boudicea.

Gerard followed that advice too. He jumped down to the bow of the boat and manned his gunner station. Everyone had something to do but Rael. She was a hunter now, and this was a fight she should be fighting too. She spied a harpoon rolling around on the deck. It must have been from the same compartment from which the demon had extracted the machine gun. Rael jumped down to grab the harpoon.

Boudicea yelled, "Where are you going?"

"I'm helping," said Rael. She picked up the harpoon. It wouldn't be much good against helicopters. Unless . . . She had an idea. "Fly," said Rael. Her wings spread out and she soared off the deck.

Gerard must have seen her. He shouted out, "I knew you were as pretty as an angel."

Rael ignored him. She flew straight at one of the oncoming helicopters. It wouldn't dare shoot her: She was their prize. The helicopter paused and hovered in midair right in front of her. Rael flew to its underside. She tossed the harpoon up into the helicopter blades. The blades directly hit the shaft of the harpoon. One of the blades shattered off the rotor, making the whole assembly unstable. Black smoke started billowing. Rael was feeling rather proud of herself. She turned to fly away just as a net hit her. The helicopter had let her get that close for a reason. It now had Rael netted like a fish and tied to a cord attached to the bottom of the helicopter.

The helicopter tried to bank and move away. It was then that the damage done by Rael had its full effect. The rotor spun itself apart. The helicopter was dead in the air without it. It hung in the air for a second. Then the helicopter started to plunge toward the black-as-night Mediterranean waters. The rope attached to the net was pulled along with it. Rael was heading fast toward the water. She was netted like a fish and now about to be swimming with the fishes. The helicopter splashed down and broke apart on impact. Rael came tumbling after and splashed down. She managed to avoid most of the debris, which was now sinking into the black abyss of the nighttime sea. There was one thing wrong here: Rael was still netted, and that net was still tied to part of the helicopter.

Rael clawed at the net. She needed to cut through before her breath ran out. They must have accounted for her claws because she was making poor progress. Time was running out. She took one last big breath before she was dragged underwater. She tried and tried but she couldn't cut the net all the way through. It must have been thirty seconds since she'd splashed down. Rael was starting to black out.

Then she saw it. A green glow moved toward her as she sank into the depths. As it reached her, she could see it was a man with a green glowstick tied around his neck. Dynami! She'd know his blue eyes anywhere, even if they weren't blue due to there only being a green light source. He had a Bowie knife with him and he was shredding the net with it. The net gave way and he jerked her out. She saw the helicopter and the net still plunging to their doom beneath her. Above her she saw only blackness. She must be very far down. She was out of oxygen; she knew it didn't matter that he was there because she'd never make it to the surface alive.

Then Dynami kissed her! Only, it wasn't so much a kiss as him forcing air from his lungs into her mouth, but she was still going to totally count it as a kiss. Their first kiss was a very bubbly one. He did another round of bubble blowing and her head started to clear, which she was almost certain was not how kisses were supposed to work, but so be it. She held onto him now and he swam them up to the surface. A couple of things flashed through her head as they rose through the water column. The first was that he could actually breathe underwater, and that second was that Boudicea hadn't been looking back longingly at the docks as they had cast off out of longing to be with her love, Amen, but because she'd been looking for the help she expected to arrive. And now it had arrived, just in time.

They broke the surface. Dynami immediately asked her, "Are you alright?"

Rael didn't reply. She embraced him and kissed him again. He couldn't stop her because he was treading water with his four limbs. Then she said, "Just needed a little more oxygen. You know, the moon does look full tonight." She leaned in for another kiss.

"Waxing gibbous, actually," replied Dynami.

There was no chance to explain to him she didn't care about the phases of the moon because another helicopter dropped from the sky and fixed its floodlight on them. Rael looked around, but Gerard and his boat were nowhere to be seen.

Rael asked, "What do we do now?"

"Wait," said Dynami.

Waiting to be captured didn't sound like an attractive plan to her. Luckily, Dynami meant wait and see what happens next. What happened next was that a battle-axe hurtled through the air and smashed through the cockpit glass of the helicopter. Rael had a suspicion the pilot wasn't okay after that impact. The helicopter lurched and then went straight into the water. Rael could hear a new sound: the sound of a jet ski across the water. Soon she saw what appeared to be a dwarf with a long white flowing beard and a pointy blue hat riding high on the waves. Dynami explained, "Here comes Archon."

Archon circled around them on the jet ski and shouted, "Argh, waste of a perfectly good battle-axe." He looked at them in the water and asked, "What are you doing in the water with that wee lass, lad? Get her up on your jet ski and let's get her back to the boat." He revved his motor and took off.

An explosion filled the night sky. Dynami said, "Don't worry, that's the fourth helicopter going down and not the boat exploding." Rael wasn't worried about that. She was more worried about being so close to Dynami again. He gently placed her up on the jet ski. Then he slid onboard. She held onto him. He revved up the motor and they were off. It was sort of romantic, riding the waves of the open sea by moonlight. If they hadn't just killed four helicopters' worth of people, that is. That specter of death did sort of dampen the romantic buzz of the evening.

Gerard's boat was idle in the water ahead of them. Rael could see Boudicea on the deck searching the waters for her. She wouldn't be too mad at her, right? After all, Rael had destroyed a helicopter and found Dynami. All in all, a successful attack. That was all wishful thinking. Boudicea scolded Rael upon their arrival alongside the boat. "There is no point in us trying to save you if you go off and try to get killed."

It was Archon who jumped to Rael's defense. He bounded off his jet ski and onto the deck. He said, "There's no better way for a lass to learn her limits than to try." He held his hand out and pulled Rael onboard. His strength didn't match his size, that was for sure. He nearly pulled Rael's arm out while yanking her onto the boat.

Gerard became peacemaker. He brought a woolen blanket and wrapped it around the soaking-wet Rael. Gerard said, "It doesn't matter now. The boat is safe, and so is my girlfriend."

Rael looked at Dynami, who seemed concerned. She assured him, "I am not his girlfriend."

Gerard corrected himself as the much taller Dynami came aboard the boat and stood next to Rael. "I am sorry, I meant to say friend that is girl. My English is not so, how do you say it, good." He then stepped away from Rael and shot Dynami a look of jealousy.

It was the demon that moved in to take Gerard's place. It came up to Rael and reached for her throat. Dynami tried to stop the demon, but Archon intercepted him. The demon pointed at Rael's neck. He asked her, "This necklace here, where did you get it?"

"From Boudicea," replied Rael.

The demon tore the Coptic cross off Rael's neck and tossed it to Boudicea. "I meant the other one."

"Oh, that one. I got it from the monks we helped. Well, actually I got it from a small boy at the oasis who said it was from the monks," replied Rael.

"He was no small boy. Likely he was a chaos demon's imp spy," confirmed the demon.

"That small boy, not human? I can't believe it," said Rael.

"Aye, believe it lass. They've been tracking you. They probably heard everything said around you since you received it," agreed Archon.

Boudicea looked concerned. The cult had not been fooled at the oasis. They'd let them get out here to open water, before attempting to extract Rael. Boudicea dropped the cross into the sea. Rael knew she'd messed up, again. Boudicea grabbed Gerard and told him, "Our plans have changed. They know where we are heading. Change our course; we're headed to Venice now."

"But the phylactery is still in London. If they come out in the open and attack because they know our plans, all the better I say," said the demon.

"Don't worry, because that *is* my plan, but since our plan is now known to the enemy, we will need a distraction in order to achieve our goals. I know someone who is very distracting, and they're located in Venice," said Boudicea.

"They say Venice is a very romantic place," said Gerard, eyeing Rael.

Boudicea grabbed him by the arm. "Romance we don't need right now; steering is what we need."

"Alright, alright," said Gerard.

Chapter 20

Venice, Italy

Rael had never been to Venice before. On her initial trip to Italy, her family had flown into Rome, spent a few days there, and taken the train up into the Alps to ski. Since her father had planned to consume her essence to gate in a demon, the holiday had not included stops to places such as Venice. Of course, that was thinking about things in retrospect, but it was likely very accurate. Things hadn't gone as planned for dear old daddy, because here Rael was. Where her father was now, she didn't know. She was headed on a collision course toward seeing him again, though. That seemed inevitable now. Such unpleasant thoughts were not what brought people to Venice. People came here for the enchanting atmosphere.

For many, Venice was the dream vacation destination, and she was sort of feeling it too. She had heard a gondola ride along the canals was the height of romance. She'd not been very interested in romance until recently. And though she wished for most any type of distraction from her fate, romantic sailing at the moment was not one of them. That was mostly because her visit to Venice had come during a living nightmare, and part of that nightmare was that she was in this gondola with the wrong man. Gerard confirmed that by opening his mouth. He complained, "I don't understand why the two of you get to sit there eating cheese and fruit while I have to do all the work."

"I'm paying you to sail us around, so sail us," replied Boudicea.

"Yes, but that was using my own boat. This is different," said Gerard.

"The only difference is that now you're wearing a costume," explained Boudicea.

"Yes, and I look ridiculous."

"You were the only one that fit into the gondolier outfit," explained Boudicea. She then slipped a cube of cheese into her mouth. The current plan was a little hazy to Rael. They'd docked Gerard's boat on a small island outside the main city. Gerard assured everyone that the dock was secure under the protection of the Knights of Malta—a boast that didn't leave Rael feeling any real comfort. The demon, though, had thought enough of it to stay behind on the boat. At least, that is what it had said, but that shapeshifting demon tended to show up wherever it wanted. It was clearly not bound by space and time as humans were.

The demon having stayed behind, the rest of the merry gang had taken a second boat to the main islands of the city of Venice. Once there, Boudicea had bribed a gondolier out of his craft and his outfit. Then they'd split up again, with Boudicea and Rael taking the gondola around town, steered by Gerard. Meanwhile, Archon and Dynami were supposed to be watching over them while following them on foot. They were all posing as tourists, because that often-repeated plan had worked so well for them to date. That was the plan, but obviously not the real plan. The actual real plan Rael didn't know. They were sailing on the canals heading somewhere important to find a distraction. It was the type of thing she knew meant she didn't know very much at all. Finding a distraction could mean just about anything. Indeed, in Venice, everything felt like a distraction from ordinary life. Rael intended to ask for more information about the real plan later, but she doubted Boudicea would give details, so she sat back and let it all happen. That was just how her life rolled these days.

They passed under a low bridge and Gerard managed to bump his head not once but twice while shoving them under it. He grumbled toward Rael, "This is going to cost you extra."

"You're not much of a knight if you charge damsels in distress extra," said Rael.

He looked down at Rael as he led them through the canal. He winked at her. "I meant . . . ah . . . anything to help a lady. You do know that the tall fellow, Dynami, he's not so attractive. A lot of ladies might think that he is, but take it from Gerard, because he is your good friend, that Dynami is not so . . . so. Yes, not so at all. After all, you know what they say about tall men like that Dynami?"

"No, what do they say?" asked Rael.

"They make for lousy lovers," replied Gerard.

"Is this conversation really necessary?" asked Boudicea.

"Of course it is necessary. I saw how she looked at him on my fine vessel as we sailed here. You probably didn't notice, but a sensitive man like me takes notice of the important things. The young woman, she can easily fall in with the wrong crowd, and I, being a knight, have sworn a duty to make sure these types of things do not happen. It was all I could do these past three days to keep those two apart. That Dynami is no knight in shining armor, I tell you. He's a lothario if ever I've seen one. A girl of Rael's age is highly impressionable, and with a strange tall young man of uncertain virtue about, why, it could have ended in disaster if not for my watchful eye. You should do better as a parent to look after her. She is bound to be . . . ah . . . disappointed if ever she were to be alone with that scoundrel."

"Dynami is not a scoundrel," protested Rael.

"Raised by a dwarf, of course he's a scoundrel. You know what they say about dwarves?" asked Gerard.

"That they have excellent hearing, are quick to temper, and can dismember a man with their bare hands," interjected Boudicea.

Gerard shifted his eyes around. He lowered his voice. "It was a rhetorical question. And I meant no ill things rhetorically toward dwarves by asking it." Gerard took his eyes off Rael for once and examined the walkways around him. Rael suspected he was on the lookout for Archon. Either way, Gerard had finally shut up. The sudden silence of Gerard was the thing she'd most welcomed in Venice so far. The continuous presence of Gerard near her the past few days had been quite the disappointment, so Gerard was only half wrong about some men being disappointing. She'd been trapped on a small boat for three days, and Dynami had done practically nothing toward her. She sighed. It was all very disappointing. She took the cheese knife and dismembered a cheese wheel in frustration.

Gerard rowed them out of the canal into a far more open channel. Across the wide channel stood a rather amazing structure. It looked almost Middle Eastern, with its arches and decorative dome. The marble and frescos around it, though, looked far more decoratively Italian. The extravagance of it all was almost gaudy. Boudicea said, "There is our destination up ahead. Gerard, move us into position along the shoreline."

Gerard replied, "I would not advise it. The Basilica di San Marco is one of the most visited tourist spots in Venice. You will hardly be able to move about unnoticed inside there. Venice is supposed to be for lovers, not fighters, so I do not wish to find a fight when no fight is needed."

"We're not going inside it. We're going under it. Rael and I are headed for the basement," explained Boudicea.

"Basement? There are no basements in Venice. There are only wooden pillars, mud, and sea beneath all of Venice," said Gerard.

"Men from Malta don't know everything," said Boudicea.

"That almost sounded like prejudice," scolded Gerard.

"Just park us in the canal next to it and I'll do the rest," instructed Boudicea.

"I'm not sure you're allowed to just park here. If I get a ticket that's going to cost you extra," said Gerard.

"I don't need you to be there long," replied Boudicea. She stood up and dove into the water.

Gerard put the pole to the side and snuck into the seat next to Rael. He scooped up some fruit and cheese while saying to her, "At last, Rael, we can be alone together. I've waited days for this moment, whereas you've waited a lifetime to be alone with a man of such virtue as myself."

"Correction, I've waited no time at all for you. Besides, a man such as you can only be virtuous by being alone," said Rael. She then dove in after Boudicea.

After nearly drowning three days ago, another underwater trip was not high on Rael's list of preferred activities. Although it did beat being in a gondola alone with Gerard. The canal water wasn't the clearest she'd ever been in, nor the cleanest, which made the experience less desirable. Still, she wanted to know what Boudicea was up to.

What she was up to was about ten feet of water right near the shoreline. Boudicea pressed on a brick marked *Intrabit.* The wall of the canal gave way. Then she swam inside the passageway that had been revealed. Rael kicked her feet and swam inside after her.

The canal wall swung shut behind her. She was in a ten-by-ten-feet stone-lined room filled floor to ceiling with salt water. Rael wasn't any better off inside here than when she was sinking deep into the Mediterranean. Then she felt a swirling current. The sea level was falling. She swam up and took a gasp of the air that was filling the upper parts of the chamber. Within minutes, the room was completely drained and Rael was on the floor soaking wet.

A door opened in the wall. Boudicea said, "Let's go."

"Where?" asked Rael.

"Out of this airlock, of course."

They walked into a white hallway with glowing white lights set into the ceiling. There were two unfriendly looking large men dressed in white outfits with black guns pointed at them. One of the men said, *"Fermati là!"*

Rael didn't need a translation. Boudicea put her hands in the air, and Rael joined her. Well, this didn't seem very promising. Footsteps echoed down the hallway. A thin man dressed in white with metal-framed glasses was running toward them. The guards with the guns just stood there pointing their weapons at Rael and Boudicea, apparently waiting for this other man to arrive. Thus, everyone waited patiently for this other man to arrive.

When he arrived, he was breathing heavily. The first thing he did was wipe the sweat from his brow with a white handkerchief. He then gave Rael and Boudicea an inspection. He clicked a ballpoint pen and went through a checklist on his clipboard. Rael looked at Boudicea, but she was just biding her time. He retracted his ballpoint after an awkward silent minute of checking boxes. He then said to them, *"Parli Italiano?"*

"We prefer English," replied Boudicea.

He said, "You're not supposed to be here. A fact that is true in any language."

"Double-check your list," replied Boudicea.

"I have, and my checklist is never wrong," he assured her.

"Giatano, bring them to me," said a disembodied female voice over a loudspeaker.

"I guess this time your checklist was wrong," said Rael.

Giatano didn't reply. He just gave Rael a hard stare. Then he stored his pen in his pocket and walked down the hallway. "This way," he instructed.

Rael whispered to Boudicea, "They seem very friendly here."

"This is not a place to make friends," Boudicea whispered back.

"Then we're doing an excellent job."

They walked down the spotless white-tiled hallway until they reached a metallic white door. Giatano scanned his retina and the door slid open. He led them into an approximately ten-by-ten-feet octagonal room. He said to them, "You will wait here. The director will be here shortly to determine what is to be done with you." He then walked to the opposite side of the room from where they had entered. He hung the clipboard on a hook, scanned his retina, and left.

Rael smiled at Boudicea. She said, "Well, now here we are, waiting. Do you know what we're waiting for?"

"Help in obtaining a distraction."

After Boudicea replied, another of the octagonal room's walls opened. A nun with a crutch limped into the room. It was Sister Isabella. Rael would have been wholly glad to see her, if she hadn't had an I-just-gutted-a-man look on her face. The sister yelled, "Strip down to your skin!"

"Strip?" repeated Rael.

"Rael, you're not a parrot; there's no need to repeat things," said Boudicea. Boudicea stripped out of her soaked cloak and Lycra outfit and tossed them on the floor. Rael started to do the same. There was something uncomfortable about being watched while undressing, but a nun watching you, well, that probably shouldn't be something that made Rael uncomfortable. And yet, Rael felt awkward about stripping in front of the nun all the same.

Once they were both naked, Sister Isabella announced, "Good." Rael wasn't sure how to gauge that remark. Frankly, she was more interested in a towel. The sister didn't offer one. She was too busy scanning her retina on another octagonal wall, in which a compartment opened. She pulled out two white gowns, which she tossed at their feet. "You will dress!"

Rael was glad to be out of her wet clothes. She would have been gladder if the gown she was wearing didn't open in the back. She kept peering around her to make sure no one could see her butt in this thing.

"Stop fidgeting, Rael," said Boudicea.

"Can't we wear normal clothes just once?" asked Rael.

"No unauthorized clothing is allowed on the cell block. Your clothing will be returned to you on your way out," explained Sister Isabella.

"Cell block? Like in a prison?" asked Rael.

"Where did you think you were, summer Bible camp?" replied Sister Isabella. She scanned her eye on another panel and the wall opened up. "Welcome to the Vatican Prison for the Paranormal Criminally Minded. Follow me and remember, strictly no magic is allowed inside the prison walls," she ordered.

"Wait, the Vatican has its own prison?" asked Rael.

"She's a nun, Rael. She's not likely to lie about a thing like prison," replied Boudicea.

They walked out of the octagonal room and straight onto a steel catwalk. Below Rael must have been a one-hundred-foot sheer drop. Lining the chasm walls, Rael could see countless steel-barred prison cells. The sister walked by a guard dressed in white. She opened a steel cage door and climbed inside a caged elevator. Rael followed inside.

Sister Isabella said to the guard, "Level nine." The guard closed the cage door and locked it. Then he activated a large metal lever and the cage started to descend deep into the chasm. "You look worried, little girl," said the sister to Rael.

"I'm just a little confused," replied Rael.

Sister Isabella explained, "The original prison was constructed by Emperor Constantine in the middle of a swampy lagoon. A nice place between the Eastern and Western empires. He had no idea of the future of this place. Like Dante's Inferno, our prison has various levels of hell. The imprisonment level varies with the danger of the criminal: spell-craft, witchcraft, devil-craft, demonic worship, telemarketing . . . . Remember, most criminals have gotten here through murder, mayhem, or worse, so be on your guard. Also, try not to look any of them in the eye, as some are known to hypnotize on sight."

"Are we really going to find help in a place like this?" asked Rael.

"We need to find a great distraction that may create a form of help for us. We are about to travel into the belly of the beast. The cult knows we're coming, so they will feel a level of comfort, and—if we're lucky—an extreme level of arrogance. We must disturb this by giving them something they don't expect. I have a two-part plan: I will pair with a saint and a sinner. The saint part will be easy to arrange. The sinner is a bit harder, but it is why we are here. A criminal coming with us—they won't expect that," replied Boudicea. It all sounded correct, and yet none of it really made sense to Rael. It didn't matter, because they'd do it anyway, no matter how she felt about it.

The elevator came to a halt. Rael looked through the steel mesh floor below her to see that there was plenty of room left to go down. The sister placed a key in the door and unlocked it. Then she swung the door open. They stepped out onto a metal railed ledge. The sister limped along on her crutch. Rael followed. They passed empty cell after empty cell until they found one that was occupied. It contained Andres de Salete dressed in a white gown, sitting on a slab of steel that served as his bed. His kind of distraction Rael had been hoping to avoid.

"I assume this is the man you wanted to see," said the sister.

"That's him," replied Boudicea.

The sister yelled at Andres, "On your feet, scum. You got visitors."

Andres looked at Rael as if he could still see heaven's gate through her eyes. It was a haunting look. She tried to step away, but Boudicea was behind her. Boudicea said to Andres, "I've come to make a deal."

Andres turned his back to them. "It is too late for that now. You had your chance. Now that I'm convicted, nothing can save me."

Boudicea said, "You can think my offer over. Let's head back up."

"Wait, don't be so hasty to accept a no from me before I've even heard your offer." Andres turned back around. "What deal can you offer me?"

"We need to borrow you. If you're a good boy, maybe something can be arranged to lighten your sentence," explained Boudicea.

"And if I'm bad?" asked Andres.

"I'll kill you," explained Boudicea.

"And if she doesn't do it, I will," added Sister Isabella.

"So, the deal is, I take you to Lebanon to let you meet my Maleficium Society contacts, and I get time off for good behavior?" asked Andres.

"No, we're heading to London, not Lebanon," said Boudicea.

"I don't know jack about the Society's contacts there," said Andres.

"I don't care if you do or don't," said Boudicea.

"I don't get it," he said.

"Don't try too hard to get it. Try harder to accept my deal," said Boudicea.

Andres came over to the bars. He pressed against them. He said, "Anything beats being in here, even being in London."

"Good, then it is a deal," replied Boudicea.

"We'll be back in touch later," said the sister to Andres.

"Don't take too long getting me out of here because there's a lot of weird people inside here," he complained.

The sister escorted them back to the elevator. She shut the door and they started to head back up. Once they were moving, the sister said, "I don't know for a fact that I can get him out of here just like that."

"You can and you will," replied Boudicea.

"I will have to run it by Cardinal Santiago. He won't like the fact you came here unannounced. Explain to me why you need Andres after refusing him once already."

"Time has changed things. I have a demon on our side who knows where the phylactery is. It's in London somewhere, and I'll need Andres if I'm to get close enough to it. I'm going to need just about everyone's help," replied Boudicea.

"You can't trust a demon at its word."

"I don't and won't, but if it leads me to the phylactery—and I have every reason to believe it will—then I must take the chance that it will double-cross me at some later point. What do you know about the Society's activities in London?"

"Next to nothing. We tried tracing the Society through Rael's father's movements. We know Rael's father is the director of a company called Velocity. But it's an empty shell of a company. All talk, no action. Worse, no leads from it to anything bigger. There has to be a Mister Big; every cult has one," explained Sister Isabella.

Rael interjected, "Dad never talked about his new job. He spent little time working, yet the money flowed in once he got the job. Odd that I never questioned it until now."

Boudicea replied, "It is not odd. It is only the blindness of youth."

"I suppose," agreed Rael.

"And what is Andres needed for in this plan you're forming?" asked the sister.

"I was wondering about that too," added Rael.

Boudicea explained, "As I've said, the society knows we are coming to London. They know we're targeting the phylactery. We need a distraction to shake their confidence and allow us time to retrieve it. There will come a time when it must look like I cannot help Rael. I will be relying on others to protect her and I know for a fact that Andres will stop at nothing to keep her alive. Andres protecting her will confuse them and give me a chance at the target."

"His motives won't be very pure," said Rael.

"Never trust anyone's motives, Rael," replied Boudicea.

"A wise idea, but a weak plan. They'll move it if they know you're after it," said the sister.

Boudicea shook her head. "They still need Rael, and if we're lucky, there will be a trap set up for us upon our arrival in London. After so many misses, it may be time for them to try and lure us in. They must be sick of chasing us by now. Yes, I am sure they will lure us into a trap now that they know we're coming after the phylactery. I'll need a distraction to spring a trap on them instead, and Andres will be part of that distraction."

"He is very distracting—perhaps too distracting." Sister Isabella warned, "He will come after Rael's essence the first chance he gets as well."

"Yes. I am counting on it."

"Is there anything else you need?"

"I need to contact the Freemasons."

"That is easy enough to do."

"I also need your help getting to London undetected."

"Is that all?"

"Yes. There will be six of us."

"Six?" asked the nun.

"We've collected a lot of help along the way."

"Then you will need room for seven, for I'm coming too. You've explained very little, but I'll see to it that it gets done. Remember, you've asked a lot from the Church, and I cannot promise the moon."

"You will get everything I asked for because I have faith," replied Boudicea.

"I never liked London much," said Sister Isabella.

"For me it will be a homecoming, though it was never really my home," replied Boudicea.

The elevator stopped. Rael didn't like the sound of this plan. She trusted the demon more than she trusted Andres. Any plan involving him was sure to go wrong. Yet there was nothing she could do about it but go along.

Chapter 21

Torquay, England

The argument in the plane's cabin had raged since they'd taken off. Heck, it had started before they'd taken off. It was still going strong two hours into the flight. The catalyst for it was that the demon had finally divulged the name of who it, or more likely Ilitar, believed was the owner of the all-important phylactery. It should have been one of those come-together moments for the team; only, they weren't really a team, so it had instead erupted within the cabin as an argument. You know what they say: Too many hunters spoil the hunt. Well, Rael didn't know anyone who'd said that, but she had a feeling it was true.

Rael was only vaguely keeping score. Sister Isabella apparently didn't trust the word of this demon, and Boudicea, who probably didn't trust the demon either, was arguing with her to at least trust it as far as accepting the name. Archon seemed to be more on the side of clobbering something—anything. Rael, who had nearly zero experience and even less influence, had lost interest in all their subtle points of view rather quickly. In the end, the name of the owner didn't matter much to her. By her incredible feat of mental logic, she knew someone had to have this phylactery and that person had to be stopped, and so they'd try to stop them, whoever they were. Thus, one cultist was very much like another to Rael at the moment. Only, the name seemed to matter a lot to all the other occupants with whom she shared the plane. She spied the demon just sitting there looking oh-so-satisfied with the fray it has started. She didn't like the demon much, but she trusted it. She knew it was correct with its facts in this matter.

Rael moved to the back of the plane and sat down. She stared out the window half in a daydream, and half wishing it was more than only half. Rael looked out on the waters of the Channel as the plane flew above it. The plane had nearly arrived at its destination unmolested during the flight. That was a rarity for Rael these days. The seat next to her groaned as Gerard sat down in it. Perhaps her optimistic side had spoken too soon. Gerard. Why was he still even around? Rael wished he'd stayed with his rusting boat in Venice.

He said to her, "You know they say too many hunters spoil the mood, and the mood on this plane is ripe like a baby's diaper. But do not worry, because Gerard's lips are like a baby's mother's lips. They can change any sour mood to be more positive."

He put his arm around her. Exactly what she had never wanted. The smell of what she assumed was a dead muskrat overcame her nose. She was pretty sure it was some sort of masculine scent Gerard had put on himself on purpose. Rael contemplated clawing his arm off her, but she figured Gerard wasn't evil, mostly. Rael instead looked over the top of her seat. She saw Dynami just sitting there next to Archon as the dwarf argued with Boudicea, the demon, and Sister Isabella. Dynami wasn't looking in her direction even a little bit. It was very frustrating. Rael inched in her seat away from Gerard's fishy lips. She replied, "Gerard, why are you still around?"

"I will tell you why. Because they confiscated my boat and threatened me if I didn't come along. How dare they threaten me! They have no authority over me. And yet they threaten. It is a terrible world we live in when people can threaten you with actions you have no interest in."

"What actions?"

"Bah, some nonsense about the possibility of me leaking valuable information on your whereabouts if I were not under their watch, they claim. Me! I would never do such a thing to such a pretty young lady. Particularly a pretty girl who had previously kissed me. No suggestions implied in that last statement—just a basic fact. The female kiss cannot be discounted for its persuasive powers."

"Sister Isabella is pretty and all, but I don't know if kissing her is such a good idea for you," replied Rael.

"Kissing the nun? You think I want to kiss the nun? I meant . . . ah, you are having a joke at my expense. Don't worry, Gerard is quite the joker. There is nothing I like more than a good laugh. Okay, I lie a little there. With a pretty girl I like more than a good laugh, and you are a pretty girl."

Boudicea grabbed Gerard by the collar and yanked him from his seat. She added, "Excuse me, Gerard, but I have to talk business with Rael."

"Speaking of business, when do I get paid for the service of using my boat?" asked Gerard.

"Out!" demanded Boudicea.

"We're on a plane. I can't go out," replied Gerard.

"Don't tempt me to show you how wrong you are on that matter," added Boudicea.

Gerard slinked off to the front of the plane, saw Archon sitting up there, and decided to find a neutral corner to sit in instead. Free of Gerard, Rael said to Boudicea, "I don't like that man."

"Who? Gerard? He's a jerk, I'll give you that, but he's a useful one. He's not been tempted to sell you out yet, so don't completely discount him. Not every jerk is evil or useless," explained Boudicea. "The thing is, we're facing a problem. The demon has finally explained to us who owns the phylactery: Ronald Bentworth. And now . . ."

"I did follow the conversation up to that point. I felt it was good to know who had corrupted my father, yet you've all been yelling at each other for two hours about it, so I take it there must be some bad news in it," replied Rael.

"You understand he's the richest man in Europe? You don't lightly accuse such a man of being a cultist. We'll need proof to approach him, and right now we have none. A demon's word counts for nothing in our circles. If we were to harm Ronald Bentworth on the word of a demon and be wrong about it, we'd all be signing our death warrant."

"What about Sister Isabella? She must know about this man. The Vatican, don't they have people in the know about stuff like this?" asked Rael.

"Our target is based in the UK. He has no known cult associations, according to the sister. The Vatican's reach in the UK is limited these days. I tell you again, no one will move on this man on the word of a demon. Not even the Order. If Ronald has been leading a cult, there's only one man in all of the UK who might know about it. We need to see him. It has been decided that if we get confirmation of Ronald being on the bent side, then we can get most of the major organizations in line with a plan of attacking him. At least maybe they will stop chasing after you long enough to go after him. They might all have different designs for you, but few will want an active cult with plans on controlling a horror in the chase for you."

"That's sort of reassuring."

"If you're reassured, it is time for us to get off the plane," said Boudicea as she stood up.

"Another parachute jump?" asked Rael.

Boudicea reached into her sleeve. She pulled out a black string bikini. She closed her cloak around her and then she opened it up. Just like that she had changed clothes. "Nope, we're about to go swimming."

"But we're flying, it's winter, and most important of all I wouldn't let Gerard see me dressed like that for a million dollars," replied Rael.

"And yet we will be going swimming anyway, so get dressed for it," assured Boudicea.

"I am not about to change into that small a bathing suit with that Gerard around," said Rael.

Boudicea said, "No choice. The plane is already slowing down. We have to jump soon."

Rael looked over at Gerard. The knight with the overactive libido had clearly already noticed Boudicea's outfit change. Well, of course he had. No choice? Hardly. Despite what Boudicea might think, one could go swimming much more modestly. The water didn't care what you wore, after all. Rael thought, *Okay, cloak, please do something modest for me.* She reached in and pulled out a white bikini. Magic appeared to have a built-in patriarchal bias.

Great. Now, how did one change into this thing on a plane full of people like Gerard without being embarrassed? She said, "I just think about changing my clothes and magic does the rest, right?"

"Something like that," replied Boudicea.

Rael pulled her cloak around herself. *Come on. Change*, she thought. She opened her cloak and she wasn't looking any different.

"Rael, don't fight your magical tendencies. Go with them."

"Maybe my tendencies want a one-piece."

Boudicea wrapped her cloak around Rael, and a second later Rael was in her new outfit. Rael now felt totally exposed.

"Why do we have to be dressed like this to swim in cold water?" asked Rael.

"Modesty isn't always a virtue; it's also a sign of fear. You have to learn to ignore your fears," replied Boudicea.

That was *an* answer but not really an answer at all. The Vatican's specially equipped Osprey rotated its engines as Archon opened the plane's door. He shouted back to them, "Lasses, get your butts in gear. We're diving in!"

Finally someone was talking sense, because Rael wanted her butt not only in gear, but also in very warm gear. A wetsuit would do quite nicely. Her butt wasn't about to get what it wanted, and thus she had a distinct feeling her butt was about to be chilled to the bone. Rael reluctantly walked with Boudicea to the open door, feeling like a condemned prisoner. They were hovering about a hundred feet off the water. Boudicea just dove in. Rael hesitated. Archon asked, "What's the matter?"

"You mean besides the fact I'm diving half-naked a hundred feet into the freezing cold rolling ocean waves?" replied Rael.

Dynami came up to Rael. He said, "It's just a high dive. It's nothing to worry about. Keep your hands and feet pointed straight as you enter the water and you'll be okay."

Gerard added, "Look at that guy getting all over you. It's embarrassing. Don't listen to him. There is no reason to jump away and deprive me of such a pretty sight."

Eww. That was all the motivation Rael needed. She jumped off the plane and into the ocean. The thing about the ocean in the winter is it is cold. She held her form as best she could as she plunged into the water, but her skin burned from slapping down onto the cold waves. Well, initially it burned. Before she could feel the full effects of hitting the ocean, her body started to numb from the cold, which was sort of a relief.

She kicked her legs and pushed herself back toward the surface. She broke through and popped her head out of the water just in time to see Dynami hit the water seamlessly. Not one bit of splash. Archon was the opposite. He landed with a cannonball, making as big a splash as possible while laughing the whole way down. The plane rotated its engines and was off. There was nothing left to do but swim for shore. Rael would have her rattling teeth to keep her company the whole swim there.

Rael grumbled as she swam, "Why do the men get to swim in wetsuits while I'm dressed like a readymade cherry-flavored popsicle?"

She had meant it to be a rhetorical question, but apparently Boudicea had heard her. "Because they're staying outside the zone—unless, that is, there is trouble inside there," explained Boudicea as she swam by.

"The zone?"

"The greater Torquay temperature anomaly zone."

Boudicea swam out of earshot and toward the shore. Rael swam after her hoping there was more to the explanation than that. She had a growing fear she'd die of hypothermia before the embarrassment of the bikini killed her. She also had a desperate need for more explanation to explain the previous one. But the fear of freezing seemed to be misplaced. The closer Rael drew toward the shore, the hotter the water got. It was a sensation, she had a feeling, that also explained better what Boudicea had been talking about. As her feet hit the sandy beach, she felt like she was in the Mediterranean waters. Then as she rose out of the water it grew even warmer.

"I don't get it. Why is it getting warmer and warmer?" said Rael.

"In the third age, when Galaxia fought Olerian at the battle of Huluxfat, a Smolt crashed here after being rended by Jehoseph's mighty sword, thus causing a temporary space–time rift that has never been fully healed," explained Boudicea.

"That's not an answer. An answer uses words that have some meaning in a language. Whereas I have no idea what the heck you just said to me," replied Rael.

The cocking of automatic guns ended their conversation before more meaningful words could be spoken. Rael realized they were surrounded by bare-chested men in short shorts with long barreled weapons. Not exactly the way a bikini-clad gal wants to be welcomed on a beach. One of them said, "You're in the wrong place, ladies. You'd better leave."

Boudicea heaved her chest out and ran her hands through her long red hair. She replied, "We're here to see General Lancaster."

All the men's eyes fell on Boudicea's breasts. Well, of course they did. It was a disgusting display, but apparently disgustingly effective. Rael heard a frail voice call out from the distance, "Perhaps, I can make a little time for two pretty ladies."

The head of the beach patrol, while still pointing his gun at them, said, "It doesn't look like you're packing a weapon in that thing, but I have to be sure." He reached to pat Boudicea down. She grabbed his gun, flipped him into the sand, pulled his gun away from him, and spun the weapon around to face him before he or his men had time to react.

"I don't need to carry a weapon on me when you kindly bring one for me," Boudicea said.

The old man's voice called out again. "Captain, never mind that bother. Bring them here. I want to see them up close. They do look like a bunch of fun."

The captain frowned in upper-class British disapproval. "Okay, ladies, the general wants to see you up close." Boudicea tossed his gun back at him, which probably annoyed the man even more.

Boudicea looked over at Rael. She said, "Let's go see the general."

"Who?" asked Rael.

That question wasn't answered. Instead, they were escorted up the beach to a cabana sporting a Union Jack-themed cover. Inside the cabana sat an old man. He looked practically ancient. He was dressed in a military uniform. His jacket was covered in medals. Upon their arrival, he put down the field glasses he had been watching them with and fumbled for his normal glasses, which were resting on the table set for tea next to him.

The general spoke. "Captain Champlain, it's a bit breezy today."

"Yes, sir."

"And what do we have here?"

"Two proper tarts, sir. I was going to send them packing."

The old man shook his head. "No need for that. They appear to be packing quite enough already."

"Sir, I must protest."

"Can't have that now, can we? Captain Champlain, these two healthy-looking specimens you found washed up on my beach are hunters of the Order if I ever saw one . . . er . . . two. And I have seen a hunter of the Order once or twice in my life before."

"Hunters are trouble, sir. I recommend sending them away at once."

"I think not. You will leave instead, and take the platoon with you," ordered the general.

"But, sir . . ."

"There are those that give orders and those that receive them. Knowing which kind of soldier you are, captain, is the key to the British military system," lectured the general. The captain apparently knew when to give in. He gave the general a salute, turned, and left.

The general turned his attention toward Boudicea. He pointed at her and said, "You there, the fiery ginger. I've seen you before, haven't I? Yes, I have. You were trailing after Divicia last I saw you. Must have been eons ago. You have a silly name, can't quite remember it. I never forget a face, though." An odd thing to say because Boudicea's face was the last place he was gazing at.

Boudicea replied, "General Lancaster, it was a long time ago when we last met."

"Me telling Pershing to stop using frontal assaults was a long time ago. Anything involving someone as young as you has to have occurred considerably more recently, almost yesterday in comparison," the general explained. He looked at Rael. "I don't know her at all. What is the deal with her?"

Rael replied, "I'm Rael Armstrong."

"Ah, that explains it. You are the Astralith everyone has been mucking about trying to win over. I had not thought you'd ever end up here on my beach. And yet . . . hmm, you must be here for a reason."

"Ronald Bentworth is the reason," explained Boudicea.

The general took his glasses off. "At my age, the blood pressure can only allow so many minutes in the presence of such beauty. Care for some hot tea and biscuits?" he asked.

"It's a hundred and three in the shade," replied Rael.

"Yes, I know it is a bit breezy today," said the general.

"We only care to learn more about Ronald Bentworth," replied Boudicea.

"I get it. No sweets because you have to keep that hourglass figure of yours. Go on, have a biscuit. I get them locally; they make them nice and firm, the way I like them."

Rael was almost sure she'd just been hit on by a dirty old man. *Almost* because there was a chance he might really be talking about the biscuits. The thing was, she could do with a biscuit. "Actually, I could go for a biscuit," interjected Rael.

"Smart girl. Figures should be left for an accountant's ledger. They should never get in the way of a good biscuit. Help yourself. Tea first, biscuit second. That's the English way. You'll find that the English way is still the best way."

Rael took a porcelain teacup and poured a cup of tea. It was hot, and the air was hot, but the cool water evaporating off her skin made a warm cup of tea sound suddenly rather nice. Maybe this old general knew something after all.

While Rael snacked, Boudicea acted as she always did. In other words, she acted with the mindset of a hunter. She was after prey again, and she wouldn't be side-tracked by thoughts of tea and biscuits. "I've met a demon who says that Ronald Bentworth is the key cultist in the Maleficium Society. I've no verification of this. He's not the kind of man you just accuse of such things, so I'd like verification."

"This demon of yours, has it got a name?" asked the general.

"It didn't offer one," replied Boudicea.

"Very cheeky. Yet you believe it all the same?"

Boudicea nodded.

"And I do too," interjected Rael.

"Do you like your tea?" asked the general of Rael.

"Oh yes, it is splendid," replied Rael.

"And the biscuits?" asked the general.

"They are very buttery."

"I do like this girl. Unfortunately, I don't like this question of yours. You seek a verification of a fact not at my disposal. Only wish that it was. I didn't like the fact that he was there in the village the day Rael was discovered to be an Astralith. Had him checked out. My operatives never found evidence against Ronald Bentworth. Met him before. Decent chap, but suspicious. You see, we English do pay attention to the paranormal grapevine."

"Then there is no reason to waste more of your time," replied Boudicea.

"However, your presence here does perhaps explain this," added the general. He reached into his coat and pulled out an envelope. He opened it. "Six tickets to a mid-winter ball presented by one Ronald Bentworth. It's at his new building, called the Vault. I was unclear why these would be sent to me, as my ball days are far off in the sunset."

Rael said, "He must have known we'd come to you seeking information."

"Yes, he knew you were coming. Spies?"

"Yes, we were spied on. It's good, though. He has already set a trap for us as I had hoped he would. That makes our next move easier," said Boudicea.

"I assume so. It is to be a frontal assault, then? I warned Pershing against them. I'm too old to join in. Still, I do believe that those tickets are the confirmation of your demon's remarks that you sought from me. I have no need for these tickets, so I will give them to you, my lady." He offered the tickets to Boudicea.

"Thank you," replied Boudicea. She took the envelope and tucked it into her bosom.

The general cleared his throat. He added, "I was hoping for a little good soldier's reward."

"Of course," replied Boudicea. She kissed the old man on the cheek. She then turned to Rael and said, "Come."

"I'm not going to kiss him, biscuits or no!" replied Rael.

"I meant come, as in we're done here," said Boudicea.

"Oh," replied Rael. She looked at the general and added, "No offense."

"I wouldn't kiss me either these days. There was a time when I did look quite the decent chap silhouetted in the gaslight, though," he said.

Rael shoved the rest of her biscuit into her mouth and scampered off with Boudicea. Asking for a reward had been the last straw. Rael said, "You know, you didn't have to kiss him. And our bathing suits are completely unnecessary. We could have worn something much more modest and with pockets to boot so you wouldn't have to put the envelope in your bosom. Boudicea, you need to get with the times. Hypersexualization is out, and so are pointless skintight outfits with plunging necklines, not wearing underwear, kissing old men, and wearing bikinis just to wear bikinis. It's time people saw you, the hunter, for who you are and not some sexualized fantasy of what you should be."

"Are you done lecturing me?"

"No, and for another thing . . . why is Captain Champlain's decapitated head lying in the sand?"

The sand around them moved. Twelve men stood up wearing camouflage. They were all well equipped, and here Rael was not even equipped with sensible clothing.

One of the men said, "Game's over, hunter. We take the girl and kill you. That's the way it is." He nodded his head and three men approached Rael.

Boudicea whispered to Rael, "Cry."

"What?" whispered Rael back.

"When in a situation like this, either flirt or cry."

Boudicea thrust her chest out and her head back and sobbed uncontrollably. It was really quite convincing to Rael. Rael wasn't at the same level in terms of acting, but she did her best. A few guys grabbed her anyway. Others cocked their weapons and pointed them at Boudicea. Boudicea sobbed, "I'll do anything, anything for you not to hurt me."

The weapons didn't discharge into her. One of the soldiers took the bait. He said, "I like the sound of that. A couple of you guys hold her while I take her up on her word."

Another soldier said, "We don't have time for this."

"I'll make time for a ripe woman like this," replied another soldier. He had more than a few agree with him.

Eww. There were men out there in the world more disgusting than Gerard, as pathetic as that seemed. Boudicea allowed the men to come upon her. She practically fainted into one of the men's arms. One of the soldiers dropped his weapon and went for the waistband of his pants. Rael could have told these guys they were playing right into a hypersexualized plot point, but she was more than willing to let them learn all about it the hard way.

Boudicea suddenly stiffened up and used leverage to flip the man she'd fainted against onto the nearest man to her. She dropped to the ground, rolled to the weapon the soldier had dropped, kicked that soldier in a place he'd probably rather not have been kicked in, and then grabbed the weapon, aimed it, and dropped that soldier with one shot, which in one way was an act of kindness because it ended his pain.

"Damn it, shoot her!" yelled a soldier. He didn't get to follow his own advice because a battle-axe inconveniently split his skull at that point.

"Do I have good timing or what?" yelled Archon.

Arrows started flying at the soldiers, who were now in full retreat behind the sand dunes—not that there was much to hide behind. Boudicea, Archon, and Dynami were mowing them down faster than they could retreat anyway.

The soldiers holding Rael weren't so fast to give up. They held onto her, probably understanding that doing so meant staying alive, as no one would dare shoot so close to her. Rael took matters into her own hands. She was a hunter herself now, after all. She said, "Fly!" She soared up into the air, dragging the two men up with her. She went higher and higher as the men realized they had clearly chosen poorly in their decision to hang on. In the ancient myth, Icarus flew too close to the sun and his wax wings melted. All Rael had to do was let the sun work very much the same way for her. The hot temperature of the anomaly made for a sweaty situation. She could tell their grip on her wasn't the most secure. And Rael's outfit didn't leave much to hang on to but slick, sweaty skin. The first slid down her sweat-soaked arm, reached the end of it, and dropped to the beach below. The second clung on a little harder to Rael, but his grip was going too. He slid down to her leg. She used her free leg to kick him off with ease. For once she'd taken care of some bad guys. That her bikini had helped by offering the men no help, she'd keep to herself. There was no point letting Boudicea get a swelled head about her fashion sense.

The rest of the soldiers appeared to be quite dead below her, so Rael flew back down to the sandy beach. Dynami ran up to her. He asked, "Rael, are you alright?"

Rael was still trying to learn all the lessons Boudicea was teaching her. Now seemed like a good time to practice one of them. Rael fainted and fell into Dynami's arms. Well, the idea had been to land in his arms. Unfortunately, he just stood there as she flopped into the sand.

Boudicea asked, "Rael, what are you doing?"

"Dynami was supposed to catch me," Rael explained.

Dynami said, "I thought perhaps you'd been injured, and you're not supposed to touch an injured person."

"Trust me, you were supposed to catch me," said Rael, standing up and dusting the sand off herself.

Archon interrupted, "Never mind that, who were these men? Cultists?"

"No, they were just mercenaries. Someone wanted us to get six tickets to a ball and sent these men along to make sure we were extra-motivated to go. They were too cheap to do us harm, but expensive enough to motivate us. That's how the setting of a good trap works," explained Boudicea.

"Quite right," added the general. The firefight had apparently stirred him from his cabana. He stabbed his cane into one of the mercenaries that was still twitching. Then he looked toward his dead captain lying on the sand. There was disapproval on his face. "Hate to see my men fall to cheap thugs. This cult must have saturated the whole place waiting for your arrival. I doubt I'm the only one who had tickets. They weren't taking chances on you not going. I could verify that for you."

"No need. It's likely true," replied Boudicea.

"I can't offer you much in the way of protection, but I will have Her Majesty's best men working on this Ronald Bentworth fellow from now on. He won't move about so freely now that I know the truth. You take care when you enter his trap," warned the general.

"We will. We've come prepared for this plot twist already," replied Boudicea.

"Have you now? You hunters never cease to amaze me."

Chapter 22

The Ritz, London

Rael was feeling a touch nervous. After successfully dodging danger for so long, a plan that involved walking deliberately into a trap didn't feel like the best of ideas. Though death could result from walking into a trap, to tell the truth she was much more nervous about how she looked at the moment. It was a silly, vain thing to be worried about, and Rael had never thought of herself as a silly, vain person; still, sometimes you do want to look the part for an event, and this happened to be one of those events.

Rael sat in what was most likely a very expensive chair inside a hotel room at the Ritz. She was trying very hard to sit still while Sister Isabella worked on Rael's face. Rael was also trying very hard to not look into the silver mirror the sister had brought with her to aid in the working. Rael had promised that she didn't want to see herself until the sister was done with the makeover. The thing was that when you've not had a proper mirror in ages, it is very hard to resist the temptation to look at yourself. That wasn't vanity speaking; that was just normal human nature, even if Rael was no longer quite as normal a human as her nature was. Rael gave in and allowed herself a little peek in the mirror.

The young lady staring back at her was just that: a lady. She didn't look a bit like Rael. She looked old . . . well, older. All this dodging death had aged her. That was silly thinking, though. Of course she looked older; that's what all the makeup did. One thing was for certain: When she offered herself up to this cult trap, she'd knock their socks off at the same time. That idea made her frown. Just this morning at the beach, she'd lectured Boudicea on how trivial all this sexualization stuff was. But she couldn't go to a ball looking like a scarecrow, now, could she? Those were just the rules of a ball. If a ball is thrown in your honor, it is expected you will show up as Cinderella—although hopefully without the need for glass slippers, as they looked incredibly uncomfortable.

"You are coming along nicely. Now, please continue to hold still," ordered the sister.

She must have caught Rael peeking. Coming along nicely? How would she know? What did a nun know about beauty and the latest fashion? Well, a lot, it seemed, given what Rael had just seen reflected back in that mirror. It was just another nonsensical oddity in a world filled with them these days. Rael said, "I don't get it. How come a nun is so good at applying makeup?"

"If you talk, your face moves, and that makes me work harder than is needed to improve your appearance. As any artist will tell you, the proper canvas to work on is a motionless one," the sister reminded her.

"I'm not a canvas. I'm a person."

"Then be a very still person!"

"Oh, sorry."

"Don't be sorry, be still. If you remain so, I will tell you why I'm so good at my job. It is because in my line of work one must know sin inside and out in order to save the souls of the sinners. Sometimes their sinning requires a little makeup for their foul deeds, and thus I know that sin all too well," explained Sister Isabella.

Rael would have nodded her head to pretend that explanation explained something, but that was the last thing she should do. It would only have incurred the wrath of the sister again. Instead, she just tried to focus mentally on holding still. Holding still was a hard thing to do, though. It was very hard to do because her whole survival these days basically came down to her not holding still. Being on the move is what kept Rael out of harm's way.

It didn't help matters that Rael was giddy with excitement at this moment in time. Technically, if she were speaking to others about how she felt, then Rael would say she totally didn't enjoy this makeover she was receiving in the least. At least, she wouldn't admit publicly to enjoying it in the least. No, to voice any other feeling would only lead to questions best not asked. The truth was, though, she was a little excited about this whole ball concept. She'd been too busy training her whole life to attend any type of formal dance before. Since the prospect of attending a future junior or senior prom was pretty much out of the window at this point, this was as close as she was going to get to a formal event.

Not that attending a formal ball thrown by a billionaire psychopath was exactly like being at prom. Although, come to think of it, from whatever Rael knew, billionaires did everything pretty much just like a high schooler did, only at a hundred times the expense. Yes, it was likely to be ten times more glamorous than a prom! Tonight's affair would be a ball to remember, which seemed very fitting, since it was a trap set up to capture her. Her essence should be worth a ball to remember as a trap. Rael would simply not walk into any trap that wasn't glamorously set up for her, because she had principles.

Speaking of principles, Boudicea walked out of the bathroom and suddenly Rael felt her own principles fall significantly. Compared with Boudicea, she was one hundred times less glamorous. That was just a basic fact. Boudicea wore an evening dress the way evening dresses were meant to be worn—at least, if you went by those red-carpet event shown on television. Not that Rael would ever admit to watching them.

Boudicea asked Sister Isabella, "Is Rael ready yet?"

"Almost," replied Sister Isabella. The nun rotated Rael on the chair and pointed her in Boudicea's direction. While Rael didn't like to think of herself as a canvas, since she was a person and not a thing, she was a person who very much wanted just a touch of that aura given off by Boudicea dressed as she was. That wasn't a bad thing, was it?

"Rael, you do look adorable," said Boudicea upon seeing the sister's work. Rael died a little inside. Adorable is never something you're looking for in a compliment while dressing for a ball—unless, of course, you're dressing cosplay for a Pokémon ball. Rael wanted to be like Boudicea. She wanted to be ravishing, breath-taking, or drop-dead gorgeous. Babies were adorable; young women dressed in formal wear should not be. She would not say a word of this to Boudicea, though, or else it would show that she cared about it all. Instead, Rael replied, "Thanks."

Boudicea explained, "Now, Rael, we're going to go over something absolutely critical to your safety tonight at the ball, so pay attention."

"Is this a hunter's lesson in physical combat?"

"In a way, yes. We're going to go over the little black dress."

"That doesn't sound combat related."

"You'd be surprised. Every woman has to have a killer black dress at her disposal just in case of need." Boudicea reached into her bosom. "Now, when in your black dress, the cleavage area is the best place to hide your essentials." She paused and reached into her plunging neckline to re-trieve her dagger. She continued, "Your weapon, a small flashlight, iodine tablets for water purification, a can opener, and fifty feet of rope can all be easily stored if you know how to pack correctly."

Rael looked down at her own cleavage and replied, "I'm not sure I have as much room up there as you."

Boudicea ignored her. She continued, "Now, bare legs are just fine un-der your black dress, but I do find that fine hose can come in handy in case the need arises to strangle a man or craft a makeshift slingshot."

"Do these needs arise often for you?" asked Rael.

Boudicea again ignored her and continued, "And a lady's shoes can be absolute lifesavers, as high-heel stilettos are very good in any fight. My left shoe can be used as a boomerang, while my right conceals a six-inch blade in the toe. With such a blade, one can easily slice the throat of a man with one swift kick."

Having said all that, Boudicea deposited an identical pair of black high heels in Rael's lap. Rael looked down at them. The five-inch thin heels seemed to be mocking her. After dealing toe to toe with devils, demons, and cultists, it was a little hard to admit to Boudicea that Rael felt more intimidated by the pair of shoes on her lap than any of those other things.

Rael replied, "I think I might kill myself just trying to walk in your shoes. You don't have any flats?"

"Flats?" replied Boudicea.

Sister Isabella slipped the shoes onto Rael's feet. She said, "Flats, indeed! Utter nonsense. These shoes are perfect for you. No princess wears flats to her first ball."

"I'm not a princess," reminded Rael.

"All women are princesses if the right prince walks into the room," said the nun. Which was a rather odd thing for her to have said. Rael tried to imagine who the right prince would have to be for Sister Isabella to become a princess. She figured it must have been a rhetorical comment, if such a thing existed. Sister Isabella commanded, "Now, stand and take a few steps for me. Being off-balance your first time on shoes such as these is perfectly normal. You will at worst fall down and chip a tooth. Which is okay, for I'm also an excellent dentist."

Somehow Rael didn't doubt those words. Rael took a deep breath. She stood up from the chair. She felt not unlike a circus clown on stilts—or worse, Frankenstein's monster. Ugh, that's what she was, wasn't she? She was all painted up in makeup and about to be marched around at this ball for the amusement of others. She took a step. She walked like the monster as well. She was too slow and awkward. This was terrible. She was a freak.

"See how the heels lift the butt and accentuate the legs?" asked the nun.

It was slightly disturbing for a nun to mention that to her. Still, Rael looked into the room's mirror, saw nothing, and frowned. She wanted to see how she looked in her outfit. She took another tentative step back toward Sister Isabella's silver mirror. She didn't wipe out along the way. She held the mirror up and surveyed herself. She began to relax. She wasn't a monster after all. Her shoes weren't as high at Boudicea's. She assumed they were equally deadly, though. She peered into her cleavage, wondering if she could pack as much heat as Boudicea up there. She probably was, as that's how magic worked. It apparently didn't just come in cloak form. She was relaxing more and more. She looked the part of a lady going to a ball. She could walk the part too—sort of. Tonight would be fun, glamorous, and an adventure. It was all going to work out. And if not, she'd only be dead again, so what was the worry? Only, Rael was worried; she couldn't help it. After running away from danger for so long now, heading toward it seemed like a slightly suicidal act.

Rael said to Boudicea, "Not to doubt our plan, but are we all sure this is the right thing to do? They're practically begging me to come to them."

Boudicea replied, "I do not know the answer. None of us do. All we know is that you can't be on the run forever. We know what we need to do to end this, and it is there at this ball for the taking. It is a chance, so we will try. They will try to stop us. The stronger of the two sides is the one that wins tonight. That is all there is to it."

She had said that calmly, without a hint of fear of her own death. It was also an honest answer, but perhaps not what Rael wanted to hear. There were two knocks on the room's door, which caused Rael's stomach to jump. Suddenly she remembered that there was more to worry about than just her life. There was also the stuff you lived life for.

Boudicea effortlessly walked over to the door and opened it. Dynami came in, and Rael forgot all about her shoe problems. Her pulse started to race a little. Of course, one couldn't have a glamorous ball without someone to take one to the ball. Dynami was dressed in a tuxedo. He really did wear clothes well. It must be his broad shoulders. Rael was slightly distracted by the sight of him and immediately took a misstep in her shoes. Forgetting about your shoes when you're balanced on top of deadly ground was a mistake. Still, it was an okay mistake as mistakes went because Dynami walked over and offered his hand in helping her off the floor. She took it, and he hoisted her to her feet. She explained to him, "New shoes. The soles are a bit slippery."

"Seeing that I'm from Atlantis, I'm used to slippery soles," he replied.

Rael laughed nervously. Then she cringed inside. Did she just fake laugh too much? Did he notice? Her hands suddenly felt sweaty. Boudicea interrupted the moment, which came as a relief to Rael. "It's time to go. The limousines are downstairs waiting for us."

"We are taking limos?" asked Rael.

"Three stretch limousines," clarified Sister Isabella as she slipped out the door of the room. Boudicea nodded her head and then exited as well.

That left Rael alone with Dynami. It was their first time alone together since floating around the Mediterranean. Given she could be dead in a few hours, it might be now or never for her and Dynami. The butterflies in her stomach obviously knew that fact as well. They were not making things any easier. Rael gave Dynami a smile. He apparently didn't notice, because he headed for the door just like the rest had. Rael scampered after him in a hurry to catch up. The shoes be damned, she was walking side by side with him down the hall even if those shoes might kill her at any minute. She really wanted to be walking hand in hand. Of course, men holding your hand was a sign of ownership. It was a way for them to exert their dominance over a woman. That's what the psychologists said. Then again, if she held his hand instead of him holding hers, that would be a completely different thing. They were going to a dance together after all, so acting like a couple was perfectly natural.

He pressed for the elevator. It arrived and they boarded it. They rode the elevator down in silence. Rael was not very good at silence. It seemed like the last thing there should be around her when Dynami was with her. "Are you nervous?" Rael asked Dynami.

"No, I've ridden on elevators many times before," he replied.

"I mean, about walking into an obvious trap with me!"

"Relax, it was a joke.

"Oh, right." She tried to fake laugh, but nothing came out. She was too nervous to laugh. "How can you be so calm when we could be killed, or worse, tonight."

"It's all part of the life of being a hunter. I'm used to it."

"I think it is very brave of you to be so nonchalant about it."

"Well, thank you, but it is all part of the job."

Right, part of the job. He was certainly brave, but not in the way that really mattered to Rael. There are times when being above it all wasn't called for. They were alone in the elevator together. He should be brave now. He should be sweeping her off her feet. Given the shoes, she'd greatly appreciate being off her feet. More than the shoes, though, he knew how she felt about him. At least, he should know. Did he know? They had kissed in the water, so he had to know.

The elevator stopped, and the doors opened. Well, if he didn't know by now, she'd let him in on the secret. Dynami started to get off and she took his hand. She led him across the lobby. If there was one thing she'd learned on this crazy adventure, it was that in life you have to take the initiative. This was, sort of, her first date with him, or anyone, and maybe her last. A tall, handsome man that she'd snuck a kiss in with while nearly drowning was taking her to a formal ball—what else could you call it but a date? Yes, it was her first date, and she looked perfect for it. . . well, probably. There was never a silver mirror around when you needed one to check up on your appearance. She paused at the front door to the hotel and Dynami opened it for her. *What perfect manners he has*, she thought.

"Thank you," she said. Then she guided him down to the curb.

The front door to the hotel opened behind them and Gerard spilled out. Rael suddenly felt less ravishing. Somehow Gerard was pulling off the little black dress look better than her. Not that he appreciated the fact. Gerard instantly complained, "Why do I have to be dressed as a woman?"

Boudicea replied, "Because we need as many eyes searching for the phylactery tonight as possible. Once all cultist eyes are on her, the rest of us go into search mode. We need to find the phylactery and take it from them. Once we have it, we've severely damaged the cult's plans. It's one man, one woman to the ball, and we're short one woman—hence your dress."

"Couldn't the nun take my place?" asked Gerard.

"You want to send a nun with a broken ankle wading into a deadly battle?" asked Boudicea.

"I had thought of that, yes. Anyway, how do we know the phylactery will even be there?" asked Gerard.

"The demon says that it is there," replied Boudicea.

"Oh, the demon. Speaking of that liar, where is the devil?" asked Gerard.

"Demon," corrected Dynami.

"Whatever it is, where is it?" repeated Gerard.

"Close by, I am sure," replied Boudicea.

"A great non-answer," complained Gerard.

"Speaking of close by, here comes your date, Gerard," said Boudicea. Archon came out of the hotel looking like a well-dressed beach ball with a long white beard.

The dwarf appeared as happy about the situation as his date. "This outfit doesn't suit me," he complained.

"Your suit looks fine," said Rael, hoping to put Archon's mind at ease a little.

"That's just it, lass, suits don't suit me at all," explained Archon.

"At least you're not the one wearing a dress," pointed out Gerard.

Archon looked Gerard over and frowned. "First date I've ever been on with a woman without a proper beard. What will my clan say about me back home?"

"Enough complaining, you two. Get into a limo," ordered Boudicea.

It must have been the sternness of her voice because they did as they were told. After they had set off, Boudicea opened the next car door. "Okay, inside, Dynami."

"Shouldn't he hold the door for me while I get in?" asked Rael.

Boudicea scolded her. "He's my date tonight, not yours."

"What!" added Rael.

"Your date is in the last limousine."

"But I want . . ."

"To live through the evening. Good, then follow my orders. Rael, it must appear as if I will not be there for you tonight. I must help find the phylactery. You are the target. You must do everything in your power to buy us time," ordered Boudicea.

"I understand," replied Rael.

"You say that with a hint of doom in your voice. Don't be so down. I will have eyes on you even when I'm not there in person. I've arranged for Wat Tyler to keep an eye on you," said Boudicea.

"Why him?" asked Rael.

"Because there's no point in you dying."

That wasn't exactly the way Rael had wanted that question answered. Wat Tyler, he was a good fighter, but not exactly trustworthy—or was he? "Then I promise not to die tonight," replied Rael.

"That's a promise I will hold you to. Remember, Rael, not to trust all that you see," said Boudicea and then shut the car door.

Rael gave one last look at the limo with Dynami as it drove away. It was hard to tell Boudicea she was more concerned about her date than Boudicea's lack of being there. What to do about Dynami? Not a word of protest from him about these arrangements. Maybe it was for the best. He was always too much into being a hunter and never after the correct game. Those were brave words that her heart wasn't exactly agreeing with.

Rael moved toward the last limousine. It was white, stretch, and detailed to perfection. She wasn't much of a car person, so she didn't care in the least for its shine. She reached for the door handle, but the door opened itself.

"Ah, so we meet again," said Andres.

How come the last person you want to see is always the person you get to see the most? He was certainly the last person she wanted to go to a ball with. She pouted and didn't care if he saw it.

"I thought Wat was to be my date," she said.

"Who?"

"Not who, Wat . . . oh, never mind." She climbed inside slightly more confused. The door shut itself and locked. The engine roared to life and they set off. "You look heavenly tonight, my dear. Which is fitting as I wanted to see heaven tonight, and with you, I think there's a real chance," boasted Andres.

"Over my dead body."

"Yes, that's how it works."

"Oh, very clever of you."

The tinted black window that divided the back seats from the front rolled down automatically. Sister Isabella leaned over the front seat. Andres backed away from her lurking presence, not that there was very far to retreat in the backseat. She said, "Andres, you are out on good behavior. Please try to remember that."

"Good behavior! When has he ever demonstrated good behavior? I mean, he's already threatened to kill me," said Rael.

"Distractions will do the darndest things; it's best to ignore them," replied Sister Isabella. She turned her attention toward Andres. She held out a wafer. She asked Andres, "Would you care to take communion?"

"I've been excommunicated," he replied.

She reached across and pinched his cheeks with her one hand. With her other, she rammed the wafer down his throat. He gagged a little. She then explained, "That wafer contains a small explosive device tied to the heartbeat of Rael. If her heart were to stop beating for any reason, things would get very bad for you, very quickly."

Andres sneered at her. "I always knew your brand of salvation was poison."

The sister ignored his reply. She asked Rael, "Are you ready?"

It was a tough question to answer. She was probably not ready at all. She wasn't sure what was in store for her tonight. She'd need forty more years or so of training to be actually ready. "I think so," she replied.

"Good. Remember, you're not required to engage the enemy, just to be our decoy. We only need you to lead them around. We need you to buy the team time until they find the phylactery. Once that's done, you're to get out of there as quickly as possible. And if anything goes wrong, don't worry, for you will have Andres by your side. And if he should fail to protect you, the Freemason should be at the ball as a backup," explained Sister Isabella.

Rael wanted Dynami and not Andres by her side. Still, this was the plan, the only one she had to work with, so she was as ready as she could be to do it. The sister nodded in approval. Then the divider window went back up. Rael looked over at Andres. He had that look about his face that told her, wafer or no wafer inside him, he was still planning to size her up for a harp and halo to go with her wings. There was no more time to worry about that because the limousine stopped.

Chapter 23

The Vault, London

The limousine's intercom blurted, "We're here!" Sister Isabella's voice normally had a way of jarring Rael to attention, particularly when it blurted out unexpectedly like that. In this case it had little effect, though. Rael's attention was already wrapped up in the location, so she barely heard the sister's words. One could hardly miss the location. She was staring out the window at a towering building. It must have been well over one hundred stories high, and each story was covered in highly reflective glass of some sort. At night, the glass reflected the LED lighting that ran up the sides of the building. Which meant that the building was providing a gaudy animated lights display right now. Those lights were luring the rich and famous to this party like moths to a flame. Cars of every make and model, excluding makes and models owned by proles, were lined up and circling around a driveway that led up to the base of this towering building.

Andres yawned as if he wasn't impressed by the display outside. "She says we're here. Fat lot you idiots know. This can't be the place. This is the Vault. It's been in the news for months. No way anything important is stashed here."

"The Vault? Then it's some sort of a bank?" asked Rael.

"Don't be stupid. The Vault is just a stupid name given to it because it is a stupid symbol of the wealth and failed masculinity of its owner, one

Ronald Bentworth. A man like that isn't into cults. He's into himself. We're obviously going to the wrong place to move in on the Maleficium Society. Where do you get your information?"

"From me," said the demon. Andres jumped in his seat at the sound of the voice. The reaction amused the demon no end. Rael was getting used to its sudden appearances, so she only jumped a little. She had wondered where it had gone off to. She knew the demon would be at the ball too. It was only a question of when it would appear. The demon continued, "You're wrong. He's the one who has been trying to use Rael's essence to gate in my dear queen Ilitar. I shall kill him tonight. I shall kill them all. Mostly Ghanal is my target, though. Ilitar wants it back home where she can keep an eye on it."

"That's the spirit. With them out of the way, I can . . . help out too," added Andres with a glint of mischief in his eyes.

"I will go now. The hunt is about to begin." The demon shapeshifted into a celebrity. Then it opened the car door and exited.

"Interesting, that friend of yours," Andres said. "Let me warn you, girl. Demons are dumb. They're not to be listened to or trusted. I wouldn't get my hopes up too high for this evening amounting to much more than a gate-crashing of poor Bentworth's ball."

"You doubt the word of a demon sent by Ilitar to stop her from being gated here?"

"I do. Self-preservation is hardly a sound basis for forming judgments. I'm an expert at this, so you'd be wise to listen to me. Not that I care if you make fools of yourselves." He smiled at Rael. "I only care about what's inside you. Here is as good a place as any for me to crack that essence of yours open and get what I want."

"Remember there is a bomb inside you."

"When you're as bent as me inside, explosions will hardly scare you off."

He was right, of course. Boudicea's plan must have accounted for that fact, though. If Rael knew Andres was speaking the truth, Boudicea and Sister Isabella would too. He was acting a little too smug at the moment. That meant he'd probably do something very distracting tonight at the ball. All of which was exactly what they wanted. Well, that was a royal "they" talking there, as Rael didn't want to be anywhere near Andres at all. Still, being the target seemed to be her current fate in life. She might as well be a target having fun at a ball if she was to be one. Her job seemed simple enough: Be the lure to draw their attention away from the other hunters. Of course, the enemy probably knew this too. It was a game of cat and mouse. Who were the cats and who were the mice was a matter of perspective.

It wasn't long before it was their turn to exit their vehicle and walk the red carpet into the Vault. The limousine pulled up to the front of the building. Two large floodlights illuminated the limousine. Then two equally large valets dressed in neon-blue tuxedos came over to open the door. One extended a meaty hand toward Rael to assist her out. Rael seized it and let him help her step out of the limousine.

"Thank you kindly," she said to the valet.

"Tickets, please," replied the valet.

Rael suddenly fell into a mild panic. The word *tickets* struck her in an annoying way. She'd not been expecting to produce a ticket at the door. They had tickets to the ball, of course, but Boudicea hadn't given Rael any of the tickets the general had handed over. She searched for Boudicea or Archon among the small crowd by the entrance, but they weren't around. They must be already inside the ball. She looked toward Andres, hoping they had been given to him. It didn't seem likely; still, they had to be some-where. Rael asked, "Do you have the tickets?"

Andres climbed out of the limousine, adjusted himself, and then spit on the ground, presumably just to be gross. He replied, "What did you ask?"

"Tickets. They need to see our tickets to the ball."

He shrugged, "Do I look like a guy who has tickets to a fancy ball?"

"But . . ." Rael looked toward the front of the limousine, hoping the sister had them, but the car was already in motion and quickly sped away from the curb before Rael could stop it.

Andres started to snicker at Rael. "What, no tickets? You mean this stupid plan of yours can't even get us through the front door? The Order and their hunters, you're all idiots led by a daffy demon's word. Sometimes I wonder how a simple man like me gets stuck in these situations."

Rael wished Andres hadn't just blurted out her status like that, but then again, everyone willing to kill her probably was well aware of who she was already. The admission of having no tickets was worse than giving away her identity, though. The valet was looking a little displeased at this moment due to Rael's lack of tickets. Her just standing there ticketless was clearly holding the valet up from offloading other people high society deemed more important than Rael. If only high society understood how wrong they were on that matter.

"No tickets means no entrance," explained the valet. "Please leave." He was looking a bit sourly at her. She figured he would become more and more sour unless tickets were produced or her exit was imminent.

"I'm ever so sorry, but there is no need for me to leave. You see, I've just misplaced them," said Rael. The valet relaxed his gruff attitude, if only a little. Great thinking. Now she'd bought herself, what, a few seconds of time? She needed to think fast where the tickets might be. Then it occurred to her: She might not have any for a reason. Why didn't she have tickets? Was this part of the planned distraction? Of course, it must be. Only, Andres was doing nothing distracting at all. He seemed quite happy to leave. It would be nice for once to know an exact plan in every detail before being in the middle of it. She might lecture Boudicea on that point later. Right now, she needed a new plan, because she was getting a little nervous as the valets were looking at her more and more like bouncers.

Rael said, "I might have left them in the limousine."

"Look, lady, I don't make the rules. No tickets, no entrance—those are the rules," the valet informed her.

"But I simply must get in. They're expecting me," explained Rael.

"Then they'll be disappointed, but you understand it is better for me that they are disappointed in you than in me for not following the rules," replied the valet.

Rael shrugged. She turned to Andres and said, "Do something!"

Andres shrugged, "What do you want me to do?"

In a flash Rael knew just what she wanted him to do. She ordered him, "Call the car because we're leaving."

Those were apparently the magic words. For no sooner had she spoken than a voice called out from the distance. "No need for tickets for those two, gentlemen!"

The valet swung around and faced the entrance, his eyes lingering for a few seconds. Something must have caught his eye because his mood toward Rael lightened up. Indeed, he waved Rael on.

The valet said to her, "You don't need to find your tickets or leave, miss. You've been approved personally. A word from that man is worth a thousand tickets."

Rael gave the valet a half-smile of politeness. Clearly Boudicea knew a thing or two about planning, because Rael had already snagged her first admirer. Rael was just glad she'd played her part correctly. Now it was time to find out who exactly she had lured. The next vehicle had already pulled up to the curb. The very important person inside that vehicle was already annoyed that Rael had taken so much of the valet's time. They beeped their horn, and the valets began working on extracting the next guest from their vehicle. Rael seized the moment and stepped onto the red carpet. The red carpet didn't appear to be made of carpet at all. The fibers inside it must have been fiber optics, because they gave off a reddish glow every time she took a step. At the end of the glowing carpet, there stood a figure waiting for her arrival. Rael stopped briefly mid-carpet and tried to see whether the face of her savior was familiar. The lighting made it hard to make out who it was that was waiting.

"Andres, do you know that person?" asked Rael.

"You mean the man at the end of this lighted shag rug?"

"Yes."

"Never seen him before, but he seems to know you."

Andres was getting more useful by the minute. Rael seized the moment to return to heading down the carpet to see who'd let her into the ball. She'd know who they were soon enough, then probably regret that fact instantly. As she strutted the red carpet, the figure at the end came into much better view. At the end of the red carpet there was standing what to all appearances looked like a short balding man. All four feet ten inches of him stood there with his suit hanging off him like readymade wear hung on a second-hand store rack. The man seemed a touch impatient at the speed of Rael's red carpet walk. He was swaying side to side and licking his hand so as to be able to work on the tufts of poorly managed hair still clinging to the sides of his head. Rael wasn't eager to hasten her speed to find out who this new man was—mostly because her shoes wouldn't allow it.

Andres whispered over her shoulder, "I take back my words. You hunters know a thing or two. I swear that's Ronald Bentworth in the flesh, and he appears to be waiting for you. If that demon was correct, here's our cultist trying to steal you from me. Fancy him being a cultist. Rich guys, they're so greedy. Don't be swayed by his lack of looks and his ample money, because your essence will always belong to me."

"That's Ronald Bentworth?" exclaimed Rael.

"Yeah, this world is filled with disappointment, isn't it? You don't have to look like a billion bucks to be worth it in this world. That's why I prefer to leave it, with your help of course."

Coming face to face with her ultimate enemy at last had never felt more disappointing to Rael. The man behind all her troubles looked like he couldn't scare a fly, but she'd learned never to judge a book by its pre-made cover art. She would have to be on her toes. The game had officially begun. Rael finished her red carpet walk and stood in front of the man who was giving this ball. She greeted Ronald, "Thank you very much for letting me inside the ball. I seem to have mislaid my tickets."

Ronald sneered at her, "Faking having no tickets, indeed! As if I wouldn't have let you into your own ball."

Rael played it cool. No reason to tell him this wasn't all part of her clever plan. She replied, "If we have to start a game this evening, I thought it best to start immediately."

"I do like an anxious girl. You're clever, Rael Armstrong—much cleverer than your father. A pity I couldn't dispose of him and keep you in his place, but it is what it is."

"My father is here?" she asked, looking around. She couldn't see him. Only photographers capturing every important person entering the ball were about. None of them bothered to click her picture. She wondered if she showed up on film. Well, there was no time for those kinds of thoughts because Ronald was the attention-needing type of guy.

"You'll meet him soon enough. It will be a touching family reunion, I'm sure. I have but one question for you: Would you like me to kidnap you now, or would you care for a dance first?"

"I do believe a dance is not too much to ask for before I am kidnapped, killed, and communed," replied Rael.

Ronald said, "I would be crazy not to take you up on that offer. Why, you could kill me at any moment. Still, being brave is favored by having a fortune, or so they say. If you or your hunters were to touch me in public, my guards would drop you half a second later."

"I only asked for a dance."

"Of course. Let me show you the rave I have put on just for you." Ronald took her by the arm and guided her into the building.

"Hey, what about me?" shouted Andres as he was left behind.

Ronald stopped and looked over his shoulder at Andres. "Yes, what about you? I hadn't counted on you being here. But one of you is very much like another, I suppose. I watched them all pour into my party. Cult after cult of desperate risk-takers. You may, of course, join in the party like the others of your ilk. Part of the fun is seeing all you pathetic hunters searching in vain, thinking you can win my game. You've lost already, and I've won. A fact, a very basic fact." Ronald apparently was satisfied he'd taunted Andres enough because he then tugged on Rael's arm and they went inside the Vault together.

The lobby was spacious. Indeed, it was one vast open space. The open space was interrupted only by an elevator complex in the middle of the lobby that connected with the floors above. This giant open lobby held the party. It was packed with the who's who of European social life. Since Rael was rarely social in Europe or elsewhere, the faces in the room meant nothing to her. She likely meant even less to them. As Ronald dragged her around the floor, to her left she saw people hobnobbing at little tables as waiters dropped tapas plates for the partygoers to taste. To her right, she saw what appeared to be an endless open bar. Dead ahead of her was the dance floor. Rael would have liked to head toward the tapas tables to get some snacks before tripping the light fantastic, but Ronald had his sights clearly set on the gyrating dance floor. It was all bright lights, bad music, and worse dancing. A house band was cranking out hits written decades before Rael was born. It was such a disappointment. When she had imagined a ball, she had thought of period dresses and music. Everything about this place felt a little too modern for a proper ball.

"Care to waltz, my dear Astralith?" asked Ronald.

She could hardly be expected to waltz to the screeching electric guitars on stage. The fact that she didn't know how to waltz, or dance at all, lowered her expectations even further. Still, Ronald looked like a man easy to humor, and he could hardly kill her while dancing on a packed dance floor.

"That would be nice," replied Rael. She hoped she'd lied adequately for the occasion. "Get bent, loser" seemed a more appropriate reply, but one could rarely give appropriate replies to one's potential murderer.

Ronald likely didn't care how she replied anyway as he'd already taken Rael by the hands and led her onto the dance floor. The tiles beneath her feet glowed as she stepped on them. For some reason the band felt compelled to belt out the song "Disco Duck" at full volume at that moment. It did nothing to make Rael want to dance and cooled her usually warm feelings toward waterfowl as well. She certainly wasn't going to get down and boogie in these shoes. Luckily, Ronald danced about as well as she expected he could do a waltz or any other dance to this music. Meaning that he mostly clung on to her for dear life as he gyrated slowly and completely out of rhythm with the music. That was a style of dancing she could easily keep up with, even in her new shoes.

While the partygoers seemed to be packing themselves in tight all around the dance floor, the area immediately around Ronald remained sparsely populated. It was almost like there was an evil aura around Ronald that acted as an effective keep-out zone. Yes, everyone here knew who he was, and because of it, they gave him plenty of space. It was almost too respectful of them. They acted as if his wealth made him some form of royalty. And the looks that guests gave to Rael from afar almost suggested jealousy. Ronald had deemed her worth an audience, and they all longed for the same experience. One could never be so famous as not to long for the attention of a man like Ronald Bentworth. Rael could have told them it was all misplaced jealousy, because the last thing Rael wanted was his attention. Indeed, she was hoping tonight would put an end to it permanently.

As Ronald slowly circled around the dance floor, she caught sight of Gerard. He looked like a complete fool dancing around the much shorter Archon. Then they passed by a man whom she could have sworn was Wat Tyler. Rael now knew where her ticket to the ball went. Boudicea had given it to Wat and now he was watching over her. That meant everything this evening was going according to plan. Probably. Next she spied a group of men dressed in black wearing black sunglasses. Were they enemy agents from America? Who else was here? Probably everyone who wanted to get her or protect her was here, as Ronald had suggested. She didn't see any demons. They'd be here somewhere, though. When Ronald threw a party, he really went all out.

As they spun slow circles on the dance floor, Ronald spoke. He asked her, "Are you to be my flea?"

Rael pulled her attention from the guests and looked at her dance partner. It took her a moment to let those words sink in. They didn't penetrate far. She replied, "I beg your pardon, but did you just ask me if I'm a flea?"

"The Empire of Rome, as great as it was, in the end was taken down by a mere flea, Justinian's flea. On that flea was carried the plague. It toppled the Roman Empire and brought about the Middle Ages."

"I'm not really feeling like an insect of any kind, thank you very much," replied Rael.

"Ah, but I think you are my flea. You wish to topple my empire, even if you won't admit it. Look at all those hunters scattered here and there; none of them will save you."

Ronald was pointing. Rael's eyes followed his hand. They landed right on Dynami, who was alone. Dynami was so elegant on the dance floor. Her heart sighed a little. With these ball things, weren't you expected to come with a frog and leave with a prince? Not that Dynami was a prince, as far as she was aware. She really had no idea of the political system of Atlantis. He could be a prince for all she knew. It didn't really matter, because he looked like a prince. Her prince. Though he was dancing without his princess!

"Are you looking to call out to your would-be savior? Boudicea, Boudicea, come kill this man for me. I can see it in your eyes. You're no match for me, but you think your friends are. Your friends won't save you. Boudicea already has gone off hunting. The rest will soon leave. I'm well informed on everything, you understand."

Rael tore herself from staring at Dynami. Ronald had said something more to her, but she'd not really listened. He was, in a word, quite the bore. She said to him, "If I told you what my plan was, would that scare you off and force you to leave me alone? No, I don't think so, because you don't leave things alone. You know our plan already. Why talk about it? Can't we just dance?"

Ronald was not one to just dance. Probably because he was so bad at it. He stopped dancing for the moment and stood on the dance floor boasting. "I'm not afraid of you. Of course, I know that you know that I know that this is a trap. You know that I know that you know I've acquired an object that could make me the most powerful man in the world. I know that you're entertaining me so that your hunter friends can slip one by one from my dance floor and go search for it throughout my building. You should know that I relish this search because I know it's a waste of their time, but they don't know that. They think they can win despite my knowing what they know I know. I know you're now mine—now on this dance floor and soon forever. Yes, soon I shall have what I really want. You must understand that you get to be Ronald Bentworth by knowing that what I know trumps what you know and that I know that for certain."

"You do sound like you know a lot," agreed Rael.

He separated from her on the dance floor. He declared, "That is because, young lady, what you see before you is perfection on Earth."

"I had wondered what perfection looked like, and now I know."

He stepped in close now, with anger in his eyes. Clearly he knew sarcasm when he heard it. Not that Rael minded much. He seized her again. He moved her around the dance floor. The music had changed, but he kept the same rhythm in his missteps. He was harder on her feet than the shoes were, if that could be believed. She was wishing they could go back to discussing how great he was—or better yet, go over and get some snacks. The next song the band belted out she didn't know, and neither was she interested in ever knowing. He kept dancing. Rael scanned the crowd. She saw no one she knew except Wat. He stayed close to them on the dance floor. The rest had left, as Ronald had known they would. Did he know Wat was to be her personal protection tonight? It was the one thing Ronald hadn't said he knew. She was doing her part. She was being a distraction. She sort of wondered what Andres was doing. Not his job, because he should have distracted Ronald a little by now.

The pace of the music quickened now. Ronald was talking. It was more of a mumbling rant. He was currently explaining something to her, but she'd forgotten to listen to most of it. It was most likely about himself, which appeared to be his favorite subject. The music was loud, and she had trouble hearing him. Not that that was a bad thing. The song changed and for a brief moment she could catch what he was saying.

"And that is how I became the apex of genetic engineering. For decades the Fascists have dreamed of a superman, and I am their superman. I am the fruit of their tireless labor."

Another song started up, and Rael longed to get off the dance floor for good. Ronald wasn't done with her. She asked him, "As a fruit, did you fall far from your tree?"

"Insolence!"

Rael didn't feel she'd been insolent enough, because he started to dance again. The hunters were gone—that was good news, right? Rael knew it was time to get on with her part of the evening. She was to play hard to get, and that wouldn't start until Ronald stopped dancing and tried to get her. The game no longer scared her because the tedium of Ronald was much worse. Rael asked, "Does all this parading around the dance floor with me satisfy your cultish desires?"

"You know nothing about me!"

"I know you'll educate me then."

"Ha!" It was the kind of laugh that held no mirth. Ronald puffed out his pigeon chest, which only brought out the turkey in him. "Do you wish to learn the truth?"

"I'm all ears . . . well, and horns."

"I've no cult desires at all, little girl. I am a leader of none and a follower of no one. You, Ilitar, the Maleficium Society are all just a means to an end."

"And what end is that?"

"Me ruling the world."

"Will you be ruling it from a very tiny throne?"

"Enough! I tire of you like a dog tires of an old chew toy. It is time. Goodbye, Rael Armstrong. Feel glad you got to meet the most incredible man in the world, me, before you died. Yes, you have met greatness, and now your life is over."

He stepped away from her. As he moved away, the dancers on the floor cleared a path as if they all feared being touched by the great Ronald Bentworth. It was then the dance floor below her opened up. It was a trapdoor. It popped open and shut so quickly that the innocent guests on the dance floor were hardly likely to see what happened. They were also the type of people who mostly wouldn't care even if they did see. To them, she would be part of tonight's show. As unnerving as it was to plunge down into darkness, it was also a relief. She'd had her fill of Ronald Bentworth, even if he wasn't very filling at all. He was really nothing more than a tiny snack. One thing was for certain: The preamble was over and the game had begun.

Chapter 24

The Vault

Rael sat on a cold cement floor deep inside the bowels of the basement of the Vault. She should have felt honored to be where she was, since probably not many visitors got to see the sub-basement of such a famous building. But her throbbing bottom distracted her from feeling any such honor, and instead she focused much more on the pain of the situation. It was likely more than just a literal pain in the butt. She guessed Ronald didn't care too much about damaging his precious cargo as she was going to be much more damaged soon enough. Well, if he had the only say in the matter. Only, he didn't have the only say in it. Rael was planning on making sure Ronald became one disappointed billionaire.

She stood up in the darkness and rubbed her bottom. The glamour of the evening was gone, that was for sure. Thus ended her sort of first date. She had gone with the wrong guy to the dance, ended up with an even wronger guy, and then been left discarded alone in the dark. She doubted she was the first woman to have a date go that way.

She tried to adjust her eyes to the blackness of the room, but she could see nothing. She took a few blind steps hoping to find a wall so she could feel her way out of this trap. Her shoes made clunking noises as she moved. That signaled that clearly her shoes were ruined. Being dropped from high above onto hard cement would do that to high heels. They were made for looking at, not for durability. She had landed feet first, then toppled down to her bottom after her shoes gave way. She was probably lucky she hadn't broken her ankles when she landed. She kicked her shoes off. She wouldn't miss them much as she preferred flats anyway. Still, there were those boomerang and knife shoe options that she'd just tossed away. She didn't really need those things, though. What she needed right now was a flashlight. She felt her upper region hoping she was packing one but came up empty. Boudicea probably had a whole candelabra up there. Well, not every woman was naturally gifted in that way.

The trapdoor had sprung so quickly Wat had not been able to do anything about it. Rael was out of personal protection for now. Had Boudicea anticipated that would happen? It hardly seemed likely, or she wouldn't have arranged to have Wat come at all.

Rael heard a door open behind her. She got the idea she was no longer alone down here, and that was likely not a good development. She turned around to see that the inky blackness was now broken. The open door had revealed a light source beyond it. Life was like that: When you got what you needed the most in a situation, you almost always got it in a form that was most repulsive.

In this case, the area behind the door glowed with soft yellow-orange light, and in that light stood a hulking silhouette. There was no surprise there. She was meant to be not a prisoner of Ronald Bentworth, but a victim, and here came her would-be executioner right on cue. She knew exactly who that silhouette belonged to because she'd seen it twice before now. She flexed her fingers—or more to the point, her demon-slaying claws on the end of those fingers. She was built to fight, and now was the time to start fighting.

She called out, "I believe your name is Ghanal. Demon of the chaos, won't you please join me?" She sounded rather brave calling it out like that. She didn't feel an ounce of that bravery. She hadn't been the most agile of fighters to date. Hopefully the demon wouldn't catch wind of her fear.

The blue demon grunted back at her. Then it took her up on her offer and came into the darkness to join Rael. It didn't seize her in its arms, though. It just stood in the darkness, waiting. Rael had a sinking suspicion as to what the demon was waiting for. She watched the lit-up doorway and waited as well. A smaller silhouette appeared at the door before too long. She would rather have fought the demon to death than face this new man at the door. She took a deep breath, and then she spoke to the silhouette. "Father, very nice to see you again."

"Brat, you nearly cost me everything!" her father shouted at her. Well, it was good to know right off the bat that Dad was still completely off the deep end. Not that she had really doubted he would be.

Rael took another deep breath. She replied, "Come now, Father, there's no reason to have such a temper. I've stopped running and come home to you. You should praise me for that action."

"Then you plan to be transformed into Ilitar like a good daddy's girl?" he asked her.

Daddy's girl, how she hated the sound of that. Maybe before all this she had been his girl. She had skied because he wanted her to. Now she belonged to nobody. She was her own person. Well, she belonged to the Order technically, but it was the idea of independence that counted, right? She replied this time with a simple shake of the head. Her father probably didn't see it in the dark. She found her voice. "I have no such plans."

"Lights!" shouted her father. The room's lights erupted around her. She was exactly where she'd thought she was. The thing about even the glossiest high-tech buildings was that behind all the flash and dash, they were pretty much like any other building. Their basements were all bare-bones cement, wiring, pipes, tubes, and ducts. In the distance was the hum of compressors. The room she was in was particularly bare-bones. This room was all cement brick walls with one exit. Clearly it was meant to be a cell of sorts.

The blue demon sighed. "We've wasted enough time talking to her. Let's get this done. Every moment we waste, she potentially could use more of her precious essence. We need every ounce of the stuff."

Her father seemed to agree on the point. He replied, "Yes, you seize her and bring her up to the summoning circle. We will begin the communion at once."

"You would kill me just for Ronald Bentworth's gain?" asked Rael. The mention of the name made her father convulse a little.

His eyes glared. He replied, "No, I do this for myself. He's helped me become powerful; he will help me grow ever more powerful. As the cult grows, we all gain power."

Rael laughed at him. "Then you are a fool. A man like Ronald doesn't do things for other people. As the cult grows, only Ronald will end up in charge. When this is over and Ilitar is here, Ronald will dispose of you all. A man like that won't share power."

The blue demon grunted, "Don't listen to her."

"And this blue demon here doesn't care about any of you, because once Ilitar is here, it will leave back to its own plane," added Rael.

The demon said, "Lies! I say don't listen to a word of them."

"Don't worry, I won't," her father assured him.

That settled it. Her father could no longer be reasoned with. Cults are like that. They get people to believe unreasonable things. Her father could only think about the power he thought he'd obtain. The essence he lost each time he tapped into Ilitar's power never scared him. As for the blue demon, she knew it didn't care either. It would be back in its own domain as soon as Ilitar was removed from it—unless Rael was up to the task of sending it back to its plane sooner than it planned. They appeared to be done talking, for they moved on Rael. There was no other hunter left to save her. Boudicea had left this part of tonight's plan up to her. It was time to find out if Boudicea's trust was well placed.

Rael lashed out at the blue demon as it tried to seize her. Her claws ripped into its scaly flesh. The demon howled in pain. Her father, ever the brave man, took a step back at the sound of the demon's howl. Rael moved to run, but there was little space to run around in this cement cell. The door was the only logical target for a flight, but her father was very near to it. No, she'd have to finish the blue demon off first. Flight was not an option right now.

"You little rat!" shouted the demon. It must have been an insult, but Rael would rather be thought of as a rat than a demon any day of the week.

She said, "Come and try to get me if you dare. My eyes are Ilitar's eyes, my horns are Ilitar's horns, my claws are Ilitar's claws. She's ruled you for near eternity, just as I will rule you too. You made me yourself. You made me capable of destroying you. That means here on Earth, just like on your home plane, you're the weaker one. Now, feel your failure."

Well, never let it be said that Rael hadn't worked on her trash-talking game. Clearly she'd hit a home run on that last remark. The blue demon went wild and lashed at her with reckless abandon. Its fists flew at her in a series of furious blows. None of them landed on their mark. Rael was a little surprised about that herself. Then again, the one thing she seemed to have learned to date was how to dodge danger. The demon had exhausted its burst of energy and appeared to be slowing its offensive. She struck out with her left hand. She aimed for its arm. She raked her claws down its arm, leaving a gaping wound. Blue blood erupted from it. It probably would have sickened her no end had it not been such a comical tint of blue.

"Stop fooling around and get her!" ordered her father.

The demon snarled in her father's direction. Then the demon shouted, "If you think this is so easy, you do it!"

"Very well," replied her father. He pulled a knife and cut his hand. The drops of blood fell into his bowl. He chanted as his essence was traded away. Out of the bowl rose a golden rope. Given all the dramatics to produce it, Rael felt unimpressed by the magical result.

"What good is that until she's subdued?" asked the demon.

"Ilitar's twine will help in the subduing. It will bind her misplaced essence here on Earth as it would on your own plane," said her father.

The demon seemed to understand. Rael didn't quite follow, but she figured it meant they could tie her up with that better than non-magical rope. She wasn't keen on being tied up again. She had her eyes on her father at that moment, which was a mistake. It was the demon that came at her again. It closed in on Rael, but this time it didn't try to hit her. Instead, it shoved her with both hands—and did so successfully. Rael was pushed into the corner of the room.

Suddenly she disliked being a rat because she was trapped like one. Rael tried to counter the move before she was completely cornered. The demon offered her as a target only its already wounded arm. It was apparently quite willing to lose the arm for the cause. Rael sank her claws down into it. The demon grimaced but didn't back off. Instead, it clamped its free hand onto Rael's hands. It drove Rael's claws deeper, but it also pinned Rael to it. It seemed to smile in delight, through the obvious pain, for having her in its grasp. It then bull-rushed forward, sweeping Rael into the corner wall. She slammed into the wall and felt the bricks behind her crack. Normal Rael wouldn't have been able to take such a blow. Thanks to this demon, normal Rael was long gone. Upgraded Rael took a licking and kept ticking pretty well these days. Rael was still trapped. It had been fun for just a second to think she was as skilled a hunter as all the rest. Now reality sank in. The demon had her, and she wasn't about to escape it.

She felt the magic rope being wrapped around her pinned wrists. It burned her flesh. She could see her father's face. There was glee on it as he started to bind her hands together.

"Hurry up. This hurts you know!" grumbled the blue demon.

"Pain is one thing no one can avoid in this world," replied her father. He looked rather smug while saying it. The smug look on his face didn't last long because a shot rang out. Her father's arm erupted with a fountain of blood. The demon's ears perked up and it spun around, dragging a still-pinned Rael with it.

In the doorway stood Andres. He said, "Come, come, don't look so angry. You didn't think I was just going to let you people use my Astralith."

Her father held his wound and yelled at the demon, "Kill him!"

The demon shrugged Rael off like an annoying tick, which was a comparison Rael felt a little uncomfortable with. It then flared its nostrils at Andres. Rael had seen this face-off once earlier. It hadn't gone well for Andres. Andres's job here wasn't to beat the demon. He was only meant to be a distraction, and he'd done that job well. The demon's hate was focused on Andres. She used the opportunity to reach on the floor to pick up the remnants of her high heels. She flicked out the blade, cut the magic rope around her hands, and then she sank the blade deep into the demon's leg before it could charge at Andres. It snarled in pain and kicked her, but she wasn't around to be hit by the kick. She was already bolting for the open door. Andres was there waiting for her with open arms. She didn't stop her momentum to get reacquainted with Andres. She ran right through him, knocking him over in the process. She wasn't going to be anyone's today. She was hers and only hers. Andres went over backwards, with her landing on top of him. She gave him a swift elbow below the ribs. That blow bought her enough time to get up and go while Andres dealt with his own pain. Perhaps that treatment had been a touch harsh for the man who had just saved her, but she wasn't second-guessing her decision based on Andres's well-known record of bad intentions.

She was rushing down a bland cement-brick corridor in the sub-basement. Overhead ran various pipes and ducts. Nowhere was there an obvious exit to get out of here. Andres had come down here, though, so there had to be a way back up to the party. The real game was now afoot. She was like the white rabbit in a dog race. Her job was to lead all the hungry hounds around on the chase. She hated the idea of that, mostly because she hated cruelty to animals.

There were footsteps behind her now. They were too loud to be created by a human. The demon was chasing after her, and not Andres. She didn't look back. She only moved forward through the maze. It was Crete all over again, only down in this maze there was no minotaur's ghost. No, this maze only had the evils she'd led down here herself.

A ding went off in the distance. It echoed throughout the corridors. It was the sound of an elevator! Only where had the sound come from? It had reverberated a lot, so she couldn't be sure. She had to guess. It had felt loudest from behind her. Perhaps from the corridor she'd just passed by. She needed to go check. She spun around to double-back on her tracks, but it was already too late. The demon was now between her and the corridor. The demon grunted at her. "Your father is dealing with that Andres fellow. He left you to me. There is no escaping fate, girl. Come quietly and I promise you a painless death."

That didn't sound like a promise she was willing to accept. The demon was correct, though. Tonight, escape wasn't on her mind. She just needed to prolong the chase as much as possible. To do that, she needed to stay one step ahead of everyone out to get her. That was made easier thanks to the demon's obvious leg wound. She taunted it, trying to get it to charge. "I promise your death will be just as painless. Now, come on, keep chasing me."

It didn't come in a rush, though. It was slowly moving toward her, stalking her like a cat. It was waiting until it could pounce. Being in its grasp again was the one thing she couldn't allow. She moved backward for every step it took toward her. She was moving further and further from that corridor that sounded like it had an elevator. She thought she was keeping their distance about even, but somehow the demon was closing the gap. It threw a fist at Rael. It never landed. Indeed, it didn't even come forward at her. A red sticky tongue wrapped around it and pulled it in the opposite direction. That was the thing about elevators: They rarely went "bing" on their own. They only made sounds when people went in and out of them. Well, that was mostly true. The elevator did have a rider, but it wasn't a person or people in this case. It looked mostly human, but the forked tongue gave away its true identity. When Ronald Bentworth threw a party, he really let all the riffraff in.

"There she is, the Astralith! These humans need her to make them stronger. The humans must not be allowed to become stronger," said the American reptilian agent.

"Look, my scaly friends, I'm not the strongest-looking thing in this hallway. My good pal the blue demon here is, and I keep it around to protect me," said Rael to the lizard people.

The demon scowled at her in disapproval of her lie. The lie was effective, though. A lizard agent said, "Don't let this blue minion give her to the weak humans. Destroy the planar minion instead."

The blue demon was not about to let itself be beaten by a couple of overgrown dimensional lizards. It reeled in the agent that had tongued it by its own tongue. It then grasped the reptile's face and slammed it into the wall. There was one dead agent now, but there were a lot more coming. Rael counted six more agents. The killing of their agent by the demon seemed to alarm them. Not that it would stop them from attacking. They surrounded the blue demon and darted their tongues at it. They scored hit after hit and were attempting to grapple the demon into submission. For the moment, they seemed to be winning. They weren't the only ones winning, however. With everyone engaged in battle but her, now was the ideal time for Rael to make a break for it, and so she did.

She headed for the corridor with the elevator, feeling quite satisfied at letting the enemy of her enemy deal with her enemy. As she rounded the corner, she quickly discovered she had a lot more enemies. More reptilian agents had come down in the elevator besides the ones engaged with the demon. That fact explained the ease of her escape, but it wasn't welcome information. She'd run right back into a sticky situation. The nearest lizard agent darted its tongue at her. It scored a direct hit on her arm. She slashed at the tongue with her claws to free herself. It was only a brief victory because three more leaped at her with the aim of catching her. They could have easily grappled her at that moment, but the sight of a thoroughly crushed reptilian agent flying past the hallway distracted them. That was followed by the deafening roar of a demon. Clearly the blue demon was not one to go down so easily. Rael took the opportunity of the distraction to claw the nearest reptilian in the face. She kicked another and tried to move toward the elevator. If she could just get inside, she might have a moment of safety. Her injuring a few of them seemed to have been a wake-up call, and now they darted at her with their tongues. It was five tongues all at once, but Rael was too quick for them all. They were stuck to each other tongue to tongue.

She reached the elevator doors and hit the call button. The elevator bell rang. Someone had just come down. Yuck, more reptilians to deal with was not what she needed. When the doors opened, no more agents came out, though. Instead, a trident came sailing out that cut the nearest reptilian to ribbons. Wat Tyler then came out of the elevator. Andres and Wat were both helping her, so maybe Boudicea's plan was working as intended. Wat retrieved his trident and was soon finishing off the lizard agents.

The last lizard agent went down and Wat said to her, "Boudicea sent me to look after you. Get inside the elevator."

Rael didn't need to be asked twice. She moved inside just as the demon rounded the corner. Any remnants of the lizard agents that had attacked it were missing, and Rael assumed them to be dead. Wat took one look at the demon and threw his trident at it. The demon took a direct hit in its last healthy leg, but the hit didn't take that much out of the demon. It bellowed in pain and then charged down the hallway toward Rael as fast as its two injured legs would carry it.

Wat turned and made for the elevator. He shouted toward her, "Up, up."

Rael looked at the elevator panel. There were countless floors to choose from. She asked, "What floor?"

"It doesn't matter," he replied as he ran into the elevator car. Of course, he was correct. Any other floor in this building was likely safer than the one they were on at the moment. Rael jammed her hand into the buttons, lighting several up; then she pounded on the close door button. The demon was a step too slow, and the doors closed before it reached them. Rael had escaped again for the time being.

With a brief second to reflect, she concluded that Wat was a better ally than Andres to end up on an elevator ride with . . . probably. She said to Wat, "The plan is for all the hunters to be searching for the phylactery. We're only to have them chase us, not to try and annihilate them."

"I'll try to find time for both," he replied with a grin. It was hard to argue with that. He continued, "It's my chance to try to pay you back for a previous mistake the Freemasons . . . well I, made. I should have trusted the rookie druid that day on the train."

"Fair enough. Consider me repaid. Do you know what's on floor thirty-eight, because that's where we're heading?"

"Not a clue."

It didn't matter because floor thirty-eight came and went. Up they continued to go. Rael looked toward Wat, but he was just as confused as she was. Wat and lucky endings didn't seem to go hand in hand. She started to hit more buttons, but they passed by all those floors too. Nothing seemed to stop the elevator from going up.

The intercom came on. Speaking over it was Ronald. "I see that you're still alive. All thanks to two hunters not doing what I planned, or are they? Those hunters aren't searching but are helping you. How unfair, how deceitful, how it all plays into my plans. Tonight has been very amusing to me so far. Perhaps you would care to amuse me further on the penthouse floor?"

It wasn't really a question. Rael was headed to the penthouse floor, whether she liked it or not, because the elevator suddenly accelerated. Faster and faster it rose. The force pulled Rael almost to the floor.

Wat cried out, "Can you stop it?"

Rael reached for the panel of buttons and started pressing them at random. They were all useless. "I don't think so."

Then just as suddenly, the elevator came to a complete stop. Rael and Wat continued on their journey because an object in motion tended to stay in motion until acted on by an equal but opposite force. This opposite force was provided by the elevator ceiling, and it truly hurt to crash into it. Her momentum now stopped, Rael proceeded to fall back onto the floor of the elevator. This was the first time since this craziness had begun that Rael was unhappy to find one rule of physics not ignored by the new normal.

The elevator doors opened. Ronald's voice came over the intercom again. "Welcome to my special floor. Guests come into it, but they never leave alive." He got a solid bellyful of laughs out and then the intercom went dead.

Chapter 25

The Penthouse Floor

The elevator doors opened, but their opening didn't exactly illuminate Rael's situation further. She sighed. It was business as usual: The open doors didn't reveal much because there were no lights inside the penthouse. Rael frowned at the sight of more blackness in front of her. She asked the intercom, "Could I have some lights, please?" There was no answer from Ronald, which in itself was a form of answer.

"Do you want me to go first?" asked Wat.

Rael shook her head. Sadly, she was getting used to being in mortal danger. Besides, she was feeling a touch braver after having survived this far. Rael stepped out of the elevator and into the darkness of the penthouse. The room she entered didn't stay dark for long. There must be something here for Rael to see or do, or else Ronald wouldn't have brought her up here. Now that she'd gone exactly where Ronald wanted her to, a red light was allowed to go on. It switched on in the distance and grew in luminosity. How Rael was supposed to feel about the situation, she didn't know, though she suspected she was supposed to be curious about that red light and what it was illuminating. Why else would Ronald have gone to all the trouble? Fortunately, Ronald's theatrics weren't for nothing, because she *was* curious about the red light.

Given that it was the only thing in the vast empty space of the penthouse, it was hard not to be drawn to it. Like a moth to a flame was the obvious way to finish that thought, but she didn't want to be the moth right about now.

Her eyes were adjusting to monochromatic light. As she stepped closer she was certain that the red light was illuminating a statue sitting on a pedestal. The statue was made of gold. That was a guess, but this was Ronald Bentworth's penthouse, so if it was made of any other metal, she'd be disappointed.

She walked across the floor toward it. A white fog drifted up around her feet. The red glow made the fog feel slightly sinister. It didn't feel otherworldly so much as like using a fog machine to generate a mood effect. Rael ignored the mood lighting and moved up even closer to the statue. The statue was about three feet tall. It was of a woman . . . well, of a female, but perhaps not exactly a woman. She had horns, claws, and four sets of arms. Rael looked over to Wat. She said to him, "I think we found the phylactery without really trying."

"No, this is not the phylactery, but you were meant to think that it was," said the shape-shifting demon as it rose out of the fog machine mist. Rael didn't jump out of her shoes that she was no longer wearing at the sudden appearance of the red demon. She was quite used to its sudden appearances by now. Wat, however, appeared ready to attack the red demon even if it was in human form.

Rael waved Wat off. She explained, "Don't be alarmed. He's with me."

"That's not a man but a demon in disguise," said Wat.

"I know, I know," Rael assured him.

The demon added, "This statue is made in the likeness of my queen Ilitar. It is no surprise that a cult dedicated to seizing her power would have a statue dedicated to her. I had hoped it would do her justice, but justice is one thing Ilitar will never get from this Maleficium Society. This looks nothing like her. Yes, it is a pale representation constructed by an untalented artist."

"Yet you are here because you thought this was the phylactery," said Rael.

"No, I would never make such a mistake. They thought I would, but I'm not like the hunters, because I'm not a fool. They are off chasing similar idols in vain. I am here for one reason. I am here for him."

That news put Wat on alert. Rael grabbed Wat by the arm and moved him behind her. "There is no need to harm him. He's helping me too."

"Not him, him," explained the red demon. It raised its finger and pointed at the elevator. After it spoke, the elevator pinged and the door opened again. The blue demon lumbered out. It was looking a little worse for wear by now. "It's time Ghanal was dealt with once and for all." The red demon circled around the statue and got between Rael and the blue demon. "Ghanal, the time has come for you to be reacquainted with Ilitar and her power. You are to return to where you came from and be punished for your insolent behavior here on Earth."

Ghanal replied, "H$s@zx, Ilitar's worst general. I should have known our foul queen would eventually send you. No servant of hers was ever more obedient than you are: weak, obedient, and a fool. Take me back to our plane if you can. Win or lose now, it matters not to me, for I would have returned there sooner rather than later. Yes, very soon I will be your new king. The girl will be used to gate Ilitar here, and you can't stop it from happening."

"I will do my part by destroying your presence here on this plane," said the red demon.

"You will try," corrected the blue demon.

Rael had the name of the red demon at last, and the red demon had been correct about it. Rael couldn't pronounce its name or even spell it. With Rael fighting alongside it, she felt rather confident that the blue demon stood little chance in the coming battle. However, the red demon wasn't interested in her help in vanquishing Ghanal. It transformed into a raging beast on all fours and then charged at the blue demon with its tusks. The blue demon did nothing to prevent the collision between them. The red demon rammed its tusks into and through the blue demon. The blue demon made no sound as it was impaled. Instead, it grasped the tusks and twisted them with its hands. It was steering the two of them by shifting its weight.

Rael moved toward the blue demon, but Wat grabbed her arm. He said, "Let them work this out."

"But this is my fight too," she insisted.

"We all have a role, and this is the demon's."

Rael relented as the struggle between the two grew more violent. The red demon bucked and kicked, but it could not free itself from the blue demon. The red demon shook its head violently, but the blue demon hung on. At last the red demon seemed to give in and stopped for just a moment. The blue demon took the chance to grasp it by the neck and began to strangle it. The red demon didn't seem to mind the chokehold. Instead, it galloped off again. It was heading full speed into the inky blackness of the greater room around them.

It was then Rael heard the sound of breaking glass. That was the thing about buildings, even monstrously huge ones built by billionaires: Their floor space was limited. Much too limited for a raging beast to just charge around. Rael couldn't hold back any longer. She broke free of Wat's grasp and sprinted in the direction from which the sound had come. She reached the end of the room. The walls were all glass panels. One of the panels was broken. Neither demon was to be seen. It didn't take a genius to guess where they were. She approached the broken panel and looked down the side of the building. It was a long way down to the ground. Down below, she saw the headlights of the cars still circling the driveway as more and more guests streamed into the party. Those cars looked like tiny ants from up here. She expected to see a little commotion down there. The impact of two demons on the pavement should have caused a stir, but there was no sign of the demons down below.

"Where'd they go?" she asked.

"They are both back where they came from by now," said Wat over her shoulder. It must be true, because nothing of this Earth could have survived that fall. Even those not of this Earth would have had a hard time living through such a plunge. "Your demon friend completed its task for its queen. Now we should complete ours. The question is, what's next for us now that you no longer need to run from the blue demon?" asked Wat.

It was a good question. The immediate threat appeared to be gone with the blue demon destroyed. That meant Rael could stop running for the moment. The question was, what should she do instead? The obvious answer was that she should start searching for the phylactery herself. It sounded like the right move even if it wasn't part of tonight's original plan. The main thing she'd learned to date in her hunter's training was that in this demon-hunting business plans changed all the time, so she probably shouldn't dwell on the original plan. The thing was, taking up the search would mean heading to a different floor, and her only way down was this broken window. She could fly down to any floor she wanted with her wings. Wat wasn't so lucky, though, so she'd be traveling alone. There was also the fact that she didn't know which floor she wanted to try next. There were enough hunters searching blindly right now. Her being one more didn't feel like it would really help matters.

She looked back through the darkness toward the elevator. There was an idea brewing in her brain. Ronald knew where the phylactery was. Maybe she could push him a little and get him to take her there. She was the bait after all. No need to go searching for the phylactery for the young woman that was the bait. He'd bring it to her. He needed to control Ilitar once he gated her here. So she was pretty sure that the phylactery had to be close to where the summoning circle was. That was guesswork on her part, yet it seemed likely. Yeah, she didn't need to search for it. Ronald would bring it right here to her. All she needed to do was play easier to catch.

She said to Wat, "I've got an idea. Let's take the elevator."

"If the elevator will allow us to use it. I think they won't let it function for us," replied Wat. He had a point. Ronald seemed to control from afar the workings inside his building, and that included the workings of the elevator. The thing was, that's exactly what Rael wanted. Rael headed over to the elevator. Rael hit the call button. It didn't immediately respond to her call. She then did what everyone does in that situation. She hit the call button a few more times as if somehow the elevator would figure out that she was in a hurry. Only, as usual, the elevator didn't figure it out because it wasn't a sentient being. It also wasn't coming for her.

"As I said, they don't want us going down," said Wat.

"That is good to know," replied Rael. She surveyed the floor again. There was nothing here but that stupid statue, and the red demon had said it wasn't the phylactery. But they still didn't want her to leave here. That meant it was here, somewhere, somehow—but where? She needed a response from the elevator to answer that. Not exactly from the elevator, but from Ronald Bentworth over the intercom. She knew he was watching and listening. She hit the call button again and banged on the elevator door. She shouted, "Come on, Ron, I want to dance some more. Come on up and dance with me, because right now I find your penthouse a bore."

"A bore?" replied Ronald over the intercom.

Rael suppressed a smile. She'd caught her fish. She continued, "Your minions have a nasty habit of not surviving meeting me. We broke your demon, and now have nothing to play with. Care to open the elevator and let us find someone new to play with?"

"You think that you're a clever girl, but I see through you. I know exactly what you want. Since you want it, you can have it," said Ronald. The elevator doors opened and Andres stepped out. Rael immediately backed away as Ronald burst into laughter. He continued, "What's wrong? Didn't you want to get reacquainted?"

"Don't worry, I did," replied Andres.

"He was talking to me," said Rael. This didn't get a reaction from Andres. He was too busy sizing Wat up. Obviously the Freemason wasn't a welcome sight for Andres. Rael wouldn't mind Wat giving Andres a trident-full of welcoming to improve his vision. That wasn't to be. Instead of seeing a battle royal, Rael felt a jolt of electrical energy delivered from behind her. Her body jerked as the electrical current flowed through her. The shocking sensation didn't last long because Wat's trident cut the wires supplying the current. She'd been hit in the back of the left leg. Rael turned around in pain to see who had attacked her. There were now eight black-cloaked figures standing behind her. Their cloaks gave their identity away as cultists of the Maleficium Society. Not the biggest surprise in the world.

Ronald chuckled again over the intercom. He said, "Did you see what I just did there? I distracted you with your own distraction and gave my men time to creep up on you in the darkness? Oh, irony, where is thy sting? In the back of your leg. Get them, boys!"

Well, obviously Ronald had turned the use of Andres as a distraction right around on Rael, but gloating about the fact like a comic villain felt beneath even Ronald Bentworth. Rael didn't care so much, because in the end this is what she wanted. Well, not to see Andres again, but the fact there were now cultists here meant that there were indeed hiding places in this room unseen by the naked eye. Yeah, the phylactery had to be up here somewhere. This was where Ronald had taken her with the elevator, this is where the cultists were, so it made sense the phylactery was up here too.

Rael didn't get to deep-think that thought too much longer because another cultist shot his stun gun at her. She didn't have time to do much more than flinch, so a direct hit seemed likely. Things didn't come to pass that way. Wat deflected the business end of the shot with his trident. Now Andres and Wat sprang into action. Wat was fighting to pay her back, and Andres was fighting to take her back, but the motives were less important than the results at the moment. The result was that three cultists went down hard very quickly. Three against five was better odds than Rael was used to. Her confidence was quickly verified when Andres dropped another one with his gun.

"You shouldn't have brought a stun gun to a fight, fellas," boasted Andres.

Wat made quick work of the closest cultist to him. You'd think watching five on your team go down fast would alarm the remaining cultists, but cults don't become cults without true believers. The tide of the battle quickly went from bad to worse for the remaining cultists as one more was felled by Wat's trident. Rael hadn't even lifted a finger and she was winning by a blowout. It was too easy. Then it occurred to her that Andres had been correct. Why bring stun guns to a battle to the death? Ronald had gotten the drop on her—and blown it by having his men be underarmed with their choice of weapon.

Rael said, "He's sacrificing them on purpose."

The fact she was probably right didn't slow down the pace of the slaughter. Indeed, Andres and Wat were pretty far from her, near the center of the room, taking down the last of the cultists. The last one went down and there was no reward for their effort. There was instead a blast of red-hot flames. They erupted out of the Ilitar statue in a wave. Wat and Andres quickly got caught in the blast. Rael was far enough away that she'd been able to dive to the floor. The blast wave went over her back. She could feel the heat of the blast wave as it passed her. When it was over, her little black dress and her team had taken a severe hit. Wat and Andres were out of action. Boudicea had set her up tonight with two protectors, one good and one not so good. Both were now out of action. She had fallen right into Ronald's plans again. She was a bit worried everything had gone as he'd planned so far tonight.

The intercom spoke again. "Looks like I just evened the odds. Not only that, but I also got rid of unneeded hangers-on. Too many cultists dilute the power of Ilitar, you understand," explained Ronald.

She understood. Rael got up and dusted herself off. She needed to prepare herself fast for what was next, because something was almost certainly coming. There wasn't much time to prepare, because she wasn't the only one standing up in the room. The blast hadn't taken everyone out. Rael saw now that the statue hadn't been the actual source of the blast: Her father had. He was standing behind the statue with blood dripping into his bowl. He'd channeled the power of Ilitar to take out Rael's allies. And, worse, he appeared ready to do it again.

"The time has come, my foolish daughter, to bring my dreams to life and your life to an end at the same time. No greater gift has ever been given by a daughter to a father. I thank you," her father said.

"Yeah, the same way you thanked Mother," replied Rael.

"She was too greedy, Rael. She wanted all the power of Ilitar for herself. She was always unhappy at the idea she'd have to share in the power. She always wanted it right now. 'When do we kill Rael?' She'd ask me that question over and over again through the years. She wanted it all; she wanted it right now. She never considered that I wanted that too. Ilitar is not a thing that you share. She had to die. You understand that, right?"

"Then Mother was in the cult too?" asked Rael.

"Of course."

The news wasn't a surprise, and yet it was painful to hear. It stung her. She hoped she would never regain another single memory of her family, because they were worthless to her now. Her past life was worthless.

The floor beneath her started to glow. Not all of it. Just parts of it. It lit up to form a large circle. It didn't end there; it kept going until it made a familiar pattern. It was a summoning circle, and Rael was standing right in the middle of it. The circle had just been unintentionally fed with the fresh blood of eight cultists by Wat and Andres. In a flash Rael understood things much more clearly. It couldn't be going worse for her.

Another figure rose from the mist now. She could make out the faint sound of a mechanical lift. There was nothing supernatural about Ronald Bentworth. He was all money and the technological things money could buy. He'd even bought the loyalty of her father. Father's loyalty had been bought heart and soul, she didn't doubt that. Ronald Bentworth appeared as giddy as a schoolgirl over the situation. Another fact not lost on Rael. Well, why shouldn't he be happy, as Rael had done everything in her power to get herself exactly where he wanted her to be? There was one quick way to still wipe the smirk off his face, and Rael had her nerve up enough to try it. She tried to lunge at the man and claw his eyes out but went absolutely nowhere. It was like her feet were stuck in cement.

Ronald asked her, "Having trouble, girl?" Rael ignored him and struggled to move her feet, but they would not move an inch. Then she felt herself weighing a thousand pounds. Maybe more, maybe a lot more. She was too heavy to stand. She dropped to the floor face up. She was lying on the summoning circle, but not of her own free will. What had happened?

Ronald explained, "We tried doing this the easy way once already. While that didn't work, luckily you lost a small part of yourself to Ilitar in the process. Just as planar rope from Ilitar's world can bind you, so too can Ilitar's phylactery control you. Not as well as it will work on Ilitar, but well enough to keep you in that summoning circle until it's over. I was tired of chasing you around, and it did feel much smarter to bring you here and use what you sought to beat you. Yes, the time has come, girl, for you to die and me to become the most powerful being this world has ever known."

Uh oh. Rael hadn't planned on this. Of course, based on all the new metaphysics she'd learned, it now felt rather obvious to her. Black flatscreens rose from below. Rael knew she was in for more bad news because Ronald Bentworth was looking even more smug after their appearance. Ronald was your classic talking villain—not that the extra time he was buying Rael by gloating was doing her any good. She was paying too much attention to him. She needed to think.

"Your hunters were very thorough in their endeavors. Each one found what they thought was the phylactery. Each one instead found a lovely little trap set up by my genius. Before I take your life from you to make me the most powerful man ever, I wanted you to see your friends die weak and pitiful deaths," explained Ronald.

Rael was feeling less pride in her trash-talking abilities now. Ronald clearly had a good trash-talking game—or at least he had a lot of game to trash talk about. The game being shown to her on those flatscreens was live camera feeds of her friends. She could see Archon trapped in a room that was slowly filling with water. She also saw Gerard surrounded by heavily armed female cultists. And then there was poor Dynami trapped in a room with a slowly descending ceiling. Each room had its own golden statue of Ilitar. They'd all been lured to their unfortunate fates by false phylacteries. It was her fault. If she'd not been born . . . it was a pointless track of thinking because she had been. Still, she felt guilty. Everything was her fault.

Ronald was talking again. Maybe he'd never stopped, but she'd turned her attention away from the screens and onto him again. She needed to focus on him because he must have the phylactery here with him. Only, there was nothing obvious in his hands.

Her father had his summoning cup with him. Was that it? The cup? It didn't sound right. Ronald would never give her father that type of power. And yet, it was her dad that seemed to be channeling Ilitar. Where else could it be? Ronald, though, wasn't good at sharing. That was a thought. She couldn't move anything but her mouth, but maybe that was enough. In an instant she formed a new plan.

Rael asked Ronald, "Will you kill my father before or after me, Mr. Bentworth?" Ronald didn't reply. An awkward silence fell on the room.

"Come, come. One doesn't just share Ilitar's power. You said so yourself. You've done your best to have us hunters thin your herd for you. After I'm gone and Ilitar is here, my father is the last of the herd, so he can't have long to live. We all know that. He'll use so much of his essence just for you in the communion to come, and it will all be for nothing."

Ronald gave a grunt. Then he said, "Ted, my old friend, don't listen to her. You know you're different. Unlike the others, you've tasted Ilitar's power already. You're worthy; they weren't."

Rael looked to her father. He wasn't paying attention to her. He was cutting himself along his arm. He was pouring fresh blood into his cup. Her father turned to Ronald and said, "She does have a point. There really can only be one." Flames jumped from his cup. They struck Ronald with force. The little toad of a man sailed a good distance and splatted on the floor. He didn't get back up after that. It was the result Rael had hoped for; only, she hadn't really believed that it would work so easily. She didn't have any more to her plan after one of them turned on the other. She didn't blame herself for that fact. Your mind can only work so fast.

Her father now turned all his attention toward her. "Now, where were we? Ah yes, ending this. It was so much easier to commune with Ghanal here. Not that I can't do it without the demon." He slit both his wrists.

"Dad, you're as likely to die from this as I am. Ronald knew that. You're not an Astralith. You don't have enough energy to do this communion," she said. She was rather certain of her opinion even if she was short on facts. She really didn't know how much essence her father had. It didn't seem to matter. He was determined to see this thing through to the end.

He started chanting:

To anoint the body and make it shine.
To choose another form and make it thine.
To drink and make thyself divine.

The summoning circle glowed with an intense red light as he continued. Rael felt her body begin to lift. Only, her body wasn't moving at all. It was her essence floating away. It was leaving her body behind for Ilitar. She was about to astral travel again. She summoned all her strength. She had one last chance to move and get out of the circle. She couldn't do it, though. All her might was not enough. In a few minutes she'd be on the plane with Ilitar and her minions. They'd be rather disappointed in her. She'd failed them in the end. When the shapeshifting demon had killed Ghanal on this plane, it had felt like victory was so near, and now it was all slipping away into the ether. She spoke in a whisper. "I've always been a failure, haven't I?"

Her body slumped. She was blacking out. In the blackness she began to see the stars. Soon she'd be drifting among them. Her mind was slipping from her. Her last thought was of Boudicea. She was . . . she was where? Rael hadn't seen her on Ronald's screens. Where was she?

"I found this rope lying in the basement. I heard this rope comes from the plane of Ilitar and can bind those who have given part of themselves to her," said Boudicea from out of the blackness.

"A hunter!" shouted her father.

"There is only one way to tear you from Rael and end the summoning, and I'm prepared to do it," said Boudicea.

Her father screamed. In a flash Rael was back—back in body and soul. She could move too—and thus, move she did. She sprang up and rushed toward her father, but he was gone. Her head swiveled around searching for him. She had heard Boudicea's voice, but from where? Rael caught a last glimpse of her father's shoes as he slipped out the broken window. He'd been dragged out by that damn magic rope he'd created to bind Rael. Channeling Ilitar had been just as damaging to him in the end as it had been for Rael. She could make a good guess as to who was on the other end of that magic rope dragging him to a fatal fall: Boudicea. There was a grappling hook imbedded in the floor by the broken window. Its appearance explained why Boudicea needed fifty feet of rope hidden down her bosom. She'd managed to climb up here. Did the fact that Boudicea knew from the start that she'd need a rope mean everything had gone according to her plan?

Rael frowned at that idea. She looked down from the broken window and saw them both falling. There was still a chance. Rael shouted, "Fly!"

She soared out the broken window using her angelic wings. She immediately plunged downward as fast as her wings could beat. She was in a race against gravity instead of time. Gravity had a disadvantage as the height of the building meant Boudicea would hit terminal velocity before hitting the ground. Rael, with active flight, was under no such constriction. This time, Rael had the time advantage. She was going to be fast enough to win. Rael flew past her father with that surprised look still etched upon his face. She finally caught up with Boudicea at the halfway point. Boudicea was on the other end of the rope, still holding it tight as if Rael's father could get away. It had been a shrewd move to lasso daddy and drag him away from the summoning circle. Rael figured that Boudicea was in the middle of committing a self-sacrifice for the greater good; only, Rael was going to go and spoil it all. It probably hadn't occurred to her that Rael might try to save her.

"Hello, Boudicea!" said Rael.

Boudicea greeted her with "Rael!"

"Have wings, will travel." In the comics the hero usually grabs the person by the heel and soars away. Unfortunately, real life wasn't as easy as the comic books. Rael was pretty sure Boudicea had enough momentum to drag Rael along with her. A quick fly-by was not an option. This was going to take work. Rael flew under Boudicea instead and caught her up in her waiting arms. They were now falling down together. To stop that, Rael beat her wings hard in the opposite direction, trying to slow their descent. Those cars circling up the driveway were getting closer and closer. The idea that her wings weren't up to the task was the kind of self-doubt Rael didn't have time for. She needed to believe. They'd be up to it. They had to be. Her wings slowed them just enough to pause them in midair. Her father passed them heading in the other direction. He wasn't going to be lucky like those demons. He wasn't going to merely head back to another plane of reality upon death.

He shouted at Rael, "Fool!" It didn't sound like a very memorable last word. Rael had no plan to remember it.

Rael said to Boudicea, "I think you can let go of the rope now." And just like that Boudicea let go of the magic rope. They began to soar upward.

"I thought it was my turn, as Divicia took his turn once for me," said Boudicea.

"Nope, we're heading up. We've still got a phylactery to secure. You can now start searching for it because I can't help but feel that you deceived me about your searching for it before."

"Me?"

"I have a feeling tonight was all a ruse. You were never planning to go hunting for the phylactery. You were always going to follow me because you knew they'd take me to it in the end. You even had Wat and Andres act as my watchers instead of you to throw them off the scent."

"Of course. I'm not a fool."

"But how did you know where I'd be?" Rael asked.

"I hid a silver acorn in your dress to track you."

"I should have guessed. From now on I'd like to know the real plan in advance."

"A proper ruse only works if everyone is in the dark."

"Another lesson?"

"The truth."

"I always like the truth. I've had enough falsehood and darkness for one lifetime. It's time to keep shedding a little light on things."

They flew back inside through the broken window. Rael set Boudicea down on her feet then quickly made her way to where her father had been standing. She found what she was looking for soon enough. Near the golden statue of Ilitar statue lay her father's cup. She held it up in triumph. "Our prize at last."

Boudicea shook her head. "No, that is not the phylactery." The statement left Rael a touch confused. But Boudicea was certain and headed over to the fallen Ronald Bentworth instead. She began to tug off his shirt.

"We're not talking to another dead naked man are we?" asked Rael.

"This is no man," replied Boudicea. She was correct. Because when Boudicea pressed on it, his chest opened up. Inside there was no blood or guts. Inside was just a small statue of a golden calf.

"He was an android!" exclaimed Rael.

"A robot," corrected Boudicea. "It was a very clever hiding spot. One only a billionaire could have afforded. Your dearly departed father thought he'd killed Ronald, but Ronald was too smart for him. Once the communion was completed, your father would have discovered the truth the hard way. Ronald is certainly clever."

"The whole fake-your-death-via-robot-body-double routine, huh?"

"Exactly."

"I thought he was a little heavy on my feet when dancing," added Rael.

"Heavy on your feet, indeed!" scorned Ronald over the intercom. "You hunters ruined everything! I was so close. So close. And yet, I don't understand how I could have been fooled. I saw the tall witch die in one of my traps and yet here she is defeating me."

Boudicea explained, "What you saw was no different than this robot. You saw what I wanted you to see."

Ronald snarled. "Me tricked by a magical illusion! Very well. And now, never let it be said I'm not a gracious loser. You will die quickly and painlessly as this building will self-destruct in one minute. You can thank me later—ah, but you won't be able to. Goodbye."

The intercom went dead. The sound of a computer counting backwards from sixty replaced it. It was as melodramatic as it was cheap. Unfortunately, the threat was also all too real. Rael said, "A minute? We'll never be able to evacuate the building in time."

"We will simply fly away. Now, move," ordered Boudicea.

"What about all the celebrities and other hunters inside?" asked Rael.

"There are some matters beyond our control, Rael, but I think you will find Archon and the other hunters are already evacuating the other floors."

"But I saw on the screens . . ."

"Not everything you see in this world is real. Ronald has his technological tricks, and we have our magic. Ronald saw tonight exactly what I wanted him to see."

That meant Dynami and the others were safe. She didn't think of Dynami first before the others for any particular reason. No, no reason at all. Still, Dynami was safe. There was relief there. They'd won. Rael started for the broken window. Then she heard Wat groan. He must still be alive. She searched quickly for Andres, but he was nowhere in sight. That seemed so typical of the guy. Rael said, "Quick, help Wat to his feet. He's one of the good guys."

"I never doubted it," replied Boudicea.

They lifted Wat up. He was a little singed but functional. "Won't three on a wing be a little tough on you?" asked Wat.

"I can do it," Rael assured him.

"Then move quickly, because the computer is already at thirty," ordered Boudicea.

They soared away just at the count of one—a fact that was only for dramatic purposes.

Chapter 26

The Order's Secret Circle

They say that everybody has a first time and that it is only natural to feel nervous about your first time. Only, *nervous* wasn't exactly how Rael felt. *Awkward* was a closer word. It was Rael's first time in the presence of the Order's high leadership. She was standing next to Boudicea inside a druid grove. It was supposedly the main grove, located in parts unknown—or at least unknown to Rael.

How she'd actually got there was sort of a mystery, as all things in cults were. The main point wasn't how she'd got there, but the fact that she was there at all. She was there as an honor—or at least to be honored. Well, she had been told this was a great honor and that few mere apprentices had ever had such an honor bestowed upon them before her. That was all well and good, and yet Rael didn't exactly feel the honor she was supposed to be feeling. She sighed and asked Boudicea, "Who am I supposed to be dressed as again?"

"Silence," Boudicea replied.

"Silence is more a what than a who."

"Silence."

"Fine, I'm dressed as silence, but she's the goddess of what exactly?"

"Silence."

"I guess that checks out then."

"No, silence!" stressed Boudicea in a slightly more authoritative tone.

Apparently Rael was supposed to feel honored, but it was a very non-verbal type of honor she was supposed to be feeling. It didn't feel fair that everyone got to make noise inside this grove but her. In front of Rael there were four masked druids standing at the trunk of the tree of Arianrhod. They were all very happily chanting. They'd been doing that for about a million years, which could have been an exaggeration. In real time it had been about fifteen minutes, but time was very much a feel thing, and Rael felt Arianrhod as a time goddess would understand how Rael felt. She understood exactly zero percent of what was being chanted, which probably contributed to the chanting feeling like such a drag. It was probably praise that they chanted—maybe even praise for her. After all, she'd been hunter number one in the whole destruction of the Maleficium Society thing, which was the theme of today's honor.

Rael reached under her mask and scratched her nose. Rael was wearing the mask of a goddess whom she was pretty sure wasn't Silence, but you could never be too sure of anything in this business. Everyone was wearing a mask dedicated to a god or goddess Rael hadn't known existed, but it was probably going to be important to get to know them now. It was all part of the new normal. It was tough enough wearing the full black Lycra outfit and magic cloak while standing outside in the sweltering jungle humidity, but did they need to force her to wear the corny wooden mask too? The answer appeared to be yes. She seemed to be the only one unhappy about it. Rael at least had gotten to choose her own mask. That is, Boudicea had told her which one to choose and then Rael had chosen it. Rael's mask depicted a ram-like thing. It felt like a rather masculine mask for a goddess. No doubt it held some special meaning to the druids that Rael would learn about in time. She did have another forty years of apprenticeship, minus a few months' time served, to learn all this new stuff, so she had time—a lot of time—to learn.

"Is this going to take much longer, because I'm awfully hot?" asked Rael.

"Rael, please pay attention."

"I have been."

"Then what is going on?" asked Boudicea.

"How am I supposed to know that?" asked Rael.

"By paying attention." That was a rather bold statement that Rael would have liked to be backed up with facts. What good could come of more attention from her given that they were just tossing silver acorns about here and there while chanting in a language Rael did not comprehend? A fat lot of nothing, she figured.

Then everyone became silent. One of the masked druids turned toward Rael and tossed an acorn at her feet. The druid said to her, "Time is but an ocean, an ocean but a tide, a tide goes in and out in a dance; thus to her, what is time?"

"I don't know. About five-thirty right now, I should think," replied Rael.

That was probably a very accurate answer, but not the correct answer. Not that the druid seemed to care. The druid looked at Boudicea. The druid nodded. Boudicea nodded. Everyone now gave a nod. Rael joined in. When in Rome, as they say. They all seemed happy with the general state of the nodding and then they all stopped. The nodding portion appeared to be over, and maybe the whole event was finished, because they each went behind a different raised monolith until all were gone from view.

"That was it?" asked Rael.

"She is coming in person to thank you," explained Boudicea. She used a tone of voice Rael had only heard from Boudicea once before, when she'd spoken to Ariadne. Still, Boudicea's words were another one of those explanations that explained nothing to Rael. It was then that Rael heard the flapping of wings. A silver-and-white-feathered owl flew into the druid grove. It chose to land on a branch of the sacred oak tree. That would appear to answer who was coming to Rael's satisfaction.

The owl must have been less satisfied because it said, "Who, who?" Of course, that was pretty much what owls always said.

"Don, the Great Mother," said Boudicea to the owl as she went down on her knees. After a few seconds, Rael felt a tug on her cloak and got the hint. She got down on her knees too. Oh, then she remembered to tell the owl who she was, or was supposed to be.

"Silence, the Great . . . Lack of Noise," explained Rael.

The owl laughed at Rael, which was a very un-owlish thing for it to do. Then it flew down to Rael's level. In an instant Rael was looking at the sandaled foot of a woman. Rael looked up to see a pale-skinned woman dressed in a gown of white with silver thread. Behind her was a radiant glow. The woman looked into Rael's eyes and Rael could feel this presence looking not just at her but inside her. For an instant Rael could feel this woman dancing through Rael's innermost thoughts. *It must be magic* was the innermost thought that Rael thought most of all. Of course it was.

The woman said to Rael, "I am Arianrhod, and you are the young lady they call Rael. A strange name. You may rise, Rael, Maker of the Noise. Rise and speak with me."

Rael stood up and noticed something interesting about this woman's dress. "You're wearing buttons!" Rael exclaimed before realizing just how stupid that sounded.

The woman replied, "Of course. You sound surprised."

"It's just that I had heard . . . you know what, it doesn't matter."

"I see within your heart the power to let go of your past. That is wise, Rael. It is, however, something I have never quite been able to do myself. I am vindictive by nature, or so say my enemies. Perhaps they are correct. It is why I have formed my hunters, for it is hardly good to be vindictive and not seek vindication. I right past injustices. You have died once, and now you are to be reborn as one of my hunters. I am glad. With you, I am most pleased."

"Oh, really? I'm flattered. It was all nothing really. I mean, it was crazy and a bit scary, but you know, we pretty much won in the end."

"You're very modest, and a touch foolish, as the young often are," replied Arianrhod. The goddess motioned Rael to get back on her knees— or at least that's how Rael interpreted the goddess's gesture toward her. Apparently, being pleased with Rael for being super-brave and stuff was over, so Rael went back to her knees.

Arianrhod got right down to business. She said to Boudicea, "Ronald Bentworth was defeated but not destroyed. He has powerful friends in high places around the world. He will bother us again. A man like that will always be a bother until he is dealt with."

"We will be watching and waiting for a time to strike back at him for all the wrong that he has done," replied Boudicea.

"As it should be," replied Arianrhod.

"I have this for you," replied Boudicea. She took the golden calf idol out from her sleeve, because where else would Boudicea hide it? In a flash of light it was gone. It was replaced by a small bundle wrapped in white-and-silver linen of high quality.

Arianrhod explained, "Without the idol, Ilitar cannot be controlled by our enemies. Rael will be safe from them for now. With the Knights of Malta, the Freemasons, and so many other cults now on your side, yes, I suspect Rael will be quite safe for the time being. Your apprentice shall be of more help when the time comes to deal a fatal blow to Ronald Bentworth. To do that, she will need a weapon. Thus, I have given you this."

"I will teach her all that I know," replied Boudicea.

"I never doubted it." In a flash the woman was gone and the owl was back. She beat her wings and flew off into the jungle. Only, she could hardly live there. She must come from another plane. This whole place must be a pocket plane, a small world between worlds. How much druid essence was spent to speak face to face with Arianrhod Rael didn't know, but she figured it was a lot. In an instant she felt really honored that so much had been spent just for her.

Boudicea picked up the package and got to her feet. She started walking out of the druid grove. Rael followed after her.

"Where are you going with my gift?" Rael took a step beyond the monoliths and found herself inside a dilapidated marble temple on top of a hill. The jungle, the druid grove, and everything else that she'd just seen was gone. She didn't even ask how.

Boudicea unwrapped the linen. Inside was a golden bound book that would fit snugly in Rael's hand. Boudicea handed it to Rael. "It is yours."

"A book?"

"Knowledge is the most dangerous of all weapons, Rael."

"Is that another lesson?"

"It is the truth, and also an emotion."

"An emotion?"

"Love, Rael. Many claim it is the best of our emotions. I will be waiting for you at the base of the hill when you are ready to continue your adventures with me. I think we shall go back to Egypt for a rest."

"I think I can go with you now. There's nothing left for me to do here. Certainly I don't love looking at old marble ruins."

"Arianrhod was correct: So silly are the young," replied Boudicea. She then smiled a wicked smile at Rael and started walking away. Boudicea walked right by Dynami sitting on the marble steps of the temple. Her path could hardly be a coincidence. Love? That was silly; she was at most mildly infatuated with the young man from Atlantis. Still . . . Rael walked over to Dynami and sat down next to him.

She explained, "I got to meet the boss."

Dynami replied, "I envy you. What was she like?"

"She was . . . she was . . . she was wearing buttons."

"Really!" he exclaimed.

"Yes."

"I never met a druid with buttons before."

"I guess when you're the boss, you can dress however you like."

"Is that all that you learned from our goddess?" he asked.

"Well, no." She showed him her gift. "I got a book from Arianrhod too."

"You're so lucky to have met her and been rewarded by her. She senses what we all sense in you," he replied.

"Oh, what's that?"

"Greatness."

"Don't be giving me a swollen head or anything like that. It's just me, Rael. Still, I shall smite my enemies in her honor by smacking the heads of my enemies with this fine tome."

"I should think our goddess probably meant for you to read it," he replied.

"It was a joke."

"I know."

She laughed; she couldn't help herself. "Would you care to kiss me now before we depart again?" she asked.

"It is forbidden for druids to kiss outside a sacred grove. When we are older and the moon is full . . ."

"I've heard of other druids that break that rule."

"I should think not. Rules are rules, and an apprentice must . . ."

She interrupted him. "Please, do not go on about the rules. We both know that you could have left my side yesterday with Wat, Sister Isabela, and Gerard had you not been waiting for something. You know, Arianrhod has the power to see into a person's heart. I think, in your case, I have that power too. You waited here hoping for a chance to kiss me."

"Archon was needed at the circle. That's why I stayed. Nothing more."

"It was me, Boudicea, and four people much taller than Archon inside there, so try again."

"I would never . . ."

"You didn't play so hard to get before. Remember, you kissed me once in the water."

"I was giving you much-needed oxygen."

Rael suppressed a smile. Of course he was. And then she'd snuck a real kiss in too, and he knew she had. He'd never admit it, though. Not next to this entryway into another reality. He was a dedicated druid right down to the lack of buttons. "I might have snuck in a kiss while I was drowning. Did you mind?"

"Rael, I feel embarrassed to say this. But one day when we're both hunters, I swear I will kiss you—no sneaking involved. Until then, there are rules and our training."

"You feel that way about me then?" she asked.

"I . . . I will when we're of age. When we are hunters, we can feel that way."

"That sounds like a long time to wait." Rael leaned over and kissed him. She went for the lips because who knew when she'd see him again? She explained, "I've learned that in life you have to take some dangerous chances because time is always against you."

Archon called out, "Come on, lad, stop all that mushy stuff. It's time we went on the hunt again."

Dynami gave Rael a longing look and then shouted after Archon. "We weren't doing anything."

"Those are the best kinds of things to be doing with the lasses, my lad," replied Archon. Dynami departed, following after his master.

Rael sighed. Love was wonderful, but far too fleeting. It was a strange family she had joined, that was for sure. She'd sort of joined it under duress, and yet it seemed so much less stressful here than with her last family. Her biological family had merely desired her power, but her new family seemed to love her in their own ways. Being loved was better than being desired. Arianrhod was right: She felt nothing in her heart for the past. It was over. Rael looked forward to the future. That felt like a lesson, but it was probably also the truth. She slid her golden book up her sleeve. She exhaled and hoped Dynami didn't know just how nervous she was. Then she started her journey down the hill. She took her time walking because today she wasn't in a race.

www.ingramcontent.com/pod-product-compliance
Lightning Source LLC
Chambersburg PA
CBHW061504120726
48001CB00004B/1213